LOST
IN
OAXACA

A NOVEL

LOST IN OAXACA

JESSICA WINTERS MIRELES

She Writes Press, a BookSparks imprint
A Division of SparkPointStudio, LLC.

Published 2020
Printed in the United States of America

ISBN: 978-1-63152-880-4
ISBN: 978-1-63152-881-1
Library of Congress Control Number: 2019911278

For information, address:
She Writes Press
1569 Solano Ave #546
Berkeley, CA 94707

She Writes Press is a division of SparkPoint Studio, LLC. All company
and/or product names may be trade names, logos, trademarks, and/or
registered trademarks and are the property of their respective owners.

To my family here and in Mexico

"The sacred is not in heaven or far away.
It is all around us, and small human rituals can connect
us to its presence. And of course, the greatest challenge
(and gift) is to see the sacred in each other."

—ALMA LUZ VILLANUEVA

CHAPTER 1

Until she hears the bus driver swear, Camille isn't worried. After all, it was only a minor accident. One minute they were chugging down a mountain switchback; the next, the tires lost their traction with the road. With little fanfare, the bus glided into the side of the mountain with a gentle thud.

Camille listens to the whine of the engine as the driver tries to back up the bus. The acrid fumes of diesel fuel seep in through the cracked windows, aggravating the headache she's had since leaving the city.

"*¡Pinche pedazo de mierda!*" the driver curses, hitting the steering wheel with the palm of his hand.

She cracks a smile. Even with her limited Spanish, she understands that he just said *goddamn piece of shit*. But then she notices the veins pulsing in his neck. There are new rings of perspiration under his arms. Her smile fades.

She takes several deep breaths, trying to tamp down her rising anxiety. It doesn't work. If the bus driver is nervous, then she should be too. She leans forward and cradles her head in her hands, listening to the rain pound the roof of the bus. What the hell is she even doing here? Why couldn't she have left well enough alone and stayed home? Now she's somewhere in the mountains

of Mexico on a dilapidated bus the color of Pepto-Bismol—
if Pepto-Bismol were blue instead of pink. And she's stuck in the
mud, to boot.

This is definitely not the Mexico she's seen splashed across the
glossy pages of her mother's travel magazines. Here, there are no
turquoise bays or white-sand beaches—no five-star hotels with
infinity pools that disappear into the ocean. There is only the
monsoonal rain, the buzz of mosquitoes, and the accordion music
playing from the tinny speakers at the front of the bus.

And this humidity! The air is so thick with moisture Camille
feels like a wet dishrag that needs wringing out. She sits up and
rolls up her long red hair into a loose knot at the top of her head.
Sweat slides from the nape of her neck and down her back.

Wearing shorts was another big mistake. Her legs are stuck to
the plastic like someone has spilled maple syrup on the seat. Grit-
ting her teeth, she focuses on the gaudy decal of the Virgin Mary
glued to the center of the bus's windshield. Her thighs sting with
pain as she slowly peels her legs from the grimy plastic. The Virgin
stares back at Camille, her half-closed eyes looking more than a
little disappointed.

The tires spin in the mud. With a bang, the engine sputters
and quits. The passengers all begin talking at once, their voices
swelling like a crescendo. Camille can't understand a word. After
four years of high school Spanish classes, she assumed she'd at least
be able to understand something. No such luck. Most of what she's
hearing isn't even Spanish.

She wants to scream. Instead, she closes her eyes and hums the
melody of her favorite Bach prelude.

She feels a light touch on her shoulder. Startled, she glances up
to see that an indigenous woman has moved from across the aisle
and taken the vacant seat next to her.

The woman begins to stroke Camille's upper arm. "S'okay,

s'okay, señorita," the old woman says, nodding. Her smile resembles a yellowed piano keyboard missing most of its ivories.

Camille is so shocked that a complete stranger is touching her in such an intimate manner that her breath catches. Even her own mother has never touched her with such tenderness. Although the heat inside the bus is sweltering, she begins to shiver.

She has no idea how old the woman is—she could be seventy or even ninety. Her skin, the color of caramel with a touch of cinnamon, is creased with deep wrinkles. A white braid coils around the top of her head like a dollop of whipped cream. Her eyelids droop so low Camille wonders if she can even see through all the excess skin. Although the material of her white dress is stained and worn, the vibrant embroidered flowers and tassels have not faded with time. Attached to a thin leather string around her neck is a pendant adorned with three small silver crosses.

Considering the intimate caressing that's going on, Camille decides she should at least introduce herself. She extends her hand and says in her best Spanish, *"Mi nombre es Camille. ¿Y usted?"*

The old woman giggles like a young girl and covers her mouth with surprisingly delicate fingers. She doesn't shake Camille's hand or even offer her name, but continues stroking her shoulder while chattering away like they're old friends. Her singsong dialect is unfamiliar to Camille, but she recognizes two words: *metropolitana* and *Americana,* which the woman repeats several times. Her head bobs up and down with vigorous approval, as if Camille is the most exciting thing she's seen since the Pope visited Mexico.

The woman starts massaging Camille's forearm, then works her way down to her wrist and fingers. Before she can pull her hand away, the woman turns it over and draws her thumb across the hardened scar tissue that spreads across Camille's right palm. She stares at the red lines crisscrossing Camille's hand, then attempts to straighten her bent fingers. She squints up at Camille, a concerned look on her face, and tilts her head in a questioning manner.

Camille's throat tightens. "It was an accident," she lies, pulling her hand from the woman's grasp. "*Un accidente.*"

The old woman gives her a look of such compassion that Camille's eyes fill with tears. She fights the urge to crawl into the woman's lap and cry.

A flash of blue light is followed by an immediate boom of thunder that violently shakes the bus. A child cries for his mother as the sky opens up again and rain pounds the roof. Without warning, the bus driver leaps up from his seat and hurries down the aisle, shouting at the passengers in rapid Spanish. Although Camille doesn't understand him, everyone else does. They quickly rise and gather their belongings. Frightened, Camille follows suit. She lifts up her backpack and slings it over her shoulder.

The roar of the rain soon drowns out the nervous chatter of the passengers as they funnel into the aisle and head toward the emergency exit. The old woman says something in her dialect and motions for Camille to follow her. The aisle is packed with so many people that Camille must wait for it to clear.

"*¡Rápido, rápido!*" the bus driver yells from the back of the bus.

When Camille finally reaches the emergency exit, she places her backpack on the floor. Steadying herself, she prepares to step off the bus.

From below, a man reaches out and firmly grasps her hand. She can't see his face, but she does notice how much lighter her skin is than his. With her other hand she quickly fumbles for her backpack, but before her fingers can grab onto the straps, the man yanks her off the bus.

The ground is slick; she loses her balance and falls facedown into the mud.

"Hey!" she shouts, getting up and spitting out a mouthful of earth.

Her once-white clothes are now covered in a reddish-brown goo. She looks around for him, her fury rising. "You don't have to be so rough!"

The next thing she knows, strong arms are grabbing her around her waist and dragging her down the road. A voice with a heavy Mexican accent yells, "*RRRRUN!*"

"What the hell?" She tries to twist away from him, but he only holds on tighter. Her sandals slip off her feet. "Let go of me, you jerk!" she shouts. "I have to get my backpack! It's on the bus!"

"Shut up and *RUN!*" he shouts, forcing her down the road.

Mud squishes between her toes, and her eyes are so blinded by the rain that she can only see blurry streaks of color as she flails along. She trips over a rock and almost falls, but before she hits the ground, his hands reach around her waist and catch her. He hoists her up onto his back and carries her down the hill.

When they are a safe distance from the bus, he sets Camille down and disappears into the rain. She looks around for him but realizes she has no idea what he looks like—she never did see his face. She couldn't pick him out of a crowd if she tried. The only part of him she'd recognize is his hand. And possibly his voice.

Camille wipes the mud from her eyes and sees that a group of passengers are staring up at the top of the road. She turns to look, and relief floods through her body. The bus is moving again! No doubt they'll be back on their way in no time.

My backpack. Everything is in there: her passport, phone, credit cards, and a large amount of cash. She can't risk losing it. She begins to hike back up the road, the rain stinging her face. Several passengers put out their arms to block her, but she moves around them.

A man calls out to her, "*¡No, señorita! Mucho peligro!*"

What danger is he talking about? She's already soaked to the skin and completely covered in mud. What more could possibly happen to her? She keeps walking.

"*Pinche Americana estúpida*," the man mutters under his breath as she moves away.

Irritated, she turns around. "Hey—I'm not stupid!" she protests, but before she can say more, a loud snapping noise draws her attention back to the top of the road.

The bus is still reversing, but now it's moving at a faster speed. She's incredulous. *Who in their right mind would drive so recklessly in this kind of weather?*

Then it dawns on her: no one is driving the bus. With a loud *whoosh*, the trees on the slope above the road begin to wave their branches back and forth. The crowd lets out a loud, collective gasp. Like a slow-motion scene from a Hollywood disaster movie, a massive wall of reddish-brown earth slides down off the mountain, carrying the bus straight toward them.

Screaming, the passengers scatter. Whether because she's in shock or because her bare feet are now cemented into the thick mud, Camille is unable to move. She squeezes her eyes shut and waits to die.

Nothing happens.

She opens her eyes. The bus has shifted its direction. The mudflow is now pushing it away from her and toward the edge of the road. For a moment, sweet relief floods her body. She's not going to die after all.

Her joy is short-lived, though. With a terrifying screech of scraping metal, the mudslide pushes the bus over the side of the road. It tumbles into the green abyss below, taking Camille's backpack and every single one of her possessions along with it.

CHAPTER 2

W hatever you do, Camille," her mother had said, "make sure you don't go wandering off alone while you're *down there*." She had finally accepted the fact she had failed to talk Camille out of traveling to Mexico by herself. Still, she'd said "down there" with a look of utter distaste on her face, as if she were talking about Skid Row or someone's dirty underwear.

It was the night before Camille was to leave for Oaxaca. She was feeling frazzled because she still hadn't finished packing for her trip. It certainly hadn't helped that she had wasted almost three hours having a "quick" lunch with her mother. In her usual form, her mother had shown up thirty minutes late to the restaurant and then insisted on ordering two glasses of wine before she would even think of looking at the menu. Five minutes after sitting down, her mother had reached into a side pocket of her Louis Vuitton handbag and pulled out a handwritten list with all of the reasons Camille shouldn't go to Oaxaca. Over the course of lunch, she'd proceeded to go over each point in great detail. By the time lunch was over, Camille had a migraine.

"Well, at least she's out of my hair now," Camille said aloud— and instantly regretted it, knowing she had just jinxed herself.

Sure enough, her cell phone began playing the haunting theme from Bach's Toccata and Fugue in D Minor, and *MOM* lit up her screen.

"Crap," Camille said, adrenaline flooding through her like she'd just downed a triple espresso.

For a moment, she considered letting it ring. But she knew if she didn't answer, her mother would show up anyway, bitching about how rude it was for Camille to ignore her calls. That she was such an ungrateful daughter, especially after everything she had done for her over the years. Camille had heard the speech so many times she could recite it verbatim.

Camille was not unappreciative of her mother's help. She was well aware that living rent-free in the estate's guesthouse was indeed a very sweet deal. After injuring her right hand during her senior year, Camille had dropped out of college. Her mother had insisted that she come back home to Santa Barbara to recuperate. When Camille balked, her mother had offered her the one-bedroom guesthouse so she'd have some privacy. Camille had agreed, thinking she'd be out of there and making it on her own within the year.

It had been fifteen years now, and Camille was still living in the guesthouse, still not making it on her own. And privacy? She didn't know what that meant anymore.

The phone continued playing Bach. Camille considered turning off all the lights and hiding in the bathtub, but there was no point. Her mother knew she was there. She always knew.

She took a deep breath and slid her finger across the screen. "Hello, Mom."

"Camille," her mother rasped, "it's your mother."

"Yes, I realize that. That's why I said, 'Hello, *Mom*.' What's up?"

Her mother cleared her throat. "I want to come over and say goodbye to you one more time before you leave for Mexico."

Camille clenched her jaw. A sharp pain shot up the back of her head. "Mom, we already said our goodbyes at lunch today. Please don't come over now. I'm in the middle of packing."

There was an uncomfortable silence. "Oh. Well, I just thought I could be of some help. If I'm going to be a bother, I'll stay away."

Camille's shoulders tightened. "Mom, you're not a bother. It's just that with all I have to do, I'm a little overwhelmed."

"Well, that's because you always do things the hard way. Let me come over and help you get organized. If I do say so myself, I'm quite the expert at packing. And I have something for you to take on your trip that I forgot to give you. I'll only stay for a bit."

Camille wasn't buying it. Her mother wanted to come over for a singular reason: to try one last time to talk her out of going to Oaxaca. Not that she hadn't already spent three hours at lunch doing just that. Highlights from her mother's list had included how dangerous it was for a single woman to travel alone in Mexico. How she would get dysentery from the water. That it was the beginning of monsoon season and there were sure to be terrible storms. Camille's personal favorite was her mother's insistence that because she was a fair-skinned redhead, she would be an easy target for those terrible "cartel people" who keep kidnapping attractive American women in exchange for huge ransoms.

"You watch yourself, Camille," her mother had warned, signaling the waiter for a third glass of chardonnay. "It's all over the news these days how Mexico is overrun with criminals. They'll take one look at you and figure out you're a rich American. Then they'll hold you hostage until they get what they want. And guess who's going to have to come up with the money to get you back? *I* am—that's who."

And then, as usual, her mother had brought up the fact that Camille hadn't always made the best choices. Since her hand injury all those years ago, she had become accustomed to having others take care of her—primarily her mother.

Camille had no problem accepting that she'd made mistakes. Some very big mistakes. She was even willing to offer her mother one final shot at trying to talk her out of going to Mexico. In her heart, she knew she wouldn't change her mind. She was going to Oaxaca, and that was that.

"Fine, Mom. Come over," she told her, pinching the bridge of her nose to relieve the pressure that was building up behind her eyes. "But please make it quick. I've still got a lot to do before I go to bed."

"I'm heading over right now," her mother said, unable to hide the relief in her voice. "I'll be there in two minutes."

Closer to forty-five minutes later, her mother let herself in through the front door of the guesthouse. Camille could hear the purposeful *tap-tap* of her mother's spectator pumps on the hardwood floor. Then she was standing in the doorway, surveying the chaos that had invaded Camille's bedroom with a sharp eye.

Camille was kneeling on the floor, folding clothes and stacking them into piles on her bed. She knew she looked ridiculous; that was another reason she didn't want her mother there. She was wearing cut-off jean shorts and a purple sports bra. The skin above her lip was swathed in a mustache of white bleaching cream. Her red hair was tied up into a lime-green bandana, lending credence to the term "carrot top." Piles of brightly colored dresses, skirts, and blouses were fanned out across the bed like a crazy patchwork quilt. An oversize black backpack blocked the doorway.

Camille quickly got up and kicked the bag out of the way, sending an array of miniature toiletries skittering across the floor and under the bed. She dove after them. "Hey, Mom, how's it going?" she asked, frantically groping under the bed for her travel-size shampoo bottles and mini toothpaste tubes. She stood up and brushed off her knees. "You look nice tonight."

Her mother ignored the compliment. "Darling," she said, standing so close that Camille could smell her Hermes cologne— as well as the fumes from the bottle of chardonnay she always drank at dinner. "What *is* that strange outfit you're wearing?" Without waiting for an answer, her mother's eyes darted around the room. "And this place is a mess. Why in God's name are you packing so many clothes when you're only going for one week?"

Her mother was wearing one of her standard linen suits, which today matched the exact gray-blue color of her eyes. Dozens of these tailor-made suits hang in her closet in a variety of muted colors—sage green, pale lavender, and mauve. Camille finds it remarkable that her mother is pushing seventy-five. Other than the slight wrinkles around her eyes, which look like the creased tissue paper you'd find at the bottom of an old gift box, she appears to be in her early sixties.

Her mother settled her gaze on the jumble of clothes covering Camille's bed.

"Maybe if you actually went on a trip with me once in a while instead of spending all your time holed up in the guesthouse, you'd know what to take with you. I'm telling you—you're completely overpacking. You should only be taking light cotton shirts, a couple of pairs of shorts, and maybe a skirt or two. You know, most tourists don't realize how strong the Mexican sun is until it's too late. The farther south you go, the hotter it gets. And isn't Oaxaca close to Guatemala? I suspect that when it's not raining the sun is going to be hotter than the blazes *down there*."

An electrical surge of irritation sent tingles up Camille's neck. Her headache pulsed in earnest. "Mom, you're still not saying it right. It's pronounced *Wah-haw-kah,* not *Ox-sah-kah.*"

Her mother sniffed. "Well, how was I supposed to know that?" She reached into a pile of thong underwear and attempted to fold them before realizing it was an impossible task. "Anyway, if I were you, Camille, I'd wear all white when you're in *Wah-haw-kah*. That way, the sun will reflect away from your pale skin. And you don't want to add any more freckles to that face of yours. You already have enough of them as it is."

Camille turned her head away and rolled her eyes.

Her mother suddenly slapped her hand to her cheek, a purple thong still dangling from one finger. "Oh—silly me! I almost forgot. The reason I came here is because I have the perfect sun hat you can borrow. You know, the one with the wide brim that I wear in the garden? I'll just run back to the house and get it for you."

Camille had reached her tipping point. "Mom, please, just stop!" she said, snatching at the thong in her mother's hand. It snapped like a rubber band, flew across the room, and landed behind the dresser. Like a petulant teenager, Camille stomped across the room to retrieve it. "I'm a thirty-seven-year-old woman, Mom. I don't want your stupid sun hat. If I need one, I'll buy it in Mexico. I believe they sell hats *down there*."

Camille reached behind her dresser and pulled out the purple thong, now dangling enough strands of red hair and dust bunnies to make a hummingbird's nest. "And you know what else, Mom?" She couldn't keep the sarcastic tone from her voice. "I think I can figure out which clothes to bring to Mexico. In fact, I might even be capable of folding my own underwear."

Her mother arched an eyebrow and tilted her head toward the dresser. "As capable as you are about cleaning *down there*?"

Camille threw up her arms and plopped down on the bed. "Okay, Mom." She sighed. "I give up. Why are you really here? I know you didn't come over just to give me an old straw hat, fold my underwear, or point out that I'm a slob. Besides, don't you need to down at least one more glass of wine before bed? You're hardly slurring your words yet."

She knew she'd gone too far, but she no longer cared. She waited for the standard angry response, but her mother merely stood there, looking troubled.

"Camille," she said, her voice subdued, "I know you believe you're doing the right thing by traveling to Oaxaca to look for Graciela. But is it *your* job to do that? After all, she didn't even have the courtesy to tell you she was leaving. I would have thought an eighteen-year-old would be mature enough to explain herself before taking off like that. I guess it just goes to show how ungrateful some people are. Obviously, Graciela hasn't appreciated all of your hard work over the past ten years."

She placed an awkward hand on Camille's shoulder—her attempt at a gesture of support. "If you ask me, you're better off without her."

Camille quickly shrugged her off; the weight of her mother's fingers seared her skin like she was sunburned.

Her mother's hand fell limply to her side. "Look, darling, I understand that you're fond of Graciela. I am too." She paused for a moment, as if searching for the right words. She sat down on the bed next to Camille. "There's something very important you need to understand. It's not your place to save Graciela. You're not her mother." She sighed. "You're just her piano teacher."

CHAPTER 3

Watching a wall of mud push her bus off the side of a cliff is far beyond what Camille's mental capabilities can handle. All she can do is take deep breaths and try to convince herself that what she just saw was a heatstroke-induced hallucination.

At least she's out of the pouring rain. As if by magic, an enormous blue plastic tarp has appeared out of nowhere. There's enough room under it for her and most of the other passengers.

She is quite surprised by how resourceful these Oaxacan people are. Within minutes, they rigged up a tarp between two trees and positioned a tall branch in the middle like a pole so the water wouldn't pool over their heads. It looks a bit crude but functions as well as any of the fancy canopies Camille's mother rents for her fund-raiser parties back home. It's a much more vibrant color too.

Camille suddenly has the urge to laugh. She imagines herself back home, standing under the tent at one of her mother's summer music soirees. A string quartet is playing Mozart in the corner of the terrace as the guests wander through the garden, sipping Champagne. All perfectly normal, except that in her imagination Camille sees herself barefoot and covered from head to toe in gooey mud. The outline of her breasts shows through her T-shirt as the wealthy music patrons of Montecito stare at her with gaping mouths.

A low chuckle begins to bubble in the back of her throat. Before long, she is laughing so hard her stomach muscles hurt. She leans over and puts her hands on her knees, her laughter modulating into soft weeping. Soon, she's sobbing uncontrollably into her mud-caked hands.

When the tears finally stop, Camille begins to hiccup. She wipes her nose with her forearm, smearing mud, now mixed with snot, across her face. The passengers stare at her like she's lost her mind. She looks down at the ground, her face hot with embarrassment, as another round of tears begins to build up again. Someone taps her lightly on the shoulder.

"Excuse me, señorita," a deep voice says. "Are you okay?"

Camille immediately recognizes the voice. It's the guy who pulled her off the bus and threw her down in the mud. The one responsible for making her look like she's been dipped in chocolate.

Forgetting her tears, she swivels around to give him a piece of her mind—but because the ground is still slick from the rain, her feet continue rotating in a circle. To stay upright, she swings her arms around like a spinning propeller, but she can't keep her balance. Her feet fly out from under her body and she goes down hard into the gooey mud, this time on her backside.

Leaning over, the man places his hands firmly under her arms. With a loud squelch, he lifts her to her feet.

Furious, she shakes him off. "Who *are* you? And why is it every time you show up I end up covered in mud?"

He smiles mischievously. Camille has the urge to shove him down in the mud so he can have a taste of his own medicine. Turning toward the other passengers, he says something unintelligible. They put their hands to their mouths and shake with laughter.

It takes Camille a moment to realize that they're laughing at her. *What an ass. Who does this guy think he is?* Sure, he's good-looking, but to Camille there's nothing worse than a guy who knows he's attractive. In his mid-thirties, with high cheekbones, coffee-colored skin, and thick black hair, he's probably used to women ogling him like he's an Aztec god. Camille finds herself irritated by his easy confidence. Especially since she currently looks like some creature that's just crawled out from the swamp.

She crosses her arms in front of her chest and glares at him. "What did you just say about me to those people?"

He presses his lips together, obviously suppressing his laughter.

Angrily, she stamps her foot, splattering mud onto the clothes of several passengers. They back away, clearly concerned with what the psycho *Americana* will do next. She points a muddy finger in his face. "Tell me what you said!"

He puts up his hands in mock surrender. "Okay, señorita—calm down." He extends his hand toward her. "First, let me welcome you to Oaxaca. My name is Alejandro Chimil." Although he definitely has an accent, he speaks perfect English, which is a relief.

She ignores his hand. "Why are all those people laughing at me?"

"It's nothing. They're just laughing at an old saying we have around here: *Otra vez la burra al maizal.*"

Camille is dubious. "That's not what you just said. I understand enough Spanish to know that you definitely said something else."

He acts wounded. "But I did say that. I just said it in our Zapotec dialect. It translates into '*Otra vez la burra al maizal.*'"

In her head she attempts to translate the words from Spanish to English. "Again . . . the donkey . . . and something about corn? What the heck does that mean?"

He pauses for a second, like he's debating whether or not to tell her. "Well, I guess it means, 'The donkey is in the cornfield again,' or something like that."

The look of confusion on her face pushes him to explain it further.

"It's what you would say when someone does the same thing over and over again and never learns. In English it translates to 'Here we go again . . .'"

He's referring to her falling into the mud a second time. "Oh, okay," she says scornfully, "I get it. I'm the donkey, and it's *my* fault that I fell in the mud when you yanked me off the bus? And it's *my* fault you just snuck up behind me and caused me to fall down all over again?"

He looks confused. "What are you talking about? I didn't sneak up on you. Look—what's your name, señorita?"

Camille knows she looks ridiculous with the mask of mud smeared across her face, but she holds up her head higher in defiance. "My name is Camille Childs. And I don't appreciate you making fun of me."

He raises his eyebrows. "Well, I'm sorry I offended you, *Camila*." He draws out the "l" in her name in a languorous manner. "But after what just happened with our bus, I thought some humor might make everyone feel a little better about our situation." He gestures toward the passengers, who are still chuckling at her behind their hands. "Which, as you can see, it has."

Camille dismisses him with a wave of her hand. "Whatever. Go ahead and make me the butt of your jokes. I don't care anymore. But you can at least pronounce my name correctly. It's Camille, not Camila."

He narrows his eyes at her. "Oh, yes?" he says. "Well, Señorita Camila, sometimes you can't always get what you want. You're in Oaxaca now, and here we pronounce things the way *we* want to pronounce them." He moves closer to her, takes a hold of one of her elbows, and places his arm next to hers.

"Look at this, Camila," he whispers, his face so close to hers she can smell his aftershave. "Don't you think it's interesting that right now you and I are pretty much the same color?" He takes both of her hands in his, turns them over, and examines the undersides of her forearms with mock seriousness. Her bent fingers are visible through the mud, but he makes no mention of it.

He turns her arms over again and smiles. "You know what? You're so dark right now that people are going to think you're a redheaded Oaxacan. Too bad for you. I guess that means no special treatment for the white lady."

He continues to hold on to her hands for a brief moment. Then, as if he's become weary of her, he releases them and turns back toward the rest of the passengers.

He looks back over his shoulder at her. "You're just like one of us now, Señorita Camila." He lets out a light, staccato laugh. "Just keep falling in the mud, and you'll have no problem fitting in around here."

CHAPTER 4

After an hour, the stormy toccata finally ends, and a tomblike stillness descends upon the mountains. The only sound is the gentle snap of the plastic tarp as it billows in the wind.

Camille has been sitting on the wet ground for so long that it takes her several attempts to get to her feet. When she finally stands up, her legs quiver like gelatin and her backside is numb. She peeks out from underneath the tarp and squints into the sunlight, her eyes stinging as if she's just walked out of a dark theatre after an early matinee. Off to one side of the road, clusters of pine trees explode into a bright blue sky, their needles sparkling like tiny crystals in the sun. Breathing in the scent of the wet earth, she looks out at green rolling hills painted with delicate yellow polka dots. Because of the storm, she had no idea how high up they had traveled until now. The magnificence of the view takes her breath away.

Enticed by the warm sun, the passengers emerge from under the tarp. They mill about in small groups, speaking their strange-sounding dialect, while Camille stands off to one side, alone. The mud on her body has dried into a tight crust, like she's wearing some sort of protective armor. She stretches out her arms and watches as miniature cracks appear in the mud. She begins to pick away at it piece by piece. She assumes everyone is either talking about their bus going over the side of the road or, more important, their rescue. After her heated exchange with Alejandro, she's afraid to ask anyone for information; they probably think she's just another pushy American used to getting what she wants. She wishes she could explain to them that the reason she's traveled all this way is to save one of their own from ruining her life.

Within a half hour, it seems as if everyone is preparing to leave. Two men take down the tarp and fold it into equal squares like a bed-sheet. The passengers begin to form an uneven line along the road.

Camille, desperate to find out what's going on, disregards her fear and walks over to the bus driver, who is busy explaining something in Spanish to the passengers. She puts up her hand to get his attention. When that doesn't work, she loudly clears her throat.

"*Perdón*," she says in simple Spanish. "Where are we going?"

He backs away from her, likely worried she's going to smear mud on him, and begins speaking rapid Spanish, pointing to the line of passengers as he talks.

She has no idea what he's saying.

"I can't understand you," she says. "A little slower, please?"

He sighs. "*Va-mos a cam-i-nar a un pueb-lito que es-tá muy cer-ca de acá*," he says, enunciating each syllable like Camille is hard of hear-ing. "*Pro-bab-la-men-te nue-ve kil-o-me-tros.*"

His voice is so loud she almost flinches, but at least she got the gist. *We're going to walk to a nearby town that is probably nine kilometers from here.*

She does the math in her head. Wait a minute—*nine kilometers?* That's over five miles! She looks down at her bare feet. How in the world is she supposed to walk five miles without shoes?

She suddenly senses a presence behind her. She turns around and looks down to see the old woman who sat next to her on the bus. The top of her head barely reaches Camille's chest. She's holding her arms behind her back and smiling like a little girl with a secret. She slowly brings her arms around to the front of her body, and in her hands dangle a pair of handmade leather sandals. They are light brown with bright red flowers painted on top. She says something in her dialect and holds them up toward Camille.

"Oh, no," Camille says, backing away. "I couldn't take your shoes."

The old woman grins even wider, making her eyes disappear into the folds of her skin. She gestures again for Camille to take the sandals.

"No, really—I couldn't—"

"Take the shoes!" a familiar voice calls out.

Alejandro.

He walks over to Camille and nods his head in the direction of the old woman. "Trust me on this one. If she's offering you a pair of huaraches, take them. You don't want to offend my tía Nifa."

"*Tía?*" Camille says, surprised. "This lady is your aunt?"

"That's what they tell me." He takes the sandals from his aunt, leans over, and murmurs something in her ear before gently kissing her cheek. She giggles and slaps him playfully on the arm. He hands the sandals to Camille.

"I can't wear these," Camille whispers. "They'll get ruined. My feet are already caked in mud, and if we're walking somewhere, they'll get even muddier. Doesn't someone have an extra pair of flip-flops or something? I'd really hate to give these sandals back to your aunt if they're covered in mud."

He gives Camille a puzzled look. "Why would you give them back to her? They're a gift. If my tía gives you a pair of shoes, she's not going to ask for them back." He points to the line of people starting to hike down the road. "Now hurry up and put them on. It's time to leave, and we've got a long way to go."

21

After walking less than half a mile, they veer off the main road and head down a narrow trail. The rain has filled the holes in the path, and the small pools of water reflect the sky like dozens of hand mirrors. Camille's matted hair stings her cheeks as it whips in the wind.

She is at the end of the line of passengers. Only Alejandro and his aunt walk behind her. She's sure they're frustrated by her slow pace, but the bottoms of the huaraches are slippery and the trail is becoming steeper. Camille is so afraid of slipping that she carefully measures each footstep, like an old woman without her cane.

Although the sandals fit her perfectly, the leather is stiff and the straps are digging into the skin above her heels. She reaches down to loosen the strap and feels the slight puffiness of newly formed blisters. She wishes she had a couple of Band-Aids.

"Camila," Alejandro says from behind her.

She shoves her feet farther forward into the huaraches and tries to walk faster. "I know I'm holding you up. It's just that my feet are killing me."

"No, you're fine. Stop for a second. My tía has something that will help you with your feet."

Camille turns to see the old woman stooping down to pick something off a spiny, cactus-looking plant growing along the trail. She snaps off a piece, walks over to Camille, and squats down.

"What's she doing?" Camille asks, feeling uncomfortable that the woman is touching her again, this time by holding on to one of her legs.

He looks down at her feet. "You're getting blisters, right?"

She nods.

"She's going to put some of the water from an aloe vera plant

22

on the back of your heels. Don't worry—it won't hurt. It will take away the pain."

"Are you sure it's not poisonous or anything?" Camille asks. "I mean, I've heard of aloe vera before, but I've only seen it in a jar at the store. Is it safe? Does it need to be sterilized first?"

He laughs. "You Americans are locos—always thinking you have to boil everything. Where do you think aloe comes from in the first place?" He crouches down and takes a plastic bottle of water and a white T-shirt out of his backpack. "What you buy in the store doesn't have much aloe in it anyway. This is the real thing, and it works."

Camille balances on one leg, and the old woman pulls the straps down from the huaraches, carefully inspecting her blisters. Alejandro unscrews the cap from the water and hands the bottle to his aunt, who pours some of the contents over the back of Camille's foot, gently washing away the mud. She uses the corner of her white cotton shawl to dry Camille's heel. Then she squeezes the liquid from the cactus onto the blister, and—to Camille's surprise—the throbbing pain instantly vanishes. She repeats the process on Camille's other foot.

In the meantime, Alejandro is ripping up his T-shirt it into several long strips.

"Are you tearing up your shirt for me?" Camille asks. "You don't have to do that. Really, I'll be fine."

He hands the pieces of cloth to his aunt, who deftly wraps them around Camille's heels and the bottoms of her feet. "It's only a shirt," he says, "and you're no good to me if you can't walk." He smiles playfully. "Besides, I think I've already carried you enough for one day. My poor back is killing me."

Camille is instantly irritated. "Well, I'm sorry I've caused you so much trouble." She shoves the huaraches back onto her mummified feet. "I wouldn't dream of letting you help me again. If I have to, I'll crawl."

"Now *that* would be something to see," he says, laughing. He helps his aunt to her feet. "Unfortunately, I don't think I have enough T-shirts to wrap up both your hands and your knees. I guess you're just going to have to walk to San Mateo like the rest of us."

"San Mateo?" Camille says, suddenly worried. "But I need to get to a town called Yalálag."

"You'll get there soon enough. And just so you know, you're not saying it correctly. You don't say the *g* at the end of Yalálag. It's pronounced 'Yalála.'"

"Whatever," she says, her tone sullen. "What does it matter?"

"It matters to me," he says, his brown eyes growing intense. "You know, Camila, you might want to be careful with what you say around here. You don't want people to get the wrong idea about you. You don't want them to think you're just another privileged white person who doesn't appreciate our culture." He takes his aunt's arm and begins to walk away from her.

How rude. Camille glares at the back of his head, deciding that she could easily learn to hate this guy.

CHAPTER 5

Dusk has laid claim to the day. The passengers' shadows are no match for the expanding darkness. In the distance, the village of San Mateo twinkles like someone has wound a strand of miniature white lights around the mountaintop. From the little Camille has been able to understand, it's not safe to continue on in the darkness. They will be sleeping here tonight.

It looks like they're on some sort of small ranch. This is confirmed when Camille catches the scent of animal manure in the breeze. The only buildings she sees are several small adobe houses and a large barn-like structure. The metal roof is so oxidized it seems possible that it could disintegrate into a powdery rust at any moment.

As they approach the barn, the smell of wood smoke is heavy in the air. It reminds Camille of the one and only time she went camping.

As a young girl, she had few friends. Her classmates mistook her shyness for snobbery and mostly avoided her. So when a girl who had just moved to town asked Camille to go on a family camping trip in the mountains above Santa Barbara, Camille was ecstatic. She begged her mother to let her go.

"Absolutely not," her mother said firmly. "Camping is much too dangerous. You could hurt your fingers. Besides, we have tickets to hear the Chatham Quintet this Saturday at the Lobero. They're playing the Brahms F Minor. And isn't that one of your favorites? It's much too late for me to find someone else to go with. The answer is no."

Although Camille loved playing the piano, it was tedious attending concerts with her mother. She was ten years old, for god's sake. She didn't want to listen to Brahms. She wanted to go camping. For three days, she pleaded with her mother to let her go, crying until her eyes were swollen. When her mother still wouldn't relent, Camille tried the silent treatment. Nothing.

Finally, she came up with a foolproof plan. She threatened to purposely hurt her fingers if her mother wouldn't let her go.

Her mother narrowed her eyes at Camille. "What do you mean, you'll hurt your fingers?"

Camille stuck out her lower lip. "I'll slam them in the car door or smash them with a hammer or something."

"Don't be ridiculous," her mother said, frowning. "You'll do no such thing."

Camille knew she wouldn't hurt herself on purpose, but her mother didn't, and now she'd planted the seed in her mind. She didn't know why she hadn't come up with the idea sooner. It worked like a charm. Within the hour, her mother had relented. But on one condition: Camille had to promise that she would never do anything to injure her fingers on purpose.

"There will be no playing with rope or sharp sticks," her mother warned. "Stay away from poison oak, and absolutely no roasting marshmallows with a coat hanger. Have someone else do it for you. It would be disastrous if you hurt your fingers."

Camille happily agreed to her conditions. Off she went, her backpack stuffed with sunscreen, bug repellent, and heavy nylon gloves.

Her mother needn't have worried. Camille ended up hating the entire experience—the sunburn, the charred hot dogs, the smell of the musty sleeping bag. The residue from the slimy creek water on her body made her skin crawl. After a day and a half, Camille—her hair and clothes reeking of smoke—sneaked off to the campground store. Using the old pay phone on the wall, she called her mother to come get her.

Within an hour, her mother arrived sporting a smug smile. The minute Camille got home, she took a long, hot bath. Her wet hair still dripping down her back, she sat down at the piano and practiced a Beethoven sonata for three hours.

The scent of smoke is overtaken by the delicious smell of cooking food. Camille's mouth begins to water.

She's about to ask Alejandro if he knows if the food is meant for them, but she hesitates. She's been intentionally ignoring him all afternoon—ever since he made that snide remark about her being a privileged white person. On several occasions he tried to initiate a conversation with her, even giving her one of his water bottles to drink. She took the water but didn't bother to thank him. She now realizes that her behavior was not in her best interest, as Alejandro is the only person around who speaks any English. She decides to suck it up and just ask him.

"Excuse me, Alejandro," she says as politely as she can, "but do you know if we're going to be eating any time soon?"

He turns around to face her. "Oh, so the American girl has finally decided to talk to me again."

Camille ignores the edge in his voice. "Well, it's just that I smell something delicious cooking. I was wondering if it was meant for us."

He doesn't even try to hide his irritation. "Who do you think it's for?" His tone is curt. "A couple of the men hiked out earlier and told the people here what happened with the bus. They knew we wouldn't make it to San Mateo before dark, so they've prepared food for us. We're going to sleep here tonight. Tomorrow morning we can walk into town and find a ride to Yalálag."

Camille is so overcome with relief she forgets she's mad at Alejandro. "Thank god. I'm so exhausted. What a day this has been! First, I almost get swept off a mountainside; then I lose all my money, my passport, and my phone. And for most of the day I've been covered from head to toe in this disgusting mud." She holds her arms out so he can get a good look at how dirty she is. "My feet are killing me, my face is fried, and I haven't had anything to eat since early this morning. I swear, I'm about to *starve to death*."

He glares at her. "Starve to death?" he says. "You're kidding, right?" He turns and stalks off toward the barn, but he only makes it a few steps before stopping abruptly and coming back to her, looking furious. "You know what? It continually amazes me how you white people think only about yourselves. All you do is complain about how hard everything is. You think the rest of the world is here to serve only you. Do you think these people here on this *ranchería* have extra food to give us? Of course they don't. They're poor people. Probably some of the poorest in the world! But they're offering to feed us and give us a place to sleep because we need their help."

Camille stands in silence, completely taken aback by Alejandro's reprimand.

He runs his hand through his hair, his voice growing more agitated with each word. "You think you know what it's like to be really hungry? Of course not. You're a rich white person who's had everything handed to you your whole life. But I know what it's like. I know because there have been times in my life when I've *really* been close to starving."

"I'm sorry," Camille sputters, "I didn't know—"

"That's exactly right—you don't know anything about it. You have no idea what I went through when I was young. Or what most of the people around here have been through in their lives. Starving is when your mother leaves you in charge of six kids for two weeks without any money to feed them. It's when you have to go out in the middle of the night to steal dried up tortillas from the neighbor's pig trough. When you have to break off the parts with the mold so the kids have something to eat in the morning. So I'd really appreciate it, Camila, if you wouldn't claim you're *starving to death*."

"It's just an expression," Camille says meekly. "I didn't mean that I was actually starving." She knows he's right. Physical hunger isn't something she's ever dealt with. But that doesn't mean she hasn't experienced suffering. She squeezes her right hand—a constant reminder of what she's lost—into a fist. She's felt Alejandro's pain, just in a different way.

A numbing weariness washes over her. "Okay." She sighs. "You're right. I shouldn't have said that. And I'm sorry. It's just that today has been really difficult for me."

She pauses, waiting for Alejandro to accept her apology. He says nothing.

She tries again. "It's just that I'm completely out of my comfort zone right now. I'm so alone here. I can't speak the language, and I don't know your customs. I realize now that coming here to Oaxaca was a huge mistake." She rambles on, unable to stop. "I should've listened to my mother and never come here in the first place. I mean, what was I thinking? How in the world I thought that I would be able to . . . that . . . I could . . . actually . . ."

The words get stuck in her mouth. Her heart begins to race, and a watery blackness seeps into the corners of her eyes. Then she floats off into the empty darkness.

A muffled voice echoes at her like it's coming through a long tunnel. Someone is lightly patting her face.

"Camila," a deep voice says, "can you hear me? Are you all right?"

She blinks several times and looks up at a circle of concerned faces. *What am I doing on the ground?*

She sits up, her head spinning. "I'm okay." She tries to stand.

Alejandro puts his hands on her shoulders and pushes her back down. "No you don't," he says, his face inches from hers. "You're not going anywhere. You just passed out. Sit right there and don't move."

Someone tucks a scratchy blanket around Camille's legs. With the pressure of Alejandro's firm hands on her shoulders, her trembling eases. He is watching her closely, but now he looks worried instead of angry.

She takes a deep breath. "Alejandro, what I said before? Well, I'm really sorry. When I'm anxious I have this habit of exaggerating things. The truth is, I appreciate everything you've done for me today."

"Shhh," he says. "I'm sorry too. Today has been rough on all of us. I shouldn't have taken my frustration out on you. Are you sure you're okay?"

She nods. Alejandro hands her another water bottle. "Drink this. You fainted because you're dehydrated. Or maybe"—he winks—"you're about to *starve to death*."

She covers her face with her hands. "I'm never going to live that down, am I?"

"Nope," he says, getting to his feet. "Do you think you could eat something now?"

Her stomach rumbles in response.

Alejandro calls out something in Zapotec to the passengers who are lining up at the barn for food.

"What did you say to them?" she asks.

He grins. "Nothing much. I just told them it's time to give this skinny redhead some food before she passes out again."

Camille is sure her face is no longer pasty white. She's so embarrassed, it's probably as red as a ripe tomato.

30

CHAPTER 6

C amille has never been so eager to sit down for a meal, but she's self-conscious about joining the others for dinner in her filthy state. As if he's read her mind, Alejandro points her toward a metal washtub off to the side of the building.

Camille removes the muddy huaraches and peels away the soiled strips of material from her feet. She tries her best to wash away some of the dirt from her face and hands with the icy cold water in the tub, then joins everyone inside the barn.

The inside of the building is dim. There are only a few kerosene lamps set around the room, but the ambiance is inviting, like that of a rustic café tucked among the trees. The dirt floor has been tamped down for so many years it feels like polished marble under Camille's feet.

The smell of home-cooked food permeates the air. Camille's mouth begins to water again. Hunks of soft white cheese, clay bowls filled with red and green salsa, and glass bottles of soda form a parade line down the center of four large wooden tables. On each table there are baskets of homemade tortillas that send up curled wisps of steam into the air.

Off to one side of the room there is a stocky, dark-skinned woman ladling soup into glazed bowls. She wears her hair in two long braids on either side of her head, and her upper body is covered in a faded red gingham apron. She fills each bowl with the fluidity of a ballet dancer. The flickering of her gold earrings in the lamplight is the only clue that she's moving at all.

She hands the steaming bowls of soup to her two solemn-faced daughters, who pass them out to the passengers. The girls are identical but slimmer versions of their mother. Both wear the same tight braids, gold earrings, and gingham aprons, although their aprons are light blue and lavender in color. The girl with the blue apron sets a bowl of soup in front of Camille. She can barely contain her delight at the sight of the food.

"*Muchas gracias*," Camille says.

Startled, the girl steps back and stares. Camille wonders if the girl's reaction was because Camille spoke Spanish. Or maybe it's because she's not used to seeing mud-covered redheads in her village.

It's a tight squeeze at the table. Alejandro and his aunt sit on either side of Camille like mismatched bookends. When everyone has been served, Camille looks around the table for a spoon, but there are no utensils in sight. She's so ravenous that she considers slurping soup directly from her bowl, but instead she watches Alejandro. He reaches into the basket and pulls out a corn tortilla the size of a dinner plate. It's toasted on both sides and spotted with flattened brown bubbles. He tears it in half, crumbles a chunk of the soft white cheese onto the center of both pieces, pours some green salsa over the cheese, and rolls up each piece into a tight cylinder.

"Here you go," he says, handing one to Camille. "Use it like a spoon."

She does what he says, and with her first bite she almost passes out again. The flavor of the rich, salty broth mixed with the crispy, cheesy corn tortilla is the most delicious thing she's ever tasted in her life.

"Oh, my goodness," she says, practically swooning with pleasure, "this is incredible. What kind of soup is this?"

He smiles. "It's good, isn't it? It's *caldo de pollo*. It's chicken soup with onion, green chilies, and *chayote*."

She shovels another large bite into her mouth. "What's *chayote*?"

He reaches into his bowl and plucks out a piece of the green vegetable. "It's a *calabaza*—squash. We use it a lot here in Oaxaca because it grows so easily in this climate." He takes another tortilla for himself and this time pours some of the dark red salsa onto the cheese.

"How come you didn't put some of that red salsa on my tortilla?" she asks.

"Because," he says, pushing the bowl away from her, "it's made with *chili piquínes*. They're way too spicy for you."

"Is that so?" she says, reaching for the basket of tortillas. "You think I can't handle the hot stuff?" She tears off a piece of tortilla, reaches across the table for the bowl of red salsa, and pours a large dollop inside.

"Camila, I'm serious. That kind of salsa is spicier than you think."

"Come on," she says, "it can't be that bad. Anyway, I'm from Santa Barbara; we have lots of authentic Mexican restaurants there. I always order my food extra spicy. Trust me, I can handle it."

Before he can say another word, she takes a big bite and swallows. It's delicious—smoky, with a hint of garlic.

"See, Alejandro? I'm fine." She is just about to take another bite when her lips begin to tingle. Then her eyes start to water, and her throat begins to burn. Suddenly, a wave of searing heat radiates up through her sinuses. She gags.

Alejandro immediately realizes her distress. He shoves a bottle of orange soda into her hand.

She gulps down more than half of it in three long swallows, but it doesn't stop the burning. She frantically waves her hands in front of her face. "Why didn't you tell me it was so damn hot? I think I'm going to be sick."

"But I did tell you!" A worried look flashes across his face. He grabs her forearms with both of his hands. "Camila," he says urgently, "whatever you do, *don't throw up.* The chilies in that salsa are so hot that if you throw up they can burn your esophagus when they come back up. You could die."

"What?" she rasps, putting her hand to her throat. "What do you mean I could *die*? Now I really *am* going to throw up! What should I do?"

"Put your hands on top of your head and take ten deep breaths. Concentrate on keeping the food down. Don't throw up, okay?"

Everyone at the table stares at Camille like she's crazy, but she follows Alejandro's instructions exactly. She laces her fingers together on top of her head and takes slow, deep breaths. Alejandro leans over and says something to his aunt in their dialect; her eyes go wide, and she places her hand over her mouth, which alarms Camille even more. *Oh, no*—even his tía knows how dire her situation is. After Camille has taken five deep breaths, Alejandro moves his hand to his mouth. His body is shaking. She turns and looks at Tía Nifa, whose body is quaking as well—and it dawns on her. They're not shaking in fear. They're trying to stifle their laughter.

"You jerk!" Camille says, punching him hard. "You're making fun of me again!"

He rubs his shoulder. "*Ay, chingaos.* You're strong for such a skinny girl."

"That's right. And there's more where that came from if you mess with me again."

He laughs again. "I'm sorry, Camila. I couldn't help it. The look on your face was worth it. Especially after I told you how spicy the salsa was and you wouldn't listen. You know, *tú eres una necia.* You're a stubborn woman."

"Tell me something I don't know," she says, licking her lips. "So I'm not going to die if I throw up?"

Alejandro dips his tortilla into his soup. "Nope. You're not going to die. But you're not going to throw up either. Your mouth is just going to burn for a while. Here, have another tortilla. *Without* salsa."

Tía Nifa gives Camille a mischievous grin and reaches up to pat her cheeks. She says something to Camille in her dialect and cackles like a witch.

"What did she say?"

Alejandro looks guilty. "I really don't think I should tell you."

"Oh, come on. At this point, nothing's going to bother me."

He shrugs. "Okay, you asked for it. She said, '*Otra vez la burra al maizal.*'"

Here we go again. That donkey keeps following Camille back into the cornfield. So far, she hasn't learned a damn thing.

Only a slight sting from the chilies remains on Camille's lips. The melodious sound of Zapotec resonates around the room, making her so sleepy that her eyelids begin to droop. The girl wearing the purple apron sets down a large platter of sugary rolls on the table. Alejandro asks her in Spanish if there's any coffee.

Camille turns to Alejandro. "How come you didn't speak to her in your dialect?"

"Because we don't understand each other's language. The dialect we speak in Yalálag is not the same one they speak here in San Mateo."

"But I thought Yalálag was close by."

He explains to Camille that there are over sixty Zapotec dialects in Oaxaca and they vary from town to town. Before the Spaniards came to Oaxaca, the mountainous villages were so isolated that each developed their own dialect. These dialects have been passed down orally through the generations.

"So you and that girl can only communicate with each other in Spanish?"

"Yes. Unless we want to speak to each other in Italian or French," he says, winking at her again.

"Very funny, Alejandro."

With a smug look he says in perfect French, "*Qui est si drole?*"

Camille is dumbfounded. "You speak French too?"

He holds up his thumb and index finger. "*Un peu.*" He finishes his coffee and swings his leg over so he is straddling the bench. "Camila, why did you come here to Oaxaca?"

"I came to look for someone."

"Who?"

"My piano student."

His eyes dart down to her hand before quickly returning to her face. Over the past fifteen years, Camille has seen that look more times than she can count. She knows he's wondering how she can possibly play the piano with crippled fingers. She moves her hands to her lap.

"Who's the girl you're looking for?" he asks.

"How did you know my student is a girl?"

"Uh, I don't know. I just assumed she was a girl."

"Her name is Graciela. I've been told she's staying with her mother in Yalálag." She brightens as a thought occurs to her. "Wait a minute—didn't you say you're from around there?"

"Yes. It's my hometown, but I haven't lived there for many years."

Camille sits up straighter. "Maybe you know Graciela? She's eighteen, kind of petite, with dark skin and long black hair?"

He smiles. "You've pretty much described every young girl within a five hundred–mile radius."

"Okay, then," she says, "how about I add that she's also a phenomenal pianist?"

He smiles. "Now, that narrows it down a bit. Why did she come back to Oaxaca?"

Camille explains the situation: Six months ago, Graciela's mother, María, who worked as a housekeeper for Camille's mother, suddenly went back to Oaxaca, leaving Graciela behind. Graciela was planning to move to Los Angeles to live with her uncle. Not wanting to lose her as a student, Camille talked her into staying with her in Santa Barbara. That way, she could finish high school and graduate with her class.

"Graciela is the best student I've ever had. She's a musical prodigy for sure. Two weeks ago, she won the grand prize in this very prestigious piano competition. They awarded her five thousand dollars—and, more importantly, the opportunity to perform a concerto with an orchestra in front of some very influential people." She sighs. "That's why I'm here. The concert is in two weeks. I have to find her and get her back home so she doesn't miss out on this opportunity. This is her one chance to make something of herself."

Alejandro looks surprised. "So you came all this way to find her, hoping she'd go back with you?"

"She has to. This concert means everything—to her and to me. Now she's disappeared without a word. And not only that, she took the prize money from the competition with her."

He looks intently at Camille. "But isn't it her money?"

"Well, yes, but that's not the point. The point is, she left without telling me."

"How do you know she's in Yalálag?"

"Because I drove down to Los Angeles to look for her at her

uncle's house. Her family was hosting some sort of religious ceremony for someone who had died. A vigil, or something like that. She told me she was going to be there."

Camille thinks back to the afternoon when she drove to Graciela's uncle's house, hoping to find her there. The run-down neighborhood was packed with so many cars, Camille had to park three blocks away. She walked through streets littered with trash. Passed houses with iron bars on the windows. There were even homeless people sleeping in the doorways of abandoned businesses. When Camille finally arrived at the house, so many people were crowded into the small bungalow that it took her over twenty minutes to locate Graciela's uncle in the backyard. Camille remembers the surprise on his face when she forced her way to the front of the line and demanded that he tell her where he was hiding Graciela.

Camille meets Alejandro's gaze. "Anyway, it doesn't matter," she says. "I was too late. Her uncle had put her on a plane to Oaxaca that morning. I've worked so hard and for so many years to train Graciela to be the very best pianist she could be. I have no idea why she would do this to me."

Alejandro studies her for a moment. "Well, maybe she's not doing it to *you*, Camila. Maybe it was something she needed to do for herself."

"What do you mean?"

"Well, maybe she had a good reason for coming back here. Some reason that you don't know about yet."

Camille considers this for a moment. "Even if that's the case," she says quietly, "she could have at least called me to let me know she's all right."

He rubs his hands together. "That's true. It wasn't right for her to leave without saying anything. But maybe she did that because she thought you would try to stop her from leaving. Or maybe it was because she didn't want to disappoint you."

Camille frowns. "Alejandro, I hardly think you can presume to know what was going on in Graciela's head. You don't even know her. But whatever her reason was for leaving, she's made a complete mess of things. And now I'm the one who has to come here and fix everything."

A shadow crosses his face. "You know, Camila," he says, getting up from the table, "you might need to wait and hear Graciela's side of the story before you decide to blame her for everything. Maybe *you* shouldn't be the one to presume to know everything about Graciela." He stares hard at her. "Maybe *you're* the one who doesn't really know her."

CHAPTER 7

Camille stands shivering in a makeshift shower that's nothing more than a cement cubicle and a bucket of tepid water. She tries to work up a lather with a sliver of soap thinner than a business card but doesn't have much success.

She is still brooding over what Alejandro said about her relationship with Graciela. What did he mean, she doesn't really know Graciela? She has been her piano teacher for ten years. How could she not know her?

She clearly remembers the day Graciela came into her life. It all began almost a year after Camille's injury. After two painful and unsuccessful surgeries on her fingers, she had fallen into a deep depression.

Her mother realized she had to figure out a way to pull Camille out of her funk. One afternoon, she barged into the guesthouse unannounced and, ignoring the fact that Camille was still in her pajamas, sat down on the couch. "Darling, I have this idea that I've been mulling around in my head for a while."

"What kind of idea?" Camille asked warily.

She cleared her throat. "Well, I've been thinking that you should begin teaching piano lessons."

Camille laughed. "Mom, I'm sorry, but that's the most

ridiculous idea you've ever had. Who in their right mind is going to want their child to study with a one-handed pianist?"

"You leave that to me, Camille. You just get yourself down to the music store and stock up on some of those beginning music books. I'm going to get you so many students you won't know what to do with yourself."

And as always, when her mother said she was going to do something, she was true to her word. Within two months, Camille had a small studio and about fifteen students, mostly at the beginning to intermediate level. They were average kids who never really practiced or showed any real musical promise. But they were *her* students, even if all of them were the children or grandchildren of her mother's Montecito cronies—people who knew what had happened to Camille's fingers and felt sorry for her.

The funny thing was, Camille began to really enjoy teaching. She looked forward to working with her students each afternoon. She made it her mission to be the best teacher she could be, no matter the caliber of the student. If her students balked at practicing Bach or Mozart, she let them choose the music they wanted to play, even if she had to listen to them butcher "Für Elise," "Clair de Lune," or "The Entertainer" for the umpteenth time. It was imperative to her that her students make music a priority and love it as much as she did.

The real problem was that they were so overextended with homework, sports, and dance classes that they had little time to practice. Camille encouraged, cajoled, and even pleaded with them to work on their pieces between lessons, but nothing worked. Before long, she began to get discouraged. She kept waiting for that one gifted student to show up—the one that would turn everything around. After almost three years of mediocrity, she had just about given up.

One evening, after Camille had experienced a particularly

rough afternoon working with several unmotivated students, her mother announced that she had a new student to add to her studio.

"Forget it, Mom," Camille told her. "It's hard enough to get through each afternoon as it is. I'm seriously thinking of quitting teaching altogether."

Her mother couldn't contain her excitement. "You can't quit now, Camille. I think I've found *the one*."

"What do you mean?"

"Well, I can hear her *soul* when she plays. And even though she's never had any musical training, the sound she was producing on my piano the other day was exquisite. It was beyond anything I've ever heard from an eight-year-old girl. Except for you."

Camille's curiosity was piqued. "Who is she?"

"Her name is Graciela. She's María's daughter."

"María, your housekeeper?" Camille said, shocked. "But María's so young. She can't be much older than I am. How can she already have an eight-year-old kid?"

Her mother took a sip of wine. "Oh, I don't know. Maybe she started early. All I know is that her husband is out of the picture. María is raising Graciela by herself."

"When did you hear her play?"

"María brought Graciela over here the other day. Graciela had a cold and couldn't be left home alone. María was going to cancel, but my bridge club was coming over for a luncheon the following day. I couldn't have my friends over to a dirty house, so I said Graciela could come along. I left to meet a friend for coffee and when I returned, I heard the most beautiful music coming from the living room. At first I thought it was you improvising with your left hand. Imagine my surprise when I saw that it was Graciela! I should've been upset that she was playing the piano without my permission, but the more I listened, the more I realized I was hearing something extraordinary."

"Who's she studying with?" Camille asked, intrigued.

Her mother had a funny look on her face. "She's not studying with anyone, Camille. Graciela told me it was the first time in her life that she'd ever touched a piano."

When Camille met Graciela a few days later, she thought her mother had gotten it all wrong. Graciela didn't look like anything special. She was just a slip of a girl with skin the color of dark caramel and buckteeth that were too big for her mouth. She stood timidly in the foyer of Camille's mother's house, wearing a faded floral skirt, cheap tennis shoes, and white knee socks that had slipped down to her ankles.

"Camille," her mother said, "this is Graciela Valera."

"Hello," Camille said.

Graciela looked down at the floor and said nothing.

"Does she speak English?" Camille whispered.

"Of course she does. Graciela, say hello to my daughter, Camille. You may address her as 'Miss Camille.' She's going to be your piano teacher."

Graciela's eyes grew big. "Hello," she whispered.

"Hello, *Miss Camille*," Camille's mother prodded. "Use your manners, Graciela."

"Hello, Miss Camille," she said a little louder.

Camille's mother steered her toward the living room. "Now, Graciela, please sit down at the piano and play something for us."

"But I don't know how to play anything," she said.

Camille felt sorry for the girl. "Mom, you can't expect her to perform when she hasn't had any formal lessons."

Her mother put her finger to her lips. "Shhh, Camille. Just listen." She turned her attention back to Graciela. "Play anything, dear. Just like you did the other day."

Graciela sat down on the bench, placed her hands on the keys, and began to play. She played little more than simple notes and patterns, but the sound she produced was extraordinary. It was as if she was piecing together, one by one, little sparkling notes on a string, creating a beautiful necklace of sound.

Goose bumps prickled up and down Camille's arms. She looked over at her mother, who gave her an *I told you so* look, and in that moment, her world shifted. For the first time since she'd lost the use of her fingers, she felt something long forgotten surge through her. It felt like hope.

As Camille attempts to wash the mud from her hair, she wonders why Alejandro believes he has the right to comment on her relationship with Graciela. Who does he think he is, telling her she doesn't really know her? It's none of his business, anyway.

She rinses out her hair with the little water she has left, realizing that she's never really appreciated the simple act of bathing before. She thinks of her spacious, white-tiled bathroom back home, where she fills the tub with steaming water and scented oil, never once considering where the water came from. How can it be that two days ago she was living a cushy life in Santa Barbara, her every need met—and then some—and now she's in Mexico, happy to have a bucket of water to take a sponge bath with? Well, a sponge bath *minus* the sponge.

"Camila, are you all right in there?" Alejandro calls out from around the corner of the house.

"Wait! Don't come in. I'm not dressed yet."

"I just wanted to check on you. You're not feeling sick, are you?"

She runs the thin towel across her body. "No, I'm fine. I'm just getting dressed. I'll be out in a minute."

Camille fumbles in the dark for the clothes she's draped over the wall. One of the solemn-faced sisters—the one with the purple apron—has given Camille an old pair of jeans and a bright yellow T-shirt in exchange for her filthy clothes. Camille has a feeling the girl will either burn them in the fire or bury them somewhere in an unmarked grave.

The borrowed jeans are acid-washed and loose around the middle. After folding the waist down several times, the pants stay up around her hips. The yellow T-shirt is also too big, so she ties a corner into a knot.

She wraps her hair in the towel and carries the bucket outside. She spies Alejandro sitting in a weathered wooden chair on the patio, his fingers laced behind his head and his legs stretched out in front of him. Next to him on the ground is an old kerosene lantern. Its yellow-orange glow draws a swarm of moths that bat themselves against the dirty glass. Standing there quietly, Camille stares at his profile. She finds it difficult to look away.

She finally sets the bucket down. "Thanks for getting me the warm water."

He sits up and smiles at her. "Feel better?"

"You have no idea." She removes the towel from her head and holds it out to him. "What should I do with this?"

"I'll take it." He reaches down to pick something up from behind his chair. Taking the towel from Camille's hand, he replaces it with her huaraches. The mud has been wiped away, and they look brand-new again.

"What's this? You cleaned my huaraches?"

"Not me. My tía. Here—she also got these for you."

Camille laughs as he hands her two Band-Aids. She promptly peels them open and sticks one on the back of each heel. She brushes the dirt from the bottoms of her feet before slipping them into the huaraches. "I bet you were worried I was going to use up all of your T-shirts," she says.

He laughs. "Not really. But in case you need more, you know

where to find me." He holds up the lamp and studies Camille's face. "Do you know you still have some mud in your hair?"

She touches her fingers to her head. "I do?"

"On both side of your face. Near your ears."

"Damn," she says, reaching for the bucket. "Now I have to go back there and wash my hair all over again. And I've used up all the water."

He slides the wooden chair in front of her. "Sit down here and lean your head back. I can get it out for you. It's not very much."

Camille freezes, unsure what she should do. It's been so many years since a man has touched her that she's suddenly nervous.

"Really, it's no problem," he says. "I'll just go get some more water."

She hesitates a moment longer. *Oh, for god's sake, Camille, what's the big deal? Just let him help you.* "Okay," she says, and sits down. As she tips her head back over the chair, her stomach flutters.

Alejandro disappears for a minute. When he comes back, he sets a full bucket of water on the ground, rolls up the damp towel, and places it under her neck like a pillow. With his left hand, he covers up her ear and trickles some water through her hair. "Camila, this mud isn't coming out very well. Where's that little bottle of shampoo I gave you?"

"I left it on the wall by the shower."

He leaves to go get it.

The sudden quiet of the night is broken only by the sound of the wind in the trees and the distant voices of the passengers back at the barn. A moment later, Camille hears Alejandro walk up behind her.

He begins to gently massage her head. The sensation is so intense that Camille almost slides right off the chair.

"Camila? Did you hear me?"

"Mmmm?" She's having trouble focusing on his words.

"I asked you if you're cold. You've got goose bumps all over your arms."

Camille's skin prickles even more as Alejandro works his way down from one side of her head to the other. He uses the tips of his fingers to loosen the mud from around her hairline, and radiating heat begins to rush through her body. Her pulse quickens. She closes her eyes and presses her fingers into her thighs. *Camille, what is wrong with you? A few hours ago you couldn't stand this guy. Now you're practically swooning from his touch.*

Alejandro pours more water over her hair. "Camila—are you okay?"

"I'm fine," she whispers. She wants to scream, *Please don't stop!*

He twists her hair into a tight rope, and the water falls to the ground with a quiet splash. He dries her hair with the towel and his fingers brush the base of her neck. More heat floods through her.

"There," he says, throwing the towel over his shoulder. "All cleaned up. That wasn't so bad, right? Now it's time to get you into bed."

"*Excuse me?*" She stands up from the chair so fast that she knocks it backward. The metal bucket goes clattering across the patio. "What do you mean it's time to get me into bed?"

He picks up the chair and stares blankly at her. "Uh . . . just that it's late and it's time to go to sleep." He looks confused. "What did you think I meant?"

"I thought you meant—I mean, I thought you were talking about—oh, never mind." She hurries across the patio to retrieve the bucket, her face burning with embarrassment. She feels like a complete fool for misconstruing his comment. She picks up the bucket and holds it in front of her body like of piece of armor. She is humiliated and disappointed at the same time.

There is a strained silence. "So where are we supposed to sleep tonight?" she says quickly. "There can't be enough beds in these houses for everyone, right?"

"Beds?" he says, bending down to pick up the lantern. "You're not going to find any beds around here. Everyone's going to have to sleep in the barn where we just ate. On the ground." He gives her a challenging stare. "You okay with that?"

Her shoulders slump, and weariness settles back into her body like an old friend. "To be honest, Alejandro, I'm so tired even the ground sounds good to me."

An owl calls out into the darkness. One long and two short beats. It's a lonely sound.

Alejandro touches the back of her arm. "Camila, is there anything else you need?"

"Yes," she says, her voice heavy. "I need this day to be over."

CHAPTER 8

C amille wakes up in the darkness. She is disoriented and unable to make sense of her surroundings. A deep, paralyzing fear laces its way up her spine like a corset, cinching tighter with each shallow breath.

The sound of snoring brings it all back to her. The moonlight coming through the open door illuminates the rows of sleeping bodies lined up around her like newly dug graves in a crowded cemetery. Then she remembers: She's in the mountains of Oaxaca, sleeping on the dirt floor of a barn. Alejandro is here, too, somewhere on the other side of the room.

The loudest snoring seems to be coming from Tía Nifa. She is rolled up next to Camille in a nubby woven blanket. A rhythmic rattle comes from the back of her throat. A thread of drool has leaked out the side of her mouth, leaving a quarter-sized spot on the ground. No longer quite so terrified, Camille lies back down and pulls her own blanket up to her chin.

She tries to recall what woke her from such a deep sleep. A remnant of a familiar melody is running through her mind. As the phrase plays out, her anxiety returns. Suddenly, in a flash of clarity, the dream comes rushing back.

Oh, no. Please, not again. Not here.

For the past fifteen years, Camille has had the same nightmare at least once a month. It always begins with her standing backstage at a concert hall, about to perform a concerto with an orchestra. From the wings, she watches as the musicians tune their instruments, her excitement growing as each instrument adds to the echoing dissonance rising up through the auditorium.

"Ready, Miss Childs?" the conductor whispers in her ear.

She exudes confidence. "Ready when you are, Maestro."

In the dream, she always performs one of her favorite concertos: Beethoven's Fourth or Rachmaninoff's Second. Even though she hasn't played any of them in years, she still knows every note, every crescendo and diminuendo by heart. In tonight's dream she was performing Mozart's Concerto in D Minor, an unusually restless piece for the typically lighthearted Mozart.

The audience applauds enthusiastically as Camille walks onto the stage, the conductor following close behind. After shaking the concertmaster's hand, she bows, then sits down on the bench and arranges her white satin dress so it flares around her feet. Her red hair is pulled back in a loose chignon at the base of her neck. Her makeup is perfect.

The conductor steps up to the podium and faces the orchestra. Holding his baton in the air, he looks expectantly at Camille. She smiles and nods to indicate she's ready. He gives a quick flick of his wrist, and the orchestra begins to play.

Camille has an immediate, visceral reaction to the music. When she hears her cue, she places her hands on the smooth keys and begins to play. The concert grand piano is so responsive to her touch it's as if she's gliding her fingertips across still water. Any nervousness she felt is now gone, replaced with a sense of absolute purpose. She is lost in a glorious world of sound and vibration.

Suddenly, something feels strange. Her right hand becomes

sluggish and her fingers tighten up, making her technique sound sloppy.

After she plays several wrong notes, the conductor angles his head in her direction, an alarmed expression on his face. Concentrating with everything she has, Camille tries to regain control. She fumbles across the keys like a beginning piano student who's neglected to practice. She frantically attempts to keep up with the orchestra, but her right hand is so numb she can barely move it.

The conductor stops the orchestra midphrase, and an awkward silence falls over the concert hall. Mortified, Camille freezes, keeping her hands on the keys. Then she feels something warm and wet under her right fingers. She lifts up her hand, and a gasp from the audience blows across the stage like a hot wind. There is blood on the keyboard.

Excruciating pain tears through her right hand. A woman in the audience screams as more blood gushes from the underside of Camille's hand. It spills across her lap and onto the floor. Soon, there is blood everywhere. All over her white dress, soaking between the keys, and pooling under the pedals of the piano.

Horrified, Camille slowly turns her hand over and feels the air leave her lungs. Right where her third and fourth fingers meet her palm, the bloodied ends of two glistening bones stick out of her skin like jagged white sticks.

She screams and screams, but only silence escapes her lips.

"Camila," Alejandro whispers, "wake up. I found us a ride to Yalálag."

She opens her eyes to Alejandro's profile, silhouetted against the faint light of dawn. The once-still bodies of the passengers are stirring like the dead coming back to life. Camille rubs her eyes and notices that Tía Nifa is gone. Only her rumpled blanket remains, as if she's removed her shroud and floated off into the early-morning light.

Alejandro pats her arm. "We need to leave for San Mateo right now. I just talked to a *paisano* here. He said his brother is headed to Yalálag in about an hour. We can catch a ride with him." He holds out his hand.

"Okay, I'm up." Still unsettled by her nightmare, Camille takes his hand and allows him to pull her to her feet. She slips her toes into the stiff huaraches. The sting of pain on her heels momentarily distracts her from the intense sensation of her skin touching Alejandro's. "What about the rest of the passengers?"

"Don't worry about them. They're not in that big of a hurry to get there. The fiesta doesn't start until tonight."

"The fiesta?"

Alejandro still hasn't let go of her hand. "You don't know about the big celebration?"

Camille shakes her head. She has the sudden urge to take Alejandro's palm and hold it against her cheek. *Stop it, Camille.* She doesn't need to complicate her life with silly ideas of romance. Her total focus must be on bringing Graciela home in time for the concert. If she doesn't, her dream of becoming a master teacher will never materialize.

She lets go of Alejandro's hand.

He picks up Tía Nifa's blanket and folds it into a neat square. Before Camille even has the chance to pick up her own, he's folded it and stacked it on top of the other one. He motions for her to follow him outside.

The morning air is chilly after the previous day's heat. Camille holds her arms close to her body to stay warm. "What's this fiesta?"

Alejandro explains that a big celebration takes place every year in Yalálag called the *Festival de San Antonio de Padua*—Festival of Saint Anthony. "Every June 13th there is a big party in honor of his death," he says. "That's why so many people were traveling to Yalálag on the bus."

Camille looks at him blankly. "Sorry, but I've never been a very religious person. Who's Saint Anthony again?"

"San Antonio is the saint of lost things or lost people. Yalaltecos pray to him to help them find the things they've lost: people, courage, love . . . sometimes even their belief in the spirit."

Camille almost laughs at the irony. "Well now, I'd call that a pretty big coincidence, wouldn't you? Not only am I looking for a missing girl, but as of yesterday, I've lost every single one of my possessions. Including my shoes." She sighs heavily. "Anyway, it doesn't matter. I'm probably too much of a lost cause for even Saint Anthony to help me."

"You're not lost, Camila," he says firmly. "You're right here, in Oaxaca. With people who are here to help you find your way. And you're alive. After what happened with the bus yesterday, *es un milagro*—a miracle, right? I mean, look around you. The rain has stopped and the sun is shining. Everything is okay. You can't be lost if you know where you are, right?"

She tries to smile, but it comes out like a grimace.

"*Vámanos*," he says, taking her arm. "We need to get you to Yalálag so you can go into the church and pray to San Antonio. I know he's helped people who are a lot more lost than you."

They walk over to the fire. The solemn-faced sisters, wearing their same blue and lavender aprons, are patting balls of masa dough into tortillas. Their faces are scrubbed clean, and their braids gleam like woven ropes of black licorice. When she spies Camille, the lavender-aproned sister wipes her hands on her apron and runs off into one of the adobe houses.

Several men are warming themselves by the fire. Alejandro shakes their hands and thanks them for their generosity. They invite Camille and Alejandro to stay for breakfast, but Alejandro politely declines. Camille stands back, finding it unnerving being the only light-skinned person around. Being unable to speak the language, let alone understand it, makes her feels like an outsider.

Still, she is thankful for the kindness shown to her by these people, so she leaves her insecurity behind and chokes out a few words of inadequate Spanish. *"Muchas gracias a ustedes por todo,"* she says, waving to the group of people around the fire. Their faces light up; they seem impressed that the *Americana* speaks a little Spanish.

As Alejandro and Camille walk toward the road, the sister in the lavender apron comes out of one of the adobe houses and bolts toward them. Keeping her head down, she thrusts a small black plastic bag into Camille's hands.

"Disculpa, señorita," she says in high-pitched voice.

Camille is not used to her unique accent and can't understand the rest of the sentence. "What did she say?" she asks Alejandro.

"She said she's sorry they're still damp."

Confused, Camille opens the bag and looks inside. Folded neatly at the bottom are her shorts, shirt, underwear, and bra— and they are no longer stained the color of coffee. In fact, they are as white as when she first boarded the bus in Oaxaca City.

Camille is touched. "She washed my clothes? I thought she would surely throw them away. And how in the world did she get them so clean?"

Alejandro laughs. "With some heavy duty Zapotec magic, I'd say. Or maybe just a lot of bleach."

"That is so sweet," Camille says, blinking away her tears before she makes a fool of herself again.

Alejandro's eyes are bright. "See, Camila? You haven't even started praying to San Antonio, and he's already helped you find something you thought you'd lost. I'd say things are starting to look up for you."

"*Gracias*," Camille tells the girl, and reaches out to hug her tiny frame. She smells of wood smoke and roasted corn. Uncomfortable being embraced by the strange white lady, the girl stiffens. Camille only holds her tighter. After a moment, the girl relaxes and even hugs Camille back a little. When Camille releases her, the girl briefly looks her in the eyes. In the light of the early-morning sun, which is beginning to rise up over the mountains, Camille catches a hint of a shy smile on the girl's lips. Then, brushing off her apron, she lowers her head and hurries back to help her sister make tortillas.

Ten minutes later, they are hiking up the twisting road toward San Mateo. The sudden realization that they've left Tía Nifa behind hits Camille, and she stops and turns toward Alejandro. "Wait a second—what about your aunt?"

Alejandro keeps walking. "Oh, she's fine. She wanted to stay and help out with the cooking. My tía is miserable unless she's doing something for someone else. If a baby's born or if someone dies, we never know how long it will be before we see her again."

He chuckles, telling Camille a story of how when he was a teenager, his tía disappeared one day without a trace. Some people thought she had gone into the mountains to pick herbs and had fallen down and injured herself. Everyone was worried; they even put a search party together to go out and look for her. The old women went to the church to light candles and pray. After a week went by with no sign of her, everyone figured she was dead. Then, one afternoon, someone saw an old woman wearing a *huipil* slowly walking down the mountain path toward Yalálag. It was Tía Nifa. She had forgotten to tell anyone that she had gone to help a woman in the next town who had just given birth to twins.

"What's a *wee-pill*?" Camille asks.

"You know the dress my Tía Nifa was wearing?" he asks. "The white one with the colorful flowers and tassels? That's a *huipil*. They're woven by hand in Yalálag." He smiles at Camille. "So you don't need to worry about my Tía Nifa. She can take care of herself. She'll go with the others to San Mateo later today, and a bus will come from the other direction and take them back to Yalálag. Or maybe she'll walk there."

They continue on in silence. The sky lightens from pale pink to purple, then light blue. The only sound is the scraping of their shoes on the road and the wind whipping through the grasses. Although Camille is exhausted, she feels hopeful. If she can find Graciela and convince her that her bad choices are going to haunt her for the rest of her life—as Camille's bad choices have haunted her—then all the struggle will have been worth it.

If she can save Graciela, then maybe she can save herself.

CHAPTER 9

When Camille and Alejandro finally reach San Mateo, the main street is completely deserted but for a young indigenous girl. She's wearing an orange cotton skirt and balances a straw basket on her head. Alejandro greets her in Spanish and she nods shyly at them. As she passes by, Camille notices there is a lump of something tied to her back with a knotted white shawl. She looks closer; sticking out from underneath the material is a tuft of thick black hair.

Alejandro shades his eyes with his hand as he looks up and down the street. "I was told to wait in front of the church. Hopefully we haven't missed him."

Camille turns and looks back at the girl with the baby. She's so young—probably not even eighteen—yet she already has a child. Camille, meanwhile, is on her way to forty, with no chance of a baby in sight.

Camille follows Alejandro across the street. They enter a large courtyard encircled by an ornate wrought iron fence. On the far side of the square is a flamboyantly painted church as blue as the syrup at the bottom of a melted snow cone. Stenciled in bright red across the front is the familiar image of the Virgin Mary.

Camille has never seen that particular shade of blue paint anywhere in Santa Barbara. If anyone were to use that color there, she thinks, the City Planning Commission, the Architectural Board of Review, or quite possibly the police would show up within the hour and slap you with a hefty fine. Then they'd hand you a roller and a can of white paint and demand it be covered over as quickly as possible.

They take a seat on a wooden bench that faces the church. Alejandro seems to be lost in his own thoughts. Camille pretends to be interested in the scenery, but what she's really doing is stealing glances at him.

She can't seem to forget last night and the intense feeling of Alejandro's hands touching her hair. Sitting next to him in the warmth of the sun, she imagines what would happen if she leaned over and pressed her lips to his. Just thinking about it sends waves of heat surging through her body.

Abruptly, Alejandro turns toward her. "Camila, can I talk to you about something?"

Her breath catches. "Sure. What's up?"

"I need to tell you something."

She straightens her back. "What is it?"

"Well, I should've told you this before, but——"

The sound of a sputtering motor cuts him off. A battered red pickup truck emerges from the alleyway behind the church. It parks, leaving the engine idling.

Alejandro quickly stands up and starts jogging toward the truck. "That must be our guy," he shouts to her over his shoulder.

"Wait—what did you want to tell me?"

He doesn't answer; she assumes he's unable to hear her over the sound of the engine.

The man with the truck does indeed turn out to be Humberto, the brother of the man Alejandro met back at the ranch. With a smile jammed full of metal fillings, Humberto tells Alejandro he'd be happy to offer them a lift to Yalálag. But they will have to wait for his mother, who is still inside the church praying to the Virgin to help heal her injured toe.

Alejandro translates verbatim for Camille as Humberto describes how a donkey stepped on his mother's toe. It's quite an elaborate story, including details of how much pus came out from under her toenail. How the nail has turned black and is now hanging by a thread. How his mother has been forced to make numerous trips to the town healer for herbs and poultices to lessen the swelling. Normally Camille's remedial understanding of Spanish frustrates her. Now she just wishes Alejandro would stop translating and shut up already.

She is relieved when the door to the church opens. An old woman, barely five feet tall and wearing a faded gray dress and a black shawl over her head, limps in slow motion toward the truck. A white bandage sticks out the front of her huarache like a golf ball.

Camille has to stifle her laughter. "Don't forget to ask her about her toe," she whispers to Alejandro.

He makes a face. "I think I've heard enough about the damn toe for today. Although it's thanks to the *viejita*'s toe we don't have to walk to Yalálag."

"Maybe we should really give credit to the Virgin Mary," Camille says, crooking her thumb in the direction of the image on the front of the church. "Without her, the old lady probably wouldn't have spent so much time there in the first place."

"You know, Camila," he says, "around here we don't really call her the Virgin Mary. We refer to her as the *Virgen de Guadalupe*."

"You do? Why?"

"Well, basically she's the same person—the mother of God. You've never heard the story of the *Virgen de Guadalupe*?"

"I just thought she was the mother of Jesus—you know, the one in the manger at Christmastime."

"Sort of," he says, and goes on to explain that in 1531 an Indian peasant named Juan Diego saw a vision of a woman who claimed to be the mother of God. To express her love and support to the people, she asked Juan to build a church in her honor in the place where she appeared. Juan went to the archbishop in Mexico City with his story. He was required to go back and ask the woman to prove her existence through a miracle. The first miracle was that she healed Juan's uncle. The second miracle was that the woman told him to pick flowers that weren't native to that region and wouldn't have bloomed during the winter. He found roses growing at the top of the hill, picked them, and tucked them under his poncho. When he went back to the archbishop, the flowers fell on the ground, leaving the image of the Virgin of Guadalupe visible on the inside of his poncho in the place where he'd carried them.

Alejandro points up at the church. "The image you see painted there is what appeared on the material of his poncho. I'm sure you've seen it many times."

Camille remembers the decal of the Virgin staring at her from the windshield of the bus. Goose bumps prickle at her neck.

"Anyway, the *viejitas* around here never have a problem finding a reason to pray. They live for that stuff." He looks up at the Virgin's bright red image on the front of the church. Putting his palms together, he bows his head and begins chanting in a quiet voice. When he's done, he makes the sign of the cross and kisses his fingertips.

"What a beautiful prayer, Alejandro," Camille says. "I really wish my Spanish was better—what did you say?"

He looks at her with a straight face, bows his head, and recites the prayer in English: "*Thank you, dear Virgin, for all that you've given us on this glorious day, especially for the old lady's toe, because without her swollen toe, Camila and I would be walking to Yalálag right now."*

She laughs. "Amen to that."

Camille is thankful they have a ride to Yalálag, although their transportation is not quite what she expected. When Humberto first drove up in front of the church, she was so preoccupied with Alejandro that she didn't notice the dozen squawking chickens enclosed underneath a dome of wire attached to both sides of the truck bed.

She gives Alejandro a pleading look. "We're not really getting in there with those chickens, are we?"

He gestures toward the cab of the truck. "You can sit inside the truck with Humberto and his mother if you want."

She looks in the window. The cab of the truck is hardly big enough for two, let alone three. If she were to sit in the middle, Humberto would have to reach between her knees to shift gears.

"No thanks," she says, stepping up onto the bumper. "I'm better off riding in back with you."

Alejandro shrugs, offers his hand, and pulls her into the cage. The chickens dart around her feet and cluck in protest. She backs as far away from the scuttling birds as possible. "Alejandro, please promise me that if these chickens start to attack, you'll save me."

He smiles and makes an exaggerated twisting motion with his hands. "Don't worry, Camila. I have plenty of experience with chickens. If they decide to go after you, I know just what to do."

The road to Yalálag is bumpy, but Camille hardly notices because the scenery is so beautiful. The hillsides, green from recent rains, are covered in patches of purple lupines and red poppies. The humidity has left with the storm, and the cool mountain air paints her skin with the softest of brushes.

"How much longer until we get there?" she calls out to Alejandro.

He grins like a little boy as they bump across a bridge spanning a river with rushing green water. "We're almost there," he says, pointing to a large white sign on the side of the road that reads *Villa Hidalgo Yalálag* in black letters.

His happiness is so contagious that Camille can't help smiling back at him. She's also confident she'll be seeing Graciela before long. She is filled with hope. Maybe San Antonio is helping her find what she's looking for after all.

CHAPTER 10

As they drive down the bumpy road into the town, Camille is intrigued that most of the houses are built precariously into the side of the mountain. They look as if they might tumble down in a cascade of adobe bricks if a stiff wind were to blow.

Farther down the road there is another large church. This one is painted a rich terra-cotta red and trimmed in elaborate white piping, like a gingerbread house whose candy has all been eaten off.

The truck sputters into a roundabout and rolls to a stop. Camille climbs out from beneath the chicken wire and picks the white feathers from her clothes. Alejandro thanks Humberto for the ride, and the little red truck bounces off on the uneven cobblestones in a cloud of exhaust.

Camille, sore from sitting on the hard wheel well, rubs her backside with as much discretion as she can muster. "Now *that* was an experience."

"A good one, I hope?" Alejandro asks.

Camille smiles at him. "Definitely memorable."

He smiles back and looks her right in the eyes. "For me too."

Camille's heart begins to beat faster. She suddenly feels shy and looks away. "Okay," she says, clapping her hands together, "let's get down to business. How do we go about finding Graciela?"

He hesitates. "We could walk around town and look for her, but that might take a while. Aren't you hungry, Camila?"

"I'm starving." She slaps her hand to her mouth. "Sorry! I did it again. Yes, I would say that I'm ravenous."

He looks relieved. "Good. See that blue house over there?" He points to a small cement house in the exact shade of blue as the church back in San Mateo. "One of my tíos lives there. He has a little *comedor*—a small café with a few tables. I'm sure they'll be happy to make us something to eat."

Camille hikes up her sagging jeans, her stomach growling. "Lead the way, Alejandro. Right now I'm so hungry, I'd pretty much eat anything that's put in front of me." She looks down at her shirt and picks off another feather. "Except maybe chicken."

The minute they walk into the small café, six ancient-looking Yalaltecos—three men and three women—look up from the table. There are noticeably perplexed that a sunburned redhead wearing retro acid-washed jeans and an oversized canary-yellow T-shirt has just walked into their restaurant.

With the men on one side of the table and the women on the other, they squint at Camille and Alejandro like a choir of confused faces. They look up at Camille's red hair, then down to her huaraches, then over to Alejandro, and then back at Camille again, like they're conducting the sign of the cross with their eyes.

A woman's shaky voice breaks the silence. "*Alejandro?*" Only then do their faces register recognition. All six simultaneously leap up from the table. An instant party erupts in the tiny room.

They surround Camille in a circle. The men wear their pants cinched up high around their waists. They shake Camille's hand; their calloused skin is scratchy like sandpaper against hers. The women are dressed in a variety of colorful aprons. They embrace

Camille with their bony arms and pat her back with light, fluttering taps. One of them reaches up to give her a kiss on her cheek, then grasps a lock of red hair between her fingers, studying it intently. She whispers something to Alejandro in Zapotec.

He laughs. "Camila, my tía just told me your hair is the same color as a *cempasúchitl*."

"A *cempas*—what?"

"It's the kind of flower we use during *Día de los Muertos*—Day of the Dead—to decorate the cemetery. You know, *flor de muerto?* Marigolds?"

"Marigolds? That's a new one. I've been referred to as a gingersnap, a fire-head, and a carrot top before, but never a marigold."

Everyone begins to talk at once, and Camille is transfixed by the sound of them speaking their native Zapotec. Like instruments playing an orchestral score, their voices blend in perfect harmony. The rhythm of their words accelerates and slows, rising and falling in pitch and timbre. Alejandro is the handsome conductor who waves his hands back and forth as he relates the story of how their bus went over the side of the road. Camille doesn't understand a single word of their dialect, yet somehow she knows exactly what Alejandro is talking about. Perhaps this is why someone who has never studied classical music can still enjoy listening to it. The mechanics don't matter. It's all about the sound of the story.

Camille stands off to one side of the room, smiling politely. The women steal quick glances in her direction as they question Alejandro about her. They wag their fingers at him as he holds his palms up in denial. Camille assumes he's explaining that they're only acquaintances who just met on the bus, but they don't seem to believe him. Camille looks away, embarrassed, but she's also a little excited. If Alejandro's family thinks there's something going on, maybe there is.

The women usher them over to a large table covered with a white plastic tablecloth and insist they stay and eat. The men chat with Alejandro for a few minutes longer before donning their straw hats and heading off to help prepare for the fiesta.

Alejandro looks a bit sheepish. "Everyone thinks we're a couple," he says. "I tried to tell them we're not, but they don't believe me."

"That's ridiculous," she says, a little too forcefully. "But other than the fact that we walked in at the same time, why would they think we're together?"

He pulls out a white plastic patio chair from the table and gestures for her to sit down. "I'm not sure. Probably because I've never been seen with a woman in Yalálag before. Other than my wife, that is."

Camille's stomach drops. "You have a wife?" She tries to hide her shock. In her mind she pictures a dark-skinned beauty with almond-shaped eyes and long black hair. Someone who speaks fluent Spanish *and* Zapotec and knows how to make a delicious *caldo de pollo*. She is instantly jealous. "I didn't know you were married."

"I *was* married. I'm not anymore."

"You're divorced?"

"No. My wife died ten years ago."

She puts her hand up to her mouth. "Oh, I'm so sorry, Alejandro. That's so sad. How did she die?" As soon as the words leave her mouth, she regrets asking.

Alejandro shifts uncomfortably in his chair.

"I'm sorry," she says. "I didn't mean to pry."

"It's all right. It's kind of a long story."

"Well, I've got the time. If you want to tell me."

He looks as if he's searching for the right words, but just as he begins to speak, one of his aunts emerges from the tiny kitchen. She carries two glazed bowls of hot chocolate and has a basket of bread tucked under her arm. After placing them gently on the table, she takes out a wooden stick with an ornate ball carved into the end from her apron pocket.

Camille watches with curiosity as Alejandro's aunt dips the stick into one of the bowls of chocolate and furiously rubs it between her palms like she's trying to start a fire without matches. Within seconds, bubbly white foam appears across the top. The room fills with the rich aroma of chocolate.

"What's that stick thing she's using?" Camille asks Alejandro.

"It's a *molinillo*," he says. "It's kind of like a blender without the electricity. The little ball at the end whips up the foam when you spin it between your palms really fast."

His aunt repeats the same action with Alejandro's hot chocolate. When she finishes, he takes a long sip and sighs. "This is the best chocolate in town. But don't tell Tía Nifa I said that. She thinks her recipe is the best."

Pursing her lips, Camille blows a cooling channel into the foam, but before she can take a sip, Alejandro tears off a piece of his bread and dips it into her chocolate.

"Wait, Camila—try it this way." He reaches his arm across the table, and his fingers lightly graze her lips as he places the piece of moistened bread directly into her mouth.

She shivers, not sure if it's the touch of his fingers on her lips, the sweetness of the hot chocolate, or both, that has provoked the response.

Minutes later, the other two women come out of the kitchen carrying plates of scrambled eggs cooked with sautéed onion, tomato, and green chilies. There is a bowl of black beans, a ball of stringy cheese that looks like mozzarella, and a stone dish filled with a dark-colored salsa. Then comes the basket of homemade tortillas.

Their hunger takes precedence over any conversation, and Camille and Alejandro eat without talking for several minutes. She waits for him to tell her what happened to his wife, but he doesn't bring up the subject. Not wanting to push, she decides to keep the conversation light.

"So, I've told you that I'm a piano teacher, but you've never told me what you do for a living."

"You never asked me."

She tears off a piece of tortilla and scoops up some black beans. "You're right, I never did. I'm sorry. We both know I've been pretty much focusing on my own problems lately. But I'm actually really interested in hearing about what you do."

He finishes his bite of tortilla and swallows. "I have my own landscaping business in Los Angeles."

"Oh, you're a gardener?"

He stops eating and stares at her. "You know, Camila, just because I'm Mexican doesn't mean you can assume I'm a gardener."

"I didn't mean . . ." Her face flushes. Now she's gone and put her foot right back in her mouth again, unintentionally spoiling their growing connection.

He sighs. "It's all right, Camila. It's not like I don't hear that all the time. People see a dark-skinned Mexican like me and they think I can't be more than *just a gardener.*"

"It's nothing to be ashamed of," she says.

"I'm not ashamed. When I first came to Los Angeles, I worked as a gardener while I went to school to learn English. I'm proud that it helped get me where I am today. After I got my college degree, I started my own business. Now I design landscaping for industrial parks and large businesses."

Camille is unable to hide her surprise. "You went to college?"

He rolls his eyes. "Is that so hard for you to believe? I graduated from Cal Poly San Luis Obispo with a degree in landscape architecture."

"Wow. That's quite an accomplishment."

"You mean for a poor Mexican like me?"

"No, that's not what I meant at all. For *anyone*, graduating from college is something to be proud of. I didn't finish college."

Now it's his turn to look surprised. "You didn't? I figured you at least had a degree in music or something."

Somewhat defiantly, she holds up her right hand and shows him her bent fingers. "I couldn't finish my senior year at USC because of this."

He stares at her for a long moment before he takes her hand in his. He turns it over and studies the red scars that line the top of her palm. His hands are warm from holding the bowl of hot chocolate.

"*Ay, Dios mío.*" He touches the hard scar tissue with the tip of his finger. "What the hell happened to your hand?"

Camille pulls her hand away from his and abruptly rises from the table. "It's kind of a long story. Maybe I'll tell you about it sometime. But right now, it's time for us to go find Graciela."

CHAPTER 11

Camille's impatience grows as she stands outside the café in the blazing sun waiting for Alejandro to say goodbye to his aunts. A sheen of sweat breaks out on her forehead. *What is taking him so long?* She crosses the street and stands in the shade of the high brick wall that surrounds the church. Glancing down, she notices that amid the gray and black cobblestones at her feet there is a round white stone with thin, fingerlike stones extending out from it like a starburst. She scans the street to see if there are more, but it seems to be the only one.

She hears the squeak of the café's metal gate. Alejandro comes toward her with a troubled expression on his face.

"Camila," he says, "there's a problem with Graciela."

Her stomach knots. "What kind of problem?"

"She's not here."

"What do you mean she's not here?"

He strokes the stubble on his chin, making a faint scratching sound. "I mean she's not here in Yalálag. My tía just told me that she's with her mother at the hospital in Oaxaca City. María is really sick."

This new information causes Camille's recent breakfast to churn in her stomach like she's just swallowed a mouthful of salt water. "María's sick? What's wrong with her?"

"They don't know yet," he says, rubbing his hands together, "but they think it's probably something serious. Maybe cancer."

She puts a hand to her heart. "Cancer? How awful. How long have they been in Oaxaca City?"

"For about five days now."

Before she can stop it, an all-consuming rage surges through Camille's body. "Five days? Are you serious?" She grits her teeth so hard that a sharp pain shoots through her jawbone. It takes all of her strength to keep from stamping her feet on the ground. She can't believe that she's traveled thousands of miles, almost died in a bus accident, and lost every single one of her possessions only to find out that she didn't even need to come to Yalálag in the first place.

"You mean to tell me that I've come all this way for *nothing?*" she cries. "That I could've simply taken a taxi from the airport to the hospital to find her? I could've avoided this entire stupid, horrible experience?" She takes the plastic bag of clothes in her hand and swings it hard against the ground. "What a complete waste of my time!" She grabs the front of her head and rocks back and forth. "Now what am I going to do?"

"The first thing you need to do is to calm down," Alejandro says, his voice low. "Getting angry about something you have no control over is useless."

"That's easy for you to say, Alejandro. Your professional career is not dependent on the actions of an inconsiderate teenager."

She looks up at him. He is staring at her in silence, his face as hard as the stones beneath their feet.

She puts her hands on her hips and turns to fully face him. "So what should we do now? Do you have any idea when the road will be fixed so we can go back to Oaxaca City?"

He cocks his head to one side. "*We?*" he asks. "What do you mean, *we*, Camila? I'm not going back to the city until next week."

"Oh, right." She shakes her head. "I meant me, of course. I'm the one who needs to get back to the city. I'm the one running out of time."

He narrows his eyes at her. "I don't think you get it, Camila. You're not the one running out of time—María is. The mother of your best piano student could be dying in a hospital right now, and all you care about is yourself. Do you have any idea how selfish you sound?"

She winces, stung by his words. "That's not fair, Alejandro. I feel awful for María. But I have to finish what I came here to do. I have to find Graciela and get her back home in time for her concert."

"Well, *lucky you*," he says, not even trying to hide the sarcasm in his voice, "my tía just told me that the road is being fixed right now. It should open tomorrow or the next day."

Camille immediately feels calmer. "That's good." She taps her fingers to her lips, calculating how much time she'll need to find Graciela and get her on a plane back to LA. "Do you know where I can find a phone? I need to call my mother and have her wire me some money."

"The phones aren't working. The lines went down during the storm. It's probably going to take a few days to repair them."

"What am I supposed to do for money, then?"

"What do you need money for?"

"Well, for one thing, I need to pay for a place to stay tonight—and food. And I need to buy some clothes. All I have are my white shorts and these ugly clothes I got back in San Mateo. I can't keep wearing this stuff. I look ridiculous."

He shakes his head. "I doubt there's one person around here who cares what you're wearing. And you don't need to pay to sleep somewhere. You can stay at Tía Nifa's house tonight. She has lots of room and probably won't be back until tomorrow. As for clothes, I'm sure she has something you can borrow. And I don't know about you, but I'm going to eat at the fiesta tonight. There'll be plenty of food for everyone."

She thinks for a moment. "Well, I guess that would be all right. Are you going to sleep at your tía Nifa's tonight too?"

"I was planning to, but I wouldn't want to make you feel uncomfortable," he says, an edge to his voice.

"Well, it's not like we haven't already slept in the same room together," she says, attempting to ease the tension with a joke. "Even though there were about forty other people sandwiched between us."

He doesn't even crack a smile. "What do you want to do, Camila?"

"Well, I guess staying at your aunt's house would be fine. Thank you."

"You're welcome," he says, his tone still somewhat brusque. "And by the way, I'm really sorry that coming here to my hometown—and *Graciela's* hometown—has been a *complete* waste of your time."

She looks down. "I'm sorry. I didn't mean it. This trip hasn't been a waste of time. I was just venting. I mean, I've met you and your tía Nifa, and everyone's been so kind to me. I'm just aggravated because I thought that once we made it here to Yalálag, it would be easy to find Graciela—that I'd bring her home and everything would go back to normal."

"Camila," he says, still sounding frustrated, "I think that you need to realize that there's no such thing as normal, or what you consider normal, around here. You can't always control everything that happens."

She sits down on a low brick wall and bows her head. "I know. But I'm so tired of all the obstacles that keep getting in my way."

He sits down next to her. "Then don't think of them like that. Think of them as a chance to learn something."

Her shoulders sag. "Easier said than done. Especially when I have this deadline looming over my head."

"And what would happen if Graciela didn't make it back in time? If her mother is that sick, she might not want to go back. How bad would it be if Graciela decided to stay in Oaxaca?"

That familiar vise of anxiety elbows its way back into the front of Camille's chest. "She has to come back with me. I won't let her throw away this opportunity. All those years of work and effort on both our parts would be for nothing if she doesn't take this chance. Her future career depends on it."

His eyes become serious. "Her future career or *yours,* Camila?" He puts his hand on her forearm. "Tell me the truth. What will happen to *you* if Graciela doesn't make it back in time for the concert?"

Camille's anxiety turns to despair. Hot tears sting the backs of her eyelids, and she leans down and covers her face with her hands. She knows that if Graciela doesn't perform at the concert, she can kiss her career as a master teacher goodbye. She'll never have another student as gifted as her.

She stands up and faces him. "Without Graciela, I'll be stuck teaching piano to uninterested students who have no real desire to study music. Students who never practice enough. Students who are only taking piano lessons because their parents insist they do. No one will know, or care, for that matter, who *I* am. That I was once really special. That I was the best."

She wipes away the tears with the backs of her hands. "I've already lost one of my dreams, Alejandro. I don't want to lose another."

He stares at her. "There are other dreams, Camila."

"Not for me," she says, her voice heavy. "I'm a piano teacher. I don't know how to be anything else."

She waits for him to respond, but this time, he stays silent.

CHAPTER 12

Camille feels her world caving in around her. If she can't get Graciela back to Los Angeles in time for the orchestra rehearsal, the student who is the runner-up will get to take her place. *I'll be damned if I'm going to let that happen*, Camille thinks, angrily. Mainly because the runner-up is Amy Chen, the top student of Camille's nemesis, Sofia Vanilovich.

When it comes to piano teachers in Santa Barbara, Sofia is Camille's greatest competition. Sofia has made it her mission to prove that she's the best teacher in town—something Camille finds ludicrous, since Sofia's students don't even play that well. Their tone quality is strident, and they lack sensitivity in their playing. Somehow, though, she gets them to practice multiple hours each day so that to the untrained ear they sound like little virtuosic prodigies. Because of that, she has a lot of supporters in Santa Barbara, even if they're nothing but a bunch of musically ignorant idiots who think that anyone who can play loud and fast has exceptional talent.

Camille has never disliked anyone as much as she does Sofia, and it's not because she can play the piano with both hands. She would be the first to admit that Sofia is an exceptional pianist, and a strikingly beautiful woman, too—tall and lithe, with icy blue eyes and short, spiky blond hair. She resembles a Russian princess. It's Sofia's attitude that Camille can't stand. Sofia is of the opinion that she's automatically a superior musician just because her parents emigrated from Russia. She's always spouting off about how great the Russian style is—how they really know how to teach music back in the homeland. Sofia acts like Prokofiev and Rachmaninoff are old family friends. It's almost comical that she's been in the US since she was three years old, yet she still speaks with an affected Russian accent.

The sad part is that she and Camille used to be friends. They studied with the same piano teacher as children and even performed duets together. But after Camille beat her out in the San Francisco Young Artists' Piano Competition when Sofia was thirteen and Camille was eleven, Sofia turned on Camille. From that moment on, she became more jealous each time Camille won another competition or when Camille was asked to perform somewhere and she wasn't. She began gossiping and spreading lies about Camille. It's become Sofia's mission in life to find every possible way to torment Camille.

Camille has known of Sofia's deviousness since they were teenagers, but the true depth of her guile was revealed a week after Sofia graduated with her doctorate in musical arts from Juilliard. Camille heard through the musical grapevine that Sofia had offers from a number of conservatories to join their faculty, yet only one year after Camille started up her piano studio in Santa Barbara, Sofia chose to move back and open her own, competing music school. Even worse, she began to circulate lies about Camille in the community. She told everyone that Camille's hand injury had made her emotionally unstable.

Camille's mother was infuriated by Sofia's outrageous behavior. One evening, after consuming almost two bottles of wine, she lost it.

"Here she is, trying to steal your students away from you," she shouted, "saying terrible things about you! And why? Because that Sofia Vanilovich has absolutely no moral character." She slurred her words so badly that Vanilovich came out as "Vanilla Bitch"—a slip that sent her into a fit of drunken laughter. From that moment on, the name stuck.

A little over a month ago, Camille ran into Sofia at a student recital held at the Bella Vista Conservatory of Music. After the recital, Camille watched Sofia make a beeline for Graciela. Camille knew she was attempting to coerce Graciela into switching over to her conservatory; she rushed to Graciela's side and put a protective arm around her shoulder.

"Oh, Camille, *dahling*," Sofia purred, her phony accent making her sound like Natasha from *Rocky and Bullwinkle*. "There you are! I thought maybe you had already left." She fluffed the top of her blond hair with her fingers. "I was just complimenting Graciela on her beautiful performance today. She plays Chopin with such lovely expression. Camille, you should really have Graciela play more of the Russian composers. Perhaps some Rachmaninoff, no? You know, I'd be more than happy to give Graciela some pointers on the Russian style, since you clearly lack expertise in that area."

Screw you, Vanilla Bitch, Camille would've shouted if Graciela hadn't been standing right there. Camille quickly moved Graciela away from her. "Thanks, Sofia. But I'm afraid we can't chitchat right now. After such a big performance, I'm sure Graciela is ravenous. I'm going to take her over to the refreshment table for a snack. Please excuse us."

"Of course," Sofia said, waving her hand in the air so that her gold bracelets slid down her arm like a glissando. "Oh, by the way, Camille, did you hear the exciting news that my student Amy Chen got accepted into Juilliard?"

Camille tried not to roll her eyes. "Yes, I did hear that, Sofia. Congratulations."

"Thank you so much," she said airily. "It's all so very exciting. She'll be starting there in September."

Camille and Graciela began to walk away, but Sofia placed a firm hand on Graciela's arm, preventing her from leaving. "And you, Graciela? What are your plans for college? I imagine it would be easy for you to get into any music school with your talent. And of course, with your *ethnicity*, you're bound to have an edge over most of the other students who are not so, how do I put it—*diverse*? And perhaps with your socioeconomic background you'll be eligible for a need-based scholarship . . . no?"

Graciela's eyes went wide with shock at Sofia's offensive comments, but she said nothing.

Damn that Vanilla Bitch! Camille had to think fast before she lost her cool. "Graciela is taking a year off to practice and enter as many competitions as possible before applying to conservatories. In fact, she's competing in the Los Angeles Young Artists' Competition next month."

For a brief moment, Sofia looked uneasy. "Of course," she said, "and I wish her the best of luck with that. You do know my Amy is also competing in that competition?"

Camille's heart sank. *Oh, great.* Amy had the technique of a well-oiled machine. She forced a smile. "Well, that's wonderful, Sofia. I guess we'll be seeing you there."

"Indeed you will, Camille. Oh—one more thing, Graciela," Sofia said, her hand still firmly attached to Graciela's arm. "I was wondering if you could answer one last question for me. It's something I've been curious about for a long time." She smiled like a Cheshire cat. "Tell me . . . what is it like to have a piano teacher who can only play the piano with one hand?"

Camille heard Graciela's sharp intake of breath. Scarcely able to believe what she'd heard, she was just about to let that Russian Vanilla Bitch have it when Graciela calmly steered her away in the other direction.

"It's all right, Miss Camille," she said, her voice strong and sure. She turned back toward Sofia. "I guess I'd have to say that it's much better to have a piano teacher with one hand who really knows how to teach than to have a piano teacher with two hands who doesn't."

And that's what Camille can't understand. How could Graciela have stood up for her like that and then run off to Oaxaca without a word? This concert is Camille's chance to prove that she still has something left to offer to the music world. After what happened to her fingers fifteen years ago, she may have lost her shot at a concert career, but she can still teach the piano, and teach it well. But unless she can find Graciela and bring her home, this once-in-a-lifetime opportunity will be gone for good. Without Graciela, she has no hope to prove that she still has what it takes to be the best.

Her eyes fill with tears as she thinks of how unfair life can be. She's been through so much already. Just when she thinks her life is starting to look up and her musical career is finally heading in the right direction, Graciela has to go and do something utterly selfish, forcing Camille to take matters into her own hands and travel all the way to these godforsaken mountains looking for her.

And now she's not even here.

CHAPTER 13

Hiking up the twisting path to Tía Nifa's house, Camille feels the backs of her calves strain with each step. She's exhausted, sweaty, and so thoroughly discouraged that all she wants to do is lie down under a shady tree, close her eyes, and forget that everything has completely fallen apart.

"See that fence up there with the black metal gate?" Alejandro says, pointing up the hill. "That's my tía's house. C'mon, you can make it. We're almost there."

The thought of climbing another steep hill makes Camille want to scream. She lets out a moan and sits down on a crumbling brick wall threaded with dead weeds. Her bad temper festers like the blisters on her heels. Between gulps of breath, she calls to Alejandro, "Wait. I have to rest."

He walks back and sits down next to her. "It's the altitude. It takes a while to get used to the thin air up here in the mountains. You've probably already noticed that Yalaltecos are never in that much of a hurry."

Camille doesn't bother to hide her grumpiness. "Well, maybe that's because they're so damn tired from hiking up and down these stupid mountains all day long."

He sighs. "Don't be such a baby, Camila. Sit and catch your breath for a minute. You'll be fine."

She wipes the sweat from the back of her neck and breathes in deeply. From this vantage point, the view of the surrounding mountains is spectacular, but the actual neighborhood is quite bleak. Most of the houses are in disrepair. The adobe bricks are crumbling, and the stucco is stained and cracked. Behind her, a flimsy fence made of wood scraps fastened with bits of wire gives her a direct view of a level of poverty she's never seen up close before.

The entire house is less than half the size of her bedroom back home. It consists of three cement brick walls with rebar sticking out of the unfinished walls. The roof is nothing more than sheets of rusted aluminum that have been haphazardly hammered together. A frayed blanket hangs in place of a front door. The yard is overflowing with junk—stacks of old wood, plastic buckets, and rolls of rusted chicken wire are piled around the property. Dozens of empty soda bottles and scraps of trash litter the ground. A frayed rope stretches across the yard, hung with dingy, worn items of clothing.

Camille wonders how people can live like this. Everything is so disorganized and chaotic. She turns away and glances up the hill at Tía Nifa's gate, praying that her house isn't as disgusting as this one.

"I feel sorry for the people who live here," she says.

"Why?" he asks, using his hand to shade his eyes from the sun.

"Well, just look at it."

He slowly shakes his head back and forth like he's disappointed in her. "Camila, this place may not seem like much to you, but someone worked really hard to pay for it. It's probably owned by some poor guy who's had to leave his wife and children here in Yalálag and go to work washing dishes in the States. It might not live up to your standards, but to them, this is home."

She wrinkles her nose. "I would think they would at least clean it up a little. Maybe pick up the trash or something."

He sighs and looks up the hill toward Tía Nifa's house. "Yeah, well—poverty can mess you up pretty badly. Your priorities change when you're struggling to survive. I don't think that's something you'll ever be able to understand." He stands up and dusts off his jeans. "Do you think you can make it up the hill now?"

"Do I have a choice?"

"Nope. Not unless you want me to leave you sitting here." His voice softens a little. "Tell you what, this part is pretty steep. Take my hand and I'll help pull you up the hill."

She slowly gets to her feet. "Or maybe since you're already so good at it, you could carry me?" she says, only half joking.

"Not this time, *mujer*," he grunts. "It's the hand or nothing."

When they finally make it to Tía Nifa's gate, Camille's legs feel like wet noodles. Alejandro reaches down behind a terra-cotta pot laden with bright red geraniums, jiggles a loose brick in the wall, reaches inside the opening, and takes out a key dangling on a thin leather string.

"My tía Nifa is a big believer in home security," he says, winking at Camille. "She thinks her hiding place is a big secret, but the whole neighborhood knows about it." He puts the key in the lock, turns it to the right, and pushes the gate open with a noisy squeak.

Camille follows him in through the gate. *Try not to judge*, she tells herself. *More importantly, keep your big mouth shut.* But when they enter the courtyard, she's so surprised she couldn't speak if she wanted to.

It's magnificent. Everywhere she looks, colorful plants and flowers explode from all corners of the patio. Trumpet flowers climb the walls like pink butterflies perched on strands of green silk. Bees buzz noisily around terra-cotta pots spilling over with golden lantana. A tangle of burgundy bougainvillea spreads out across the adobe walls like the piping on a child's birthday cake. It looks like something out of *Alice in Wonderland*.

"Oh, my," she says, trying to take it all in at once.

"You like it?"

"Alejandro, this is incredible!" Camille turns around in a complete circle so she doesn't miss anything. "I had no idea what was behind this gate would be so spectacular. Is this all your design?"

He grins, unable to hide his pleasure. "Yes. It's pretty, isn't it?"

"It's exquisite. And so colorful! Some of these flowers I've never seen before in my life."

The house, constructed in the traditional Mexican style with white stucco and a red-tiled roof, abuts the mountainside. A covered porch runs along the entire front of the house. Wire baskets of cascading red flowers hang from the beams over a large wooden table and a set of chairs. Alejandro walks over to a wall fountain made of cobalt-blue-and-white tiles set into a diamond pattern and plugs in the electrical cord. The water begins to bubble in a soothing rhythm.

"This is paradise," Camille gushes, "and the best part about it is that it doesn't even seem like someone designed it. It seems natural, like everything just grew here on its own."

His eyes shine. "I wanted it to feel like a private oasis."

"It does. From out on the street, I'd never have guessed what was in here. It's like opening a present that's been wrapped in plain brown paper and discovering a beautiful gift inside."

He looks pleased. "Thank you, Camila. I appreciate that. Here, let me help you with your things." He takes the black plastic bag out of her hands. "Since my tía isn't here, I guess I'll be the one taking care of you."

"Thank you," she says, feeling her mood improve. She heads toward the house. "Is the bathroom this way?"

"Uh, no." He turns and points to a small cement building bordered by several banana trees on the opposite side of the property. "It's over there. Don't put the paper into the toilet—put it in the trash can. The plumbing around here isn't the best."

Camille makes a beeline for the bathroom. Inside, there is a toilet and a small sink. Next to that is a shower nozzle over a drain in the floor.

As soon as she unzips her jeans, something black skitters across the floor. She leaps up with a shriek and jiggles the door handle, but it won't open.

Alejandro rushes over to the door. "What's wrong?"

"There's something hideous crawling around in here, and the door won't open!" She begins to kick the metal door.

"Camila, don't force it. I'll open it from out here."

Alejandro finally gets it open, and Camille rushes out to the patio holding her pants up around her waist. She hears something hit the floor with a thud. A moment later Alejandro comes out holding one of his huaraches in his hand.

"It was a scorpion. But don't worry, I killed it with my shoe. It's safe to go back in now."

She shivers as she sits back down on the toilet, not sure if it's because of the cold porcelain or because she can still see the smashed carcass of the scorpion on the floor. There's no toilet seat, and the bowl is so wide she has to hold on to the sides to avoid falling in. There is also no toilet paper. Instead, a wire ring hanging from the wall is pierced with a thick wad of magazine pages that have been cut up into squares. She yanks off a sheet that includes the partial face of an attractive Latina woman with heavily made-up eyes.

She washes her hands with a hunk of purple glycerin soap and, finding no towel, dries them on her shirt.

Outside, Alejandro is waiting for her by the front door. "Come on in," he says, smiling. *"Mi casa es su casa."*

The inside of Tía Nifa's house is old and smells a bit musty, but compared to the poverty Camille saw down the street, it's practically luxurious. The walls are whitewashed and the floor is covered in large squares of black tile—cracked in places, but clean.

Alejandro leads Camille into the open-air kitchen first, which is connected to the patio through a wide archway. A table covered with a blue plastic tablecloth sits in the center of the room. An older-model, root beer–colored refrigerator stands alone in the corner.

Without thinking, Camille walks over and opens the refrigerator door. She wrinkles her nose as a waft of sour-smelling air hits her in the face. Instead of food, she counts five pairs of leather huaraches and a pair of brand-new white tennis shoes stacked in neat rows on the wire shelves.

"Whoops," she says, trying not to laugh. "Sorry."

Alejandro covers his eyes with his hand and shakes his head back and forth. "Typical," he says. "I bought this refrigerator for my tía over ten years ago, but I don't think she's ever plugged it in. What you're looking at right there is a very expensive shoe closet."

Camille walks out to the kitchen patio and points to what looks like a barbecue pit with a large plate on top covered in a layer of flour. "What is that?"

"That's the *comal*," he says. "It's an outdoor stove—it's like a big plate where the food is cooked. It's made of clay, and we put lime on it so the tortillas don't stick to it. Most Yalaltecos cook all of their food outdoors on a *comal*."

Back inside, Alejandro shows Camille Tía Nifa's bedroom. The walls are painted a warm rust color. A queen-size bed covered with a bright blue-and-yellow cotton bedspread and matching pillows takes up most of the room. Hanging from the ceiling is a swath of sheer mosquito netting that encloses the entire bed in a filmy canopy. On either side of the bed are two wooden end tables, each with its own old-fashioned glass lantern. Against one wall is a large wooden wardrobe with an ivy plant set on top, the green vines twisting down almost to the floor. Alejandro opens the wooden shutters that cover the window and the sun spills in, bathing the room in a wash of warm light.

Camille smiles. "For some reason, I'm getting the sense that you had something to do with the decor of this room as well."

Alejandro puts his hands in his pockets and looks as if he's mentally checking off each improvement that he's made. "It's true. Every time I come back here to visit my tía, I always do something to help her fix up the house. I plant something in the garden, fix the roof, whatever needs to be done. A couple of years ago, I told her I wanted to make her bedroom really nice. I painted it and went to the city to buy her a new bed. The last day I was here, I finally finished everything and brought her in to see the room. She began to cry because she was so happy. Six months later, I came back for a surprise visit and arrived before dawn. Not wanting to wake her, I let myself in. There she was, sound asleep on a *petate*—a straw mat—on the floor of the main room."

"She didn't like her new bed?"

"I don't know. I don't think she ever actually slept in it. Later on, she admitted to me that she thought the room was too fancy for an old woman like her. She treats it like a museum and only comes in here to visit sometimes. This morning before we left the *ranchería,* she told me she wanted you to sleep in here tonight."

A warm sensation spreads through Camille's chest. "She said that? I thought she didn't like me that much."

"Oh, she likes you all right. If she didn't, you wouldn't be standing here right now."

They walk into the main room of the house. It could be the living room, although it has no furniture except a table that's pushed up against one wall and acting as some sort of a makeshift altar. High on the wall above it hangs a black-and-white photograph of a serious-looking young couple wearing traditional clothing. In addition to her *huipil*, the woman in the photograph has a black headdress wrapped around her head. Both the man and the woman stare into the camera with unsmiling faces; their expressions looked carved from ancient stone.

The woman in the photo is familiar. "Is that your tía when she was young?" Camille asks.

"Yes. That picture was taken of my tíos on their wedding day— I think it was sometime in the early 1950s. Did you notice that they're standing in front of the same church where we were dropped off this morning?"

"Amazing." Camille smiles and turns her attention to the altar, which is spread with a white cloth embroidered in delicate blue and red flowers. Two plastic vases are stuffed with bunches of flowers that withered and died long ago. There is an upside-down painting of what looks like a Catholic saint holding a small child. Camille reaches over to turn it right side up, but Alejandro grabs her by the wrist, stopping her.

"Don't," he says. "Leave it that way. It's supposed to be upside down."

"Why?"

"That's a picture of San Antonio de Padua. Remember, the saint we were talking about earlier? For this time of celebration, you're supposed to turn his picture upside down until you find what you're looking for. When you find it, you turn the picture right side up again."

"Oh, sorry. I had no idea. What do you think your tía Nifa is looking for?"

Alejandro pauses for a moment. "I'm not really sure. But I'm the closest thing she has to a son, so I think it has something to do with me." He points to a faded Polaroid photograph of himself as a young man with his arm around a pretty young woman. They both stare at the camera, as unsmiling as his aunt and uncle.

Camille studies the photograph. "Is that a photo of you and your wife?"

"Yes—that's Araceli. That picture was taken in Los Angeles when we first got married."

"She was so pretty."

Alejandro suddenly looks sad.

"Back when we were eating breakfast, you were about to tell me what happened to your wife . . ."

He turns and looks at her. "And you were going to tell me what happened to your fingers."

Camille nods.

"Tell you what—why don't you go out to the patio and take a short nap in the hammock? I'm going to take a shower and change my clothes. When I'm done, we can talk. I think both of us have very long stories to tell each other."

CHAPTER 14

The distant sound of a flute floating up the hillside gently pulls Camille out of a deep sleep. She only intended to take a quick nap, but her exhaustion was no match for the gentle swinging of the hammock.

"*Hola, dormilona*," Alejandro says, startling her.

She bolts upright, and the hammock pitches back and forth. She tries to get out but finds herself thoroughly entangled in the web of knots.

"You scared me," she says, trying to pull the sides of the hammock apart. Her actions only make it swing more violently.

He laughs. "Need some help?"

Camille continues to thrash about while he stands there patiently. "Seriously, Alejandro," she says, irritated. "This is getting old. Every time you show up, I act like some idiot who can't take care of herself."

Alejandro grabs the sides of the hammock to stop the swinging. "It's never easy getting out of there for me either. Maybe if you stopped fighting, you'd be able to get yourself free."

"Fine," she says, crossing one foot over the other and settling herself back into the hammock. "I give up."

Alejandro pulls a wooden chair over from the patio and places it under the tree so he's sitting right next to her. "Here," he says, holding up a cold bottle of water. "I walked down to the market while you were sleeping."

He looks like he just stepped off the pages of GQ Magazine. He's wearing a pair of faded Levi's and a cotton shirt with the sleeves rolled halfway up his arms. His hair is damp from showering, and the scent of soap and shampoo coming off his body is intoxicating. Those recent iniquitous thoughts come back into her mind as she imagines pulling him into the hammock with her.

Camille reaches through the ropes like a prisoner behind bars and takes the water. It is ice-cold and delicious, and she gulps more than half of it in one long swallow. She wipes her mouth with the back of her hand. "So what's the plan for tonight?"

"Do we need a plan?" he asks.

"I guess not. How about if I just tag along with you? I was thinking it would be fun for me to experience the real Yalálag."

"I thought that's what you were already doing," he says, his eyes teasing. "But if you need a plan, I've got one. First we'll go to the fiesta and eat, and then we can go down to the square and listen to the *banda*. I'll teach you the traditional dance of Yalálag."

"That sounds wonderful," Camille says, feeling a twinge of excitement as she pictures herself dancing with Alejandro. Looking down, she makes a face at her garish yellow T-shirt and baggy jeans. "The only problem is that I don't have anything to wear."

Alejandro scratches the back of his head. "I actually found a dress in my tía's closet that will probably fit you. I put it on the bed."

The thought crosses Camille's mind that the dress may have belonged to Alejandro's wife. "Is it one of Tía Nifa's dresses?"

"I'm not sure. I've never seen it before." He studies her face for a moment. "It's not Araceli's dress, if that's what you're thinking."

"No, no—I wasn't thinking that," she says, her lie obvious to both of them.

Alejandro leans back in the chair and crosses his legs. "Araceli wouldn't have worn a dress like that anyway. She was born in LA, so she wasn't really traditional like most Yalalteca women. She liked to buy her clothes at Macy's."

Camille is relieved he's finally brought up the subject of his late wife. "How did the two of you meet?"

"Oh, you know. We'd see each other at all the fiestas around town. I knew who she was because all Yalaltecos know each other—here and in LA."

"Were the two of you pretty young when you got married?"

"I was twenty and she was eighteen. I'd been in the US for about three years, and I was doing really well in my English classes. One of my teachers told me I had potential, but back then I couldn't go on to a university without a green card. Araceli married me so I could become legal, get my papers, and finish my education."

Somehow, this information makes Camille feel lighter inside. "So the two of you didn't really marry for love?"

He looks thoughtful. "Well, I did love her, but more like a sister. She was my closest friend. Without her help it would have been so much harder. And I know she loved me, too, but I really think she just wanted her freedom. I was the solution for her to get out of her parents' house."

He tells Camille how after they got married, they rented a room in a large, run-down Victorian near downtown Los Angeles with about fifteen other Yalaltecos. The paint was peeling and the roof sagged, but their room was spacious, with high ceilings and a large bay window that looked out over the street. He had his gardening job, and Araceli worked at her parents' bakery. When he wasn't working, he was attending classes or studying at the library. He was also responsible for supporting his family in Yalálag, so he was under a lot of pressure.

"You were working to support your family *and* going to school?"

"I had to. They needed my help. But I also knew that nothing was going to stop me from finishing my education. After I was done at LA City College, I applied and got into Cal Poly, San Luis Obispo. They have a great landscape architecture program there."

"So did you and Araceli move to San Luis together?"

"No," he says, sighing. "That's what I wanted to do. I thought it would be the best way for us to start a new life together, but Araceli didn't want to leave LA. She and her parents decided that she should move back in with them while I went to school by myself."

Alejandro unscrews his water bottle and takes a long drink. "I think her parents felt bad that they were separating us, so the summer before I left for Cal Poly, they took us on a trip to Oaxaca. Araceli had only been to Yalálag once before, when she was a baby. Even though we were already legally married in the States, her parents insisted that we get married by the priest at the church here."

"That must have been really special," Camille says, feeling a pang of jealousy.

He hesitates. "Not really. Araceli didn't like it here. She was bored. And my mother, who was still living at that time, didn't like Araceli at all. She thought she acted too *gabacha*—too white."

Camille wonders what Alejandro's mother would have thought of her. "So after you got back from Oaxaca, you moved up to San Luis all by yourself?"

He nods. "I worked on a small farm so I didn't have to pay rent."

"You must've been really lonely without Araceli."

He pauses a moment. "No, I was so happy to be in school, and with all of my studying and working I didn't really have time to be lonely. Araceli, on the other hand, was tired of working at the bakery. She was doing nothing to improve her own life, and I was so far away. I felt guilty. I told her that when I was done with school, everything would change. I'd move back to LA and start my own business, and we'd have money to do what we wanted."

"Did that make her feel better?"

"Not really. I think she finally figured out that she shouldn't have married me in the first place. She was young and pretty, and I couldn't give her what she wanted—whatever that was. After a while, I heard that she was going out with some guy in LA. I wasn't mad, though. I understood why she did it."

"Still. It must have really hurt that she cheated on you."

"What hurt the most was that she didn't tell me the truth," he says. "I really hate dishonesty."

"So you came back to LA when you were done with school and started your own business? Were you and Araceli still together?"

"After I moved back to LA we finally talked, and we decided to stay married. We agreed we would just live apart for a while and wait and see what happened." Alejandro leans back in his chair. "For almost two years, while I worked trying to save a little money so I could start my business, we lived apart. We met up once in a while to talk and spend time together. During that time, we grew closer. We weren't *together,* if you know what I mean, but somehow we became better friends than we'd been before." He stops talking for a moment and stares off across the garden.

"How did she die?" Camille asks gently.

Alejandro leans forward and places his hands on his thighs. "One Saturday night, there was this big quinceañera at a salon near downtown. I had a cold, so I didn't go. In the middle of the night I got a phone call from her father. He was crying hysterically. I'd never heard him like that before. He told me that Araceli had been hit by a car when she was crossing the street after leaving the party. She was thrown up in the air and hit her head when she landed."

Camille puts her hand to her chest. "How awful," she whispers.

"It was bad. She was in a coma for over a week. We kept praying that she would wake up. Then the doctors told us she

93

was brain-dead and there was nothing they could do. We had to take her off life support. Two days later, she died. She was only twenty-four."

Reaching through the hammock, Camille places her hand gently on his arm. "I'm so sorry that happened to you and her family."

He puts his other hand on top of hers and then quickly removes it, like he's just touched a hot stove. "It was a long time ago."

"What happened to the person who hit her?"

"Nothing. He was some rich guy from Beverly Hills with a good lawyer. They claimed it was just a terrible accident, even though the guy ran a red light. There was an insurance settlement, and it paid me a lot of money because I was Araceli's husband. I didn't want the money. I thought her parents should have it. She was their daughter, after all."

Alejandro looks like he's on the verge of tears, but he takes a few deep breaths and composes himself.

"When I got the check from the insurance company, I went over to the bakery to give it to her parents. They couldn't believe it. They wanted me to keep some of it so I could start my landscaping business. I kept telling them no, but in the end, they convinced me to take part of it."

He sits up in the chair and rubs his hands together. "Not only did Araceli get me my green card and make it possible for me to get an education, but her death was the reason I was able to start my business. Here I am, a poor Zapotec Indian from the mountains of Oaxaca who now has his own successful landscaping business. All thanks to his dead wife."

Camille wants to comfort him, but she doesn't know what to say.

The silence is broken by the sudden din of chattering voices. Like a parade, a large group of people strolls by the gate. Alejandro walks over and peers after them.

"Where's everyone going?" Camille asks.

"They're going to the fiesta. It's time to eat some *mole negro*."

"*Mole negro?*" Camille says. "That's the dark, chocolatey sauce, right?"

"Yup." He smiles. "Are you hungry?"

"I'm starv—" She stops herself and rolls her eyes. "Sorry! Yes, I'm hungry. Let's go eat."

"But what about you, Camila? I've done all the talking, and you haven't told me any of your story."

"I'll tell you about it later," she says. "We've had enough sadness for one afternoon."

She pokes her arms through the opening in the hammock. "Now, if we're going to go eat some delicious *mole negro*, you're going to have to help me out of this hammock. And as much as I don't want to admit it, Alejandro, there's no way I can get out of this contraption without your help."

CHAPTER 15

"If I keep eating this way," Camille says, "I'm going to get fat." She reaches around and loosens the tie in the back of Tía Nifa's dress, relieving the slight pressure around her waist. She is pleased that the dress, a periwinkle blue with pink and purple flowers embroidered across the front, turned out to be quite lovely—and it fits her perfectly.

Again, she has stuffed herself beyond reason, polishing off a large plate of stewed chicken and savory white rice covered with a rich, dark *mole negro* sauce. She's never tasted anything so delicious in her life. Looking for a clean spot on her once-white paper napkin to wipe her mouth with, she says, "You know, I thought nothing could compare to that chicken soup we ate back in San Mateo, but this *mole* is by far the most delicious thing I've ever eaten."

"Well, you never know, Camila—even with all that mud washed off, you might turn out to be part Oaxacan after all."

"I doubt it," she says, running a finger along her plate for one last taste of the spicy sauce. "But if I was from here, I would eat this stuff as often as possible. How do you make it?"

Alejandro wipes his mouth and pushes his plate away. "I'm sorry to tell you that I never took the time to pay attention when my mother made it. I know there are three or four kinds of chilies in it. Onions, garlic . . . I think there are nuts too. Maybe almonds and peanuts? There's Oaxacan chocolate. Oh, and *tomatillos*, those small green fruit that look like unripe tomatoes. *Mole* is pretty complicated to make. I remember that it used to take my mother and my tías many days to prepare it."

Camille takes a sip of her soda and looks around the table. "Hey, how come no one's talking to each other?" she whispers.

"Well . . . I would say that Yalaltecos are pretty quiet as a people. Especially when they're eating."

"Then how come you talk so much?"

He laughs as he reaches for his bottle of Coke. "Well, I've always been different. I'm more like my mother. She really liked to talk— and laugh and gossip too. My father was the complete opposite. He was very quiet. He only spoke when he had something important to say."

"Is your father still living?"

"No. He died of a stroke when I was sixteen. He had just returned from California, where he'd been working picking lettuce. He was only home for about a month when it happened. It was so strange. One minute he was standing in the kitchen talking to my mother, and the next he was on the ground, unconscious. He was a lot older than my mom. Almost twenty years. But still too young to die. After that, I had to leave Yalálag for Los Angeles. I had to get a job to help support my family."

"You couldn't find a job here in Yalálag?"

"There's really not much work here, unless you own land or have a skill like making huaraches. Even then, it's hard to get by. That's why so many Yalaltecos have gone to Los Angeles—or *Oaxacalifornia,* as we call it."

Camille laughs. "Clever name."

"We call it that because so many Oaxacans have migrated to

California. Did you know that there are more people of Yalalteco descent living in Los Angeles than there are right here in Yalálag?"

Camille is dumbfounded. "Seriously? Where do they all live?"

"All over, really. Mostly near Koreatown. And they live pretty much the same kind of life there that they lived here in Yalálag—with the same customs—except that they now live in apartments and houses instead of adobes."

"I know where Koreatown is—Graciela's uncle lives there, in this little run-down bungalow off Normandie Ave. I was just there a week ago when I went to go look for her."

Alejandro opens his mouth like he's about to say something but then changes his mind.

"Do you live in Koreatown?" she asks.

"No, I live in Arlington Heights. It's next to Koreatown."

Camille tries to imagine what kind of place Alejandro would call home. "Do you live in an apartment?"

"No, a house."

"Whose house is it?"

Something flickers in his eyes. "I live in my own house."

She is unable to hide her surprise. "You own your own house?"

A flash of annoyance crosses Alejandro's face. "Camila, why is it so hard for you to believe that I could own a house? Is it because you come from a place where the Mexicans don't own houses—they just clean them?"

"No . . . I didn't mean . . ." She quickly changes the subject. "So who owns this whole open area right here?" she asks, sweeping her arm in a wide arc.

"It's owned by the people in this neighborhood," he says. "Everyone helped to build it by giving money or labor, so they get to use it when they want. Celebrations are very important to Yalaltecos. We'll find any reason possible to have a fiesta—a wedding, baptism, quinceañera, or the birthday of a Catholic saint like San Antonio. And these parties can go on for days and days."

"But aren't most of the people here pretty poor?" She looks around at the run-down houses on the hillsides. "How can they even afford to pay for all these parties?"

"*Ay, mujer*," Alejandro says, looking exasperated. "Look, you've got to realize that these parties are extremely important for our culture. They help bring everyone together. Because so many of us have left Yalálag, there's the worry that we're losing our traditions. So we have these fiestas to honor our saints, like San Antonio. It helps bring us all back together again. It allows us to value who we are as a people."

Camille is intrigued. "So where do all these people from Yalálag work in Los Angeles?"

"Most of the men have jobs in restaurants as cooks or busboys. Usually the women work cleaning houses or taking care of other people's children."

"Oh, like Graciela's mother," she says. "I always wondered why María moved from LA to Santa Barbara to work for my mother."

He stares at her. "You never asked?"

"No . . . she was just there cleaning the house one day."

Alejandro shifts in his chair. "So you're telling me you don't know María's story?"

Camille shakes her head. "No, not really."

"But I thought you were close to Graciela. I mean, you've been talking about how she's your best piano student and you've been helping her out all these years. Giving her lessons for free, letting her move into your house. You're basically supporting her, right? You talk like she's part of your family, but you don't know anything about her or her mother?"

Camille feels her face grow hot. "Well, you know how it is with the language barrier and everything. My Spanish isn't very good, and María doesn't speak that much English, so it was kind of difficult to have a real conversation with her. We didn't talk that much."

He looks perplexed. "Okay, so let me get this straight. María is the mother of your very best piano student who lives with you, and you *never talked that much?*"

Camille doesn't have an answer for him.

"Camila, didn't you think it was important for you to get to know María? Especially since her daughter is such a big part of your life? And what about Graciela? She speaks English. Why didn't you talk to her?"

Camille feels herself growing defensive. "Well, that would have been awkward, don't you think? I didn't want to pry or seem like I was intruding into her personal life. I'm her piano teacher; it's my duty to keep our relationship on a strictly professional level."

Alejandro looks stunned. "Graciela is a teenage girl whose mother has left her in your care. Don't you think that maybe she's needed you to be more to her than just her piano teacher?"

Camille puts her shoulders back. "You know, Alejandro, I really feel like you're judging me. I mean, María was the one who left Graciela behind. Did you know she left for Mexico on some family emergency without even telling me or my mother? She just left one day, so we helped Graciela out by taking her in. Yes, in hindsight I see that I should've talked more openly with María. And Graciela, for that matter. Perhaps if I had done that, Graciela wouldn't have left the way she did. But I was only doing what I thought was right for her."

"Right for her, or right for you?" He slams his hands down on the table and abruptly gets to his feet. "*Gracias,*" he says to the other people sitting at the table.

"*Provecho, provecho,*" they answer back in unison. They wear surprised looks on their faces as he walks away.

Camille gets up from the table. Not knowing what to say to the people still sitting there, she ends up giving them an awkward bow before rushing after Alejandro.

"Alejandro, wait!" she calls. "What's wrong? Are you mad at me?"

He lets her catch up. "No, Camila. I'm not mad at you, I'm just frustrated with how you act sometimes. You always think you know what's right for other people. Like your way is always the best way. You pretend that everything you've done for Graciela is because you're a generous and kind person. But in reality, you're just doing it all for yourself."

"What do you mean by that?"

His face hardens. "*Díme la verdad*, Camila. Why don't you just admit that everything you've ever done for Graciela has been to help save your own career?"

Camille is instantly furious with him again. "God, what is wrong with you? You have absolutely no idea what you're talking about. You don't know anything about what I've done. For years I have given all of my time and energy to help Graciela, never charging her one cent, so that she could be the best pianist possible. I only wanted to help give her a chance for a better life."

"*A better life?*" He throws his hands up in frustration. "What makes you think you gave her a better life? Do you think it was easy for Graciela to grow up in Santa Barbara, isolated from her family in Los Angeles? Away from her culture, practicing the piano for hours every day? For what? So she could make you look good as a piano teacher? So your dreams could come true? Maybe the reason Graciela left was because she decided that the life you had to offer her wasn't the life she wanted."

Camille is so furious she can barely spit her next words out. "You can go to hell, Alejandro. You don't know *anything* about me or Graciela. None of this is any of your damn business, anyhow!"

His nostrils flare. "I know more than you think. And I'm making it my business."

Camille puts up her hand. "You can just shut your mouth right now. I'm done talking to you."

Her mounting anger propels her away from the party. Down below in the square, she can hear the band starting up with a lively polka. As if the tubas are mocking her, their *oom-pah-pahs* match her footsteps in perfect sync as she marches down the steep path.

"Camila!" Alejandro calls out from behind her. "Where are you going?"

She ignores him and continues down the hill, stomping to the beat of the booming drums.

CHAPTER 16

Camille strides through the shadows of the steep streets that twist and turn toward the center of town. The heavy soles of her huaraches weigh her down like she's crossing the river against the current. There is a scream stuck in the back of her throat, and if she doesn't get it out soon, she may choke on it.

Several times, she glances back up the road, expecting to see Alejandro following her, but there's nothing there except the sound of lonely crickets calling out from underneath the nearby rocks. *Well, screw him and his holier-than-thou attitude.*

She has no idea where she's going. She figures her best bet is to follow the sound of the music.

When she finally reaches the main square, the band is in full swing and the dancing is well underway. Camille looks for a place to sit down amid the rows of hard wooden benches that line the perimeter of the square. A dozen or so old women with cotton shawls draped over their heads are scattered throughout the benches. Their dark eyes follow Camille as she searches for a place to sit. She avoids eye contact with them, hoping they won't try to talk her. All she wants to do is sit by herself and ferment in her indignation.

Why am I so concerned with Alejandro's opinion of me in the first place? She hardly knows him. Why should she care so much about what he thinks? He certainly is handsome, and she'll freely admit she's attracted to him. But he's also proved he can be a know-it-all jerk. So why does she feel as bereft as a teenage girl who's been abandoned at the dance by her prom date?

Unable to shake off her anger, she slumps down on the bench and tries to gather her thoughts. It's impossible to think clearly, though; the music is so loud that her molars are actually vibrating.

That's another thing that intrigues Camille about this remote mountain town. How is it possible that so many people don't even have running water or working toilets, yet there's a large symphonic band? She would expect to find indigenous instruments here, of course, like the flute she heard earlier. Maybe even a drum or two. But a large brass band? And the music doesn't even sound indigenous. It sounds like German polka music.

She watches as the townspeople happily dance around the square, their movements also reflecting a European influence. The dance seems to be a hybrid of an old-fashioned waltz and some sort of Native American dance. The dancers clasp their hands together and swing their arms in a seesaw motion from side to side while they make little hops with their feet. This must be the traditional dance Alejandro was planning to teach her tonight.

She massages the top of her head with her fingers. *Oh, to hell with Alejandro and his stupid dancing. I don't even care anymore.*

A bowlegged old man wearing the standard local outfit—a straw hat, gray pants, and huaraches—limps past her, oblivious to her presence. He suddenly stops and lifts up his face as if he's caught the scent of something in the breeze. Turning around, he spies Camille, and his face lights up with delight. With a glass bottle of a pale-colored liquid in one hand and a stack of cups that look like they've been made from small gourds in the other, he hurries over to Camille as if she's his long-lost friend.

Speaking cheerfully in Zapotec, he smiles at her with a mouth filled with more holes than teeth. His face is covered with a thick coating of bristly white whiskers. They glow luminescent against the rich caramel color of his skin. Camille has no idea what he's saying, but she gives him a quick nod and then looks away. She hopes he'll leave her alone.

"Hey, lady," he says. "You *Americana?*" He waves the bottle in the air. "Lady? Hey, lady . . . you want the mezcal?"

The music is so loud that Camille isn't sure what he's talking about. She puts her hand behind her ear, angling her head to hear him better.

"Lady, you want the tequila?" he asks in a louder voice, holding up the bottle and making a pouring motion with his hand.

Camille finally realizes he's offering her a shot. "*No, gracias, señor,*" she says. "I don't drink."

He puts his face so close to hers she can smell the liquor on his breath. "You sure, lady? *El mezcal de Yalálag es muy bueno.* You try a little bit, no?"

Camille is about to refuse him again, but she hesitates. Long ago, because of her mother's drinking, she made the decision to never go down that road. Now, she finds herself thinking, *Why the hell not?* Earlier she told Alejandro that what she wanted to do tonight was experience the *real* Yalálag. Here's her chance to sample a real taste of the culture. She tried *mole* and loved it. Who's to say she shouldn't try some mezcal as well?

"Sure, why not?" she tells the old man. "I'll have a little."

He smiles and his watery eyes shine. The deep creases in his face disappear, and Camille catches a glimpse of a younger, once handsome man. With a surprisingly steady hand, he pours the pale liquid into a cup and hands it to her. She takes a small sip and almost gags. It tastes like gasoline, or at least what she imagines gasoline tastes like.

"*No, no, no,* lady," he says, shaking his head back and forth like Camille is an errant child with whom he's greatly disappointed.

"You don't drink the mezcal like that—you drink the mezcal like *this*." He pours another shot into one of the cups in his hand, lifts it to his lips, and swallows it down in one swift motion, then thumps his chest with his fist. "Ahhh . . . *es muy bueno*."

"Okay, okay, I get it," she says, bringing the cup of mezcal up to her nose. The pungent fumes burn her sinuses like she's just taken a whiff of ammonia. She holds up her cup in a mock toast and drinks it down in one quick gulp.

A second later, she realizes her grave mistake. "Holy crap!" she cries, but she is barely able to get the words out—her throat is ablaze. She begins to cough, and her eyes water. She thinks this must be *worse* than drinking gasoline. Even worse than that salsa she sampled back in San Mateo.

When she finally stops coughing, she uses her forearms to wipe away the tears that are streaming down her cheeks. "*Muy fuerte!*" she croaks, sounding like a two-pack-a-day smoker.

His eyes are full of amusement. "*Sí, lady—es muy fuerte, pero es muy bueno, también.*" He holds out the bottle to her again. "You take more the mezcal? *Sí?*"

Camille begins to relax as the warmth of the alcohol spreads throughout her body. She finds that she's suddenly feeling much better. Not only is the hard ball of anger in her throat softening, but her recent fight with Alejandro has also begun to disappear into a hazy memory.

"Who cares what that judgmental ass thinks about me, anyway?" she mutters under her breath. "I don't need him. I don't need anyone."

Almost at once, all the stress, frustration, and disappointment of the day—of her entire trip to Oaxaca, for that matter—disappears into a glorious wash of tranquility. Everything is now all right with the world. She decides that she likes this mezcal stuff—*a lot*.

"*¿Por qué no, señor?*" she says, holding out her cup. "*Más, por favor.*"

He throws his head back and cackles with happiness. "You

speak the espanish *muy bueno*." He's still chuckling under his breath as he pours her another shot.

This time, Camille tosses it back like an expert, without flinching.

The man gives her a toothy smile, pats her lightly on the shoulder, and tips his hat. Moving on, he offers his mezcal to the guests who have just begun to fill in the empty benches.

Camille sits up and looks around, noticing that the lights surrounding the square are so much brighter now. She's no longer shivering, and her feelings of despair have completely vanished. *So this is what being drunk is like. Not bad. Not bad at all.* Camille finally understands why her mother loves her chardonnay so much. Maybe she should have followed in her footsteps long ago.

As the band's music vibrates through her body, Camille taps her feet on the ground. Everything around her is bursting with vibrant color and sound. She feels honored to be a part of this new and exciting experience while wearing this very pretty dress and watching these wonderful people dance their native dance. She decides that she's falling in love with Yalálag—the clothing, the food, the music, the dancing. And the people here are so kind. Especially Tía Nifa. After every stupid thing Camille has said or done, Tía Nifa still told Alejandro that she wanted Camille to sleep in her special museum bedroom tonight. That makes Camille adore her that much more.

A rueful laugh escapes Camille's lips. There's still one Yalalteco she doesn't like at all right now. *He's a self-righteous jerk who can't keep his big mouth shut. He doesn't know anything about anyone.* She thinks back to the curse words that rolled out of the bus driver's mouth as he tried to get the bus out of the mud. She crosses her arms in front of her and quotes him verbatim in perfect Spanish. "*Alejandro es un pinche pedazo de mierda.*"

She laughs heartily. "Yep," she says with conviction. "Alejandro is a goddamn piece of shit."

CHAPTER 17

Camille is still brooding about what a jerk Alejandro is when a young man wearing a purple-and-gold Lakers jersey walks over and stands directly in front of her, blocking her view of the dancing. Numerous vinelike tattoos creep up from under his shirt and curl around his neck. With his closely shaved head and small gold hoop earrings, he looks as out of place as Camille.

But as the mezcal has brought out such powerful feelings of camaraderie toward everyone here in Yalálag, including this guy who resembles a gangbanger from East LA, Camille decides it would be rude not to speak to him.

"*Buenas noches,*" she says, giving him a dazzling smile. Her words are as thick as gravy on a hot stove. He doesn't smile back, just looks at her with a penetrating stare. She assumes he speaks only Zapotec.

"Hey, buddy," she says, thinking he won't understand, "knock that chip off your shoulder and smile, why don't you? Life's way too short to be so damn serious all the time." A drunken giggle escapes her mouth. She turns her head away so he doesn't think she's laughing at him.

"Do you want to dance?" he asks in perfect English.

"Oh, crap—you speak English! That's *wunnerful,*" she says, her words slurring. "And as a matter of fact, today is your lucky day. I do wanna dance!"

This is her opportunity to learn this dance without any help from Alejandro. *I'll show him.* In her eagerness she stands up so quickly that the light bulbs strung around the square flicker like yellow strobe lights at a disco.

"Whoa," she says, feeling dizzy. She grips her dance partner's forearm to avoid falling down. "Hold on a sec, buddy. Let me just stand here for a moment and get my bearings, okay?"

He grabs her roughly by the shoulder to steady her.

"Okay, I'm good," she says, trying to unhook herself from the pressure of his fingers. "You can let go now."

He abruptly takes her hand and leads her out into the middle of the square.

"I'm not really sure how to do this dance!" Camille shouts over the loud music.

His face is expressionless. "I'll show you."

They end up in the middle of a large group of people who are moving around in fast circles. The loud music, coupled with the motion of all the spinning bodies, makes Camille feel even woozier.

"Pay attention," he says, stretching Camille's arms out wide. He begins to snap her wrists from side to side while taking little hopping steps with his feet. After a few minutes, she is able to follow it well enough to more or less blend in with everyone else.

She scans the area, looking for Alejandro. She wants to prove that she doesn't need him to show her how to do this dance. She doesn't need him at all. *Where is he?*

Her dancing partner is holding her hands so tightly that it's becoming painful. He's also looking at her with such intensity that she's beginning to feel frightened. She decides that when the music stops, she'll go back to her bench and sit down. Unfortunately, the music doesn't stop. Every time the band starts to diminuendo and the dancers begin to move at a slower pace, she waits for the final cadence, filled with relief that it's finally over, but then the cymbals start to crash again and the band begins to play at an even faster tempo.

Camille groans inwardly. The blisters on her heels are stinging, and she needs to get off her feet. They're now dancing so fast that the *mole* she ate is sloshing around in her stomach like a milkshake in a blender. The warm, relaxed feeling she had just a few minutes ago has turned to dread. If she doesn't sit down soon, she's likely to throw up in front of everyone.

Miraculously, the music finally ends. She lowers her arms and begins to walk away, but her dance partner has other ideas.

"Let's go again," he says, tugging on her hand.

"Uh, no thank you," she says, trying to untangle her fingers from his. "I'm really tired."

He begins to lead her back onto the square as the band starts up again with another lively polka. "C'mon, I want to dance with you again."

Her head is spinning. "No, really, I'm not feeling well. My stomach hurts."

He presses his lips together, and his eyes grow flat. "You're just saying that because you don't want to dance with me anymore."

Obviously. "No, really. It's not that. It's just that my stomach is upset, and I need to sit down. Like right now."

He continues to hold on to her hand. "Okay, I'll wait. We can sit down right here until you feel better, and then we can dance together again."

Camille wonders why this idiot can't take a hint. "Uh . . . what's your name?"

He stands up a little taller. "Jesús. But my friends call me Little Chuy."

"Look, Chuy . . ."

"*Little Chuy*," he corrects her.

She tries to pry her hands away from his, but he won't let go. She begins to feel desperate. "Look, *Little Chuy*, I appreciate that you took the time to teach me the dance, but right now I really need to sit down."

Her head is spinning like she's on a merry-go-round, and her stomach is way past queasy. As his grip tightens, all the good feelings she had before disappear. She's had enough of this guy. Exasperated, she pulls her arms down and out, twisting away from his grasp. She slowly backs away from him. "I'm leaving now."

Like a light has been turned off, his face darkens into a misshapen mask of anger. "What's your problem?" he says, loud enough for several people to overhear. "You think you're better than me? *Fucking white bitch.*"

Camille is stunned. She has no idea how to respond to such hateful words. She feels herself growing angry. "Are you serious?" she says, putting her hands on her hips. "*Better than you?* That's the most ridiculous thing I've ever heard."

Her comment only fuels his rage. He comes closer and pokes a stiff finger at her chest. "Why you think you're better than me? You think 'cause you're white you're fucking special? I was doing you a favor to dance with you, bitch. You might be hot, but ain't nobody else gonna wanna touch you with those fucked-up fingers of yours, anyhow."

Camille's stomach lurches. Her anger boils up like a pressure cooker about to explode. Before she can stop herself, the scream hiding in her throat since her fight with Alejandro comes out with a vengeance.

She moves right up to him and slaps his still-pointed finger away from her chest. "Don't you touch me, you jerk—I'm not afraid of you!"

He's so caught off guard by her sudden aggression that he backs up several steps.

"Take it easy, *esa*," he says, glancing around to see if anyone is watching. As Camille gets closer to him he looks around for an escape route, but the benches are now completely filled with people. Unable to find a way out, he sits down. He crosses his arms in front of his chest and glares at her.

Camille raises her voice so that he and everyone else standing nearby can hear her above the sound of the band. "Oh, I've known guys like you before, *Little Chuy*," she hisses. "You're nothing but a misogynist bully. Always trying to prove to the world that you're a man. Far from it, I'd say. You're just a stupid little boy—just like your stupid name suggests." She rambles on, the mezcal making her bold. "Seriously—if you're such a big, strong man, why the hell do you call yourself *Little* Chuy? Maybe it's because you're describing another part of your anatomy?"

A deep flush rises up through his tattooed neck and onto his face. Camille leans forward and pokes her finger into his skinny, concave chest. "I've wasted enough of my life on losers like you, and I'm *done*." Her voice is strong and sure. "It's time for you to leave, asshole."

He opens his mouth as if he's about to say something, then clamps it shut.

She raises her eyebrows. "What's wrong, Little Chuy? You scared or something?"

Camille leans down and puts her face as close to his as possible. From a distance people might even think they're starry-eyed lovers about to kiss. And then, as if she's planned it all along, she does the one thing that will make him think twice before treating a woman like this again: she opens her mouth and projectile vomits a mixture of mezcal and *mole negro* all over his purple Lakers jersey.

CHAPTER 18

C amille's hands are trembling. It's either from of all the adrenaline coursing through her blood after unleashing her pent-up
anger on Little Chuy, or it's because she's just emptied the contents
of her stomach all over him.

There's nothing like the smell of barf to scare someone away,
and Little Chuy has run off like a Chihuahua with his tail between
his legs. Two pretty teenage girls take a hold of Camille's elbows and
lead her back to her bench. Someone hands her a cold bottle of water.

"*Gracias*," she says to no one in particular. She drinks down half
of the bottle in one long swallow. Before she can stop herself, a
loud burp escapes her mouth. Leaning over, she cradles her head in
her hands as the two girls begin to gently rub her back in a circular
motion.

"Please forgive me for everything," she tells them in broken
Spanish.

One of the girls pours some cold water on the edge of her cotton shawl and leans in close to Camille. "*No, señorita*," she whispers,
"*gracias a usted*." She wipes Camille's face and says something in
Spanish so fast that Camille doesn't catch all of it. She does hear
Chuy and *cholo* several times. Camille assumes the girl is pointing
out that the guy is bad news.

Camille hears her name being called from across the square. *Oh crap.* It's Alejandro. Her first instinct is to hide so he won't see that she's been drinking. Hoping to blend in, she quickly grabs one of the girls' white shawls, covers her head with it, and hunkers down between them. She doesn't take into account that her legs are so white they shine like two fluorescent beacons in the night.

Alejandro spots her and rushes over, sweaty and out of breath. "Camila—what happened to you?" he asks, kneeling down in front of her. "I heard that you were in a fight. Are you okay?"

"That was fast." Camille keeps her head covered by the shawl and enunciates each syllable so he won't notice she's drunk. "How did you find out?"

"The people around here don't move very fast, but the gossip sure does. I heard someone saying something about a redhead and a fight. Who else could it be but you? I ran here as fast as I could."

One of the teenage girls begins speaking to Alejandro in rapid Zapotec, her voice rising with excitement as she describes what happened. Camille knows the girl has reached the end of the story when she places her hands on her stomach, leans over, and makes a loud retching noise.

Alejandro turns back to Camille, his face concerned. "Did that guy hurt you?"

"No. I'm okay. He just scared me a little."

He gets to his feet. "You stay here with these girls. I'll be right back."

"Where are you going?"

"I'm going to go find that *pinche cholito* and let him know that what he did was not okay."

"No, no, no—please don't do that," she pleads. "Please just stay here with me. The truth is, I sort of handled the situation . . . in my own way."

Camille pictures Little Chuy covered in dark brown *mole* sauce and can't help but giggle. She quickly covers her face with the shawl to stifle her laughter. Before she can stop herself, she lets out another loud burp.

Alejandro looks at her curiously and moves closer to her. She feels a wave of heat. This time it's not because of the mezcal but the warmth of his body so close to hers. He pulls the shawl away from her face, and the touch of his fingers on her skin makes her tremble. He leans in close to her face. *Oh god, here it comes—he's finally going to kiss me.* She closes her eyes and waits to feel his lips touch hers.

He takes a whiff of her breath instead.

"Camila," he says, "have you been drinking?"

She opens her eyes and blinks several times. "Um . . . no?" She looks up to avoid his gaze.

He takes her chin in his hand and forces her to look him in the eye. "Tell me the truth, Camila."

"Well, maybe just a little."

"A little what?"

"A little mezcal."

"*Mezcal?* Are you kidding me, Camila? Do you know how strong that stuff is? How much of it did you drink?"

"Only two little shots."

He smacks his forehead with his hand. "Well, no wonder you threw up. The mezcal around here is super strong. What were you thinking?"

"I was thinking that I wanted to experience the real Yalálag. And I was thinking that I was mad at you for being so mean to me about Graciela."

"So you decided to get back at me by getting drunk?"

"I was not trying to get back at you," she says, the words like glue on her tongue. "It's just that I am unaccustomed to drinking alcohol. I was unaware that it would affect me in such an adverse manner."

Alejandro looks at her like she's lost her mind. In her attempt to cover up her drunkenness by being verbose, she only sounds more like an idiot.

"Look," she says, smiling, "I'm really feeling much better now. Especially since these two lovely young ladies have been so kind to me." She stands up and curtsies toward the two young girls. In the process, she loses her balance and almost falls to the ground. Alejandro catches her just in time. "Whoopsy-daisy," she says. "My legs are a still a little rubbery because of all the dancing I've been doing."

The two girls begin to giggle; their laughter sounds like a duet of trilling piccolos. Alejandro puts his arm around Camille's waist to support her.

"Camila, you have to be more careful how you act around here," he says sternly. "That Chuy guy you were dancing with? He's some *cholo* who grew up in LA. He's involved in gangs and has come back here to sell drugs or smuggle people across the border. This guy is probably dangerous." He looks her straight in the eyes. "From now on, please just stay close to me. Don't go running off alone into the dark."

Oh, I'd like to stay close to you. The heat of his body burns into hers. For some reason, the anger she felt toward him earlier has completely dissipated.

"I'm so sorry, Alejandro," she whispers into his ear. "I keep getting myself into these awful situations. But do you know what he said to me? He told me that he was doing me a favor by dancing with me. He said no one would want to ever hold my hand because of my fingers." Camille starts to cry. "He was so mean to me."

"Don't listen to that guy, Camila. He's just some stupid *pendejo*. Now, come on—let's get you back to Tía Nifa's house so you can sleep off that mezcal."

"No, wait. Not yet. Can we just dance together one time? Please? I learned how to do the traditional Yalálag dance. I really want to show you."

"I don't think you're in any condition to dance right now."

"Please?"

His face softens. "Only if you sit down for a while and sober up. Then we'll see."

"Fine. I'll sit here and behave myself for as long as it takes me to stop being drunk. Then we'll dance together, okay?"

He takes her arm and guides her back down onto the bench. "Are you always this pushy? Wait—that was a dumb question. Of course you are."

"Only when I want to get my way."

"Okay, Camila. You'll get your way. *This time*. I will dance with you, but first you have to promise not to throw up on me."

"I'm not sure I can make that promise, Alejandro. You'll just have to take your chances."

He laughs. "Well, you know what, Camila? I think maybe I'll take that chance, just so I can watch you dance like a real Yalalteca."

Someone hands Camille a cup of strong black coffee. After a while, the cool evening air slips down the mountains and clears the mezcal cobwebs from her head, sobering her up faster than she deserves. The music slows down again. Several young men holler out from the balcony on the other side of the square; their whoops and catcalls encourage the musicians to play faster. Soon the music swells to a climax. The dancers whip around the square in a frenzy until the final two chords crash down.

"*Dun-dun*," Alejandro sings in unison with the last two notes.

"Five-one," Camille adds, conducting in the air with her hand. He gives her a puzzled look. "What do you mean, *five-one*?"

"That's what you were singing when you went 'dun-dun.' You know, the dominant chord to the tonic chord? The *authentic cadence*?"

117

He looks lost. "Camila, I can tell you anything you need to know about gardening and landscaping, but music—forget it. The only thing I know about music is that I like to listen to it. And dance to it."

The music teacher in Camille feels the need to explain it to him. "Well, an authentic cadence is when the five chord moves to the one chord. I would say it occurs 99 percent of the time at the end of every piece of Western music ever composed."

Alejandro gives her a blank stare.

"You have no idea what I'm talking about, do you?"

"Nope."

"Okay, listen . . ." Her head is still a bit foggy from the mezcal, but she tries to think of an easy way to explain it to him anyway. "You know what a scale is, right?"

He nods. "I guess so."

"*Do re mi fa sol la ti do*," she sings. "Okay, now—the first note, *do*, is called the tonic note. That's the note that sounds finished and restful. It's the root of the 'one' chord or *tonic* chord. And the fifth note of the scale, *sol*, makes up the five chord or the *dominant* chord. That's the chord that sets up the tension. Often included in the dominant chord is the seventh note of the scale—*ti*—which is called the *leading tone* because it leads your ear back to the tonic—the resting note."

A glazed look comes into Alejandro's eyes. He covers his mouth with his hand and yawns noisily.

"You're not getting any of this, are you?" she asks.

He shakes his head. "I speak three languages fluently, but music is not one of them."

"Right. I'll try and make this easier for you to understand. Okay, take the song 'Happy Birthday.' Everyone knows that song. If I sing the first three lines and leave out the last, the song doesn't sound finished."

She begins to sing again:

"*Happy Birthday to you,*

Happy Birthday to you,
Happy Birthday, dear Alejandro . . ."

She stops and pauses. "See? If I stop there, the song is left up in the air and makes you feel uncomfortable. It doesn't sound complete. Our brains like to hear the music go back to the tonic note because we like that restful sound where everything is finished. That's why the endings of most musical compositions end with an authentic cadence—the five chord to the one chord. It's announcing '*The End.*'"

"So when I sing '*dun-dun*' at the end of a piece of music . . . I'm actually singing an authentic cadence?'"

"Yes!" She claps her hands together. "And to think, all this time, you never even knew that."

He looks amused. "And now that I know what an authentic cadence is, my life is complete."

"Very funny."

He looks thoughtful for a moment. "What if the music *doesn't* end with an authentic cadence?"

"Then without a doubt, there's something more to come. In all music, the dominant chord is needed to set up the tension, because without that tension—without that sense of something being unfinished—there'd be no resolution. The music would just end up sounding monotonous. Music needs those ups and downs to keep us interested in what's going on."

"Kind of like life."

She looks at him. "You're right. Music is just imitating life."

The band suddenly starts up again with a fast-paced number. Camille stands up and smooths the front of her dress. "Hey, Alejandro, I have a really good idea. As there's been quite a bit of tension going around this evening, why don't you and I try to find our own resolution?"

He raises his eyebrows. "And how should we do that?"

Camille holds out her hand. "Let's dance."

CHAPTER 19

As they dance around the square, Camille senses that Alejandro is watching her closely. She hopes it's because he's more concerned with her welfare than whether or not she's going to throw up on him too.

The band is playing an old-fashioned waltz that brings back memories of her childhood. The music sounds vaguely like the tune that played on the pink jewelry box she treasured so much as a girl—the one with the pirouetting dancer that spun around in endless circles on top of a satin-covered box. An image of that dainty ballerina pops into her mind. At this moment, she is no longer Camille the former musical prodigy who has lost her ability to play the piano. Nor is she Camille the piano teacher who needs to prove that she's still worthy of others' admiration. She is simply *Camila*, the half-drunk ballerina who is spinning around in circles of her own making. Falling for a man she's known for less than two days.

The music finally ends for the evening. Alejandro and Camille stand together at the edge of the square, both out of breath from dancing for so long. Without the music blaring, the quiet of the night seems to open up wide, and an awkward silence falls between them. They turn to each other and speak at the same time.

"Sorry," Camille says. "What did you say?"

"I said the color of that dress looks really pretty on you."

She looks down. "You think so? I hope Tía Nifa isn't upset that I'm wearing it."

He smiles. "Oh, she won't be. It will make her happy to see you in it. She'll probably end up giving it to you."

Camille laughs. "First her huaraches, and then this dress? If I hang around here long enough, who knows what I'll get next?"

He raises his eyebrows and gives her a crooked smile. "I guess you'll just have to wait and see."

Camille feels her face grow warm and quickly changes the subject. "When do you think Tía Nifa will get back to Yalálag?"

"I doubt she'll be back before tomorrow morning." He turns away to stifle another yawn with the back of his hand. "Camila, are you getting tired yet? It's getting late."

"I'm exhausted. But my plan is that if I stay up late enough, I'll be able to bypass the whole hangover thing in the morning."

"I don't think you have to worry about that. With all the dancing you've done, any mezcal you had left in your system is long gone by now." He holds out his hand. "*Vámanos*—let's go home."

As they walk away from the square, Camille notices that a group of townspeople are watching them with curiosity. They're probably wondering what's going on between the girl with the marigold hair and the handsome Yalalteco. Camille is nervously wondering about that too.

As they near the top of the hill, the sky flickers with bright blue light, followed by a loud rumble of thunder. Another storm is moving in over the mountains.

By the time they arrive at Tía Nifa's gate, the wind has picked up and the air is thick with the scent of ozone. Lightning continues to flash every thirty seconds, and thunder booms across the peaks like timpani drums.

Alejandro quickly finds the hidden key and opens the gate just as a downpour lets loose on top of them. Camille shrieks and covers her head with her hands as they run under the porch roof and out of the deluge. Heavy gusts of wind send the wind chimes into a riotous scherzo of pentatonic tones.

Alejandro looks up at the sky. "Bad timing. I hope the storm doesn't last too long."

"I don't mind it." She grins. "I actually love a good thunderstorm. Unless I'm stuck on a bus about to go over a cliff."

He laughs. "Don't remind me."

She looks up at the sky. "Okay, wish me luck. I'm going to make a run for the bathroom."

"Okay. I'll meet you back inside the house. There's a new toothbrush on the edge of the sink for you."

She puts her hand to her heart. "Are you insinuating that I have bad breath? I'm utterly offended."

"No," he says, laughing, "I was just trying to be a good host. Anyway, I put it in there before we left. Before I knew you were going to turn out to be such a *borrachita*."

"What's that?"

"A drunk."

She makes a face and slaps him lightly on the arm.

The rain is coming down so hard that her dress gets soaked on her way to the bathroom. Turning on the light, she sees that Alejandro has left her more than just a toothbrush. There's also a bottle of purified water, a miniature tube of toothpaste, a mini-hairbrush, and a package with something white inside. She picks it up and laughs aloud. He's bought her two pairs of women's granny panties, size small.

When she sits down to use the toilet, something moving along the floor catches her eye: a long line of red fire ants trailing in from a crack at the bottom of the wall. This time, she doesn't react, only watches. It looks as if the ants have been quite industrious all evening. Piece by piece, they've removed the corpse of the scorpion that Alejandro smashed earlier with his shoe. The ants march in a straight line, each carrying an oversized piece of the scorpion on its back, struggling with the weight of the load but not letting anything stop them from doing what they're meant to do. *Now's that's the spirit*, she thinks. *Never give up.*

She runs the brush through her hair, washes her face, and scrubs her teeth for at least five minutes. Never has she gone so long without brushing her teeth, and just being able to get that sour taste of mezcal out of her mouth feels momentous.

Just as she's spitting the last bit of toothpaste into the sink, there is another loud clap of thunder. The light bulb hanging from the ceiling hums for a second and then blinks out. In the dark, she fumbles for the latch and opens the door without a struggle.

"Alejandro?" she calls out over the sound of the raging downpour. There's no answer, so she decides to make a run for it. When she reaches the house, she slips her feet out of the soggy huaraches and attempts to wring out as much water as possible from her hair and dress before going inside.

In the main room, the scent of sulfur lingers in the air. Alejandro has lit the candles on the altar, and the flickering orange light makes the shadows dance on the walls. Camille stands completely still, feeling the water drip down her legs and onto the tile. She stares at the upside-down image of St. Anthony on the altar, regretting her lack of faith. She'd like to believe that everything that's happened to her is all part of a bigger picture. That there's some divine plan she has no control over, and if she prays hard enough, all that's been lost can be found again.

Her body begins to tremble from the cold. She's got to get out of her wet dress. *Where is Alejandro?* She heads toward the kitchen to look for him. As she walks through the doorway, the candlelight falls away and the rain on the roof is deafening. She can't see or hear him—and as she takes another step forward, she runs smack into him, so hard that she almost falls backward onto to the floor.

"Whoa," he says, putting his arms around her waist to keep her from falling. "Camila—I'm so sorry. I didn't hear you come in. Did I hurt you?"

She shakes her head. The feeling of his arms around her waist is so thrilling, it leaves her unable to form any coherent words.

She expects him to let her go, but he doesn't. He gazes at her with a strange intensity in his dark eyes.

"You're soaking wet," he says, his voice barely above a whisper. She can feel his warm breath on her face.

She tries to speak, but the words are trapped in her throat.

"Camila . . . I . . ." he says, his voice dropping down almost an octave. "I wanted to say . . . I need to tell you something . . ."

"What is it?" she manages to whisper.

He looks right into her eyes and opens his mouth, but instead of answering, he places his hand behind her head, pulls her mouth to his, and kisses her with such intensity that she can barely stand. His mouth is as hot and sweet as a cup of Oaxacan chocolate.

In that moment, Camille decides to let go and stop fighting. She gives in to the miraculous sensations and lets Alejandro kiss her. And she kisses him back, too, because she couldn't stop herself if she tried.

He envelops her in his arms and presses his body to hers. He slowly draws his mouth across the sides of her face, her eyelids, and down her neck with such gentle ferocity she thinks she may pass out again. Her entire body is on fire; she realizes there's absolutely no going back now.

"Camila," he says, almost growling. "You are so beautiful." He tugs the sleeves of her wet dress down off her shoulders and kisses her neck and chest before moving back to her mouth again.

Camille's trembling intensifies, either because of her wet dress or because she's so aroused—probably both.

Alejandro stops kissing her for a moment and takes her face in his hands. "You're shaking. You need to get out of that dress."

A flash of lightning explodes through the windows. The subsequent thunder shakes the house like an earthquake. Without saying a word, Camille reaches down, takes a hold of the hem of her dress, and yanks it over her head. She drops it on the floor and stands there in the candlelight, completely naked but for a pair of white granny panties, size small.

Alejandro devours her with his eyes. "*Ave Maria purísima*," he whispers before picking Camille up in one swift motion and carrying her into the darkness of the bedroom.

CHAPTER 20

Camille lies on her back in Tía Nifa's bed, so relaxed that she can barely move. The soft glow of the lantern on the bedside table has turned the mosquito netting into an eerie orange vapor that floats above the bed like a spirit. The bulk of the storm has moved on to the next mountain range, and light rain taps on the roof in a steady rhythm. She is thankful it's dark, because she can't wipe the self-satisfied smile from her face. How could she not have realized what she was missing out on all these years?

Alejandro traces his fingers across her chest and stomach in a fluttering motion that raises goose bumps on her skin. "Are you okay?"

She closes her eyes and sinks deeper into the soft bed. "You have no idea," she murmurs. "That was *spectacular*."

He leans over and places a gentle kiss on her lips. "*You're* spectacular," he says in his heavy accent, rolling the *r*'s out like soap bubbles from a child's wand. Desire rolls through her again and she turns on her side, pressing her body against his.

"Let's do it again," she whispers in his ear.

"*Sí, mi amor*," he says, pushing his mouth down on hers like he can't get enough.

Another hot wave of desire rolls through her body. Suddenly, there is a loud crash from the other end of the house. A woman's high-pitched voice calls out something in Zapotec.

"*Ay, Dios*," Alejandro says, rolling off of her. "It's my tía."

Camille sits up and frantically arranges the sheet around her naked body. "But I thought you said she wasn't getting here until tomorrow!"

He jumps off the bed and grabs his jeans. "I guess I was wrong. My tía is sometimes—how do you say it—*unpredictable*."

"Jandro . . . *Jandro?*" Tía Nifa calls out, her voice growing louder as she approaches the bedroom.

Camille pulls the sheet up to her eyes and hides like a little girl who's been caught with her hand in the cookie jar.

Tía Nifa appears in the doorway and stands completely still. In her white *huipil* and with her hair dripping across her shoulders, she looks like a frightening apparition. She narrows her eyes at a bare-chested Alejandro, who's jumping around trying to pull on his jeans. She then turns toward the bed and spies Camille peeking out from under the covers. Her hand flies up to her mouth, and her eyes go wide.

Oh, crap—here it comes. Camille grits her teeth and waits for Tía Nifa to rant and rave and toss her out into the street.

Instead, the old woman throws her head back, lets out a whoop of joy, and begins to skip around the room, singing and clapping her hands together as the orange tassels on her *huipil* explode like miniature fireworks. In what resembles religious ecstasy, Tía Nifa spins around the bed, her wet hair spraying Camille's face with a fine mist like an automatic garden sprinkler.

Camille blots her face with the corner of the sheet. "*What's going on?*" she silently mouths to Alejandro.

Alejandro looks amused. "I think she's doing her happy dance."

Half a minute later, Tía Nifa ends her frantic waltz. She comes over to the bed, where Camille is cowering in naked embarrassment, and reaches over to embrace Camille and kiss her on both cheeks. She spews out a stream of words that Camille has no chance in this lifetime of ever understanding. *"Ushkenot, ushkenot,"* she repeats over and over as she rocks Camille back and forth.

Camille turns her head and looks imploringly at Alejandro. "What is she saying?"

"She's thanking you," he says, fastening the last button on his shirt.

"Thanking me? For what?"

He looks a bit embarrassed. "Um, she's thanking you for being here with me. Actually, the exact translation is closer to 'Thank you for making love with my nephew.'"

Camille puts her face in her hands. "Oh, my god. I don't think I've ever been so mortified in my entire life."

"Don't be, Camila. I'm not." He gives her one of his wicked smiles and raises an eyebrow. "In fact, later on—if it's all right with you—I'd like to continue what we just started. You know, maybe give my tía another chance to thank you."

Camille's face burns; she thinks it must be as flaming red as her hair. She slides down under the covers. "Well, you know where to find me," she mumbles from under the sheets.

It's the middle of the night, and Alejandro is talking to Tía Nifa out in the main room. The rise and fall of their animated conversation is like listening to an operetta in a foreign language without the libretto translation. It's driving Camille crazy that she can't understand what they're discussing. Up until a few minutes ago, they were laughing and joking around. Now it seems the conversation has taken a turn and Tía Nifa is chastising Alejandro for doing something wrong.

The voices peter out, and he comes back into the room and closes the door.

"Is your aunt mad at you about something?" she asks. She feels guilty that they're sleeping in her comfortable bed while Tía Nifa has to sleep on a straw mat on the floor. "Are you sure it's okay that we're staying in her room?"

He looks preoccupied with something. "I tried to tell her we'd sleep on the floor out there, but she said she wants us to use her room."

"Why was she yelling at you?"

He sighs. "Oh, you know how it is. She has her opinions about my life. And she never holds back from telling me how to live it."

Camille lets out a sardonic laugh. "I can relate. I've got the same problem with my mother."

Alejandro quickly removes his clothes and climbs back into bed. He pulls Camille close to him; his skin is cool to the touch. "*Ay*, Camila, you're so warm. Now, where were we?"

A faint flash of lightning illuminates the room for a moment. Within seconds, there is another strong rumble of thunder. The rain begins to come down harder as the storm spins back around and hovers over the house.

"Oooh," she says, snuggling closer to him and wrapping her legs around his. "We never get storms like this back home. This whole thing is exciting for me."

"What's exciting? That you're in bed with a *guapo* like me, or the thunderstorm?"

She playfully bites his neck. "The thunderstorm, of course."

"Very funny." He leans over and brushes the hair off her face. "You know, the storms arrived early this year. Usually the heavy rain doesn't come until the middle of July. I think maybe you brought the rain with you."

"I love this kind of weather," she tells him. "When I was a teenager, I spent six weeks in Colorado at the Aspen Music Festival. It was actually one of the best times of my life. Mostly because my mother wasn't there breathing down my neck. That summer I won the grand prize in the student concerto competition. I was selected to play my concerto with the festival orchestra."

"Wow. How old were you?"

"Sixteen. It was a pretty big deal. My mother even flew out to Aspen to attend the performance. On the day of the concert, this violent thunderstorm rolled in. That wasn't anything unusual for the mountains of Aspen, especially in the summer. But this particular one was really intense. The concert took place in this outdoor structure—really just a gigantic white tent. I was playing the Ravel Concerto in G Major—are you familiar with it?"

He snorts. "What do you think?"

"Oh, right. Sorry. I guess you don't listen to much classical music, do you?"

"Not really."

"Well, you should listen to this concerto sometime. It's a wonderful piece. Ravel was an Impressionistic composer, but this particular piece is full of jazz idioms and driving rhythms. I have a feeling you'd like it."

Camille adjusts the pillow behind her neck. "Anyway, in the middle of the first movement there's this section where the orchestra gets really loud. Right then there was a flash of lightning, immediately followed by a big boom of thunder directly above the tent. It came exactly at the climax of the music, like it was part of the score. The power went out, and the audience made this loud gasp. But the orchestra just kept right on playing like nothing was wrong—so I did too."

Camille closes her eyes, reliving the memory. "By the time I started the second movement, which has this very restful and lyrical quality to it, the thunder had stopped. The rain was coming down in this gentle rhythm, which fit perfectly with the mood of *that* movement. Then the craziest thing happened: when I started playing the final movement—which is fast and rhythmic—the thunder and lightning came back again just as the brass instruments began to play fortissimo. It was wild. People talked about it for days."

Alejandro looks thoughtful. "Weren't you scared playing in front of all those people?"

"Not really. By that time, I had performed in so many concerts that I was used to it. I mean, I still got a little nervous before every concert, but once I started playing I would just get lost, like I was in this dreamlike zone. I sort of became one with the music. It was like there was no separation between my body and the notes. It's kind of hard to explain. It's almost like having a spiritual experience. You know what I mean?"

"I think I understand."

"Anyway, tonight's storm reminds me of that performance. I'll never forget it."

He sits up, leans on his elbow, and gives her an intent stare. "You really miss it, don't you?"

"Miss what?"

"The concerts, the performing—all of it."

Camille is quiet for a moment. "Yes, I do miss it. But to be honest, there's a lot of it I don't miss. All those hours of practicing, the intense preparation for concerts. I hated dealing with all those insecure musicians with their big egos. That part I don't miss at all. But what I do miss is being able to sit down at the piano and play Bach or Schumann, or any composer, for that matter. I miss that feeling of transcending my ordinary existence through the music."

"But you can still play with one hand, right?"

"Yes, of course. There are even pieces that have been composed for the left hand only. For me, though, it's not enough."

Alejandro is quiet for a moment, then asks, "What happened to your fingers, Camila?"

131

She doesn't answer.

"Please tell me."

"They were broken," she whispers.

He leans on one elbow and looks her straight in the eyes. "How? Was it an accident?"

"No." She holds out her hand to show that she can no longer straighten her fingers. "It was on purpose."

A shocked look on his face, he picks up her hand and gently massages her knuckles. "Who broke them?"

"Jack did," she says.

"Who's Jack?"

"He was my boyfriend."

Camille hears Alejandro suck in his breath. "But why would he do that to you?"

She closes her eyes and swallows hard. "Because I let him."

CHAPTER 21

Jack blasted into Camille's life one week after she turned seventeen. It was her last summer at home before heading off to the University of Southern California, where she had been chosen as one of four candidates for their prestigious Artist Diploma program. Camille had wanted to study at Curtis or Juilliard, but her mother had strongly encouraged her to choose USC, her own alma mater. She wanted Camille to keep the family tradition going. This pretty much translated into "Since I'm paying your tuition, you're going to go where I tell you to go." Camille went along with her mother's wishes only after her mother promised her she could go anywhere she wanted for graduate school.

That summer, Camille's mother was set on Camille attending a six-week-long music program at the Bella Vista Conservatory in Santa Barbara. She was also insisting that Camille audition for a full merit scholarship. This meant that even though Camille's mother had more money than she knew what to do with, she wouldn't have to spend a dime on Camille's summer tuition. If she received the scholarship, Camille would be the youngest pianist in the history of the school to do so.

The problem was, Camille never wanted to attend Bella Vista in the first place. What she wanted was to get as far away from Santa

Barbara—and her mother—as she could. So when her mother told her she had scheduled an audition for Bella Vista, she pitched a fit worthy of a three-year-old.

"Are you kidding me, Mom?" she whined. "I don't want to go to Bella Vista! It's way too close to home. This is my last summer before college! I want to go somewhere far away, like last year." She racked her brain, trying to come up with a plan to get out of the audition. "Bella Vista won't accept me, anyhow. Their age requirement is eighteen. There's no way they're going to let me in. And even if I did get in—which I know I won't—we have way too much money for me to get one of their merit scholarships. And don't you think those scholarships should go to someone who really needs the help?"

Her mother rolled her eyes. "For god's sake, Camille," she said irritably. "Could you just spare me the bleeding heart act for one minute? Of course we don't need the money. That's not the point. The point is that since I became a board member at Bella Vista, I've worked my fingers to the bone fund-raising for them. It's about damn time they showed me some small gesture of appreciation." She picked a nonexistent piece of fluff off of her suit jacket and brushed off both sleeves. "And that one small gesture is that they've made an exception with the age requirement this year. You're now eligible to audition. Not only for their summer program, but also for one of their merit scholarships."

"Well, that's just great," Camille muttered under her breath. It all sounded overly suspicious to her. She wouldn't put it past her mother to pull the necessary strings to get what she wanted.

Much to her mother's dismay, Camille was growing up. She had straightened her frizzy hair, traded her ugly wire-rimmed glasses for contacts, and learned how to apply makeup. She no longer resembled a gangly Irish setter puppy whose paws were too big for her body. She had managed to transform herself into a graceful red swan that the boys couldn't help but notice. Her mother thought her social life would distract her from her practicing; Camille knew that was why she was making her stay close to home.

For over a week, Camille butted heads with her mother about attending Bella Vista. But even though she put up her best fight, her mother wouldn't give in this time; it was going to be Bella Vista or nothing that summer. So she finally relented and went to the audition.

From the moment she sat down at the piano, it was clear that the faculty knew she was the daughter of their revered Nanette Childs. They were acting more nervous than Camille felt, obviously worried that she wouldn't be good enough for their school. She considered botching the audition on purpose, but in the end she decided to give it her all and prove to them just how good she was. When it was over they were all smiles, clearly astonished by the caliber of her playing.

A week later, Camille got her formal acceptance letter in the mail. That night, her mother, after consuming an entire bottle of chardonnay in less than an hour, let it slip that she knew Camille was going to get in all along. What she wasn't expecting was that the faculty would actually fight over who got to have Camille as their student.

"We may not need the money," her mother said, walking unsteadily to the wine refrigerator to pull out another bottle, "but those idiots over there at Bella Vista were very smart to finally give me what I deserve. Without my help, they'd be nothing. Ten years ago, Bella Vista didn't have a pot to piss in. They had nothing but mediocre students and run-of-the-mill faculty. It was *pathetic*."

Camille knew there was no point in arguing with her mother when she was drunk, but she had to try. "But Mom, I don't want to go! I'm going to be the youngest student there. All the college kids are going to think I'm some show-off prodigy. They're all going to talk about me behind my back like I'm a freak."

"Oh, stop it, Camille," her mother said, using the back of her hand to wipe some drool off the corner of her mouth. "Don't be such a drama queen. The only reason anyone would gossip about you is because they're jealous of your musical ability."

"That's another reason! Everyone will hate me. They're all going to think that I just got into Bella Vista because of you—*which is totally true*. I already told you I want to go back to Aspen this summer."

Her mother wagged a perfectly manicured finger at her. "Absolutely not. There's no way I'm sending you back to Aspen this year. You already won their concerto competition last summer. That makes you ineligible to win again. If you can't compete, what's the point of going back?"

Camille pounded her fist on the table. "The point is that all my friends are going to be there!"

"Friends?" She smoothed a strand of hair off her forehead. "You mean 'boy' friends, right? Well, you can just put that idea right out of your mind this instant. You don't have time for anything but practicing. You have to prepare for Bella Vista's concerto competition. And you have to win it too."

Camille fumed. "The only reason you want me to go to Bella Vista is so you can control what I do. You only care about showing me off to your snooty Montecito music friends."

Her mother's mouth set itself in a tight line. "You might want to remember that those snooty Montecito friends of mine are *your* friends too. And they're the ones who have the contacts to pave the way for your concert career, whether you like them or not."

Camille glared at her. "You can't make me go."

"Oh, I can't?" She arched one eyebrow so she looked slightly lopsided. "We'll just see about that."

As she knew she would, Camille ended up at Bella Vista for the summer. Since it was so close, she continued living at home, and her mother drove her to campus each day. She was correct about the older students ignoring her, but she pretended not to care. She spent most of her time in the practice rooms or wandering around the conservatory's sizable oceanfront acreage.

Even she had to admit that Bella Vista had a lovely campus. The property, originally a private estate, had been bequeathed to the music school over a hundred years earlier. Although improvements had been made since then—namely, the addition of a large auditorium and state-of-the-art practice rooms—the main house still retained its original Santa Barbara charm with its pink paint and red-tiled roof.

While the estate was picturesque, it was Bella Vista's lush gardens that made it extraordinary. After practicing all morning long, when she couldn't bear sitting at the piano a minute longer, Camille would take a break and explore the grounds. There were so many wonderful things to see: The secret hiding places created by the boxy mazes of Eugenia hedges. The cushiony beds of blue periwinkle that grew under the scrub oak trees. There was even a reflecting pool, complete with lily pads and bright orange koi fish. The scent of the blooming pittosporum trees was so heavy it was like the air had been laced with perfume. Camille loved the brick pathways that crisscrossed through the grass like a Victorian board game. She often imagined that the algae-covered statues on the lawns were forgotten game pieces that had been frozen in time. As she sat on the lawn and listened to the other students practicing chamber music inside, she felt like the star of her own movie.

At the beginning of her second week at Bella Vista, Camille was on her way toward the Old Recital Hall. The venue was the original living room of the estate but was now used for recitals and student master classes. Camille was unusually tense. She was scheduled to perform in her first master class in about fifteen minutes. She knew she had to prove to the other students that she was worthy of being at Bella Vista. She was so nervous, the butterflies in her stomach were swarming like wasps. She wiped her sweating palms on her skirt.

As she rounded the corner of a building, she smelled the sharp tang of fresh-cut lumber and wet paint. She passed by a group of men working on the dilapidated gazebo that stood near the Old Recital Hall, and a young man of about twenty caught her eye. He was tall and blond and had a lit cigarette dangling from his lips. There was something about him. Camille couldn't help but stare at his rippling muscles as he pounded nails into the wood.

As if he sensed she was watching him, he abruptly turned and looked directly at her. He took a long drag off his cigarette, his gaze never leaving her face. Even as he tilted his head back and blew out a stream of blue smoke, his eyes were still on her.

Camille's stomach turned over and her heart began to race. With that one look, she forgot all about the master class. She felt weird inside, like she was on the verge of losing control. Surprisingly, she found she liked the feeling. For the first time in her life, she felt alive away from the piano. She tried to look away from him, but his gaze held hers like they were tethered by some invisible cord. As she stood there, paralyzed, she knew that whatever happened from that moment on was completely out of her hands.

"Camille!" A muffled voice called out her name as if it were coming through a thick fog.

She ignored it and kept her eyes on his face.

"*Camille!*" The voice became shriller. "Do you hear me?" It was her mother, shouting from the doorway of the Old Hall. "Hurry up! You're late, and the master class is about to begin!"

Coming out of her stupor, Camille turned toward the sound of her mother's voice. She had a scowl on her face, but Camille could see that there was something else there too. Fear. Her mother was afraid that something beyond her control was happening.

"I'm coming," Camille called. She turned back to the blond guy, expecting to see his gaze still focused on her face, but he wasn't even looking in her direction any longer. Her heart sank. He had gone back to pounding nails, banging his hammer in a precise rhythm like he had never even taken any notice of her.

Like she was nothing to him.

CHAPTER 22

The master class was a complete disaster. Camille had been performing in competitions and recitals for years, and she'd never once fallen apart so badly. She'd actually blanked out at one point and left out a large part of her piece.

She tried to blame it on the fact that it was the first time she'd ever performed in the Old Recital Hall. The formality of the room was intimidating; the grand decor had not changed since the early 1900s. Elaborate tapestries and Baroque-style gilt mirrors still hung on the walls. Cut glass chandeliers dangled from molded ceilings that spread out above the spacious room like smooth white frosting on a wedding cake. Two black concert grand pianos stood side by side on risers in front of the original stone fireplace. There were no carpets on the scuffed hardwood floors, and every cough or restless twitch of the audience echoed so noisily through the room that people spoke in hushed whispers or said nothing at all.

Camille also considered the possibility that her breakdown had occurred because she was being so closely watched by everyone in the audience. Not just her mother but also her mother's platinum-haired, Chanel-scented Montecito cronies who sat alongside her in the first row. According to her mother, Camille needed these people to help launch her solo career. Her ultimate goal, therefore, was to demonstrate to them that she had what it took to succeed in the concert world.

Any of those excuses would have sufficed, but the truth was, Camille knew exactly why she'd fallen apart. It was all because of the blond-haired guy.

She'd been playing the Brahms Rhapsody in G Minor, and her performance had started out better than she'd expected. The tone of the piano was warm and responsive. The acoustics in the cavernous room were perfect for a Romantic piece such as the Brahms. Halfway through, she began to relax. *No problem, Camille—you've got this.* Then she caught a whiff of cigarette smoke wafting in through the open French doors.

For a split second, Camille allowed herself to get distracted. Glancing up over the piano, she looked outside and saw a tall figure standing against the wall. A chill went up her spine. It was that blond-haired guy. He was out there, smoking a cigarette and listening to her play. Her stomach dropped, and the room began to spin. Sweat dripped down her back. Suddenly, she froze, her hands stopping midair.

She fumbled around the keys, unable to figure out where she was in the music. In sheer desperation, she jumped to the end of the piece, leaving out almost an entire page. She was mortified. And she was sure her mother was dying a slow, painful death right there in the front row.

Immediately following the master class, her mother pulled her outside to the parking lot and made her get into the car with her. "What the hell was that?" she demanded, unable to hide the fury on her face.

Camille tried to hold back her tears. "I'm sorry, Mom. I don't know what happened."

Her mother practically spat out the words. "Well, I do. You

blew it because you lost your focus. Now, I don't know what's going on inside that hard head of yours, but I'm well aware of the fact that something is distracting you." She narrowed her eyes at her. "Whatever it is, you'd better put it out of your mind right now and get back to work. You get it together right now, because I don't *ever* want to be embarrassed like that again."

She shoved the key into the ignition and started the engine with a roar. "I suggest you get over to the practice rooms and study your music thoroughly. Figure out what the hell happened with the Brahms."

Camille sat there and stared sullenly out the windshield.

"*This instant!*" her mother screamed.

Camille jumped so high that she almost hit her head on the roof of the car. "God, Mom—calm down!" Fat tears began to roll down her cheeks, and she scrambled out of the car. "You don't have to yell. I'm going!"

I hate her, she thought as she watched her mother's Mercedes squeal out of the parking lot. She didn't care that Camille felt terrible about her performance. She only cared about what others thought.

She wiped the tears away with the palms of her hands. *Screw it*. Screw the practice rooms, screw the Brahms. And screw her mother. She was tired of trying to be the perfect daughter all the time. She wanted to be a normal teenager for once. She wanted to hang out with friends and go to parties—go out on a date with a boy. She was sick of working so hard. For what? To make her mother look good in front of her snobby friends?

She realized she needed to get away from Bella Vista to clear her head. She had a couple of hours to kill before the evening chamber music concert; she decided to take a walk on the beach. She went to the bathroom, changed out of her dress and high heels into shorts, a tank top, and sandals, then headed out.

As Camille got closer to the water, she felt her anger dissipating. It was a dazzling June afternoon. The seasonal fog that typically burned off by late morning had not yet rolled back in for its evening encore. The Pacific unfurled out in front of her like a glittering sapphire carpet.

As she walked, she watched the monarch butterflies with their orange-and-black stained-glass wings flit in an out between the date palms and eucalyptus trees that lined the road.

She sat down on a stone wall that ran parallel to the shore, kicked off her shoes, and wriggled her toes down into the cooler sand. Staring out over the ocean, she didn't think about the Brahms, the master class, or about how much she hated her mother. She had only one thing on her mind: the handsome blond-haired guy, and how it had felt when he'd looked into her eyes.

As she gazed out at the water, she heard the sound of a motorcycle stopping and parking nearby. Footsteps crunched on the road and then stopped directly behind her.

"Hey," a deep voice said, "didn't I see you at the school back there? Aren't you one of the music students?"

She jerked her head around. *Oh, god.* It was him. He was even better-looking up close. He was over six feet tall, with evenly tanned skin, a square jaw, and just the hint of a cleft in his chin. He was wearing a brown leather jacket and had a ratty backpack slung over his shoulder. The red top of a pack of Marlboros peeked out of the front pocket of his T-shirt.

"Uh . . . yes," she stammered. "I'm . . . uh . . . I'm a student there."

"What do you play?" he asked, casually dropping his backpack on the sand next to her feet. He took off his jacket and threw it over the wall. His bronzed arms were covered with a layer of blond hair that looked so soft and fine Camille wanted to reach out and stroke them like she would a cat.

She stared at him, so flustered she had forgotten his question. "I'm sorry—what did you say?"

The corners of his mouth turned up slightly. "What instrument do you play? The violin? Or maybe you play the piano?"

"Oh. Yes. I'm a pianist."

"I heard some pretty good tinkling of those ivories back there at the school a while ago. Was that you I heard?"

"Maybe," she said, not wanting him to know that she was the pianist who had messed up so badly.

He sat down next to her. "What's your name?"

She couldn't place his accent, although she knew he had to be from somewhere on the East Coast—possibly New York or Boston. "Camille," she said.

He held out his hand. "I'm Jack." His skin was rough and calloused. As he wrapped his fingers around hers, a shock of electricity moved through her body.

"Hi," she managed to squeak out.

He unzipped his backpack and pulled out a brown glass bottle. "You want a beer?" He snapped off the twist top and flicked it onto the sand. He drank down half the bottle in one long swallow.

"No, thanks," she said. "I have to head back to Bella Vista in a little while. I'm supposed to turn pages for another pianist at a chamber music concert tonight."

He turned to look out over the ocean. "Too bad. I was going to ask you if you wanted to take a ride with me on my bike."

"On your motorcycle?" she asked. "Where?" His eyes were so blue she couldn't look away.

"I don't know—just up in the hills around Montecito. I like to ride around and look at all the fancy houses. Flip off all those rich assholes."

"Oh." Camille was surprised by how easily the curse word slid out of his mouth. She wondered what he would think if he knew that he'd probably ridden down her street. That she was one of the "rich assholes" he'd flipped off.

"So, you up for it?" he asked.

"Um . . . I can't. I really have to get back to Bella Vista."

He playfully poked his finger at her arm. "C'mon, Camille. You know you don't want to go turn pages or whatever it is you're doing over at the school. It's so nice out right now. Come take a ride with me."

Camille knew the minute his finger touched her arm that she was going to go with him. She glanced at her watch. "If I'm back before eight, I guess it would be all right."

"*No problemo*," he said, sucking down the remainder of his beer. He turned his head and let out a loud belch. "I'll get you back in plenty of time." He put on his jacket. Even though there was a trash can just a few feet away, he left his empty bottle sitting on the stone wall.

He straddled the motorcycle and handed Camille a grimy helmet. "Here—wear this. I wouldn't want you to get hurt if we had an accident or something."

The helmet smelled of sweat and stale cigarettes. It was too big, making Camille feel like a ridiculous astronaut.

Jack turned the key and the engine rumbled noisily. He jerked his head toward the back of the motorcycle. "Well, get on."

She climbed up on the bike, unsure of where to put her hands. She finally reached back and grabbed the metal bar that jutted out from the end of the seat.

He craned his head back around and looked at her strangely. "What are you doing?"

"What do you mean?" Camille's voice was muffled by the foam inside the helmet.

He reached around behind him and pulled her wrists so that her arms were encircling his waist. "Now hold on tight and don't let go."

"Okay," she said, feeling his hard stomach muscles pressing against the underside of her forearms. It felt good.

He turned his head back around toward her again. "One more thing."

"What?" Was he going to ask her to get down off the bike because she was too much trouble?

"How old are you?"

Camille's heart skipped a beat. She couldn't tell him she'd just turned seventeen. He'd think she was just a kid. She entwined her fingers and tightened her arms around his waist, pushing her breasts against his back. "I'm eighteen." The lie slid out of her mouth like a well-practiced scale.

He grinned. "That's what I was hoping." Without looking, he gunned the motor and swerved sharply out into the lane.

They sped across the railroad tracks and wound their way up into the hills, passing the gated driveways of Mediterranean-style mansions that rose up from the silvery-green chaparral. When they reached the top of the ridge, they stopped and looked down. The lights of the Santa Barbara harbor twinkled in the fading light. The sky turned pink, and the sun fell behind the ocean.

Camille looked at her watch again and saw that it was almost eight o'clock.

"I think you're going to be late," Jack said, giving Camille an easy smile. He took another beer out of his backpack, opened it, and held it out to her.

She hesitated.

"What's wrong?" he asked. "You don't like beer?"

Camille had never had alcohol before, but she didn't want him to know that.

"Sure I do," she said, reaching out for the bottle. She took a long sip. It was lukewarm and tasted bitter, but she drank it anyway. At that moment, she didn't care about anything except being with Jack. She wanted to be as far away as possible from Bella Vista, the piano, all of the pressure. More than anything, she wanted to be away from her mother.

Jack reached inside his backpack and pulled out a sandwich wrapped in greasy white paper. Smiling, he handed Camille half of an Italian submarine. "Dinner's on me tonight."

They sat on a flat boulder and ate the vinegary sandwich, passing the warm beer back and forth. Jack told Camille all about himself. How he had come out to Santa Barbara from New Hampshire to go to the University, then dropped out after only two quarters because his grades had slipped. He talked about his family back East and how he missed New England, especially the change of seasons. He complained that Santa Barbara just had one long, continuous summer. He told her how he'd been working as a carpenter for almost a year, trying to save enough to go back to school. How the rent in Santa Barbara was so expensive that he was barely making it.

They watched the stars come out. When it got too cold, he wrapped his leather jacket around Camille's shoulders. Then, without warning, he leaned in and kissed her. He tasted of beer and cigarettes, but Camille didn't care. She was being kissed for the first time in her life. So what if he was a little rough and his whiskers scratched her chin? He was kissing *her*, and that was all that mattered.

As they looped their way back down the twisting roads into Montecito, Jack stopped at an intersection near Camille's house. She realized that she wasn't ready for the evening to end. She took off the helmet and tapped him on the shoulder.

She pointed to the left. "See that gate with the two big trees on either side?" she asked. "That's my house."

He whistled. "You're kidding me, right? You actually live *there*?"

He pulled the motorcycle up to the wrought iron gate and turned off the engine.

"Do you want to come in?" Camille asked.

His eyes widened. "What about your parents?"

"It's just me and my mom. And she's probably already gone to bed. Besides, we have a guesthouse. We could go hang out there for a while."

"What if your mom wakes up and hears us?"

Camille pictured her mother passed out on the couch in the living room with an empty bottle of wine on the coffee table. "I don't think that will be a problem. My mother is a very sound sleeper."

"Well, okay, sure," he said, taking her hand and helping her off the bike. "Let's go."

Later on that night, as Camille lay awake in the darkness, she felt a little guilty that she hadn't made it back to Bella Vista for the concert. The pianist she was scheduled to turn pages for was probably pissed off at her for not being there.

She figured she had a pretty good excuse for not showing up, though.

She'd been just a little bit occupied losing her virginity in the darkened bedroom of her mother's guesthouse to care much about turning pages for anyone.

CHAPTER 23

Camille knew her relationship with Jack had to be kept a secret. The best way to keep her mother from getting suspicious was to go back to playing the role of the obedient daughter. The one who practiced for hours and showed up on time to her classes and rehearsals. The one who kept her mouth shut and didn't whine or complain. She even apologized to her for her terrible performance at the master class. She promised to work harder so it would never happen again.

Her mother was noticeably pleased with her sudden change in attitude and pretty much left her alone after that. Little did she know that right under her nose, her seventeen-year-old daughter was having sex every night with a horny twenty-two-year-old in the bedroom of her vacant guesthouse.

It was so easy for Camille to deceive her mother. All she had to do was wait around for her to polish off her second bottle of chardonnay. It usually took no longer than fifteen minutes for her to pass out on the couch after that, and then Camille slipped out the back door and headed to the guesthouse, where she met up with Jack.

Most nights, she brought snacks she'd pilfered from the pantry and Jack supplied the beer, and they watched a movie—or at least started watching one. While Camille would take only a few sips of beer, Jack would polish off the whole six-pack within the hour. Then, whether they had finished the movie or not, Jack would invariably make his move and lead Camille into the bedroom for sex.

Their secret trysts continued throughout the summer. Camille found herself in a state of euphoria, like she was sitting in the front seat of a thrilling roller coaster ride. Sometimes, when she had a break from lessons or rehearsal, she would seek Jack out as he worked around the Bella Vista campus, pretending that she'd run into him by chance. He would be wearing his tight jeans, a tool belt slung low around his hips, and her stomach would flip with excitement at the sight of him. He rarely acknowledged her. The most she got from him was a nod of his head—or a quick wink, if he was feeling generous. He explained to Camille that it wouldn't be wise to let anyone know what was going on between them. With her mother being on the Bella Vista board, he could lose his job for socializing with a student.

He also made it clear that their relationship was only temporary. "No ties, Camille," he'd say. "We're just having some fun."

She was fine with that. As long as she had him all to herself in the evenings, she wasn't about to complain. Camille felt like the luckiest girl alive that a guy as cool as Jack wanted to have fun with someone like her.

Even with the distraction of a secret boyfriend, Camille practiced harder that summer than she ever had in her life. She spent the majority of her days preparing her music for Bella Vista's concerto competition.

She had chosen to audition with the Schumann Piano Concerto in A Minor. It was a piece she had originally learned when she was fourteen. On the advice of her teacher, she had put it aside until she was more mature and could fully understand the deep emotion of the piece. Now that she had lost her virginity and considered herself a real woman, she felt ready to do justice to the big, romantic concerto. Camille loved how the singing melodies twisted and turned their way through the score. How the piano part intertwined with the clarinet part, and how the mood changed from melancholic to dramatic within a few bars. Even with Jack distracting her in the evenings, she managed to find extra time during the day to devote to practicing.

Her diligence paid off in full. She ended up winning first prize in the concerto competition.

Camille could barely contain her excitement about winning the competition. That night as she and Jack snuggled together in bed, she told him that the following week she would be performing with the Bella Vista Orchestra as their featured artist.

"Oh, yeah?" he said. "Good for you."

He didn't seem impressed. Camille chalked it up to the fact that being a non-musician, Jack had no concept of what a big deal this was. She laid her head on his chest and pressed up against him. "You know, if you wanted, I could get you a ticket and maybe you could come hear me play. The concert is this Saturday night at eight. How about it?"

His body tensed. "I can't come. I already have plans."

She sat up and leaned on one elbow. "What kind of plans?" She was slightly hurt that he didn't understand how important this concert was for her.

"I don't know," he said vaguely. "Just plans."

"But couldn't you change them?"

He quickly got out of bed and pulled on his boxer shorts. "Camille," he said, his voice flat, "I already told you I have plans. Don't question me like that. I can't go, and that's that." He grabbed his cigarettes and lighter off the nightstand. "Be right back. I'm gonna go have a smoke."

She lay there, tears stinging her eyes. How could he not understand how important this was to her? This was a huge deal, and he was acting like it was nothing. She got up to use the bathroom and began shivering, as Jack had left the French doors wide open. Without even thinking about it, she picked up his baby-blue Brooks Brothers shirt and wrapped it around her naked body like a robe. It smelled of nicotine and aftershave. When she came out of the bathroom, Jack was standing there staring at her, a strange look on his face.

"What's wrong?" she asked.

"Why are you wearing my shirt?" he said in a voice she barely recognized.

She pulled her arms in close to her body. "I don't know. I was cold, so I put it on to go into the bathroom."

"Take it off."

She was confused by his strange behavior. "What's wrong?"

"Take my shirt off right now," he said, his jaw tight. "That's my shirt, and I paid good money for it. I don't appreciate you touching my things without asking."

At first Camille was merely surprised that he was making such a big deal about it. Then she began to get angry. *What a jerk.* Here she'd gone and invited him to her big concert, and he acted like he couldn't care less. Now he was making a huge fuss over her wearing his shirt.

"Geez, Jack," she said, roughly pulling off the shirt and tossing it to the ground. "Why are you getting so pissed off? It's only a shirt."

His face turned red, and he pointed to the ground. "Pick it up, Camille," he growled.

"You pick it up," she said, irate now. "It's your stupid shirt."

Before she even realized what was happening, Jack had grabbed her arm, twisted it behind her back, and shoved her roughly up against the wall. His other hand went around her throat so tightly she could barely breathe.

"Are you going to pick up my shirt *now*, Camille?" he said, his lip curling like a snarling dog.

With his hand around her throat she couldn't speak, so she just nodded. He let go and shoved her down to the ground. Still in shock, she managed to pick up his shirt and hand it to him, her hands shaking with fright. He took the shirt and gently snapped it in the air several times, as if he was trying to shake off her scent. He then brought it up to his nose and inhaled deeply. Satisfied, he put it on and buttoned it slowly, like he had all the time in the world.

Camille stood there, naked and trembling, trying to hold back her tears, as he put on his pants, dug his keys out of his pocket, and opened the bedroom door.

Before he left, he turned around and leveled his eyes at her. "Camille, don't you ever fucking disrespect me like that again."

She nodded in silent acquiescence.

"Good girl," he said, and walked into the living room, leaving the door open.

Letting out her breath, Camille sat down on the bed and pulled the cold sheet up around her shivering body. She heard the front door swing open.

"Camille?" he called out.

Her heart pounded. Maybe he felt guilty about what he'd just done and was going to apologize.

"Yes?" she said, keeping her voice even.

"I'll see you tomorrow," he said, as if nothing had happened. "Same time."

Looking back, Camille realizes she should have told her mother what Jack had done. But she thought she was strong enough to end the relationship herself. The next day, she made the decision that she wouldn't meet him at the guesthouse. *The hell with him*, she thought. *I'm not letting anyone treat me like that.*

The following day, her piano lesson at Bella Vista had ended early, as her teacher wasn't feeling well. She headed over to the parking lot to wait for her mother to pick her up. She found an unoccupied bench under a shady Monterey pine and was taking her music out to review her teacher's notes when she felt a hand on her shoulder.

Startled, she turned around. There was Jack, looking as forlorn as a lost puppy.

"Hi, Camille." This was the first time he had ever spoken to her on campus.

Without a word, she turned back around, put her music back into her bag, and ignored him.

"C'mon, Camille, please don't be mad," he said, coming around to sit down next to her on the bench. He gently took her hands in his. "I'm really sorry about last night. I didn't mean to lose it like that. It's just that when you told me about you winning that contest, I started thinking that the summer is almost over. I'm just really upset that you're going off to college in a few weeks. I'm really bummed that I'm not going to be able to see you anymore."

Her heart leapt. Did that mean he was going to miss her? That maybe their relationship meant something more to him than just having some fun?

"The thing is," he continued, "when we first started hanging out together, I thought it was just going to be for a few weeks. But it's been over a month, and now I'm beginning to have these strong feelings for you." His voice caught. "I don't know what I'm going to do without you. Please don't leave me, Camille."

He looked so earnest, Camille knew there was no way she could stay mad at him. "Oh, Jack." She sighed. "It's all right. Just don't scare me like that again, okay?"

He reached out, gathered her into his arms, and held her tight against his chest. "I swear to God, Camille," he whispered into her ear, so softly she almost didn't hear him. "I promise I'll never do anything to hurt you ever again."

CHAPTER 24

The morning of Camille's Bella Vista concert, her mother came into her room and stood at the foot of her bed. It was just after dawn, and the glow of the sunrise turned the white cotton curtains a soft shade of pink. She had been at the guesthouse with Jack until about four that morning, so she awoke groggy from lack of sleep. Upon slowly opening one eye, she saw that her mother was staring at her intently.

"What do you want, Mom? It's so early."

She was visibly cross. "I need to discuss something with you."

Camille moaned. "Can't it wait until later? I want to sleep in."

"No, it can't wait, Camille. I just got a call from one of the neighbors. He said he saw a man leaving the guesthouse before dawn this morning. He was going to call the police, but then he saw a young girl follow the guy out. He thought it might've been you."

Oh, crap. I'm caught.

"Was it you, Camille?"

Camille rubbed her eyes and thought about coming up with some sort of lie, but she decided against it. She was tired of sneaking around. It was time to be straight with her mother. She and Jack loved each other. Why should they have to hide it from the world?

"What if it *was* me?" Camille asked.

Her mother didn't flinch. "Well, then, I guess I'd want to know who you were with and what you were doing in the guesthouse in the middle of the night."

Camille looked right at her. "Are you sure you want to know?"

She swallowed. "Yes, I'm sure."

Her mother kept her face perfectly still as she proceeded to tell her all about Jack. How he was one of the crew that worked fixing up the Bella Vista campus, and that they'd been seeing each other all summer. That even though Camille was moving down to Los Angeles to start school in a few weeks they were still going to try to keep their relationship going because they were deeply in love. When she mentioned that Jack was twenty-two, her mother's mouth fell open.

"Camille, what in the hell are you thinking?" her mother asked, her voice rising. "He's twenty-two—that's five years older than you."

"I don't care. I love him."

"Love him? Don't be ridiculous. Your relationship with this man is against the law!"

"What do you mean, *against the law?*"

"I mean you're underage. If he's having sex with you, I could easily have him arrested for statutory rape."

Camille sat up in bed. "*Rape?* What are you talking about, Mom? He's not raping me! I want to have sex with him."

Her mother scowled, unable to hide her revulsion. "It doesn't matter what you want, Camille. You're a minor, and I'm responsible for you. You're too immature for this kind of intimate relationship. Especially with a man five years older than you. I forbid you from seeing him any longer."

Camille's fury surged. She had been under her mother's thumb for far too long. "I swear to God, if you try to prevent me from being with Jack, I will never speak to you again. I'll—I'll run away. I won't go to college or ever practice the piano again! I mean it, Mom."

Her mother sat down on the bed, her face stern. "Be reasonable. You're only seventeen—he's *twenty-two*. Don't you think it's strange that a man his age wants to be with a teenager? That's sick."

"It's not sick! You just can't understand real love because you never loved anyone before—not even my father. But I love Jack! We're soul mates!"

Her mother clapped her hands together like Camille was a misbehaving puppy. "Stop it this instant, Camille. You have absolutely no idea what you're talking about. I cannot allow you to behave this way. Not with your entire life in front of you. You're about to go off to college and meet new people and have new experiences. Why you would want to tie yourself down to one person when you're so young is beyond my comprehension. Especially to someone who is uneducated, works as a day laborer, and probably has no real goals in life. Except maybe to find his meal ticket with an underage girl from a wealthy family."

Camille began to cry from frustration. "You're such a snob. You don't even know him and already you're judging him. But I know him. *I love him.*"

"You don't know what love is, Camille. And you're going to call him up today and tell him it's over."

"No."

"Yes, you are. I mean it, Camille."

"No, Mom. I don't care what you say. I'm not breaking up with him. It's my life, and I'm going to do what I want for once." She lay back down on the bed and pulled the comforter up to her neck. "Hey, I have an idea. How about if instead of performing tonight, I just use that time to pack up my stuff and get out? I'll go stay with Jack at his place."

Her mother suddenly looked nervous. "Don't be stupid, Camille. You can't back out of the concert now. That would be disastrous for your career."

There was no way Camille was going to miss performing her concerto that night, but her mother didn't know that. "I could care less about the stupid concert," she lied.

Her mother stood up and smoothed her skirt. "We'll talk about this some other time. You need to rest up for tonight. I'll leave you alone now."

Camille burrowed down deeper into the bed. "*Yes!*" she silently mouthed when she was safe under the covers. It was just so easy to manipulate her mother. She would go to the ends of the earth to avoid doing anything to jeopardize Camille's musical career. Even if it meant giving Camille exactly what she wanted.

And what she wanted was Jack.

That evening, Camille performed the Schumann concerto for a packed house. She played so brilliantly that she received a standing ovation that went on for over five minutes. At the reception following the concert, she watched, annoyed, as her mother traipsed around like a queen bee, basking in the glow of her daughter's success. Her cronies, wearing their designer gowns, buzzed around her mother as if she were the one who had performed in front of all those people instead of Camille.

Camille looked for Jack in the crowd, but he hadn't shown up. She had to admit she was disappointed, and a little hurt. But later that night, she arrived home to find a bouquet of wildflowers— yellow sour grass and candy orange nasturtiums—tied to the front gate with a piece of string. A note was written on a piece of scratch paper and tucked among the wilting blossoms. *Sorry I missed it. Next time. Love, Jack.* Camille's heart soared.

Camille's mother rolled her eyes and muttered something about *not even having enough class to show up or buy real flowers*, but said nothing more. Camille assumed her mother had decided it was better to leave it alone and hope the relationship would simply fizzle out over time.

She knew that would never happen.

For the remainder of the summer, Camille continued to regularly sneak out at night and meet Jack at the guesthouse. If her mother knew, she played dumb. And soon enough, it was time for Camille to pack up her things. She was headed to USC to begin her freshman year of college.

Camille's mother had decided it was best that she not live in one of the freshman dorms, believing the social aspect of college life would distract her from practicing, so she'd purchased a two-bedroom condominium near campus and had it completely furnished. She referred to it as an "opportune real estate investment," even though they both knew she'd bought it solely for Camille to use for the next four years.

The day after Camille moved in, a glossy black Steinway grand piano arrived. Camille could practice at home and avoid having to wait in line to use the practice room pianos on campus.

At first, Jack called Camille every day to tell her how much he missed her. After a few weeks, however, the calls became less frequent. And even though she was making new friends, she missed him terribly.

She decided to invite him down to USC one weekend for a visit. She was performing in a chamber music concert, and she thought he might like to come hear her play. He could even meet some of her new friends.

Jack seemed annoyed that she had even asked. "You know how

busy I am with this new painting job," he said, sounding exasperated. "And you should know by now that this classical music stuff really isn't my thing. I don't get it." He suddenly became quiet. "The truth is, I've been doing some thinking. I've had a lot going on lately. I think it's probably best that we don't spend as much time together anymore."

She almost laughed. Jack had to be joking—they hadn't seen each other in over a month. Then it dawned on her. "Oh my god, Jack. Are you breaking up with me?"

"Uh, well, I think that would be the best thing," he said. "At least for right now."

"But—don't you love me anymore?"

"Sure I do. It's just that I'm really busy." There was an uncomfortable silence. "Listen, I gotta go. I'll talk to you later."

Camille couldn't believe he would dump her over the phone like that. She spent the weekend in bed with a broken heart, crying and stuffing herself with ice cream and potato chips. But by Monday morning, she was feeling stronger, thinking maybe she would survive after all. And by Thursday afternoon, she was sure of it. She even made plans with friends to go to dinner and a movie that Saturday.

On Friday morning, she opened her front door to find a homeless man sleeping on the front porch. She grabbed her phone to call the police. Then she recognized the ratty brown leather jacket. It was Jack. He was dirty, disheveled, and passed out cold.

When Camille was finally able to rouse him and get him into the house, she could smell the sickly sweet odor of alcohol emanating from his body. He tearfully explained that he had lost his job and gotten kicked out of his rented room after failing to pay rent for two months.

"I didn't have anywhere to go," he said, his voice thick with tears. "None of my friends would take me in. So I came here. I just need a week or so to get my shit together, Camille—to find another job. Could I stay here with you?"

She didn't hesitate. He obviously needed her. "Of course," she said, reaching out to put her arms around him. "You can stay as long as you want."

He stayed for almost four years.

CHAPTER 25

For about six months after Jack moved in, he was wonderful. He did laundry, shopped for groceries, and even cooked dinner several nights a week. While Camille went to class or stayed home to practice, he looked for work, but he never had much luck finding anything. Sometimes Camille would come home around noon to eat lunch and there he would be, sitting in front of the television, an ashtray full of cigarette butts and several empty beer cans on the coffee table. On weekends he would often hit the bars, and he sometimes came home so drunk he could barely walk.

One Sunday evening he showed up at the condo with three sketchy-looking guys in tow. They stayed up all night long, partying. Camille was terrified that the neighbors were going to call the police, which would inevitably mean her mother would find out that Jack was living there. The following morning, she was so exhausted that she couldn't help lashing out at him.

"I would really appreciate it if you wouldn't invite a bunch of lowlifes over to party when I have to get up for class in the morning," she snapped. "I couldn't sleep at all last night. I really think—"

Before she could even finish her sentence, his hand came out and struck her so hard across her face that she landed in a heap on the kitchen floor. "You fucking bitch," he said, his face turning red with fury, "don't you ever talk about my friends like that again." He leaned over and raised his arm as if to strike her again. "Nobody talks to me like that."

She could smell the alcohol fumes on his breath, and she realized he was still drunk from the night before. "I'm sorry," she cried, covering her face with her arms. "I'm so sorry. Please don't hit me." She began to sob.

He turned and kicked the kitchen cabinet so hard the wood splintered. "You fucking better be sorry."

Jack's angry outbursts began to occur more often—always when he was drunk. He would take offense at something Camille said and berate her, sometimes shove or hit her. He would then storm out of the condo and not return until later that night or early the next morning. When he did, he was always full of regret and apologies and tearful promises that he would never do it again. He blamed his behavior on the alcohol. He always told Camille he couldn't help it, that the booze turned him into a different person.

"I swear to god, Camille," he told her every time, "I'm going to stop drinking. I don't like what it does to me."

Camille was naive enough to believe him and stupid enough to forgive him. She felt he was a wounded soul—a lost little boy who just needed someone to help him find his way. Her love was the only thing that could save him. But no matter what she said or did—no matter how much love and support she gave him—within the week he would go right back to drinking again. And with the drinking came more violence.

Camille learned to watch what she said around him, making sure never to criticize or nag. She encouraged him to keep looking for work, even though it seemed that every time he got a new job it only lasted a week or two. He always had some excuse: his boss was a jerk, or he'd been fired for showing up late because he was hungover from partying the night before.

One time, he told Camille he was done with California and wanted to go home to New Hampshire. She cried and begged him to stay, but he left anyway. After a few months, his parents kicked him out. He called her collect, saying he couldn't live without her. He begged her to take him back, and of course she did; she even purchased his plane ticket back to Los Angeles.

For almost three years, Camille put up with his physical and verbal abuse, never telling anyone what was going on. She always held on to the hope that her love would change him. To get through each day, she began to focus more intently on her musical studies. She diligently prepared for her senior piano recital, which was scheduled for the following spring. She entered competitions and won first prize in several of them. She was beginning to make a name for herself as an up-and-coming artist.

As Camille began looking into graduate schools, Jack's drinking escalated further. She tried to stay out of his way, never knowing what would set him off. Several times she had to sneak out of the condo in the middle of the night to go stay with friends because he was being so violent. They began to ask questions. Camille withdrew further into herself, leaving the house only for class or rehearsal. She was so anxious that she developed stomach problems and began losing weight.

One morning, Camille woke up in the music library after falling asleep in one of the study carrels. She'd gone there the night before to escape Jack's abuse. The previous week she had failed a midterm after Jack had kept her up all night, threatening to beat her up. Sitting there in the library, her eyes gritty and her body stiff and sore, she realized she was sick of it all—the daily fighting, the constant fear and worry. Jack wasn't worth the effort anymore. It dawned on her that she was finally done. She wanted him gone.

That night, she gathered the last bit of courage she had and told him to leave.

He put his hands on her shoulders. "I swear to you, on my honor, I will never drink again. I know things have gotten out of control. But I love you, and I know you love me. We can work this out. Just give me one more chance." He began to cry.

She felt nothing but contempt for him. "No, Jack. I'm sorry, but I can't do this anymore. You have until Saturday to get your stuff out and find somewhere else to live."

In the meantime, Camille went to stay with a friend whom she had confided in about everything that had been happening. For the first time in a long while, she felt safe.

As the deadline for Jack's moving out approached, Camille began to feel lighter inside. Gone was the sense of dread hanging over her head. Gone was the constant churning in her stomach. Her appetite returned, and she felt like she could breathe again.

She waited an extra day before going back to the condo to be sure that Jack was gone. It was a Sunday evening in late November, and the air had a crispness to it that was rare in Los Angeles. She had just finished up a rehearsal with a singer, and as she walked back home from the practice rooms, she smelled the tangy scent of chimney smoke in the air. A sudden sense of excitement ran through her. She couldn't wait to be alone in the condo. She wanted to straighten up the place without Jack being there—do laundry, wash dishes, and then take a long, hot bath.

She let herself in the front door, tossed her keys down on the coffee table, and headed toward the kitchen. Suddenly, she caught a whiff of fresh cigarette smoke in the air.

Crap. Jack was still there.

Her skin suddenly felt too tight for her body. She knew instinctively she had to get out. She spun around to head back toward the front door—and stopped in her tracks, because right there in front of her was Jack.

His eyes were filled with such rage that they had morphed into dark black pools. By the crazed look on his face, Camille knew he was drunk out of his mind.

He was swaying on his feet, and at first it was difficult for her to understand his slurred words. "So, the little princess is back. Bet you weren't expecting to see me still here, were you?" He laughed low in his belly, like a madman. "So you thought you could just kick me out like that, did you, Camille?"

"Jack," she whispered, frozen with fear, "what are you doing here?"

"What are you doing here? What are you doing here?" he mocked her in a high-pitched voice.

She began to tremble. "You need to go. Please." She started to back away toward the kitchen.

With surprising quickness he crossed the room and smacked her across the face with the back of his hand. She almost lost her balance but managed to remain on her feet by holding on to the wall.

"I'm not going anywhere, you bitch," he snarled.

"Jack," she said, trying to remain calm, "just go. We can talk about this tomorrow."

His face became even more twisted with rage and he hit her again, this time so hard that she went flying onto the floor. The metallic taste of blood filled her mouth. He got down on all fours and breathed his hot, boozy breath into her face. It smelled like overripe fruit left on the ground to rot. "Get up, you fucking whore," he whispered in her ear.

Camille covered her head with her arms. He grabbed her under her armpits and dragged her toward the sliding glass door that led to the condo's small patio.

"You think you can get away with kicking me out?" he shouted. "After everything I've done for you? You little bitch. You have someone else now, don't you? Do you think I don't know what goes on when you say you've got rehearsal? That I don't know you're out sleeping with other guys? Just because everyone says you're this great piano player, you think you're better than me? Bullshit!"

"Jack, please," she begged, even though she knew he was so far gone that there was nothing she could do to calm him down.

As he pushed her toward the glass door, she thought he was going to do what he'd done many times before—throw her outside and lock the door. Instead, she watched in confusion as he opened the door with one hand and held her wrist against the opening with the other, pinning it so the fingers of her right hand were splayed against the metal doorframe.

"Jack!" she screamed. "What are you doing? Jack—stop!"

Before she could even comprehend what was happening, he grabbed the handle of the sliding glass door and slammed it against her hand, instantly crushing her fingers.

The pain was excruciating. She tried to scream, but nothing came out but a faint squeaking sound. She tried to break free from Jack's grasp, but he was too strong. Three more times, he opened the sliding glass door wide. *Slam, slam, slam.* Her blood was splattered across the glass, and her fingers were in shreds. When he finally stopped, she collapsed onto the cold tile, protectively holding her throbbing hand up in the air so it wouldn't hit the floor.

That's when Camille saw how bad it was. Her hand looked like it had just gone through a meat grinder. Blood spiraled down her arm like the red stripes on a barbershop pole. She stared in disbelief at her hand, willing her brain to move her fingers, but nothing happened. She slowly turned her hand around and saw why. Like twigs that had been snapped in half, two grayish-white bones were sticking out of her palm. She felt herself slipping into unconsciousness.

"What did I do?"

Jack's racking sobs roused Camille from her stupor. She opened her eyes. He was kneeling on the ground next to her, holding his head in his hands. "Shit, Camille, I'm sorry. *I'm so sorry.*" He wiped snot from his nose with the back of his sleeve. "I didn't mean it! *Christ!* Why did you have to choose your piano career over me the way you did? You should've put me first. That's why I got so pissed. That's why I did it. Oh, my god. I'm so sorry!" He began to beat his fists on the floor, his brief remorse instantly replaced by a more intense anger.

She was so terrified, she lay there without moving a muscle.

He got to his feet. "Say something! Admit this is all your fault!"

She tried to speak, but her terror prevented her from forming any words. She kept her eyes on his face, praying that he wasn't going to kill her.

He looked down at her bloodied hand. His face instantly contorted into another mask of unbridled rage. "You made me do this. I couldn't help myself. It's your fault! And now that you can't play the piano anymore, none of your fucking music friends are going to want you around. I'm the only one who will want you. I've finally got you all to myself." He got to his feet with a triumphant smile and kicked her hard in the ribs. "You need me now. You're never, ever going to leave me."

Before the heavy curtain of unconsciousness closed before her eyes, she heard him speak one last time.

"You're my bitch now, Camille."

CHAPTER 26

After two consecutive nights of less than three hours' sleep, two shots of mezcal, and the fact that she and Alejandro stayed up most of the night talking—*and doing other things*—"refreshed" is not exactly how Camille would describe herself at the moment. But she is happy. The sun is streaming in through the shutters, wrapping the walls of Tía Nifa's bedroom in yellow ribbons of light. For the first time in ages, the coming day feels like a present waiting to be opened.

Camille is relieved she told Alejandro the full story of what happened with Jack. She's never told anyone all the details except for her mother. For some reason, telling him made her feel better.

He listened without asking any questions. When she got to the end, he reached out and held her tightly in his arms.

"What happened to Jack?" he asks quietly. "Did he go to jail?"

"Yes," she says. "Right after it happened, the friend I'd been staying with came by the condo to check on me. She found me unconscious on the floor and called 911. By that time Jack had locked himself in the bathroom. I was pretty out of it, so they put me in an ambulance and took me to the hospital. I found out later that the police had to break down the bathroom door to get him out. He was arrested and charged with felony assault and resisting arrest."

"How long was he in jail?"

A heavy weight fills her chest. "One night," she says, quietly.

"What? Only one night? After what he did to you? That's crazy. Why so little time?"

Camille turns on her side and buries her face in Alejandro's neck. "While he was locked in the bathroom he'd found an old bottle of pain medication I'd hidden in a makeup bag. It was left over from when I'd sprained my ankle. There was at least twenty pills left in it, and he swallowed them all. Then he stashed the bottle behind the toilet so the police didn't know he'd taken them. They assumed he was drunk, so they left him in the jail cell to sleep it off. The next morning, they found him unresponsive. They tried to revive him, but it was too late. He was gone." She swallows the knot in her throat. "Even after what he did to me, I still wish I'd been able to tell him goodbye."

Camille sits up in bed and rubs her eyes. Alejandro is nowhere to be seen. He must've left quite a while ago because the sheets on his side of the bed are cool to the touch. Stretching her arms up over her head, she feels aches in the strangest places throughout her body. Her head is foggy and her stomach is churning. Never having had one before, she wonders if this is what a hangover feels like.

She is unsure if she should venture out into the house or stay and wait for Alejandro to return. She really needs to use the bathroom, and *soon*. She doesn't want to face Tía Nifa without Alejandro here, but the need to pee takes precedence over any embarrassment she might feel after having been caught in bed with her host's favorite nephew. Although Tía Nifa did seem pretty ecstatic about it last night.

She opens the mosquito netting and steps onto the cool tile floor. After throwing on her white shorts and shirt, she pokes her head out the door. "Hello?" she says, her voice barely above a whisper. "Alejandro?"

No one answers.

She slips through the main room and out onto the patio, where the birds are performing an early-morning prelude. The smell of wet earth and tangy wood smoke lingers in the air, tickling her nose. Still laden with droplets from last night's rain, the flowers sparkle in the sunlight like colorful costume jewelry. She steps into her damp huaraches and hurries off toward the bathroom.

Staring at her reflection in the mirror above the sink, she is surprised by the beautiful woman staring back at her. Her hair is a wild red mane, her cheeks are rosy, and her eyes are sparkling like jade cat-eye marbles. *I look like a disheveled French ingenue who's just rolled out of bed after a drunken night of wild lovemaking*, she thinks, and lets out a laugh.

She remembers what she and Alejandro did last night, and a wave of desire radiates through her body. She holds on to the porcelain sink and takes several deep breaths, trying to convince herself that she must have dreamed the whole thing. Then she touches her fingers to her swollen lips. *Oh, yes—something most certainly happened last night.*

Then regret hits her so hard she feels dizzy. *Damn it!* This whole thing with Alejandro—whatever it is—is only going to distract her. She came to Oaxaca to do one thing: find Graciela and get her back home. Now she's gone and complicated everything. Not only has she developed feelings for Alejandro but she also went and told him the story of what happened to her fingers. Even worse, she slept with him.

She groans, pulls her hair off her face, and twists it into a tight knot at the back of her head. On the floor near her feet is a faint mark on the cement where the body of the smashed scorpion was yesterday afternoon. The fire ants didn't give up. They've carried off every single bit of the scorpion's shell, leaving nothing but an oily stain on the floor. *Now, that's how you get it done.* A sense of renewed determination fills her chest. She decides that nothing—not even Alejandro—is going to stop her from finding Graciela and getting her home in time for the concert.

As she's brushing her teeth, she hears the whine of the metal gate and the sound of animated voices. Alejandro and Tía Nifa have returned.

"*Camila?*" Alejandro shouts from across the patio. "Are you up?"

She quickly spits into the sink. "Over here," she calls out, her heart beating rapidly. *Nip this in the bud, Camille. Tell him right away that last night was all a mistake.* She steps out onto the patio.

"Good morning," Alejandro says, his eyes bright. "Did you sleep well?"

God, he is so handsome. She starts to answer him, but before she can get any words out, Tía Nifa rushes over and grabs her in such a tight embrace that she nearly knocks her to the ground. Wearing the same soiled *huipil* that she's had on for the past three days, Tía Nifa smells of sweat and unwashed hair. Over her shoulder is a red woven bag bulging with fresh produce. As she rocks Camille back and forth in her arms, the stems of some unrecognizable vegetable sticking up out of the bag repeatedly smack Camille in the face.

Trying to hold back his laughter, Alejandro hurries over, takes the bag off his aunt's shoulder, and gently sets it down on the table. Tía Nifa reaches up with her tiny fingers and begins to stroke Camille's cheek, speaking in rapid Zapotec, as if Camille is capable of understanding everything she says.

Camille turns toward Alejandro and gives him a pleading look.

He swallows. "Well, first off, she's telling you that she's going to make coffee and breakfast for you." He pauses for a moment. "And, uh . . . after that . . . well, she says she wants you to go with her to the *curandera*. She wants you to have a *limpia*. A cleansing."

"First of all, what's a *curandera?*"

"She's like a medicine woman. I guess you could call her a healer."

"And a cleansing?" Camille asks, discreetly lifting one arm to sniff her armpit. "Do I smell bad or something?"

He looks uncomfortable. "No, no—it's not like that. She wants you to have a cleansing so you can be healed." His eyes dart down to her right hand.

Camille is suddenly suspicious. *"Healed?"*

Tía Nifa keeps her eyes on Alejandro's face as she takes Camille's hand and sandwiches it between her small, rough ones. As she did back on the bus, she begins to knead Camille's fingers, like she's trying to loosen up the tightness.

Alejandro takes a step closer. "My tía believes that if you let the *curandera* perform a cleansing ritual on you, you'll be healed."

Camille sucks in her breath and snatches her hand away from Tía Nifa's grasp. She steps back and crosses her arms defensively in front of her chest. "That's absolutely ridiculous, Alejandro. There's nothing that can be done for my fingers. I've had two intricate operations already—performed by the best hand surgeons in the country. Neither one of them was able to do anything to help me." Her anxiety level rises. "You've seen it," she says, holding up her fingers and attempting to move them back and forth. "I can hardly bend my fingers with all of this scar tissue. How can you think that some silly ritual could fix them? I'm surprised you're even suggesting it."

"It wasn't my idea, Camila," he says softly. "It was my tía's. She insists that it will help. To be honest, I don't believe that a *curandera* can heal your fingers. But I do believe that these cleansing rituals can help heal you in other ways. I think you should try it, if only for that."

Camille raises her eyebrows. "Oh, so now you're insinuating that there's something wrong with my head?"

"I really can't get inside your mind or your heart," he says, keeping his voice calm. "I don't know what kind of pain you carry around. But I do know that when someone suffers from an experience like you did, it changes you. After everything you told me last night, I know for a fact you were deeply traumatized. This cleansing ritual is more about helping your mind than your body. Although my tía will tell you they're always related."

Tía Nifa nods her head in vigorous agreement, as if she perfectly understands what Alejandro has just said. She cocks her head toward Camille in a questioning manner. Not wanting to upset her, Camille acknowledges her with a half-hearted smile. Satisfied, Tía Nifa reaches up to pat Camille's shoulder, then heads over to the kitchen area to prepare breakfast.

Alejandro takes Camille's hand. "So, what do you think? Will you go with us to see the *curandera?*"

"I don't know. I'm skeptical about all this New Age hocus-pocus stuff. I don't really think it will help me in any way."

Alejandro clears his throat. "Ah, just so you know, this type of ritual has been used in Yalálag for thousands of years. You might not want to refer to it as *New Age hocus-pocus.*"

"Oh, right. Sorry. Well, you know what I mean."

Camille watches Tía Nifa crouch down and light the fire under the *comal*, gently blowing on the flame. Since she sat next to Camille on the bus, the older woman has been nothing but kind to her. A sudden rush of love for her fills Camille's heart, and she feels herself relenting. "Well, your tía has been so good to me over the past few days, I can't very well deny her this one small request. I guess I'll go, if it means that much to her."

Alejandro grins and draws Camille into his arms. "*Gracias*, Camila. That will make her so happy."

His chest is warm, and his strong arms are a perfect fit around her waist. Her brain is telling her to push him away and explain that what's happening between them is completely insane. She can't possibly dive into a relationship when she has to focus on finding Graciela. But her heart won't listen.

Oh, the hell with it, she thinks. She'll tell him later that it's all a big mistake.

Right now it just feels too good to let go.

CHAPTER 27

The cleansing ritual is nothing like Camille expected. For some reason, she imagined it would be like going to a spa, with flickering candles and the scent of lavender in the air.

Instead, she finds herself kneeling on a straw *petate* in a smoky, incense-filled room. The little *tienda* is packed with so many items there is hardly room for the four of them to squeeze in between the clutter. There are woven baskets stuffed with dried herbs, shelves lined with colorful votive candles, and religious figurines in all shapes and sizes. Thin paper packets of medicinal powders are stacked between brown bottles coated with dust. Hanging from the wooden beams are bunches of dried leaves tied with string that look like shriveled-up bridal bouquets.

Camille finds the chaos overwhelming. She takes a deep breath, trying to calm herself. The *curandera*—an old woman who is a smaller and more wrinkled version of Tía Nifa—approaches her. The woman takes a sip from a small plastic cup, purses her lips, and spits a fine mist directly into Camille's face.

"What the heck?" she says, reaching up to wipe away the sticky spray. She whips her head around to look at Alejandro and Tía Nifa; they are practically hidden amid the mess of jars and packages that line the back wall of the store.

"Shhh," Alejandro says, putting his finger to his lips. "*Cálmate*, Camila. Let the *curandera* do what she needs to do. Just relax."

"Do you think it's easy to relax when I'm kneeling on the floor while some woman spits on me?" she whispers back loudly. "And what the heck is that stuff she's spitting on me?"

"I'm surprised you don't recognize the smell by now." She can hear the amusement in his voice.

"What do you mean?"

"It's mezcal."

She groans. "*Ugh*. Serves me right."

The *curandera* takes another long sip from the cup and walks around so she's standing directly behind Camille. She lifts up Camille's shirt, leans over, and sprays her back. Then, as if she's speaking in tongues, she begins to chant rapidly in Zapotec.

Camille has no idea what she's saying. It must be good, though, because from across the room, Tía Nifa grunts in tacit approval.

After Camille's chest, thighs, and arms are covered in the sticky spray, Alejandro walks over to the *curandera* and whispers something in her ear. She picks up Camille's right hand and peers at it as if she's studying an artifact. Holding Camille's bent fingers against her sagging breasts, the *curandera* rolls her eyes upward, mumbling again in Zapotec. She then places Camille's fingers as flat as they will go across her forearm. She takes another long sip from the cup.

"*Pffftttt*," she hisses, spraying the entire mouthful on the back of Camille's right hand. An unexpected burning sensation travels up Camille's arm and into her chest. It's somewhat like an electrical shock, but not as painful.

"Why is my arm tingling?" she whispers.

"That's a good sign, Camila," Alejandro says. "That means your heart is opening up."

Oddly, his comment pleases her. She closes her eyes and takes another deep breath.

After spraying the remaining parts of her body, including the soles of her feet, the *curandera* begins to roll something cold and hard along Camille's head and neck. The feeling is not unpleasant.

"What's she doing now?"

"She's passing a raw egg over your body to draw out the evil spirits," Alejandro says in a low voice. "When she's done, she'll crack it into a glass of water. Then she'll read it to find out what's going on inside of you."

Camille is doubtful. "Really? You mean to say that just by looking at the egg, she can tell what's wrong with me?"

"*Ay, mujer,*" Alejandro says, sounding impatient. "Yes, Camila, *she can.* Now, *por favor,* stop talking and let the *curandera* do her work."

She sighs and lets her shoulders drop. The *curandera* rubs the egg across Camille's face, arms, and chest, and the constant chattering in her head finally ceases. Before long, all she can hear is the wind rustling the leaves of the mango tree outside the door. She can't see Alejandro or Tía Nifa, but knowing they are right across the room makes her feel safe. She falls into a trance.

As if she's dreaming, hazy clips of her life begin to play out in her mind. She flashes back to age seven and sees herself wearing a white taffeta dress and a pair of black patent leather shoes as she performed her first Haydn concerto with an orchestra. She feels the thrill when the audience stood up and clapped for her. Then her mother's face comes into view. Set with a frown of disapproval, she slaps the back of Camille's head, "*Play it right, Camille! Play it right!*" Then her mother's body morphs into Jack's. His eyes seethe with violent rage, and his hand is raised to strike her. *No, no, no! This is too much. I don't want to think about this anymore!* She lets out an involuntary moan and opens her eyes.

Alejandro is there, his concerned face hovering above her.

"Are you all right, Camila?"

"Is it over?" she asks. Her mouth is dry, as if she's just taken a bite of a green banana.

"Almost," he says softly. "The *curandera* just needs to finish up with the herbs."

The lingering smoke from the incense makes Camille's eyes water. The *curandera* shakes a bouquet of fresh basil and rosemary above her body. The potent fragrance makes her think of her mother's garden back home. She is suddenly homesick. Tears prick at her eyes.

"What is *wrong* with me? I just can't keep it together lately."

"Camila," Alejandro says, moving closer to her, "for once, why don't you just let it out?"

A hard lump forms in her throat. "Let what out?"

He leans down, places the palm of his hand against her cheek, and whispers, *"Just let it out."*

Camille doesn't know if it's because of the mezcal, or the chanting, or a spell the *curandera* has cast on her, but Alejandro's words are all it takes for something inside of her to crack open. Before she can stop herself, she begins to wail. The pain of the past fifteen years flows out like raw sewage from a broken pipe.

Embarrassed by the sounds coming from her mouth, she tries to get up and run out of the room, but her legs are so rubbery that she falls back down onto the straw mat.

Alejandro crouches down and puts his arms around her shoulders. *"Sí, mi amor,"* he says in a soothing tone. *"Está bien.* It's okay. Just let it out."

She buries her head in his neck and sobs. Tía Nifa strokes her hair, murmuring like a mother singing a lullaby to her baby.

Camille cries until she has nothing left. When the tears stop and she's finally able to catch her breath, she hears the crack of an egg. Looking up, she sees the *curandera* standing in front of her with a clear glass in her hand. A single orange yolk is suspended in the egg white.

The old woman points to a tiny red spot on the edge of the yolk. She gestures toward Camille and says something to Alejandro and Tía Nifa in Zapotec.

"What's she saying about the egg?" Camille says, her voice raw. "Am I healed?"

Alejandro clears his throat. "She says that you have a lot of evil spirits inside of you, Camila—a lot of negativity. But she also says that the egg white is not too thick. This is a good sign. It's like a fog that will burn off when the sun rises higher in the sky. She says that little red spot on the yolk means that in time your sun will grow brighter. That you will have the chance for a new beginning. A new life. But first, you need to forgive."

She thinks for a moment. "Forgive?" she asks. "Who do I need to forgive? Of course—it must be Jack. No wait, maybe it's my mother. Do I need to forgive my mother?"

Alejandro turns and asks the *curandera* a question. She taps the side of the glass and points at Camille.

"What does that mean? Who do I need to forgive?"

"It's you, Camila," he whispers. "She says you need to forgive yourself."

CHAPTER 28

After leaving the *curandera*'s store, Alejandro and Camille walk in comfortable silence toward the center of town. Tía Nifa has gone off to help prepare food for the celebration. She tells them she will meet them back at the house later that afternoon. Before leaving, Tía Nifa cried and held on to Camille for such a long time that Alejandro had to practically pry her arms from around Camille's waist.

Surprisingly, the cleansing has made Camille feel more comfortable in her body. It's as if she's been wearing too-tight jeans for the past fifteen years, and now she's finally put on the right size. The scenery around her seems brighter and more in focus. The clouds appear to be backlit with white light, and the mountains are as plush as a green velvet sofa. Even the bougainvillea blossoms look like they've been cut from red tissue paper and glued onto the vine.

Camille is relieved that Alejandro isn't peppering her with questions. She's still confused about the whole *limpia* experience. Especially the part about needing to forgive herself. She has no idea what she ever did that needs forgiving.

As they turn a corner and approach the church, the sound of ringing bells startles Camille. There is a high-pitched whistling sound, and then a loud boom above their heads. Alejandro pulls

Camille back against the wall that surrounds the church. Three young boys rush past them like colts galloping back to the barn.

"That was close," Alejandro says, pointing to the sky. "Look, Camila—the celebration for San Antonio is beginning. It always starts off with the rockets."

With the phosphorous scent of gunpowder hanging in the air, the pealing of the church bells ceases. A band down at the other end of the street begins to play. As the musicians march toward the church, the music builds to a dramatic fortissimo, and another loud set of booms echoes across the town. A group of old women wearing cotton shawls and carrying buckets of gladiolas shuffles in through the church gates.

Alejandro taps Camille on the shoulder. "See that *viejita* over there?" He points to an old woman holding a clay pot billowing white smoke. "That's *copal*—do you smell it? That's the same incense that the *curandera* burned during your cleansing."

"What's *copal*?"

"It's a sap that comes from a tree. They burn it in the church during mass too."

Camille raises her chin and inhales. "It smells earthy. Almost primitive."

"It is primitive," he says. "It's been used for rituals here in Yalálag since before the Spanish came."

The band plays another short phrase and stops. It's immediately answered by the high-pitched sound of an indigenous flute. The musicians argue back and forth until the church bells enter into the fray, creating a surging cacophony of dissonance. When it ends, the band marches back out of the church courtyard and down the street.

"Where are they going?" Camille asks.

"Not far. The priest will lead them down a few blocks, and then they'll come back. Do you want to walk with them?"

"Actually, I was wondering if it's possible for us to go inside the church."

He looks around. "There's going to be a special mass for San Antonio later on, but I don't think anyone is in there right now. Let's wait until everyone leaves, and then you can go in for a quick look."

When the crowd is gone, Alejandro pries open the heavy wooden doors. "You go in by yourself, Camila. I'm going to wait out here."

"Okay. I just want to see what it looks like. I'll be right back."

He touches her lightly on the arm and smiles. "Don't forget to say a prayer to San Antonio."

The minute Camille steps into the church, the musty smell makes her feel as if she's traveled back in time to the Middle Ages. The building is narrow, separated by tall posts painted a seafoam green that rise up like pillars on either side of the space. The only light comes from a square window placed high above the altar.

Camille's footsteps echo as she passes the rows of wooden pews, moving toward the front of the church. Above the altar there is a portrait of San Antonio, surrounded by several large bouquets of flowers and dozens of lighted candles. Unlike the painting at Tía Nifa's house, this likeness of San Antonio is turned right side up. He is wearing a brown habit and is bald but for a strip of hair around the outside of his scalp. In his arms he holds a young child whose small fingers rest lovingly on his cheek.

Camille feels foolish praying to a Catholic saint when she's not the least bit religious. She's relieved that Alejandro decided to stay outside.

Clearing her throat, she speaks softly. "Okay, San Antonio, I've been told that I'm supposed to pray to you to help me find something I've lost. The problem is that I've lost so many things. I wouldn't even know where to begin."

Her eyes begin to tear up again. She's cried more in the past three days than she has in the past decade.

"Alejandro told me about you and said that I should pray to you to find what I had lost. I thought that all I needed to do was ask to find Graciela. I thought that if I could get her home for the concert, everything would fall into place. I'd have the life I've always dreamed of having." Her voice catches. "But now I'm not sure about anything. I have all these strange new feelings inside of me. I'm not even sure I know what it is I'm looking for anymore."

She pictures Alejandro standing outside the church, waiting for her. A warm feeling spreads through her body. She wouldn't be standing here right now if he hadn't helped her off the bus and saved her life. She thinks about his brown eyes and sweet smile. How kind he is to everyone, especially Tía Nifa. She loves how he teases her and makes her laugh. Then she thinks about what they did in Tía Nifa's bed last night, and her knees go weak again. *What is going on? Is this love?*

She looks up again at the portrait. "Hey, San Antonio," she whispers, "I think I just figured out what it is I've been looking for all this time. I think he's standing right outside the door of this very church."

Awkwardly, she bends down on one knee, and though she's not sure if she's doing it right, she makes the sign of the cross with her hand and kisses her fingers. She offers up a silent prayer of thanks to San Antonio. Then she rises to her feet and heads out into the light.

Alejandro holds the heavy door of the church open for Camille.

"So, what did you think?" he asks. "Did you pray to San Antonio?"

Instead of answering him, she puts her hands on either side of his face and kisses him hard on the mouth.

"*Ay, Dios.*" He takes a quick look around to see if anyone is watching. Then he presses her up against the door of the church and passionately kisses her back. "Wow," he says, almost panting. "Do I need to thank San Antonio for that?"

"Nope. He actually told me you were a liar and not to trust you."

For a split second, a look of alarm passes over his face.

Camille slaps him playfully on his arm. "I'm just teasing. The truth is, you're so irresistible it's impossible for me to keep my hands off you." She puts her arms around his neck and hugs him tightly.

Holding hands, they walk toward the square, where a bustle of activity is taking place. An outdoor market has been set up with booths and tables. Blue and white tissue paper flags are strung diagonally across the square. Old women wearing *huipiles* sit behind woven mats spread with baskets of fresh produce. There are piles of mangoes painted with streaks of red, spotted bananas, and clusters of mandarin oranges with dark green leaves. Red-and-black clay pottery, handmade clothing, and leather goods are for sale as well. Lively music plays over a loudspeaker.

They wander over to a table under a large white tarp where there are various types of food for sale, including steaming tamales wrapped in dark green banana leaves, pots of thick hot chocolate, and freshly baked bread. A young girl stands behind a portable *comal*, her forehead glistening with perspiration. She expertly forms balls of *masa* with her tiny hands, then places them on an iron press and flattens them until they are paper-thin. The tortillas sizzle as she lays them on the hot surface of the *comal*.

"She's making quesadillas with *flor de calabaza* and *quesillo*," Alejandro says. "You've got to try one. They're so good." He holds up two fingers to the girl.

Camille watches the girl layer thin strips of Oaxacan cheese on top of the tortillas, then cover them with a mound of yellow flower blossoms before folding the tortilla in half. When the cheese has melted, she opens the quesadillas with the tips of her fingers, ladles a spoonful of green salsa inside, and then wraps them in a piece of brown paper.

Alejandro pays her, and they sit down on the cement steps to eat.

The quesadilla is delicious—crunchy on the outside and warm and cheesy on the inside. Without a hint of shame, Camille wolfs it down in under a minute and licks the grease from her fingertips.

"Oh, that was so good," she says. "Are those nasturtium blossoms?"

"No, they're from the *calabaza*—squash plant," he says. "They taste really good with Oaxacan cheese." He stands up and dusts off his hands. "Do you want to go watch the dancing now?

"There's more dancing?"

He laughs. "Camila, you haven't seen anything yet—we're just getting started. During this celebration, Yalaltectos do nothing but dance, eat, and pray. All kinds of dances have been planned over the next week for the *Fiesta de San Antonio*. When I was young, it used to be a much smaller celebration, but now that so many Yalaltecos have migrated to Los Angeles, the parties here have grown much bigger."

"Why do all these people believe so deeply in San Antonio?"

"Mainly because they believe he's helped them. When Yalaltecos leave here to migrate to the States, they pray to San Antonio and ask for his help with their journey. They promise him that if he helps them cross the border without getting caught by ICE or if he helps them find a job in LA, they will return someday and honor him with gifts of money to pay for improvements to the town."

It's hot and crowded under the tent where the dancing takes place. There are twelve dancers, all men. Camille is surprised to find that half of them are wearing short skirts, long-haired wigs, and high heels. The other half are dressed like tourists, sporting Hawaiian shirts, baggy shorts, and high-top tennis shoes. Their faces are covered by opaque masks painted with black-outlined eyes and glossy red lips. As the men clomp awkwardly back and forth on the dance floor, they shake their backsides in a semi-sexual dance. *Okay, this is weird*, she thinks. She wants to ask Alejandro what's going on, but the band is so loud she knows he wouldn't be able to hear her.

When the dancing finally ends, it takes a long time for Camille and Alejandro to exit the tent. Many people want to stop and chat with Alejandro. Camille is well aware that she's on the receiving end of quite a few curious looks.

"What was that strange dance we just saw?" she asks when they walk outside. "I was sort of expecting it to be a little more traditional."

He grins. "Oh, that was just one of the many dances that Yalaltecos perform during the celebrations for the saints. What they were doing was making fun of the people who have left Yalálag and moved to Los Angeles."

"Why do they make fun of them?"

"Because when those immigrants return here to visit, they sometimes act more Americanized. You know, like they're better and more successful than everyone else. They stop wearing traditional clothing and act superior. So the dancers here in Yalálag dress up like Americans to make fun of them. It's supposed to put them in their place. To show them they're no better than the people who still live here."

"Oh, I get it—kind of like a social commentary on the changes that have taken place here." Camille chuckles. "That's funny."

"That's it exactly. Yalaltecos are proud. When they feel that someone is making them look bad, they mock them with a particular dance. There are all kinds of these dances. They added a new one recently—*Danza de los cholos*—which translates to "Dance of the Gangsters." It makes fun of the younger kids who get involved in gang culture in LA and then bring it back here to Yalálag."

An image of Little Chuy's angry face flashes before Camille's eyes. She sees his bald head and the black tattoos that climb up his neck.

A chill runs down her spine.

CHAPTER 29

After spending a good part of the afternoon wandering around the *mercado*, Alejandro and Camille hike back up the hill to Tía Nifa's house. The recent rains have coaxed a carpet of tiny green shoots to sprout up along both sides of the street. The sky is as blue as a brand-new, waxy crayon.

"Is there any chance I can take a shower when we get back to your tía's house?" Camille asks, wiping the sweat off the back of her neck. "I'm still sticky from the mezcal."

"Sure. You take a shower, and then we'll just relax for the rest of the afternoon." He nudges her with his elbow. "Maybe take a little *siesta* or something."

She raises her eyebrows. "Or something?"

"What?" He feigns innocence.

"You don't fool me, Alejandro. I know what you're getting at." She looks directly at him. "Lucky for you, I'm in the mood for a good, long nap right now."

Entering through the gate, Camille catches the scent of blooming jasmine in the breeze. They sit down together at the table, where Tía Nifa has set out a wooden bowl of small green fruit.

Alejandro deftly cuts one in half and hands Camille a piece. "Have you had *guayaba*—guava—before?" He takes a bite and the juice runs down his chin. "*Ay, que rico.*"

Camille shakes her head. "I never have."

He motions for her to take a bite. "Go ahead. Have some— you'll love it."

The inside of the guava is a dark pink color, and as she bites into the flesh the tropical sweetness explodes across her tongue. Sighing, she leans back and puts her feet up on one of the chairs. "It's been such a lovely afternoon. I want to thank you again for taking such good care of me over the past few days. I honestly don't know what I'd have done without you. And I want to apologize again for having been such a thorn in your side."

"A thorn in my side? What do you mean?"

"I know I've been hard to deal with. I'm always saying the wrong thing. If I'm not fainting or bursting into tears, I'm complaining, starting a fight with you, or getting drunk on mezcal."

He takes her hand and laughs. "All of that may be true. I guess at times you have been *un espino en mi lado*—a thorn in my side, as you say. But you've made this trip home a lot more interesting for me than it ever has been before." He looks directly into her eyes. "Especially last night."

A thrill shoots through her and she squeezes his hand. "It's funny, but I feel like a different person now. At first I didn't believe that the cleansing ritual would help me in any way. Honestly, I thought it was going to be a big waste of time. But now I feel stronger. And like there's this feeling of calm inside of me."

"I'm glad to hear that, Camila. After everything you've been through, you deserve to be happy." He slices another guava open and, as he hands her half, studies her face. "You know, you really have changed a lot since the first time I saw you. And to tell you the truth, you didn't make a very good impression on me. I had a feeling you were going to be . . . ah . . . how can I say it? *Difficult?*" He smiles. "But then, when you turned around and looked in my direction and I saw your face for the first time, you just looked like a scared little girl. You were so sad and beaten down. I felt sorry for you, even though I was angry at the way you were acting. And then the sun came out from behind the clouds, and it made your red hair light up like fire, and your eyes were so green. I thought to myself, *Ay, Dios—this redheaded American girl is so beautiful.* I knew right then I wanted to get to know you."

"Really?" she says, pleased. "You thought that about me?'

"Yes, I did. I still do." He leans forward, puts his hands on either side of her face, and kisses her softly on the mouth. Camille can taste the sweetness of the guava on his lips.

She slowly pulls away from him. "But wait a second. I'm confused here. Didn't we meet for the first time during the storm? I mean, you never saw me before you helped me off the bus, right? And the sun didn't come out until hours later, when I was still soaking wet and totally covered in mud. So how could you have seen my red hair shine in the sunlight?"

For a moment, Alejandro doesn't move. Then he slowly begins to rub the back of his neck. "Ah . . . well . . ." He has an odd look on his face. He sits up taller in his chair. "Okay, listen, Camila. I've been meaning to tell you something for a while now, but there's never been a good time. I tried to tell you when we were in San Mateo, and then again last night, but . . ."

Her mouth goes dry. "What is it?"

He takes a deep breath and lets it out. "When I helped you off the bus during the storm it wasn't the first time I saw you."

She is relieved it's not something worse. "When, then? When I got on the bus in Oaxaca City?"

"No. I saw you before that. In Los Angeles."

"You saw me at the airport? Were we on the same flight? How come you didn't tell me?"

He places his hands on the table. "No, not then. I saw you a week before that. At the vigil. When you went to look for Graciela at her uncle's house."

"What?" she says, surprised. "You were there?" She thinks back to how rudely she behaved that afternoon, and her face flushes with shame.

He nods almost imperceptibly.

"What were you doing there? Do you know Graciela's family?"

He doesn't answer her.

Camille pushes her chair back and stands up as a hot gust of apprehension threatens to knock her over. "Tell me, Alejandro. Do you know Graciela?"

He leans over and puts his face in his hands. "She's my niece."

"Your niece? You mean María is your sister?"

He speaks so quietly that Camille almost doesn't hear him. "María is my first cousin."

"Wait, wait, wait . . ." She holds up her hands. "I'm totally confused here. Are you telling me that Graciela is a close family member, and you *knew* I was looking for her all this time? And you didn't bother to tell me you were related to her?"

He stares down at his feet. "I'm sorry, Camila."

"But . . . why didn't you say anything? I mean, what's the big deal about me knowing that you're related to Graciela?"

He sits there, looking miserable and saying nothing.

Then it dawns on her. Alejandro didn't say anything because he never wanted her to find Graciela in the first place. The realization hits her with such force that she feels as if the wind has been knocked out of her.

"Oh my god," she says, "how could I have been so blind? This whole plan was concocted to keep the pushy piano teacher away from Graciela, right? You followed me here from LA to keep tabs on me, didn't you? To prevent me from finding Graciela and bringing her back for her concert."

He looks up again. "I didn't follow you, Camila. I was already planning to come back here to visit my tía. I had already bought my plane ticket to Oaxaca when you showed up at Victor's house looking for Graciela. You were acting crazy that day—yelling at Victor and making a scene. After you left, Victor asked me to keep an eye out for you in case you showed up in Oaxaca. He wanted to make sure that you didn't cause any problems for Graciela. It was just luck that we ended up on the same bus to Yalálag together."

"*Luck?*" Camille says, incredulous. "Are you kidding me? I shouldn't have even been on that bus! I could've *died* during that mudslide." She feels sick to her stomach. "I can't believe you let me board that run-down piece of junk and come all this way. And even worse, you didn't try to stop me when you knew Graciela was already in Oaxaca City the whole time. You let me travel all the way here just to keep me away from her. Then you kept up this big lie the whole time? You even took me to bed knowing that you were deceiving me!"

Alejandro's face falls. "Camila," he says, rubbing his hands along his thighs, "you have no idea how sorry I am. But you've got to understand that a week ago I didn't know you at all. I thought I had to protect Graciela from you. She's having a hard enough time now that her mother is so sick. You trying to talk her into going back to California would've been too much for her to handle."

Camille presses her lips together. "Well, I guess your plan worked out quite well for you. How very fortunate for you that the bus got stuck in the mud. You couldn't have planned it any better if you tried. It's just too bad I didn't go off the cliff with the bus. Now *that* would've made everything easy for you."

He looks distraught. "Camila, please. I feel terrible about

what's happened. Really, I do. You've got to know that I would never purposely do anything to hurt you."

Her voice catches in her throat. "That's hard to believe. You act like you're so decent and moral. You claim to hate dishonesty, yet you're nothing but a big liar yourself." She covers her mouth with her hand and takes a deep breath. "You put my life at risk, Alejandro. I could've died on that bus. And all you had to do was tell me where Graciela was in the first place."

Alejandro hangs his head and says nothing.

Her voice becomes hard. "I was honest with you. I opened up and told you things that I've never told anyone before. God, I'm such a fool. Why did I think I could trust you? I should've known better."

"Please forgive me," he says, his eyes pleading. "You've got to know how sorry I am."

"No," she says, feeling the perspiration bleed at her temples. Her throat is so thick with despair that she can barely get the words out. "There's no way I can ever forgive you for this, Alejandro."

CHAPTER 30

Camille stares at Alejandro in stunned disbelief. How can it be that up until a moment ago, she actually thought she was falling in love with him? After what Jack did to her, she willingly closed herself off from love, choosing instead to live an isolated life. Now she finally finds the courage to open up after all these years, and this is what happens.

It suddenly dawns on her that she's sick and tired of relying on others to help her. A fierce determination seizes her, and she decides she no longer wants or needs anyone's help. She is perfectly capable of getting on a bus to Oaxaca City and finding Graciela on her own.

She pulls her shoulders back. "I want to ask you something. And I would appreciate it if you would tell the truth this time."

He looks up at her, his face a mask of misery.

"Are the phone lines still out?" she asks.

He doesn't answer.

"And are there still no buses running because of the road?"

When he finally speaks his voice is flat. "The phones lines aren't working yet, but the road has been fixed. The buses will probably be arriving in a few hours."

Her face hardens into stone. "And just when were you going to tell me all this?"

"Tonight."

"Oh, I see. I suppose you wanted to get me into bed one more time before you said anything."

His face drops. "No, Camila—that's not why. I waited to tell you because I didn't want you to leave. Because I wanted—I feel—"

"I don't care how you feel. It doesn't matter anymore. I'm leaving Yalálag today, and I'm not coming back. And as much as I hate to have to ask, I need one more favor from you."

He looks suddenly hopeful. "Anything."

"I need to borrow money from you for a bus ticket. When I get to the city, I'll figure out how to wire the money back to you."

Looking defeated, he slowly reaches into his pocket and pulls out a thick roll of pesos. He peels off several bills and places them in her hand. "Here. That's enough money for a bus ticket and whatever else you need."

"Thank you. I'll find a way to pay you back."

"It's nothing." He glances away and rubs his eyes before looking up at her again. "Camila, please. Can we just talk about this some more?"

"What is there to talk about? It's all been said. You did what you thought was right. Now it's my turn to do what I think is right. I'm going back to Oaxaca City on the next bus."

He gets up from the table and presses his hands together like he's praying. "Let me go with you, then. I'll take you right to the hospital where Graciela and María are. I know the city, and I can show you exactly where to go."

She steps away from him. "No. I'm going there by myself. I need to do this on my own."

His shoulders slump like an old man's. "But what about

everything that's happened between us? You can't tell me that you don't feel something for me."

"Whatever it was I felt for you was an illusion. You saved me when I needed saving. That made me believe what was happening between us was something meaningful. But you know what I've just realized? I don't need saving anymore. I'm perfectly capable of taking care of myself. I don't need you after all."

He looks so despondent that her throat tightens and she feels her resolve weaken. She wants to throw herself into his arms—but then she thinks of how he lied to her.

"I'm going to walk back to town and wait for the next bus," she says, "but first I need to get my things."

She heads back inside the house to retrieve the few items she left in Tía Nifa's room. After grabbing the plastic bag from the bed, she walks back through the main room. The altar looks different, as if it's been spruced up. The dried flowers have been replaced with yellow gladiolas and freshly cut pink roses. The normally dark room glows with dozens of flickering candles. Something else is different, too—Tía Nifa's portrait of San Antonio has been turned right side up.

She also notices that the Polaroid of Alejandro and his late wife is missing. She looks down to the floor to see if it's fallen off the table, but it's nowhere in sight.

As she turns to leave, she catches sight of something bulky propped against the wall off to one side of the altar. She takes a few steps closer, and she opens her mouth in shock. *What the hell?*

It's her black backpack, encrusted in a shell of dried mud. She's so astonished that she forgets how angry she is and calls out, "Alejandro, come here!"

She lugs the backpack into the middle of the room, inadvertently hitting the side of the altar and almost knocking the candles over onto the floor.

Alejandro runs inside the house. "¿Qué pasó, Camila?" he asks. "What is it?"

She frantically brushes the dried mud off the backpack. "This is my backpack! The one I lost when the bus went off the side of the road. I can't believe it's here." She suddenly stops what she's doing and looks up at him with accusing eyes. "Did you know about this?"

"*What?* No. I've never even seen it before." He crouches down on the floor and reaches for the zipper. "Here, let me help you with it."

"No," she says, sliding it away from him, "I can do it by myself."

Some of the nylon material is caught in the zipper. She struggles to get it open, but the harder she pulls, the more it jams. Frustrated, she punches the backpack with her fist. Small pieces of grit fly up into her face.

She rubs her eyes. "Damn it! I don't know why I'm bothering to open it, anyway. I'm sure someone has already rummaged through it. I just hope that my passport is still here." She tugs at the zipper once again.

Alejandro puts his hand on her arm. "Camila, please let me help you."

She snatches her arm away. "I don't want your help!"

With one more tug, the zipper finally comes loose and slides open with ease. Camille reaches her hand inside and feels around until her fingers find a plastic bag. She pulls it out and is shocked to see that not only is her iPhone still there, the plastic bag has completely protected it from all the mud. She holds her finger on the button until the apple lights up. She can't believe it still works.

Digging deeper, she finds her passport and, finally, her wallet. She opens the clasp, expecting to see that all of her cash and credit cards are gone, but not a single item is missing. Even the eight hundred dollars she exchanged for pesos at the airport in Mexico City is still there.

Camille is overcome with relief. "Everything's here," she whispers.

"Why wouldn't it be?" he says.

She ignores his question. "How do you think my backpack ended up here?"

"I have no idea. Maybe my tía knows."

Just then, the patio gate swings open with a squeak. A moment later, Tía Nifa is in the room, pointing to the backpack and chattering to Alejandro in excited Zapotec.

"Does she know how it got here?" Camille asks.

"She says that when she arrived home earlier this afternoon, there were two men waiting at the gate with the backpack. They found it at the accident scene when they were searching the bus."

"But how did they know it was mine, or where to find me?"

"She's not sure," he says. "Maybe they looked at your passport photo and asked around. There probably aren't too many redheaded American women around here."

"I still can't believe it."

"It's definitely a miracle." Alejandro nods his head in the direction of the altar. "It looks like San Antonio really did help you find something you lost."

"Yes, he did," Camille says, thinking that she may have found her backpack, but she's lost something even more precious. She reaches into the pocket of her shorts and holds out the pesos he gave her. "Here, you can have the money back. It seems I don't need it after all." He reluctantly takes the money and shoves it into his pocket. She takes a five-hundred-peso bill out of her wallet and tries to put it in his hand. "This should cover what you've spent on me while I've been here."

He places his hands behind his back. "Please. I don't want your money."

"Take it. I don't want to owe you anything."

He looks as if he's going to cry. "No, Camila. I won't take it."

She places the bill on the altar and covers it with a glass candleholder. "Well, if you won't take it, I'll just leave it as a donation for San Antonio."

Tía Nifa shoots worried looks back and forth at Alejandro and Camille, clearly sensing that something has changed. Like a little girl whose parents are quarreling, she tries to distract them by cheerfully pointing to the portrait of San Antonio and then back at Camille. She rushes over and grabs Camille in a tight embrace, speaking rapidly.

"What's she saying?" Camille asks.

"She's telling you that she turned San Antonio's picture right side up because of you," he says. "She says that after all this time, she's finally found what she's been looking for."

Camille hugs Tía Nifa back. Her tears spill out onto the top of the old woman's silvery braid. "Please tell your aunt that I have to go," she says, her voice quavering. "That I'm so sorry about everything. Please tell her how much I appreciate what she's done for me." She leans down, kisses Tía Nifa's wrinkled cheek, and then quickly twists away from her embrace.

Alejandro looks despondent. "Wait. Please don't go. *Please.* Let's work this out together."

Camille picks up her backpack and throws it over one shoulder.

"Please tell Tía Nifa how much I love her," she says, and strides out the door.

CHAPTER 31

It's been over an hour, and Camille is still waiting for the bus to arrive. The hot sun has intensified the sour smell of mezcal coming from her body, and she wants a shower more than she's wanted anything in her life.

She hears it before she sees it—the whine of worn-out brakes and the sputtering of a diesel engine. Another ramshackle bus, this time a rusty white, chugs down the hill and parks in the roundabout. Its engine idles noisily as its passengers disembark and collect their belongings from the roof of the bus—which, to Camille's surprise, includes several chickens and a live pig in a crate. She climbs the steps into the sweltering bus.

After choosing a window seat in the middle, she places her backpack on the empty space next to her and slides the window open as far as it goes. There is no breeze. She fixes her eyes on the open door, certain that any minute Alejandro is going to show up looking for her. Her optimism wanes as each new passenger boards and it's not him.

When the bus driver takes his seat, Camille almost gets off the bus. She wants to run up to Tía Nifa's house and tell Alejandro that she forgives him. Instead, she digs her fingers into her thighs and forces herself to stay put.

As the bus climbs the hill back toward the main road, Camille turns around and watches the red gingerbread church disappear from sight. Has she really only been here two days? This morning, when she stood in front of San Antonio and asked him to help her figure out what she was looking for, her heart was filled with so much hope. How foolish she was.

Before turning onto the main road, the bus stops to pick up several more passengers who are waiting in front of a small market. Camille sticks her head out the window for some fresh air and spots a group of young men congregated around a wooden table, drinking beer and eating chili-covered pork rinds from greasy paper bags. Every single one of them is dressed in a white tank top, sagging pants, and high-top tennis shoes.

Camille is about to pull her head back inside the bus when one of the group—a bald, skinny young man—abruptly turns around and looks directly at her. His lips are stained a bright red from the chili powder. He squints at Camille—and his eyes flash with surprised recognition, quickly followed by a look of such pure hatred that Camille's breath is taken away.

She's puzzled as to why he's glaring at her with such animosity. Then she spots the familiar vinelike tattoos creeping up his neck.

Her body goes cold, and she is suddenly afraid. It's Little Chuy—the *cholo* from the dance last night. She yanks her head back inside the bus and drops down in her seat. She breathes a sigh of relief as the bus door closes with a squeak behind the last passengers, and the driver pulls onto the road.

As the bus gains speed, Camille figures it's safe to sit up again. She peeks out the open window to make sure Little Chuy isn't still watching her from in front of the market.

An angry voice curses in Spanish from just below her. She is so startled that she hits her head on the metal window frame. Rubbing the sore spot, she again peeks out the window—and her heart moves into her throat. Little Chuy is running alongside the bus. He screams at her with his red-stained lips, furiously pumping his fist in the air, his posse trailing close behind him. He looks Camille right in the eyes. "*¡Pinche puta pelirroja!*" he yells, spitting out the words like his mouth is on fire.

This time Camille's Spanish is sufficient enough to understand exactly what he said—*Fucking redheaded whore.* She hunkers down even lower in her seat, willing the bus to gain speed, but they are stuck in low gear, headed up another steep hill. She hears a loud thumping noise. Little Chuy is pounding his fist against the side of the bus. Several passengers turn and look at her with worried expressions.

"You think you can get away from me, you bitch?" he screams through the window. "*I'll fucking kill you!*"

Camille is sure the bus driver is about to stop the bus to find out what the ruckus is all about. Terrified, she lowers her head and covers her ears with her hands. *Please don't stop the bus, please don't stop the bus*, she prays with all her might.

Finally the bus begins to gain speed. Camille garners enough courage to raise her head and look out the back window. Sweet relief floods through her. Little Chuy and his friends are no longer chasing her. They stand in the middle of the road in a cloud of dust, furiously gesturing at the back of the bus. The look on Little Chuy's face is the most chilling. Even from this distance, Camille can sense the intensity of his rage. This time, he was going to really hurt her. Perhaps even kill her.

She shudders, thinking how ironic it is that she almost lost her life on the way into Yalálag, and now she just about lost it on her way out.

Camille is jerked awake when the bus goes over several speed bumps. She looks out her window and sees San Mateo's familiar blue church silhouetted against a sky saturated with hues of coral, pink, and lavender.

A dark-haired man wearing faded jeans and a white button-up shirt is sitting on the bench in front of the church. Camille's heart soars. It's Alejandro; he's somehow managed to get here before the bus. She slides open the window as fast as she can.

"Alejandro!" she cries. "Over here!"

The man on the bench turns his head toward the bus, a quizzical expression on his face, and she realizes she's made a terrible mistake. This man has a mustache and looks nothing like Alejandro. Embarrassed, she brings her head back inside the bus and ignores the curious looks from the other passengers.

The bus driver parks in front of a market across from the church and turns off the engine. Desperate to change into clean clothes, Camille heads to the door, where she asks the driver how long they'll be stopping and where she can find a bathroom.

"We leave in fifteen minutes," he says. "The bathroom is in the market."

"*Gracias, señor.* I'll be right back."

Inside, she finds the door marked "*Baño.*" Upon entering, she almost gags at the sewer-like smell that permeates the windowless room. She'd light a match to cover the stench, but she's afraid the lingering gas would ignite the place and blow it into a pile of rubble.

She slides the bolt across the door, then holds her breath as she removes her white shorts and T-shirt. She's eager to wash the stickiness from her body. There are no paper towels, only a rust-stained porcelain sink with a faucet that trickles out a thin stream of water. In desperation, Camille holds her dirty T-shirt under the water and hurriedly runs it over her face, arms, and neck. She doesn't bother with her feet, which are so coated in grime that her toenails look like they've been painted with brown polish. She changes into clean clothes and shoves the dirty ones into the bottom of her backpack.

Before leaving the market, she purchases a bottle of water, a cheese sandwich, and some gum. As she pays, she hears the sound of tittering voices. Behind her are two indigenous girls, their heads so close together that their noses almost touch. One of them has a sucker in her mouth, and the other holds a half-eaten mango in one hand. Camille recognizes them immediately, as they're wearing the same purple and blue gingham aprons they had on the other night. She is well aware that she's the subject of their whispered conversation.

Suddenly overjoyed to see their familiar faces, Camille reaches out and grabs them both in a tight bear hug. When they begin to squirm she reluctantly releases them.

"*Hola, muchachas,*" she says, smiling. "*¿Cómo están ustedes?*" They cover their mouths with their hands, look down at the ground, and begin to giggle.

In simple Spanish, Camille tells them how much she appreciated their kindness toward her the other night. She thanks them for washing her clothes and asks them to please tell their mother how delicious the food was. They are both such precious little girls—so innocent and shy. On a whim, she removes two thousand-peso bills from her wallet—she calculates that they are worth somewhere around fifty dollars each—and holds the money out to them.

"This is for you. For taking such good care of me the other night."

Wide-eyed, they shake their heads in unison. Their braids swing back and forth like horsetails swatting at flies.

"Please," Camille says. "*Para la familia.* Give it to your mother if you'd like. *Por favor.*"

The smaller girl, the one in the lavender apron, slowly reaches out her hand for the money. Her older sister grabs her by the wrist and roughly pulls her outside the store, chastising her in their dialect.

Camille hears the sputter of the bus's engine. She hurries out after the sisters and tries one last time to get them to take the money. When they still refuse, she quickly folds the bills in half and tucks them into their apron pockets.

"*Muchas gracias, niñas*," she calls out, already running back toward the bus. "*¡Adios!*"

Before the bus drives away, Camille looks out the window and sees the two sisters, still standing outside the store. They're examining the blue bills, their mouths open in astonishment. Fifty dollars is nothing to Camille—maybe the cost of a lunch date in Montecito or the price of a concert ticket. To these sisters, she imagines it's a small fortune. She feels the corners of her mouth turn up. The gnawing pain in her chest eases ever so slightly.

The bus drives headfirst into the fading light. Since there's no point in looking out the window at scenery she can't see, Camille sleeps the entire way back to Oaxaca City. When they finally arrive, the noise of idling buses and the glare of the station's fluorescent lights make her head throb. She has no idea which direction to go to find a hotel this late at night.

Before she can ask someone for help, a short, balding man with a protruding belly approaches her. He flicks a lit cigarette onto the sidewalk and deftly extinguishes it with the tip of his shoe.

"Taxi, señorita?" he asks, reaching out for her backpack. "I take you to hotel?" He opens the back door of a taxi and holds out his arm.

"Okay," she says, "that would be great." She slides into the back seat of his cab. It smells of mildew and cigarette smoke. "Can you recommend a good one?"

"*Sí, señorita*," he says, studying her. "You pay high?"

Camille isn't sure what he means. "I'm sorry?"

"You pay high for expensive hotel or not so much?"

She doesn't think twice about it. After roughing it over the past several days, the thought of a soft bed in a luxurious hotel is more than a little tempting. "I will most certainly pay high."

He grins and starts the car. "Very good, señorita. I take you right away to very good hotel. *Casa de los Monjes.*"

Camille has no idea what the name of the hotel means except that it's a "house" of something.

The taxi driver, who introduces himself as Miguel, keeps up a lively chatter and points out the cultural attractions as they bump along the narrow one-way streets. Camille is so exhausted she only halfway listens to him. Taking her phone out of her backpack, she checks for phone service. She doesn't know whether to laugh or cry when she sees there are eighty-seven missed calls from her mother.

The taxi pulls up in front of a nondescript building painted in a soft cappuccino color that is illuminated by the warm glow of the street lamps. Miguel holds open the heavy glass door for Camille. Once inside, he takes charge and speaks to the concierge on her behalf.

The lobby of the hotel is charming. Painted a buttery yellow, every wall is adorned with framed artwork, ornate mirrors, and light sconces that throw intricate designs onto the walls. An elegant wrought iron banister curves up to the second floor. There are statues of angels and cherubs on tabletops and set into glass cases with mirrored shelves. Directly behind the counter is an oil painting of a priest wearing a brown robe who looks surprisingly like San Antonio. It suddenly dawns on Camille what *Casa de los Monjes* means—House of the Monks. She might consider it a positive sign if she believed in all that San Antonio nonsense.

After generously tipping Miguel and the concierge, Camille settles herself into her room. She soon finds herself submerged up to her neck in the most gigantic claw-foot tub she's ever seen. She's laced the steaming water with half a bottle of fragrant bath oil, and it's a relief to soak away all the grime, sweat, and sticky mezcal that she's been wearing like a second skin.

She knows she should be thrilled to be in such a lovely room. A room that includes a soft bed, a working toilet, and even an air conditioner. She should be proud that she made it safely back to Oaxaca all on her own. She should be ecstatic that she's one step closer to Graciela. She should be all of these things.

Instead, she's utterly miserable.

She washes her hair and scrubs her skin raw with a washcloth. Then the tears come. Heavy, racking sobs that pour out of her like torrents of mud gushing down off the mountainside.

She takes a deep breath and lowers her head under the water. Opening her eyes and looking up at the light through the murky water, she decides that perhaps she should just stay right there, safe and still in this quiet cocoon of nothingness. She braces her feet against the side of the tub so she won't float back up to the top. Closing her eyes, she holds her breath and waits for oblivion. Then the faint sound of Bach's Toccata and Fugue comes at her from behind the bathroom door.

Her mother is calling.

CHAPTER 32

Wearing nothing but a towel, Camille sits on the edge of the bed, her wet hair dripping down her back. For five minutes she stares at the phone in her hand. She knows she can no longer avoid talking to her mother. She presses the call button.

The phone rings only once before her mother picks up.

"Camille—is that you?" There is an edge of hysteria in her mother's voice that Camille hasn't heard before.

"Yes, Mom—it's me," she says. "I'm in a hotel in Oaxaca City."

"Where on earth have you been? I've been calling and calling you! I was worried sick. I thought you'd been kidnapped! Or worse, that you'd been in an accident—gone off a cliff somewhere in the middle of nowhere!"

Camille would laugh if she wasn't so tired.

"Why didn't you call me?" her mother demands. "Is it that difficult to pick up a phone and call your mother? I was going to give you one more day to get in touch with me. Then I was going to call the American consulate in Oaxaca. That is, if there even is one."

"Take it easy, Mom. I'm fine. I ran into a few problems while looking for Graciela. I didn't call you because I didn't have any phone service."

"That's no excuse," her mother says with her usual irritation. "And Graciela? Is she there with you at the hotel?"

"No. I haven't found her yet."

"You haven't found her? Then what in God's name have you been doing all this time?"

"I've been looking for her! She wasn't where she was supposed to be. Tomorrow I'm going to see if I can find her at the hospital."

"The *hospital?*" Her mother's voice rises an octave. "Why would she be at the hospital? Did something happen?"

Camille tells her mother the story of how she traveled all the way to Yalálag to look for Graciela, only to discover that she and María were in the hospital in Oaxaca City the whole time. She leaves out the part about the bus going off the side of the road and what happened with Little Chuy. She doesn't mention Alejandro either.

"What's wrong with María?" her mother asks. "And why did it take you so long to get back to the city? Tomorrow makes five days that you've been gone."

"There was a big storm and the road got blocked, so I had to wait in Yalálag longer than I expected. And I'm still not sure what's wrong with María. It might be cancer."

She hears her mother suck in her breath. "Cancer? Oh, dear god. Poor María."

"I'm hoping to find out more in the morning when I go to the hospital. I just wanted to let you know that I'm okay. I'll call you tomorrow night with any news."

Her mother clicks her tongue. "So, you got stuck in the mountains because of a big storm, did you? Well, you can't say I didn't warn you about those monsoons, Camille. I clearly recall telling you that traveling *down there* was going to be dangerous. And now you've gone and wasted all this time."

Camille's annoyance flares. "Mom, why do you care if I've

211

wasted time? Didn't you try to talk me out of coming here in the first place? I distinctly remember that you were the one who told me that I was only Graciela's piano teacher. Not her mother."

Her mother takes a long sip of something. "That may be true. I did think it was too dangerous for you to travel alone to Mexico. But as long as you're there, you might as well get a move on and get Graciela back here as soon as possible. That Sofia Vanilla Bitch has smelled a rat. I've heard through the grapevine that she's been asking questions about why you and Graciela have disappeared all of a sudden."

Camille tries to tamp down the anxiety swelling in her chest. "What have you heard, exactly?"

"That Sofia thinks that this might be her big chance to get her student to take Graciela's place for the concert. She's already spoken with the symphony conductor and told him that Graciela is missing." Her mother's voice becomes more agitated. "You know that if Graciela doesn't show up in time for the rehearsal next Thursday, we're in trouble, don't you? Sofia's student will get to take Graciela's place."

"You think I don't know that, Mom?" She forces herself to take a calming breath. "There's still almost a week before the rehearsal. If I can find Graciela in the next day or two, I can get her back in plenty of time."

"I really hope you're right, Camille."

"Me too, Mom. Okay, I'll talk to you later—"

"Camille, wait a second," her mother says, her voice softening. "I want to tell you—I want you to know I'm relieved you're all right. I was so worried. And I promise that I'll do what I can here to keep Vanilla Bitch from causing any more trouble. You just figure out how to get Graciela back home, okay? And you call me if you need anything. Anything at all. See you soon, darling."

Camille tosses her phone on the bedside table, crawls under the covers, and pulls the sheet up to her neck. *Now that was different.*

Was her mother actually being supportive? *I'm so tired, I must be imagining things.*

Desperate to sleep, she turns over in bed and closes her eyes. She sees only Alejandro's face, and a vise tightens around her heart. The tears come again, but before she can even get started on another good cry, her overwhelming exhaustion prevails and hurls her headfirst into oblivion.

Before going downstairs, Camille applies extra makeup to cover her puffy eyes. After she eats a quick breakfast of toast and coffee on the hotel patio, she is ready to go look for Graciela. She heads out to find a taxi.

She is standing in front of the hotel and contemplating which direction to go in when a battered orange-and-white taxi pulls up to the curb. A familiar-looking man gets out of the cab, waddles around it, and opens the passenger side door.

"*Buenos días, señorita,*" he says cheerfully.

Camille is delighted that it's Miguel, the driver from last night. The hotel concierge must have alerted him that she needed a taxi.

He smiles broadly. "Where I take you today, señorita?"

"I need to go to the hospital," she says.

His face darkens. "You are sick?"

"No, no—I'm fine. But I need to find someone who's a patient there."

He bows slightly. "I take you now right there."

Twenty minutes later, they walk into a small but modern-looking hospital. The lobby is immaculate, and the walls are painted with colorful murals depicting Oaxacan culture.

When Camille gives her María's name, the admitting nurse

looks up apologetically at her. "I'm sorry, miss, but this person is not here." She then says something quietly to Miguel in Spanish.

He turns to Camille. "Señorita, maybe the friend you look for is not here. She is in other hospital?"

"There's another hospital?"

"Sí. This hospital here is *privada*—private. There is other hospital. *Hospital General de Oaxaca.* It would be unexpected for your friend to be at that hospital. Maybe there is mistake and she is there?"

"I don't know," Camille says, dismayed. "I guess we'll just have to go over there and find out."

She soon discovers that the narrow streets of downtown Oaxaca were not designed for congested city traffic. Even with Miguel's skillful maneuvering behind the wheel, it takes another thirty minutes before they reach the General Hospital.

Camille's heart sinks when they pull up in front of a large cinderblock building. A long line of dejected-looking people snakes out from the front entrance and curves around the block.

"You can drop me off here," Camille says.

"But I come with to help you, señorita," he protests.

"No, that's okay, Miguel," she says. "I'm not sure how long it's going to take me to find my friend. You go on." She reaches into her wallet to pay him, but he waves her away.

"I return in three hours, no? You pay me when I take you back to hotel."

"Are you sure?" she asks. "What if you can't find me?"

"Then I come to Hotel de los Los Monjes," he says, smiling.

"*Muchas gracias,* Miguel. You're very kind."

After talking briefly to a security guard that can't be older than eighteen, Camille discovers that the people standing in line are not hospital patients. They are family members waiting to visit their loved ones. Only one visitor per patient is allowed in at a time. Everyone must wait outside on the sidewalk until it's their turn.

The line seems to be made up exclusively of poor, indigenous Oaxacans. There's no place for anyone to sit down except on the ground. Families have laid out blankets and mats where they wait while their small children either play quietly or sleep away the boredom.

It takes Camille almost an hour to work her way through the maze of people to the front entrance.

A stocky woman sits alone at the front desk. She is wearing a plain navy-blue dress and a gold wristwatch. Her short haircut is so severe it looks like she has a brown helmet perched on her head. Camille approaches her and receives a glare full of distrust.

"I'm here to visit María Valera," Camille says in the best Spanish she can muster.

The woman produces a clipboard layered with a thick sheaf of dog-eared papers and scans a list of names for a few seconds before stopping her finger midway down. She spews out something in rapid Spanish.

Camille has absolutely no idea what she said. She switches to English. "I'm sorry, but I don't understand you."

Her glare intensifies. "¿María Valera *es su familia?*"

"Is she my family? No, no—she's a friend."

She puts her clipboard down on the desk. "*No familia, no visita.*"

"What? Are you serious? But I really need to see her."

"*No familia, no visita,*" the woman repeats in a louder voice.

"Please. It's imperative that I speak to her. Could I at least leave a message?"

The woman ignores Camille and motions to the people next in line to step up to the desk. Thinking fast, Camille opens her wallet and takes out a hundred-peso bill. She holds it right in front of the woman's wide, stony face.

In a loud, clear voice she says, "*María Valera es mi familia.*"

In a flash, the woman grabs the bill and stuffs it into her pocket. "*Tercer piso*," she says, thrusting a pen into Camille's hand. Camille scribbles her signature on the clipboard next to María's name.

"Third floor—how do I get there?"

The woman points down the hall to a large staircase covered in worn linoleum.

"*Treinta minutos*," she says sternly.

Camille practically runs up the stairs before the woman changes her mind.

Camille has no idea where to go. The ward is like a maze; she walks around peering into rooms looking for María and Graciela, but she finds only unfamiliar faces. She wants to ask someone for help, but the nurses working on the floor look so busy that she doesn't want to bother them.

After spending over twenty minutes wandering around the crowded floor, she has worked up a sweat. *This is ridiculous. I'm never going to find María without a room number.*

Reluctantly, Camille heads back down to the lobby to ask for the exact room number from the rude lady with the clipboard. As she turns the corner in the direction of the stairs, she runs smack into a patient in a wheelchair and goes sprawling onto the tile floor, her kneecaps hitting the ground with a dull thud.

"Oh my goodness," she says, picking herself up from the dirty floor. She hastily brushes off her hands and knees. "I'm so sorry—I didn't see—"

"Miss Camille?" a quiet voice says.

Camille looks up in stunned disbelief and almost falls to the ground again. Standing right in front of her, pushing María in a wheelchair, is Graciela.

CHAPTER 33

Unable to stop herself, Camille begins to cry with relief. She is shocked by Graciela's appearance. She has purple half-moons under her eyes, her skin is sallow, and her normally lustrous black hair hangs limply across her shoulder in an untidy braid.

Camille reaches out to hug Graciela and feels the outline of the girl's bones poking out from underneath her white cotton dress. Graciela doesn't return the embrace; she just stands perfectly still, her arms at her sides. She is obviously in shock that her ordinarily undemonstrative piano teacher is not only in Oaxaca, but is also squeezing the breath out of her and crying into her neck.

When Camille is finally able to regain control, she steps back and places her hands on either side of Graciela's face. "I can't believe it's really you," she says. "You have no idea how relieved I am to have found you."

Graciela opens her mouth to speak, but nothing comes out—probably because she's having a difficult time recognizing the new *Camila*, a woman who openly shows her emotions and cries at the drop of a hat. Up until now, she's only been acquainted with the restrained *Miss Camille*, who is always in control. Unbeknownst to Graciela, that Camille ceased to exist when a certain blue bus went off the side of a cliff.

Camille turns to María, who is dressed in a hospital gown and has a frayed white cotton blanket wrapped around her shoulders. Other than looking a little tired, Camille is surprised to see that María looks quite robust for someone dying from cancer. "María— *¿Cómo está usted?* How are you feeling?"

María smiles broadly and reaches out to grasp her hand. "Miss Camille—I so happy you are here. This is big surprise, but I so happy to see you." Tears begin to stream down her cheeks.

Now it's Graciela's turn to cry. This causes Camille to start up again. Before long, they are like a trio of sopranos crying in harmony, accompanied by the noisy chaos of the hospital corridor.

Graciela is the first to recover. She wipes her eyes with her hands, then retrieves a wrinkled tissue from of her pocket and gently wipes the tears from under her mother's eyes. María turns her face up toward her daughter, and, smiling, she takes Graciela's hand in hers and presses it against her own cheek. It is such an intimate maternal gesture that another lump forms in Camille's throat.

She is suddenly furious with herself. How could she have assumed that Graciela was thinking only of herself when she left Santa Barbara? It's obvious that she is nothing but a devoted daughter who has come back to Oaxaca to take care of her sick mother. Like a flash, it hits her: she won't try to talk Graciela into coming back with her. It would be unconscionable to ask her to leave her mother under such dire circumstances.

"Miss Camille," Graciela says, finally finding her voice, "what are you doing here in Oaxaca?"

"I came here to find you," Camille says. "I wanted to talk you into coming back home so you could perform in your debut concert."

Graciela's mouth opens with surprise. "You did? Wow. I can't believe you came all this way just for me."

"Of course I did! You're my best piano student. I thought I had to keep you from throwing away this opportunity." Unable to hide the sarcasm in her voice, she mutters, "Although according to Alejandro, I only had my own selfish motives in mind."

Graciela knits her brow together. "Who's Alejandro? Are you talking about my tío Alejandro?"

Camille's heart begins to pound as she thinks about him. "That's the one," she says bitterly. "He told me I only wanted you to come back for the concert so I could further my own teaching career. He accused me of being selfish." She feels herself welling up again and quickly fans her hand in front of her face. "Anyway, enough about Alejandro. He's the last person on earth I want to talk about right now."

Graciela looks confused. "But how do you know my tío Alejandro?"

Camille lets out a sigh. "I met him on the way to Yalálag."

Graciela's eyes go wide. "You went to Yalálag?"

"Yes. I've just spent the last four days there."

At first, Graciela looks stunned. Then her face lights up, and she lets out a full-throated laugh. Embarrassed, she quickly covers her mouth with her hand, but as she turns her head away, her body begins to shake.

"What's so funny?" Camille asks. She assumes this apparent hysteria is the result of all the stress Graciela has been under.

"I'm sorry," Graciela says, still laughing, "I'm just having a hard time imagining *you* in Yalálag."

"Well, I was there, all right," Camille says, lifting up one pant leg. "And I've got the huaraches to prove it."

Graciela looks down at Camille's feet. "Oh, my gosh! You're wearing huaraches from Yalálag. That's crazy!" She begins to laugh again. She points at Camille's feet and says something to her mother in Spanish. María smiles and nods approvingly.

"I still can't believe you went all the way to Yalálag to find me,

Miss Camille. That was just so nice of you. How did you even know where I was?"

"From your uncle Victor in Los Angeles." Camille sighs. "You know, Graciela, when you first left I was so angry with you. I thought you had gone on a whim. That you were just acting like some spoiled teenager. That you never considered what missing the concert would mean for your musical career." She places a hand on her student's shoulder. "But now, seeing you here with your mom, I understand that you came for all the right reasons. I realize now how important it is for you to be with your mother . . ." She turns her head away from María and whispers, "During her final days."

Graciela gives Camille a strange look. "Her final days? What do you mean?"

Camille keeps her voice low. "You know, to be here with your mom, because she's dying from cancer."

Graciela breaks into a huge grin. Camille once again thinks that she has most certainly lost her mind. "But that's the good news," she says, "that's why I was crying earlier. We just found out this morning that my mom doesn't have cancer after all. She's okay! The lump in her breast isn't malignant. It's just a benign cyst. She gets to leave the hospital today. She can go back to Yalálag tomorrow."

"That is such wonderful news!" Camille cries. "So you'll be returning with her to Yalálag?"

Graciela hesitates. "Well, that's what I was planning to do. But now that I know my mom is okay, I was thinking that maybe I could somehow go back and perform in the concert after all."

Camille has to fight the urge to jump up and down right there in the hallway. "Are you serious?"

"I really want to do it, Miss Camille. I love playing the piano so much. The only reason I left to come here was because I was so worried about my mom. I feel so bad I didn't say anything before

I left . . . I just didn't know how to tell you. I thought you'd be so mad at me and never want to talk to me again. I didn't know what to do, except to leave. I'm really, really sorry."

Camille squeezes Graciela's hand. "I'm not mad at you. I'm just thrilled that you want to go back with me. This is absolutely the best news I've had in days." She begins to form a plan in her head. "Tell you what: I'll go back to my hotel room and make airline reservations for the two of us for tomorrow. Then in a couple of hours, I'll come back here to pick you and your mom up. We can all go out for a nice dinner. The two of you can stay overnight at the hotel with me. There are two beds, and there's plenty of room."

A look of dismay passes over Graciela's face.

"What's wrong?" Camille asks. "You don't want to come back to the hotel with me?"

"No, it's not that."

"What is it, then?"

Graciela bites her lip and says nothing.

"Please, Graciela, tell me."

"I can't go on the airplane with you."

"Why not?"

She looks down. "I don't have an American passport," she says, so quietly Camille almost doesn't hear her.

"Oh, no! Did you leave it back in Yalálag?"

"No." Her voice is even tinier now. "I don't have one."

"What do you mean you don't have one?"

Graciela looks down at the floor. "I'm not an American citizen," she says. "I don't have my papers. I only have a Mexican passport."

Camille feels the blood drain from her face. "But I thought you were born in Los Angeles."

"I was born in Yalálag. I came to LA when I was four years old."

"But how did you come to the States if you didn't have a US passport?"

"My mom crossed the border with me."

Camille is aghast. "When you were only four?"

Keeping her head down, Graciela nods.

It takes Camille a moment to digest this new information. "So you've been *illegal* all these years?"

Graciela looks up, a pained expression on her face. "*Undocumented* is a better word. But yes."

"Sorry—*undocumented*. I swear I had no idea. Is this why you didn't want to apply for college right away? Because you knew you'd have trouble getting in without the proper documents?"

Graciela nods again. "DACA—the Dream Act—makes it easier for someone like me to go to college, but now that we have a new president who wants to deport everyone, my mom and I thought it was best to wait. She's afraid that if I enroll in college, they'll find me more easily and I'll get deported. Plus, I don't have any money for school. And I can't get any federal student loans."

Camille paces the hallway. "I just wish you would've told me about this sooner, Graciela. I'm sure I could've helped you somehow. Okay, let's see. What if we go to the US consulate here in Oaxaca and ask for permission for you to travel to the US? I could vouch for you."

Graciela takes a deep breath. "It's not that easy, Miss Camille. It takes months—sometimes years—to get a visa to go to the US. You even have to prove that you own a house here in Mexico so that they know you'll come back."

"So what do we do, then?"

Graciela looks as if she wants to say something but remains silent.

"Please, Graciela—if you have an idea, I'd love to hear it."

"I could cross again."

"What do you mean, *cross again*?"

Graciela looks up. "You know, sneak over the border."

"By yourself?"

"No," she says, "we'd have to hire someone to take me. And it would be pretty expensive. I think it costs around seven thousand dollars right now. But I still have the five thousand I won from the competition, so I could use that to cover most of it. I guess I could ask my family for the rest."

"You haven't spent your prize money?" Camille asks. "I thought you would've used it to come here."

"No, I still have it. My tío Victor gave me money to pay for my plane ticket and to pay for the hospital for my mom. They didn't want me to use my prize money. They said I had earned it with all of my hard work, and I should keep it for myself."

"Well, that's extremely generous of them," Camille says, taken aback. "They certainly must care deeply about you."

Graciela smiles. "They do."

"Well, I'm not going to let you use your prize money either. The money part isn't going to be an issue. The question is, do you even know anyone who does this sort of thing?"

"I don't personally," she says, "but my tío can find a *coyote*. He knows people."

"A *coyote*? You mean someone who leads you over the border?"

Graciela nods.

Anxiety tickles the base of Camille's neck. "But isn't that dangerous?"

Graciela frowns. "Sometimes it is. I've heard some really terrible stories. My cousin's wife was beaten and raped when she crossed a few years ago. Sometimes people get left by themselves in the desert and they run out of water, and then their family never hears from them again. And if you get caught by *la migra*—the border patrol—they'll put you in a detention center for who knows how long."

"Oh, my god." Camille pinches the bridge of her nose. "This

is a total nightmare. First of all, we don't have that kind of time. Secondly, I'm terrified something bad is going to happen to you."

"Well then," Graciela says in her most optimistic voice, "I guess we'll just have to find a really good *coyote*. Someone who can get me across on the first try."

CHAPTER 34

When Miguel spots Camille in front of the hospital, he swerves over so fast that his tires squeal against the curb. He hurries out of the cab and opens the back door with a flourish befitting a toreador. "*Buenos tardes, señorita*," he says, holding out his arm.

"Perfect timing, Miguel," she says. She scans the line of dejected-looking people one last time, feeling only relief that she is finally leaving this place. She steps aside to allow María and Graciela to get into the cab first. Before they even reach the door, Miguel sticks his arm out like a barricade and snarls at them in Spanish. They look over at Camille in alarm.

"What's the matter?" Camille asks, surprised that Miguel has such a look of distaste on his face.

"Señorita, I tell these women that this is your taxi and they can wait for the next one."

"But Miguel, these women are my friends. They're coming with me."

His eyes widen. "*Perdón, señorita.*" He bows slightly. "I did not understand."

Camille nods distractedly and gets into the cab. She has only one thing on her mind, and that's how she's going to get Graciela over the border and back to LA in less than a week. If Graciela gets caught by immigration at the border, they're both doomed.

She is also worried about Graciela's lack of preparation for the concert. She hasn't had access to a piano in Oaxaca; her concerto will need practice. As they won't be leaving for Tijuana until sometime tomorrow, it's imperative that Camille find a piano for her to practice on, preferably by tonight.

As they pull up in front of the hotel, Camille turns to Miguel. "Do you know of a place nearby where there's a decent piano I could use?"

"A piano? *Sí, señorita.* There is very large black piano at the *Museo de las culturas de Oaxaca.* The museum is few blocks away, next to the Church of Santo Domingo. Sometimes they have the concerts there. If I may ask, why you need the piano?"

"My student has won a very prestigious piano competition," Camille says with pride, "and her debut recital is coming up next week. Unfortunately, she hasn't been near a piano for almost two weeks. She really needs to practice her music."

He smiles, showing teeth stained yellow from years of smoking. "Then you are lucky to have asked the right person. My cousin Silvia works at *el museo.* I will talk to her to see if is possible for your student to use the piano after the museum closes."

"Oh, Miguel—really? That would be wonderful."

He takes Camille's arm and helps her out of the taxi, leaving María and Graciela to fend for themselves. "I go speak to her right now," he says. "I return soon and let you know what she says."

Camille is more than grateful. She thanks him profusely and pays him triple the fare.

Later on that evening, after Camille has reserved two plane tickets to Tijuana and purchased María's bus ticket back to Yalálag,

Camille takes Graciela and María out to dinner. They dine at a lovely open-air restaurant bordering the *zócalo*—main square—at the center of the city. Smiling tourists stroll under the cool umbrella of laurel trees as a brass band plays traditional Oaxacan music. There is laughter and the scent of delicious food in the air, but Camille hardly notices. All she can do is think about Alejandro. She wishes she was strolling arm in arm with him around the *zócalo*, listening to the lively music. When the waiter takes their order, she makes the mistake of asking for the *mole negro*. With the first bite she's immediately transported back to Yalálag. Her throat closes up with grief, and she begins to cough. She puts her fork down.

"What's the matter, Miss Camille?" Graciela asks, looking worried. "You don't like the *mole*?"

Camille wipes her mouth with her napkin. "Oh, no, it's delicious. I guess I'm a bit overtired. And to be honest, I'm nervous about what's going to happen over the next few days." She says nothing to Graciela about Alejandro.

"Please don't worry, Miss Camille. It's going to be fine. Just two weeks ago, one of my cousins got through. I think my chances are good."

Camille covers Graciela's hand with hers. "I'm so sorry you have to go through this, Graciela. I've been thinking about it a lot."

"Thinking about what?"

"That it's not fair. You've grown up most of your life in the United States. I mean, you're basically American, right? You read, write, and speak English fluently, you've been educated there. You've worked hard all these years with your music to make something of yourself. Yet you can't get back into the country you've called home since you were four years old. Now you have to come up with an exorbitant amount of money and put your life at risk just to get across the border so you can go home."

Graciela stares out across the square with a faraway look in her eyes. "I know," she says quietly. "It really sucks. And if I told you how many people I know who are in the same situation, you'd never believe me. With Obama, at least we had some hope. Now, it's all changed. They say they'll leave the Dreamers alone, but nobody really believes it."

Fortunately, Camille has received permission from Miguel's cousin to use the piano after hours. After settling an exhausted María in the hotel room for a rest, she and Graciela walk down to the museum where Miguel and his cousin Silvia are waiting.

"Thank you so much for allowing us to use the piano," Camille says.

Miguel smiles formally and gives her a slight bow. "It is our pleasure to serve you," he says, surreptitiously glancing up and down the street as if he's waiting for someone. Finally he speaks. "*Disculpa, señorita,* but where is your student?"

Camille is puzzled. "What do you mean?" She gestures toward Graciela. "This is my piano student, Graciela Valera."

A look of surprise flashes between Miguel and Silvia. "This girl is your student?" he asks. "*Perdón, señorita*, my mistake. I thought you talked about someone else. I expected someone, ah—different."

Camille isn't quite sure what he means, but for some reason, his comment leaves her feeling disconcerted.

Silvia unlocks the heavy door, and the four of them climb a staircase to the main level of the museum. They step onto a wide outdoor hallway that looks down upon the open courtyard below. Miguel explains that the building is a former monastery and the Oaxacan government has spent millions restoring it to its former glory. It now houses a museum with ancient Oaxacan artifacts, a periodicals library, and a botanical garden filled with native flowers and plants.

It is cool and tomblike inside the museum. Their footsteps echo as they walk through the cavernous stone hallways. Near the library, Camille is surprised to find a concert grand piano in excellent condition positioned in an alcove set into one of the walls. After Silvia unlocks the fallboard, she is thrilled to see it's a newer model Steinway.

Silvia informs them they can stay for one hour. Graciela sits down at the piano and warms up with some scales.

"Oh, Miss Camille," she says, her face glowing. "This is a really nice piano. It's so responsive." Her eyes sparkle. "It feels so good to play again. I didn't realize how much I missed it until this very moment."

She begins to play the opening chords of the Rachmaninoff Second Piano Concerto. Camille can hardly believe Graciela has been away from the piano for two weeks. She has remembered every single note. The sound of the piano echoes through the magnificent archways behind them and floats out into the summer evening. As Graciela's delicate fingers ripple up and down the keyboard, Camille can almost hear the orchestra's lush harmonies swelling. She glances over at Miguel and his cousin. They are clearly impressed by Graciela's prowess at the piano.

Miguel walks over. "Señorita," he whispers, "I would have never thought that *una indígena morenita* could learn to play the piano so beautiful like this."

Camille smiles with pride. "She is wonderful, isn't she?" A moment later, she realizes what Miguel has called Graciela: an *indígena morenita*—a dark-skinned indigenous girl. Is he implying that because Graciela is Zapotec she is less capable of being a superior musician than a light-skinned person? Camille is suddenly irritated, and it dawns on her: when Miguel said earlier he was expecting Camille's student to be something "different," what he meant was *white*, like her. Her anger intensifies. Here they are in a place where the ancient culture of Oaxaca is revered, yet Miguel considers Graciela to be inferior because she is indigenous.

An hour later, after Graciela has finished practicing, Camille is still unable to shake off the mounting anger she feels. *If Alejandro were here*, she thinks, *he would say something to Miguel and put him in his place.*

When it's time to leave the museum, Miguel offers to give them a lift back to the hotel in his taxi.

"Thank you, Miguel, but it won't be necessary," Camille says, her tone short. "I think we'd prefer to walk."

He bows again. "As you wish." He smiles expectantly with his crooked yellow teeth, obviously waiting for another large tip. Camille merely offers a curt *"gracias"* before putting her arm around Graciela and leading her down the steps to the street.

Out in front of the museum, a crowd has gathered. A large band, complete with tubas and bass drums, plays lively music as it marches down the cobblestone street. A colorful parade of brightly costumed characters walking on stilts and wearing papier-mâché masks follows close behind. They swing their arms in time with the music like awkward, lumbering giants.

After the parade passes, Graciela puts her hand on Camille's arm. "Do you mind if we go into the church next door for just a moment? I want to light a candle and say a prayer before we leave Oaxaca."

Camille looks up at the church. Darkness has fallen behind the Iglesia de Santo Domingo. Like a golden oil painting that has been propped up against a midnight-blue sky, the floodlights have illuminated the church in a wash of ethereal light. She nods her head.

"Of course, Graciela. We could use all the help we can get."

Inside the church, Camille is captivated by the elaborate fili-greed ceiling, which is covered in gold leaf. She smiles, thinking that Bach would have felt right at home here.

Burning *copal* and the cloying scent of tuberose mingles with the musty air inside the church. Graciela and Camille make their way toward the main altar, where yellow tapered candles flicker on either side of a long wooden table. A handful of people are scattered throughout the pews, their lips moving in silent prayer. Camille moves into a pew in the middle. She motions for Graciela to go up to the front by herself, then looks around for portraits of San Antonio. She doesn't see any, but as long as she's here, it wouldn't hurt to say a prayer.

She bows her head. "Okay, San Antonio," she whispers, "I've never been a follower of yours. I didn't even know who you were until recently. And I still can't decide if I believe in you or not. But if for some crazy reason you do exist, I want you to know that I'm a little ticked off. I really don't appreciate how you handled the whole Alejandro thing. But right now I'm going to put all of that aside and ask for your help anyway." She grips the pew with both hands, leans over, and places her forehead on the smooth wood. "San Antonio, if you help me get Graciela safely over the border, I promise you that exactly one year from now, I will return to Yalálag. I will honor you in a very special way. I promise I'll do something really big for you."

Camille lifts her head and watches Graciela light a candle on the altar. Her delicate hand rises up and across her chest, and she solemnly kisses the tips of her fingers. Camille's heart fills with emotion. The tears slip out and run down her cheeks.

"Please, San Antonio, I'm begging you. Graciela is a good girl. She deserves this chance. Please help me get her home."

Camille rises from the pew and waits for Graciela to make her way back down the aisle. Graciela's cheeks are also wet with tears.

231

When she sees Camille watching her, she smiles so sweetly that for a moment Camille imagines the statue of the *virgincita* has come to life. A deep sense of hope suddenly fills her chest.

"Don't do it for me, San Antonio," she whispers, wiping her eyes. *"Do it for Graciela."*

CHAPTER 35

Their plane arrives in Tijuana around ten o'clock in the morning. Walking through the concourse with Graciela, Camille is pleasantly surprised to discover that the airport is clean and modern looking. But as soon as they climb into a cab and start driving toward downtown, she feels like she's landed on another planet.

Like a Polaroid snapshot that has faded over time, everything has a yellowish-brown cast. The dry hills, the run-down buildings, even the trees look as if they're covered in a film of dust. The streets are filled with so much colorful chaos that it makes her head spin. She suddenly longs for the tranquil order of Santa Barbara.

Using Camille's cell phone, Graciela calls her uncle Victor in Los Angeles. He tells her he's working on finding someone to help get her over the border as quickly as possible. In the meantime, he's advised them to wait at a particular hotel—the Hotel Paz. The irony is not lost on Camille: the hotel is located on the corner of a congested intersection where the sound of revving engines and honking horns is constant. The air is so laden with the smells of diesel fuel, fried grease, and raw sewage Camille doubts anyone could find peace at this hotel, let alone get a good night's sleep.

Graciela informs Camille they're supposed to wait in the hotel room for someone to contact them. Camille pays for the room, hoping it doesn't have any roaches or bedbugs. This whole process seems pretty sordid to her, but knowing nothing about sneaking someone across the border, she doesn't question it.

They climb the stairs to the second floor and settle into a room complete with cracked tile floors, a broken air conditioner, and two lumpy beds.

By five o'clock, the *coyote* still hasn't called. Even though Camille is so nervous that she can't imagine eating anything, her rumbling stomach disagrees.

"Let's go grab a bite to eat," she says. "Why do we need to wait in this stuffy room? I can just as easily take my phone with me."

"I guess that's okay," Graciela says. "But it's probably best to stay close by. Just in case."

They walk down the block to a small café that looks relatively clean. It's more than halfway full of people, so Camille figures the food must be good. They slide into a small booth upholstered in cracked red leather and order chicken tacos, beans, rice, and bottles of Coke.

Camille tries to eat when the food comes, but her stomach is in knots. After taking only one bite of her taco, she feels nauseated. Sipping her soda through a pink plastic straw, she watches Graciela pick at her food.

She clears her throat. "Do you mind if I ask you a personal question?"

Looking uncomfortable, Graciela wipes her mouth with the corner of her napkin. "I guess so."

"Why did you and your mom leave Los Angeles to come to Santa Barbara to work for my mother?"

"You don't know?" Graciela asks.

"No," Camille says, confused.

Graciela hesitates. "It was . . . because my mom wanted to keep me safe."

"Safe from what?"

She looks down at her plate. "From my father."

"Why? Did he do something to you?"

She looks uneasy. "Not to me. To her."

Camille pauses for a moment, then gently asks, "What did he do?"

Graciela is silent for so long that Camille decides to let it go.

"Graciela, forget I asked. You don't have to talk about it if you don't want to."

Graciela raises her head. "If I tell you, do you promise not to tell anybody?"

"Of course."

She takes a deep breath. "He used to get drunk. Like almost every night. Sometimes he beat her up."

Camille sighs. "I didn't know. I'm so sorry you and your mom had to go through that."

"I was really little . . . only around six. I don't really remember all that much. The night I remember the most is when he came home so drunk that he tried to get into bed with me."

Graciela looks so miserable that Camille puts up a hand and says, "Really, Graciela. You don't have to tell me if you don't want to."

"Nothing happened," she says quickly. "I mean, he tried to do something, but my mom came in and stopped him. But that's when he went crazy and started attacking her. He broke her nose and knocked out two of her teeth. The neighbors in the apartment next door heard me screaming. They called the police. He got arrested."

"Oh, Graciela, I'm so sorry."

"My mom was so afraid that when he got out of jail he was going to try to kidnap me. She thought he'd take me back to Mexico and hide me there. She didn't know what to do. So when my tía told her about a job at a house in Santa Barbara, she decided to take it. One night we left without telling anyone. My tío Victor and my tía Rosario were the only people who knew where we were."

"That's when your mom started working for us," Camille says softly.

Graciela nods.

"So where's your father now?"

"He got deported after he got out of jail. I think he's in Mexico City."

"You don't talk to him at all?"

She shakes her head. "I haven't seen him since that night the police took him away."

Camille takes Graciela's hands in hers. "I've said it over and over, but I'm so very sorry. I know how it feels not to have a father because I grew up without one too. And I also know how it is to be in an abusive relationship. I'm sorry that you've had this sadness in your life. But I'm also thankful that your mom was smart enough to protect you."

Camille moves her rice and beans around on her plate but can't seem to get the fork up to her mouth. "I feel badly that I didn't know about your situation. To be honest, I didn't try very hard to find out much about you. I thought my role as your piano teacher was to keep a distance between us. That it was somehow more professional of me to keep our relationship on a superficial level."

Graciela looks up at Camille. "Your mother knew what happened," she says. "I thought she told you."

Camille pushes her plate away and signals the waitress for the check. "Well, that's no surprise. My mother doesn't always tell me everything. But it's really my fault for not asking. As your temporary guardian, I should've made more of an effort to be closer to you, to really get to know you and your mom. It was my responsibility, and I blew it."

Graciela's eyes begin to tear up. "Miss Camille, it means so much to me that you're saying that. For such a long time, I wished I could talk to you about the things that worried me, but I was afraid to tell you. I really appreciate everything you've done for me and my mom over the years. Because of you, I've had so much more happen in my life. Especially with my music. That's changed everything for me."

Camille squeezes her hand. "I'm glad you feel that way. Okay, from here on out, we talk to each other about everything, all right? We're in this together. Like family."

Graciela squeezes back, and Camille feels the incredible strength in her tiny fingers. "Yes, Miss Camille—like family."

The waitress boxes up their leftover food, and Camille pays the check. As they walk out of the café, she notices a boy and a girl with dirty faces sitting on the curb in front of the restaurant, their clothes wrinkled and grimy. They can't be much older than eight or nine. They stare longingly at the boxes of food in Camille's hands.

Camille looks away so as not to spook them. "Graciela," she says in a low voice, "those children look lost. See if they're all right. Ask them where their parents are. But be careful. Don't scare them away."

Graciela walks over, slowly kneels down on the ground, and murmurs to them in Spanish. A moment later, she turns back to Camille. "They say they're here in Tijuana all by themselves. Their mother lives in Los Angeles, and they rode the train all the way here from Honduras. Up until yesterday they were with some neighbor woman from their village. Now she's disappeared, and they don't know what happened to her. They haven't had anything to eat since yesterday."

"Oh, dear," Camille says. "Poor things." She squats down next to them on the sidewalk, opens her box of leftover tacos, and motions for them to take the food.

They scarf it down in less than a minute. Camille tells Graciela to keep an eye on them while she runs into the market to buy more food. When she returns, she asks Graciela if they should call the police.

"I'm not sure if that's a good idea, Miss Camille. The police probably won't do anything except send them back to Honduras. If their mother lives in LA, maybe we can call her and help get them together again."

"Hmm . . . okay. See if they know their mother's phone number."

Graciela says something to them in Spanish. Without skipping a beat, they recite a ten-digit phone number in perfect unison.

Camille smiles and hands the phone to Graciela. "Well, I guess that answers my question. Let's give their mom a call."

Graciela taps in the number and holds the phone to her ear. "No one's answering."

"Maybe she's not home. Leave a message."

"There's no voice mail. It just keeps ringing. What should we do?"

"Well, we can't just leave them here in the street. Ask them to come back to the hotel. We can try calling her again in a little while."

Graciela nods and speaks calmly to the two children. At first, they seem reluctant, but they're finally convinced they'd be better off with them in a hotel than all alone on the streets of Tijuana. They slowly get up from the curb and take Graciela's hands.

On the way back to the hotel, they pass a *ropería* filled with a colorful display of children's clothing.

"Give me a minute, Graciela," Camille says. "These kids can't keep wearing those filthy clothes. I'm going to buy them some new ones."

Twenty minutes later, after also stopping at a small pharmacy, they walk back to the hotel. The children's arms are laden with shopping bags full of new pajamas, underwear, pants and T-shirts, tennis shoes, toothpaste, and toothbrushes. Most importantly, Camille has purchased plenty of food.

When they reach the room, Camille dumps the heavy bags onto the bed. "Tell the kids that they have to take a bath before they can put on their pajamas. Then they can eat something." She slaps a hand to her head. "I don't even know what their names are." She kneels down on the carpet so she's eye level with them. "*¿Cómo se llaman ustedes?*"

They look at her with wide eyes, surprised that the American lady speaks Spanish.

Camille points to the girl first.

"*Me llamo Alicia Moreno de la Cruz,*" she says formally.

"*Mucho gusto, Alicia,*" Camille says, shaking her tiny hand. She points to the boy. "*¿Y tú?*"

For the first time, he smiles widely, showing a gap where his two front teeth used to be. He sticks out his hand, his tiny fingernails still caked with little half-moons of dirt. Puffing up his chest, he says with pride, "*Mi nombre es Alejandro.*"

Camille feels her face begin to crumble. "Of course it is," she says, just loud enough for Graciela to hear.

Graciela studies Camille for a moment, as if she's just figured something out. She has a look on her face that Camille has never seen her wear before. It might even be a smirk. "Isn't that a coincidence, Miss Camille?" she says in a singsong voice, her eyes teasing.

Camille avoids her gaze and begins to empty the contents of the plastic bags onto the bed. "What do you mean?" she says, trying to sound casual.

"I mean, don't you think it's a funny coincidence that this little boy has the same name as my uncle?"

Camille feels her face redden. "Not at all. In fact, I'd say it's probably a pretty common name."

Graciela raises her eyebrows and tries to look innocent. "Whatever you say, Miss Camille. But the only other person I know with that name is my tío Alejandro. You know, the one you met in Yalálag?"

If Camille didn't know Graciela so well, she would swear she just winked.

CHAPTER 36

Time slows to an adagio as Camille waits for the phone to ring. Both children have bathed and donned their new pajamas, and they are now happily watching cartoons, their fingertips stained a fiery orange from the entire bag of chili-covered tortilla chips they just consumed.

Camille is in awe of the resiliency of these two young children. Only a few hours ago, they were hungry and alone on the streets of Tijuana. Now they're transfixed by Scooby-Doo on the television, which is equally annoying in Spanish as it is in English.

After insisting they each eat a banana, Camille takes the junk food away and sends them into the bathroom to brush their teeth and wash their hands. Within minutes, they're fast asleep under the rough white sheets, wrapped up like little mummies, with only their faces showing. Lying on the lumpy bed with the sounds of two snoring children next to her, Camille has no illusions she'll be able to get any rest. Yet the minute her eyes close, she falls into a deep sleep.

She dreams she's back in Tía Nifa's garden. The rain is coming down in torrents and she is back behind the ropes of the hammock, like a wild animal caught in a trap. The rain lashes at her face, but it is not cool and refreshing. Instead, it scalds her skin like a shower that's been turned on to the highest setting. She tries to pry open the entangled ropes, but no matter how hard she fights, she can't free herself.

Panicked, she calls out for Alejandro to help her. Powerful hands reach in and grab her wrists and pull her out of the hammock. At first, she is overjoyed that Alejandro is rescuing her. But something isn't right. The sour odor of cigarettes and beer overwhelm her. The hands pulling on her wrists are dry and rough. Suddenly, she realizes it's not Alejandro holding her—but Jack. She is paralyzed with fear as he moves his hands down to her fingers and begins to squeeze. "Where you been, baby?" he murmurs. "I've missed you."

Terror steals her breath away. She tries to pull away from him. "Alejandro! *Help me! Please help me!*" Her cries come out like whispers.

Jack begins to tighten his grip on her fingers. "No one's going to save you, Camille. Not this time." She screams again, but nothing comes out.

From a distance, she hears the familiar sound of Graciela's voice. She wakes up to someone tugging on her hand.

"Miss Camille—wake up! Your phone is ringing!"

It is Graciela's uncle calling. Camille hands the phone to Graciela, and after a detailed conversation in Spanish, Graciela disconnects and tells Camille that the *coyotes* are coming to the hotel early tomorrow morning.

She shakes her head. "It's not good news. My uncle says there's more agents at the border than usual. It's supposed to be really hard to cross right now. They are rounding everyone up and putting them in detention centers."

Camille's heart sinks. "Oh, no. We can't let that happen. What are we supposed to do now?"

Graciela is silent for a moment. "My uncle did say that there are safer ways to get over to the other side, but it's a lot more expensive. And I don't know where I'd get that kind of money."

"How much are we talking?"

She looks grim. "Thirteen thousand dollars."

"For *one* person?"

She nods. "Instead of walking through the hills, they would hide me in a car or a motor home. Or maybe we'd go in a boat or something like that. It's more money, but it would be a lot faster. And safer."

Camille pauses to think for a moment. She has almost ten thousand dollars in her savings account, but she'll have to borrow the other three thousand from her mother. Her mother is not going to like this.

Screw it. It's only money.

"I don't care how much it costs. Call your uncle back and tell him to set it up." She looks over at the sleeping children. "But wait a second—first we need to figure out what to do with these kids. Can you try calling their mother again?"

Graciela makes the call. Someone on the other end must have answered because she starts speaking in Spanish.

"Miss Camille," she whispers after a moment, "it's her—it's their mother. Her name is Luz." She walks over to the bed and gently shakes Alicia and Alejandro awake, telling them their mother is on the phone.

"*¿Mami?*" Alicia says, still half-asleep. When she hears her mother's voice, she begins to cry. After little Alejandro gets on the phone, he won't let go of it. Graciela has to pry it from his hand to recover it.

After spending another few minutes talking to Luz, Graciela hangs up with a worried look on her face.

"What's wrong?" Camille asks.

Graciela hands the phone back to her. "Their mother doesn't

know what to do. The woman from their town—you know, the one the kids were with? Well, she was the one who knew someone to help the kids cross. Now that she's missing, Luz doesn't know who to call. She's desperate. She wants to know if there's any way we can help her. She says she has over four thousand dollars saved and is working on raising more. She's just having a hard time getting all the money together."

Camille groans. "God, will this ever end?" She looks at the children sitting on the bed, their pajamas rumpled and their eyes still wet with tears. Her heart breaks for them. *They're just kids. They didn't ask for any of this.* There's no way she's leaving them behind in Tijuana. She'll get down on her knees and beg her mother for the money if that's what it takes.

She turns back to Graciela. "Okay, this is what we're going to do. You're going to call your uncle back right now and have him arrange to get you *and* the two kids over the border—the *expensive* way. Don't worry about how much it costs. I'll get the money somehow."

Graciela looks stunned. "But that's almost forty thousand dollars, Miss Camille."

"I know it is. But it's worth it to me to get you over quickly and safely. And these poor kids have been through enough already. None of this is their fault. Why make it harder on them?"

After Camille gets the children back to sleep, she steps outside onto the balcony and calls her mother, explaining the situation about Graciela being undocumented. She then tells her about the two children.

"You're joking, right?" her mother says. "I understand your desire to help Graciela get home. But now you're telling me that you want to bring two children as well? How much is this going to cost you?"

Camille pauses. "Here's the thing, Mom. It costs around

thirteen thousand dollars per person. I'm going to need to borrow thirty thousand dollars from you."

"*Thirty thousand dollars?*"

"Mom, just listen——"

"Have you lost your mind, Camille? Now, I will help you come up with the money for Graciela. But for two children you found on the street? Whom you don't even know? Absolutely not. Darling, they are not your responsibility!"

Camille wants to scream at her mother, but she restrains herself. She has to somehow get her to agree to loan her the money. "Mom, please just listen to me for a minute. I have to help these kids. This situation is *not* their fault! They've been through so much already. All I want to do is reunite them with their mother. If I don't help them, who knows what will to happen to them."

There is silence on the other end, so Camille keeps talking.

"Mom, if you do this for me, I promise I will never ask you for anything ever again. Please. It would mean so much to me if you would help me this one time. And I swear, I will pay you back every penny."

No answer.

"Mom——are you there?"

"Yes, I'm here."

"Will you do it? Will you loan me the money?"

Her mother lets out a long sigh. "Oh, I suppose."

Camille wants to jump up and down, but she's afraid the balcony might collapse under her feet. She pumps her fist in the air instead.

"But Camille, what really concerns me are these smugglers—they've got to be a dangerous sort. In fact, the whole affair just seems incredibly risky. Isn't there some other way?"

"No, Mom. This is our only option. Unless you want to come down here and hide the three of them in the trunk of your Mercedes—and I don't think that's a feasible solution."

"Maybe not, but it would be a lot less expensive."

Camille is dizzy with relief. "I can't thank you enough for this. Would you be able to meet me in LA sometime tomorrow and bring me the money?"

"Will these smugglers take a personal check, or do I need to get a cashier's check?"

Unbelievable. "It has to be cash."

Her mother snorts loudly. "I'm only making a joke, Camille. I'm not that dumb. All right, darling. I'll see you tomorrow. Please be careful. Don't go and do anything stupid."

She sighs. "I think it's a little late for that."

By seven the next morning, the four of them are dressed and ready to go. Not wanting to leave the room in case the *coyotes* show up, they nibble on some of the leftover chips and cookies from the day before, washing them down with bottles of lukewarm Coke Graciela has brought up from the hotel lobby.

Around eight o'clock, there is a quiet rap on the door. Graciela lets two people, a man and a woman who both look to be in their midthirties, into the room. They don't smile or shake Camille's hand; instead, they thoroughly inspect the room, like they're anticipating an ambush. The woman even looks in the bathroom and checks the closet. Her dark coffee eyes, rimmed in heavy black eyeliner, stare at Camille with suspicion. Camille half expects the woman to frisk her.

Camille angles her head toward Graciela and whispers in jest, "I think she forgot to check under the bed."

The woman scowls. "Hey—you want our help or not?" she says in perfect English. "You think this is some game? We don't know you. All we know, you could be some *gabacha* cop who works undercover for *la migra*. How are we supposed to know? The only reason we're here is because this girl's uncle"—she points to Graciela—"is somehow related to my brother-in-law. We barely know any of them. We're just doing this as a favor."

A very expensive favor, Camille almost blurts out. "I'm sorry," she says instead. "I tend to make jokes when I'm nervous."

The woman glares at Camille. "Watch what you say, then."

Camille nods her head a little too enthusiastically. "I know, I know. I'm so sorry."

"Are these the kids?" the woman asks, glancing impassively at the children, who are sitting quietly on the edge of the bed.

"Yes. This is Alicia and her brother, Alejandro."

The woman doesn't smile or even acknowledge them. She goes on to explain that Camille probably won't hear from them for at least a day or two, depending on how the crossing goes. As soon as Graciela and the children arrive in Los Angeles, she'll call and let Camille know where to pick them up.

"You know it's going to cost thirteen thousand dollars for each one," she says, giving Camille a long, hard look.

"Yes, I realize that."

She acts surprised, almost as if she expected Camille to bargain with her. Placing her hands on her hips, she nods in the direction of Graciela and the two children. "If you don't have all the money with you when you pick them up, we'll bring them right back here to Tijuana. So don't try anything."

"Don't worry. I promise I'll pay you the entire amount."

"You better." The woman nods to the man, indicating it's time for them to leave.

"Wait," Camille says. "Before you go, I have a question. What if something happens and they get caught at the border?"

"We'll call you." She holds out her cell phone. "Put your number in here."

Camille inputs the numbers slowly, making sure to not make

any errors. She feels sick to her stomach. She's purposely handing Graciela and the children over to two people she knows absolutely nothing about. Graciela takes the two children by their hands and moves toward the door. Before she can stop herself, Camille's eyes fill with tears.

Without thinking, Camille grabs the woman's hand. "Please take care of them," she begs, desperation in her voice. "Please don't let them get hurt." The two children see Camille crying and begin to wail in solidarity.

She expects the woman to snatch her hand away in disgust, but instead she does something quite unexpected. She warmly squeezes Camille's hand, then turns to the children and speaks calmly to them in Spanish. They stop crying, and she says to Camille in a reassuring tone, "Everything is going to be okay. I promise nothing bad will happen to them." She lets go of Camille's hand and slides her finger across the screen of her phone. "What's your name?"

The heaviness in Camille's chest recedes just enough for her to take a shallow breath.

"My name is Camille," she says. "But you can call me *Camila*."

CHAPTER 37

Crossing the border from Tijuana into San Diego turns out to be much easier for Camille than she expected. Just another perk of being an American citizen with light skin. Camille waits for the immigration officer to grill her as to why she's been in Mexico, but he only casts a cursory glance at her passport and asks her if she has anything to declare. She tells him no. Without even looking up, he waves her through the gate like a bored policeman directing traffic.

In San Diego, she rents a car and heads north on the 5 Freeway toward Los Angeles. Pressing the radio's scan button, she searches for some classical music. It lands on a Spanish-language station playing a romantic ballad sung by a man with a velvety, soulful voice. Camille can't understand all the words, but she knows he's singing about heartbreak because the word *corazón* is included in almost every line. She reaches over to change the station but instead turns the volume up full blast. As the music builds, the ache in her own heart swells. She can barely see out the windshield because she's crying so hard. When the singer reaches the final cadence, Camille realizes that what she had with Alejandro is over too. They had their authentic cadence in Yalálag, and now there's no more music to come. She turns off the radio and drives on in despairing silence.

Two hours later, she spots the Los Angeles skyline rising up out of the desert basin like an array of crystal decanters set on a tray. She follows the GPS's directions to the downtown Ritz Carlton, where her mother has booked a room and will meet Camille later this afternoon.

As she pulls up to the valet, Camille can't help but think about the opulence of this hotel—how the price of staying here for one night would probably feed a family in Yalálag for a good three months.

Walking through the pristine lobby, she feels oddly out of place, like she no longer fits into this world of privileged luxury. At the moment, of course, she doesn't—she's a disheveled mess. Her eyes are red, her clothes are wrinkled, and her hair is a tangled, unkempt mop. As she approaches the front desk, the concierge eyes her with suspicion. Camille slings her backpack across her shoulder, lifts up her chin, and smiles with false bravado.

It is obvious the concierge has a superiority complex. Impeccably dressed in a navy Ralph Lauren suit, white shirt, and red silk tie, he places his manicured hands on the counter in a pretentious manner. "May I help you, miss?" His tone suggests that the last thing he wants to do is help her with anything.

"I'm here to check in."

Pursing his lips, he cocks his head to one side. "Do you have a reservation?"

"Uh, yes. It should be under my mother's name." She begins to babble, feeling obligated to explain herself. "You see, I've been out of the country for a week trying to track someone down in Mexico. Thank goodness I found her too. But everything that could go wrong, went wrong. I was in this horrific storm where our bus went off the cliff, and I was stuck in this small village in the mountains. Now I have to wait for this person to get to LA, and I have no idea how long it's going to take. Anyway, my mother is supposed to have called to make the reservation for the room so we have a place to stay while we wait. "

"Name?" he asks.

"Her name? Well, her name is Graciela, but I don't see why you'd need to know her name . . ."

The roll of his eyes is almost imperceptible. "Under what name is the *reservation?*"

"Oh! Of course. Sorry. The reservation should be under the name Nanette Childs."

He quickly looks up. "Mrs. Childs, you say? Why, I know that name. I believe Mrs. Childs stays here quite often."

"Yes, she likes this hotel."

"She's your mother? Hmm . . ." He blinks twice, as if he's skeptical of her story, and turns his attention to the computer screen, his fingers clicking away on the keyboard like he's practicing his staccato technique. "Ah, here it is," he says after a moment, sounding surprised. He raises his eyebrows in a failed attempt to appear sincere. "I'm afraid I'll need to ask you for some form of identification before I can allow you access to the room. Just for the sake of security. I'm sure you understand."

His request is not unreasonable, but his supercilious attitude is getting on Camille's nerves. "Of course," she says. She hoists her still-dirty backpack up onto the ledge so that bits of fine dirt crumble off onto the burnished counter. He quickly pulls a folded handkerchief out of the inside pocket of his jacket and wipes the counter like a persnickety librarian dusting bookshelves. He takes her license and holds it gingerly between his two fingers.

"I'm terribly sorry," he says, looking back and forth between

Camille's face and the photo on the license, "but this likeness doesn't resemble you in the least. Might you have any additional forms of identification?"

Now it's Camille's turn to roll her eyes. *What is this jerk's problem?* She knows she's not looking her best after having traveled all the way from Oaxaca, but this guy has gone too far.

She hands over her American Express Gold Card. "Maybe you'd feel better if I just went ahead and paid for the room with my own card? Or if you have a razor blade handy, perhaps you'd prefer I sign something in blood?"

He looks at Camille in horror before realizing she's being facetious. "That's not necessary, Miss Childs," he says, handing her card back with a phony smile. "The reservation has been secured with your mother's credit card. Let me just call the bellhop to take you up to your room."

"No, thank you. I've just got the one bag," she says, slapping her hand against the side of her backpack with enough force to cover him in another fine spray of dried mud. "I think I can manage."

Camille takes the elevator up to the twentieth floor, where she lets herself into a stark but sleekly decorated room in soft gray tones with a spectacular view that looks out over all of West Los Angeles. After taking a twenty-minute shower, during which she washes her hair with a luxurious coconut-scented shampoo, she wraps herself in the soft hotel robe and gets comfortable on the couch. She shouldn't expect to hear anything from the *coyotes* so soon, but she checks her phone anyway. No missed calls.

She hasn't eaten since early that morning; she picks up the hotel phone and orders room service. A scant thirty minutes later, a gourmet lunch of poached salmon with lemon-caper herb sauce, scalloped potatoes, and crisply steamed green beans arrives at her door.

After three bites, she loses her appetite and covers the food back up with its metal dome. She suddenly longs for a bowl of steaming *caldo de pollo* and a crispy homemade tortilla.

Her cell phone rings; the screen shows an unfamiliar number. An instant shot of adrenaline moves through her body. Could it be the *coyotes* calling?

"Hello?" she says, her voice tight.

"Camille, *how are you?*" She immediately recognizes the pseudo-Russian accent: *Sofia Vanilla Bitch.*

Sofia is the last person Camille wants to talk to right now. "Hello, Sofia. How did you get this number?"

"Well," she says, her nasal voice grating, "I ran into one of your piano students. She said you've been out of the country. As no one has seen or heard from you for over a week, I talked her into giving me your cell number. It's not like I didn't try calling your home number first. I did—multiple times, at that. But no one bothered returning my calls. I even stopped by, but no one was home. It was almost as if you had disappeared off the face of the earth. I was beginning to get concerned."

Sure you were.

"Anyway," Sofia prattles on, "I was just wondering how things are going with you. Has Graciela been working hard on her concerto? I'm so looking forward to hearing her perform the Rach II with the Philharmonic next Saturday. I must say, it was such a surprise for everyone when they announced that she had won the grand prize. I don't think anyone had a clue that she could possibly win."

What a bitch. Camille imagines her hands reaching in through the phone, coming out the other side, and grabbing Sofia's skinny, birdlike neck in a tight squeeze.

"Now, Camille, you are aware the rehearsal with the LA Phil is this coming Thursday, right?"

"Of course I am, Sofia. Graciela is more than prepared for both the rehearsal and the concert. We'll be there."

There is a brief silence on the other end. "I hope that you would tell me if there's anything amiss. If there is, maybe I could help you in some way."

"Why would I need your help, Sofia?"

"Well, my cleaning woman knows someone who knows Graciela's family. She said something about you taking a trip to Mexico to look for Graciela? I thought perhaps Graciela had gone there and had some trouble getting back in or something."

Camille's skin prickles. "Sofia, I have absolutely no idea what you're talking about. There's nothing going on. Graciela and I will both be there at the rehearsal on Thursday. Now if you'll excuse me, I've really got to go. There's someone at the door."

"Camille, *wait.* I——"

Camille hangs up the phone just as her mother lets herself into the room.

"Who were you talking to?" her mother asks, slightly out of breath. She drops her white leather Louis Vuitton bag on the chair by the door and leans a bulky briefcase against the wall. "Was that the smugglers? Have they made it across already?"

"No, Mom. It was just Sofia."

Removing her pale lilac suit jacket, her mother scowls. "That Vanilla Bitch is relentless. I think she might be on to us, Camille. She's not going to leave us alone until she sees Graciela with her own two eyes. We may have a problem on our hands." She walks over to the couch, sits down, and puts her hands on either side of Camille's face. "Oh, my dear, I must say, it is *such* a relief to see you."

Her hands are cool and smell of expensive, flowery lotion. Camille's throat begins to close.

She studies Camille's face. "Good god, Camille, you look terrible. Your eyes are all puffy! Your skin is peeling. And I've never seen so many freckles on your face. For God's sake—didn't you wear sunscreen? I distinctly remember telling you to take my sun hat with you, and then you got mad at me for suggesting it! I guess it serves you right for not listening to me."

Camille is so dejected that she can't even come up with a snarky response.

"What's wrong, darling? You're so quiet. Did something happen to you while you were *down there?*"

Camille opens her mouth to tell her mother that she's fine and that she has everything under control. Without her meaning them to, her arms fly out and reach around her mother's frail shoulders. Unable to stop herself, she falls with all of her weight into her mother's perfumed neck.

"No, Mommy. I'm not all right," she says, bursting once again into tears. "I'm a complete and utter mess."

CHAPTER 38

Camille clings to her mother like a little girl who's just been found after wandering off alone in the department store. Her mother holds her stiffly, noticeably uncomfortable in the role of nurturer. "That's enough now, Camille," she says, disentangling herself from her daughter's embrace. "You're getting my blouse all wet."

Camille pulls away. "Geez, Mom. Don't go out of your way to be supportive or anything."

"Oh, hush, Camille. You know I'm not interested in all that mushy stuff." She primly crosses her legs and leans forward. "What I *am* interested in is hearing all about what happened to you in Mexico. Go on, now. Tell me everything!"

Wiping her nose on the sleeve of her robe, Camille hiccups once before launching into her story. Her mother listens raptly as Camille recounts the past week in Oaxaca: The torrential rain in the mountains. Tía Nifa's unexpected kindness. How Alejandro pulled Camille off the bus and then threw her into the mud. How the mudslide pushed their bus right off the road, forcing them to walk through the mountains, sleep on the ground at the ranch, and ride in the back of a pickup truck loaded with chickens. About Alejandro, and how they finally made it to Yalálag, only to find that Graciela wasn't even there. She describes her fight with Alejandro and how he accused Camille of being self-serving. How she was so angry that she got drunk on mezcal.

Her mother's eyes almost bulge out of her head. "You got drunk on tequila? Good Lord, Camille, I'm shocked! And, I may add, a bit disappointed. I can't believe I missed out on witnessing *that* milestone in your life." She chuckles under her breath. "Now that's something I would've enjoyed seeing for myself."

Camille is perplexed that her mother seems more excited that she got drunk for the first time than she is by the fact that she almost died in a mudslide. Her gleeful reaction delivers that familiar rush of irritation through Camille's body. "You can just wipe that smirk off your face," she snaps, "because getting drunk was a one-time thing for me. It's never going to happen again."

Her mother's eyes twinkle. "*Never say never*, Camille."

"Mother, listen to me. I guarantee you, there is absolutely no chance that I will get drunk—on mezcal or anything else—ever again. Once was enough. Unlike you, I'm not a *lush*."

Camille immediately wants to take the words back. "Wait. I'm sorry. That was really unkind of me."

Her mother sighs and massages her forehead with her fingers. "Well, perhaps a bit unkind, but certainly not untrue. God knows I've hardly set a good example for you over the years." She reaches over and pats Camille's leg. "But I do hope there's still time for me to redeem myself in your eyes. Now, go on with your story."

Camille holds nothing back: She tells her mother all about the altercation with Little Chuy, and how she threw up all over him after he got rough with her. How Alejandro found her and they danced together. She even tells her how they spent the night together in Tía Nifa's bed while the storm raged outside.

This last part is finally enough to rattle her mother. "What? You slept with him? After knowing him for only two days? I'm not sure that was a good idea."

Camille's face crumples. "Whether or not it was a good idea doesn't matter now. It's over."

"Oh, dear. What happened, darling?"

"Only the worst possible thing," Camille says, hating that she sounds like a heartbroken teenager. "There I was, stuck in this isolated village high up in the mountains of Oaxaca, and even though I tried to fight them, the feelings I had toward Alejandro kept growing more intense. Not only is he handsome, he's also smart. He graduated from Cal Poly in San Luis Obispo and owns his own landscaping business. He's fluent in Spanish and English. He even speaks a Zapotec dialect. At first I couldn't stand the guy. Then, as I spent more time with him, I found I was really beginning to like him. Maybe even more than just like him."

"So what went wrong?"

"Well, listen to this: *After* our night together, Alejandro admitted to me that he knows Graciela. She's his niece, for God's sake! He *knew* she and María were in Oaxaca the whole time, and he never told me. Not only that, he was planning on keeping me away from Graciela for as long as possible."

Her mother sits up straighter. "Graciela is Alejandro's niece?"

"I know, right? Can you believe that?" Camille runs a quick hand through her damp hair. "Graciela's uncle Victor actually asked Alejandro to keep an eye on me to prevent me from finding her. He didn't want me to talk her into coming back home. Alejandro let me climb aboard that bus knowing the whole time that Graciela was right there under my nose in Oaxaca City. I keep thinking that I never should've been on that bus in the first place. I could've died in that accident. No matter what feelings I have for Alejandro, that kind of betrayal is unforgivable."

"Camille . . . I very much doubt this Alejandro fellow could've known there would be such a huge storm. Let alone a mudslide. Did he explain to you why he didn't tell you where Graciela was?"

"He said it was because he didn't know what my motives were. He said that with María being so ill, he needed to protect Graciela. He didn't want her to be pushed into doing something she didn't want to do."

"Well, that sounds reasonable to me."

"What do you mean?"

Her mother sighs. "I know firsthand what happens when you push someone into doing something they don't want to do. Perhaps he only wanted to protect his niece—wanted Graciela to make up her own mind about what *she* wanted. If that's the case . . ."

Camille stares at her in disbelief. "Mom, whose side are you on?"

"Well, of course I'm on your side, darling. I just think you should look at it from Alejandro's point of view as well."

"But he flat-out lied to me!"

She shrugs. "So he lied to you. Big deal. People lie all the time. It's part of life." She stares at Camille without blinking. "Sometimes people lie, and there are life-changing consequences."

A wave of shame moves through Camille. "Why don't you just come right out and say it, Mom? It's obvious you're referring to how I lied to you about Jack. You're insinuating—"

"I'm not insinuating anything, darling." Her mother waves her hand in the air, then places it on her chest. "You know, I've also got to take responsibility for what happened all those years ago. I'm to blame as well. I tried to control you and ended up pushing you right into the arms of that horrible man. And even though he ruined your career, he did *not* ruin your life."

They sit in silence for a moment.

"I wish I could go back and do it all again," Camille whispers. "I wouldn't make the same mistakes this time."

"I wish you could, too, darling. But, as life would have it, we can't go back. Things don't always happen the way we want. But we can learn from them and move on. Yes, Alejandro lied to you.

But if he hadn't lied, you never would have climbed aboard that bus. And then you never would have had that incredible adventure, now would you?" She takes Camille's hands in hers. "Tell me the truth. Does the fact that he lied really change how you feel about him?"

Camille bites her lower lip and says nothing.

"Well," her mother says, squeezing Camille's hands, "That's what I thought. In fact, I knew from the moment I walked into this hotel room that there was something different about you. Even with that mopey face and those swollen eyes, you're blooming like a newly opened rose. You may think you're more miserable than you've ever been, but in my opinion, you've never looked happier." She leans forward and places her hands on Camille's knees. "So you say this Alejandro has a landscaping business? Hmm. Do you think if you tell him I'm your mother, he'll give me a deal on redoing my garden?"

They spend the afternoon watching an old black-and-white movie on television. Too nervous to eat much, they nibble on snacks from the hotel minibar. Camille's anxiety grows as each hour passes without word from the *coyotes*. Her mother is antsy too. Camille keeps expecting her to open one of the miniature bottles of white wine in the mini-fridge, but she sticks to plain mineral water.

By four o'clock, there's still no call from the *coyotes*.

"Camille, I can't wait around here any longer," her mother says, putting on her linen jacket. "I've got to get back to Santa Barbara. I have tickets to the symphony tonight, and I just know the freeway is going to be jammed." She pulls a lipstick out of her purse and stands in front of the mirror, expertly applying a layer of soft pink to her lips.

For the first time ever, Camille doesn't want her mother to

leave. "Do you really have to go, Mom? Couldn't you just skip the concert this time?"

Her mother picks up her purse and holds it under her arm. She has a distasteful look on her face. "Well, I'd certainly prefer to avoid it, especially seeing as tonight's program is all contemporary music. You'd think they could throw in some Beethoven or Mahler, but it's all going to be this hideous dissonant stuff. Not only that, the soloist is some curly-haired millennial violinist from Seattle. Can you believe this guy prefers to wear a ghoulish black turtleneck instead of a tuxedo? He moves around on stage like a crazed poodle in heat." She shakes her head. "He's set to perform this Philip Glass concerto. I'm sorry, but this minimalist stuff makes me think of the soundtrack to some European car commercial. Honestly, what was the conductor thinking? I'm telling you, Camille. Sitting through that will be more painful than getting my mustache waxed."

"Then don't go," Camille says. "Stay here with me while I wait for Graciela."

Her mother purses her lips. "I wish I could. But you of all people know that I don't go to these concerts for the music. I go there to be seen—to *schmooze*. As a Bella Vista board member, I have to nurture my relationships with these wealthy music patrons so they're more inclined to open up their wallets and support the arts. If I don't show up tonight, people will wonder where I am, especially that *Vanilla Bitch*. We have to make sure she doesn't figure out that Graciela is here in this country without permission."

She picks up the briefcase and places it on the coffee table. "Here's the money you asked for. The combination to the briefcase is my birthday. Now you be careful, Camille. That's an awful lot of cash. People will do crazy things for that kind of money."

Camille stands up and tightens the sash of her robe. "Mom, thank you so much for doing this. I'll repay you as soon as I can, I promise. With interest."

Her mother checks her hair in the mirror. "Don't worry about it, darling. My interest payment will be the exquisite pleasure I'll experience seeing Vanilla Bitch's face at the concert when she watches Graciela walk out on that stage. That alone will be worth loaning you all that money."

CHAPTER 39

The buzzing of Camille's cell phone yanks her out of a fitful sleep. She squints at the screen—*No Caller ID*.

"Hello?" she says, her mouth dry.

"*Camila?*" It's a man with a heavy Mexican accent.

For a split second, Camille thinks it's Alejandro. Her heart begins to race. Still groggy, she sits up in bed. "Yes—yes," she says. "This is Camila."

"*¿Ya tienes el dinero?*"

"*What?* Who is this?"

"You got the money to pay for the girl and the two kids?"

"Oh! You're calling about Graciela! Is she here already?"

"*Sí.* We got her and the two little kids. You got the money?"

Sweet relief spreads throughout Camille's body. Graciela has made it over the border. She's *here*! And it only took one day. *Finally, my luck is changing!*

"Yes," she practically shouts, giddy with excitement, "I have the money! Of course I have it. Where do I go to pick them up?"

He coughs loudly into the phone. "You know where is Pico and Vermont?"

"I can find it."

"There is restaurant on corner there called *El Pequeño Oaxaqueño.*

You go to alley behind the restaurant. In the back. You come alone and bring the money. Be there at seven."

Camille squints at the numbers on the clock and sees that it's 5:38 a.m. "Okay. I'll be there. But what if I can't find you—"

He hangs up the phone without answering.

Camille leaps out of bed and throws on her clothes. She quickly brushes her teeth and pulls her hair into a messy ponytail before grabbing her cell phone and the briefcase and heading out the door. With the morning rush hour, she's bound to hit traffic.

Camille is surprised to find there are hardly any cars in sight on the freeway. *Oh, right—today is Sunday.* Since leaving for Oaxaca almost a week ago, she's lost all track of time. She reaches the intersection of Pico and Vermont in less than ten minutes. The neighborhood is on the run-down side, filled with shabby-looking storefronts locked up with security gates. With all the signs in Spanish, it's almost as if she never left Oaxaca.

She parks a block up from the restaurant and checks her phone. She's forty-five minutes early. She cracks her window, and a waft of warm, sugary air slides in through the opening. Her stomach growls. A few doors down there is a Mexican *panadería.* The lights are on, and a placard in the window says *"Abierto."* She could use a hot cup of coffee right now.

She gets out of the car, holding the bulky briefcase tight against her body, and scans the street to see if anyone is watching her. Satisfied that no one's around, she hurries to the shop door and walks in.

The inside of the bakery is cozy, painted a bright coral color and decorated with dozens of framed photographs on the walls. A glass case packed with an array of delicious-looking breads and pastries runs along one side of the narrow room. Behind the counter, a stocky, middle-aged woman with a black braid streaked with white is busy filling the coffee maker. Covering her dress is a familiar-looking light-blue plaid apron. With her round face, almond-shaped eyes, and high cheekbones, she looks as if she's just stepped right off the cobblestone streets of Yalálag.

"I help you, miss?" the woman asks, probably wondering what this redheaded white woman is doing in her bakery at dawn on a Sunday morning.

Camille points to a corkscrew pastry dusted with cinnamon sugar. "This one, please. And a cup of coffee." She looks around and notices a man sitting nearby dipping a piece of bread covered in toasted seeds into a small bowl of hot chocolate.

"Wait a minute." She gestures toward the man. "I've changed my mind. I think I'd like some of that hot chocolate instead. And I'll have a piece of bread like that as well."

"*¿Pan de Yalálag?*" the woman asks.

Camille nods, and stands and watches the woman as she ladles thick hot chocolate from a blue enamelware pot into a glazed bowl. She cradles the cup with her fingers on the bottom and her thumb hooked over the rim, holding it with the ease of a mother about to rinse her baby's head in the bath. After setting the bowl on the counter, she dips a *molinillo* into the chocolate and spins it between her palms. A frothy layer of foam threatens to spill over the sides. Camille is immediately transported back to the *comedor* in Yalálag. The pain in her chest is so swift that she has to turn away.

On the wall behind the counter there is a large black-and-white photograph of a mountainous village with a familiar-looking church in the center. Goose bumps prickle up and down Camille's arms when she recognizes the place where, less than two days ago, she prayed to San Antonio.

Camille points to the photograph. "I know that place," she tells the woman. "I was just there."

The woman looks at Camille with skepticism.

"No, really," Camille insists, "I just came back from Yalálag. I visited that very church." For whatever reason, Camille needs this woman to believe her—to somehow acknowledge that they are connected to each other in this small way.

The woman comes out from behind the counter and places the bread and hot chocolate on a small table. "Is true you really go to Yalálag?"

Camille nods enthusiastically. "Yes, I was really there."

The woman's face lights up. "That is the town where I from. Is beautiful place, no?"

Camille smiles. "Yes, it is."

"You go to the *Fiesta de San Antonio?*" she asks.

"Yes! I ate *mole* and watched the dancing and everything. It was wonderful."

The woman's eyes twinkle. "*Ay, que bueno. La Fiesta de San Antonio* is very good party. Lot of dancing." She walks back around the other side of the counter. As an afterthought, she turns around and says, "Is good you not get stuck in that big storm, no? When the bus go off the road and the mountain come down. That was very terrible accident. You lucky you not on that bus."

A sardonic laugh almost escapes Camille's mouth. She tears off a piece of bread, dunks it into the bowl, and pops it into her mouth. She savors the rich chocolate flavor. "Oh, yes," she tells the woman, "you could say I'm *extremely* lucky."

The bell rings above the door. The woman in the apron nods toward Camille. "*Con permiso,*" she says, moving away and turning her attention to a short, stocky man who has just entered the bakery. She greets him in what sounds like Zapotec.

Camille finishes her chocolate and bread before checking her watch. She has ten minutes before she's due to meet the *coyotes*. She places a five-dollar bill under the empty bowl, picks up the briefcase, and heads toward the door. *"Muchas gracias,"* she calls out to the woman, but she has gone into the back of the bakery.

Near the door, there is photograph hanging on the wall that she didn't notice before. A dark-haired young woman wearing an elaborate turquoise gown stares solemnly into the camera. Her lips are painted a deep burgundy, and a silver tiara is perched atop a cascade of black ringlets.

Her face is so familiar. Peering closer, Camille reads the inscription at the bottom of the photograph, where *"Mi quinceañera"* is written in looping calligraphy. Underneath that is a name: *ARACELI*.

A chill travels down her spine. *Araceli.* Of course. The girl in the photograph is Alejandro's dead wife. The woman behind the counter must be Araceli's mother. Camille takes a deep breath. There must be dozens of Mexican bakeries in this part of town. How is it she had to choose this one?

She opens the door to make her escape, but not before looking up and examining the wall of photographs one last time. At the top, to the left, she sees it: an eight-by-ten color photograph of Alejandro and Araceli standing together in front of the red gingerbread church in Yalálag. They are dressed in what Camille assumes are the traditional wedding clothes of their village. Alejandro is wearing a white shirt and pants, and Araceli has on an embroidered *huipil* and a black headdress. They both have on handmade leather huaraches.

The temperature inside the bakery suddenly rises twenty degrees. Camille begins to feel faint. She rushes out onto the sidewalk, sits down on top of the briefcase, and puts her head between her knees.

After a minute or so, the dizziness recedes. She stands up slowly, clutching the briefcase against her body as if she's cradling a sleeping baby. She looks up at the front of the bakery. Written in bold red letters are the words *Panadería Yalalteca*.

The irony is not lost on her. Here she is, thousands of miles away from Yalálag, yet she still can't escape from Alejandro.

CHAPTER 40

Other than a scraggly-haired mop propped up against the back door like a wallflower waiting for a dance, there is no one behind the restaurant. The low early-morning clouds have yet to burn off, and Camille waits uneasily in the damp air. *Where are they?* She checks her phone again and sees that it's almost seven fifteen. Perhaps she misunderstood the man on the phone. Maybe she's waiting in the wrong place.

Camille heads toward the front of the building to see if there's anyone inside the restaurant. Suddenly, two slicked-up sedans with fancy silver rims race in from both directions. They park diagonally across the alley, like trained soldiers executing some sort of covert operation. Six men, all of them with shaved heads and tattooed bodies, leap out of the cars. They form a constricted circle around Camille.

A stocky man of about forty with a potbelly, a handlebar mustache, and baggy khakis approaches her. He is so short his head only comes up to Camille's chin.

"You Camila?" he asks.

"Yes," she croaks. A copious amount of saliva fills her mouth; she swallows it down. She glances around for Graciela and the two children but doesn't see them.

"Where are they?" Camille whispers. Maybe these guys don't have Graciela and the kids after all. Maybe this is a setup to abscond with her forty thousand dollars.

His eyes move to the briefcase under her arm. "You got the money?"

"Yes." She holds tightly to the briefcase. "It's right here. But first I need you to tell me where they are."

"They're close," he says, coolly scanning the alleyway. "Soon as we see the money is all there, we're gonna bring them to you."

Reluctantly, Camille punches in the combination. The sound of the lock clicking open echoes against the buildings like a gunshot. Camille hands him the briefcase, and he passes it to another man, who takes it into one of the cars to count it. The rest of the men stand in formation around Camille, leaning back on their heels and glaring at her. Their menacing reticence makes her so uncomfortable that she feels compelled to break the silence.

She crosses her arms in front of her chest. "So, uh . . . are any of you guys from around here?" As soon as the words leave her mouth, she regrets how stupid she sounds.

One of them rolls his eyes and laughs with disdain. "You wanna know if we from around here? Hell, no—we ain't from this shitty neighborhood." He slaps his chest with the flat of his hand. "Don't you recognize me? I'm one of those famous movie stars that lives in a big mansion in Beverly Hills. My boys here— Shorty and Beto—they're big shot music producers. They live in Bel Air. We just do this kind of work on the side so we can hang out with our homies."

He points to a skinny, sleepy-eyed boy of about eighteen. "And Juanito lives in West Hollywood because he's a big *hoto*." The other men start to snicker.

"Shut up, man," Juanito says. "I don't live in West Hollywood."

Another one pipes up, "No, *ese*—remember? Juanito moved to

that beach house in Malibu with his *novio*. But he still comes back here to visit sometimes 'cause he can't get good tacos down there!"

As they hoot with laughter, Camille's face grows hot. The short guy with the mustache hurries over and puts up his hand.

"*Cállense, cabrones*," he says with authority. "Keep it down. You're gonna wake up the whole neighborhood." He glares at Camille. "You too. No talking."

She clamps her mouth shut.

A few minutes later, the man counting the money calls out from the car. "*Ya*, Paco, it's all here."

The taut circle around her loosens slightly. Paco takes a phone out of his pocket, turns away from Camille, and makes a call in Spanish. She strains to hear what he's saying, but his voice is too muffled for her to make out the words. He looks up at her and nods. "Okay, they're coming."

About five minutes later, the crunch of tires on the potholed alleyway breaks the ominous silence.

"They're here," Paco says. Two more cars park on either side of the alley with engines idling. A dark-haired woman with heavy makeup gets out of the car and helps two young children climb out of the back seat. When Alicia and Alejandro see Camille, they let go of the woman's hands and run over to her. She enfolds their tiny bodies under her arms.

"Where's Graciela?" Camille ask the woman, recognizing her as one of the *coyotes* who came to their hotel room in Tijuana.

"She's over there," the woman says, pointing down the alley. Camille turns to see a young, bald-headed man open the back door of a black car. Graciela steps out of the back seat and into the alleyway.

"Graciela!" Camille calls out. "Over here!"

Graciela grins at Camille and gives her a thumbs-up sign. Camille is so relieved to see her that she barely notices that the bald young man has turned around and is standing perfectly still, staring at her.

The sun peeks through the moving clouds, temporarily blinding her. The next thing she hears is a man shouting out across the alleyway, *"Hell, no!* I ain't handing nobody over to that white bitch!"

Camille instantly recognizes the voice. *No, no, no! This can't be happening.* She feels paralyzed; the horror seems to unfold in front of her in slow motion. She watches as Little Chuy roughly shoves Graciela into the back seat of the car and slams the door.

"NO!" Camille screams, unable to run to the car because the two children are clinging to her sides. Terrified, she cries out to Paco, "Get her! Please get her!"

"¡Pinche Chuy cabrón!" Paco yells, running toward the car. Little Chuy is too fast for him; he jumps into the driver's seat, guns the accelerator, and reverses back through the alley before screeching out onto Pico Boulevard. There is nothing left but a dissipating trail of car exhaust and the smell of burned rubber in the air.

"Oh, my god!" Camille screams. "Where's he taking her?"

"¡Vámanos!" Paco yells to the rest of the men, and they quickly climb back into the remaining cars. Over his shoulder he yells back at Camille, "You stay close. We'll call you."

"Stay close?" she cries. "But where—*here?"*

He doesn't answer her. The three remaining cars peel out of the alley. Camille is left standing alone with the two children.

Camille is not about to stay there in the deserted alley, but she has no idea where to go. Should she take them back to the hotel? Maybe she should call the police? No. If they find Graciela, she could be arrested and detained. Camille stamps her foot. *Crap!* She wishes Alejandro were here. If only Camille had his phone number, she could call him in Oaxaca. He'd know exactly what to do—

The bakery! The woman at the bakery—Araceli's mother—is bound to have Alejandro's phone number. Camille can go back

271

there and ask her to call Alejandro. She quickly takes the children's hands, practically dragging them up the street toward the bakery while trying to comfort them as best she can.

When they get inside the bakery she sits them down at a table and mimes for them to stay put. The bakery is empty and there is no one behind the counter. "Hello?" Camille shouts. "Is anyone here?"

A voice calls out from the back—"*Momentito, por favor.*" Araceli's mother comes out and gives Camille a warm smile. "You back. You need something else?"

Camille tries to catch her breath. "Do you know Alejandro Chimil?"

She gives Camille a funny look. "*Sí,*" she says. "I know him."

Camille's hands are shaking. "I need you to call him right now. Please. I need to talk to him *right now.*"

"Okay." The woman plucks a cell phone from out of her apron pocket, presses a button, and begins speaking rapid Zapotec into the phone. With a surprised look on her face, she hands the phone over to Camille.

"Alejandro?" Camille gasps.

"Camila, what's going on? What are you doing at the bakery?"

"Oh, my god, Alejandro. Something terrible has just happened." She begins to cry, barely able to choke out the words as she explains how Little Chuy has kidnapped Graciela.

"Stay right there, Camila," he says. "I'm coming right now."

"Right now? But wait—you mean you're here in LA? I thought you were still in Oaxaca!"

"I decided to come back early. Now, don't go anywhere. I'll be there in a few minutes."

Camille hands the phone back to the woman and falls limply into a chair. She is drunk with sweet relief. *Alejandro is here.* He'll know what to do. He can fix this mess.

In the meantime, Araceli's mother has brought out donuts and hot chocolate for the children. Both of them sport foamy mustaches, and their chins are dusted with powdered sugar. Oblivious to the drama going on around them, they happily gorge themselves on the sweet treats. Araceli's mother briefly places her hand on Camille's shoulder. "Is okay, señorita. Don't worry. Alejandro is good man. He will help you."

Exactly eight minutes later, the bell above the door jangles with the sweetest-sounding music Camille has ever heard—and in rushes Alejandro.

CHAPTER 41

Camille runs over to Alejandro and flings her arms around him.

"I really messed up this time," she says, her voice catching. "I'll never be able to forgive myself if something bad happens to Graciela."

The smell of him—a woodsy aftershave mixed with the scent of fabric softener instantly soothes her. "It's all right, Camila," he says, his breath warm against her neck. "We'll find her. I've already talked to Victor. He's in contact with Paco, and they're out there looking for her right now."

She pulls away and looks him in the eyes. "But what if Little Chuy hurts Graciela? He hates me so much that he might do something to her to get back at me." She quickly tells him the story of how Little Chuy chased after the bus and threatened to kill her.

He presses his lips together. "I knew this guy was going to cause some trouble. I never thought he'd do something like this, though. Maybe he's just trying to prove that he's in control. *Damn.* I wish I'd taken care of him when we were in Yalálag."

"I'm so sorry, Alejandro. I really screwed everything up."

"Camila, this isn't your fault. We've used these *coyotes* many times to get people across. This has never happened before. I don't think any of them realized how crazy this Chuy guy is."

He walks over to the table where the two children are busy coloring on the back of a paper bag with a red ballpoint pen. "So," he says, smiling, "Victor mentioned to me that you've made a couple of new friends. Are these the two *chamaquitos* you've been hanging around with?"

Camille gently places a hand on each of their heads. "Alejandro, meet Alicia and *Alejandro*."

He raises his eyebrows. "*Ay*, Camila, you've had your hands full of Alejandros lately, haven't you?" He greets the children in Spanish and then turns back to Camille. "They seem to be okay. You should probably give their mother a call to let her know that her kids are safe. Do you have her number?"

Camille picks up her cell phone, locates the number, and hands the phone to Alejandro. "Will you talk to her? Her name is Luz."

He makes the call. When he's finished, he sits down next to Camille at the table. "She's on her way. I'll wait until she gets here, and then I'm going out to look for Graciela."

"I want to go with you," she says.

"No, Camila, it's too dangerous."

"But I want to help!"

"I don't think it would be good for Graciela if Little Chuy sees you."

"Oh, right." Her frustration subsides. "That makes sense. Should I wait for you here in the bakery, then?"

"My house is only a few minutes away. You can stay there until we get Graciela back." He places his hands on the table, his face serious. "I need to tell you again how sorry I am for not being honest with you. I feel terrible about it."

She covers his hands with hers. Together, they're like *café con leche*—coffee and milk. "I know you do, Alejandro. I'm not mad.

I understand why you did it. You were trying to protect Graciela. And . . . I'm to blame as well. I never should've run off like that. I should've given you time to explain yourself further."

He begins to massage her hands with such gentle intensity that she closes her eyes. "You know, I did come after you. But by the time I got down to the square, the bus had already left."

She opens her eyes. "You did? I was waiting for you to show up. What happened?"

"I had to take my tía to the clinic. Right after you left, she started having heart palpitations."

Camille covers her mouth with her hand. "Oh, no! What happened? Is she all right?"

"She's fine. It turned out to be an anxiety attack. She was really upset that we were fighting. When I told her I was going to go find you, she suddenly got better. But after you left, there were no more buses. I had to wait until the following afternoon. By the time I got back to Oaxaca City, María had checked out of the hospital. I got on the next plane to Los Angeles, thinking that's where you were headed. It was only after I landed here and talked to Victor that I found out you were in Tijuana helping Graciela cross." He reaches over and lightly caresses her cheek. "So I've just been waiting for you to show up."

The bell above the door jangles again. Camille glances over to see a band of petite women storm the bakery as if they're on a mission. They look like sisters, or possibly first cousins, all of them with short, curly hair, full lips, and round cheeks. Upon seeing the children, the one in front falls to her knees on the floor. *Luz*. She lets out a cry of such relief that it takes Camille's breath away.

"*Ay, mis hijos, mis hijos,*" she wails.

Alicia and Alejandro rush from the table and fly into her arms. The three of them rock back and forth together on the floor. Camille is so moved by the sight of their reunion that she chokes up.

Alejandro puts his arm around her shoulder and pulls her close.

"See what you did, Camila?" he whispers. "Now that's what I'd call generous. And worth all that money, wouldn't you say?"

Camille wipes her eyes with the palms of her hands and laughs. "This emotional drama has got to stop. And *soon*. I've cried so much over the past week I'm going to get dehydrated."

"You don't need to worry about that, Camila. You've been saving up those tears for a long time. I think you've barely used up your reserves."

Luz gets up off the floor and approaches Camille. "You are the lady who bring my children?"

"Yes," she says, reaching out her hand. "I'm Camila. I'm so happy to meet you, Luz."

Luz takes Camille's hand and begins to cry silently, the tears dripping off her chin like rivulets of rain sliding down a windowpane.

Camille pats her arm. "Please don't cry. I'm so happy I was able to help reunite you with your children."

"You are my angel," Luz says, reaching out and pulling Camille into a tight embrace. "I don't know what happen to my kids if you don't help them. I never forget you for this."

A woman hands Luz a padded manila envelope. Luz holds it out to Camille. "Here is four thousand dollars for my kids. I pay you the rest when I can."

Camille looks at Luz's thinning hair and the dark circles under her eyes. The constant struggle of poverty has worn her down and aged her beyond her years. She doesn't take the envelope. "No, Luz. I don't want it. You keep it. Use it for Alicia and Alejandro."

Luz stares at her, uncomprehending. She tries to force the envelope into Camille's hands. "No, señorita, please. Take the money. I no let you pay."

Camille shakes her head. "No. I don't want it. You've got your children to take care of now. You need it more than I do."

Luz looks ready to insist, but then her shoulders sag with relief. "Thank you, señorita. You are such good person to do this." She turns to her children and tells them something in Spanish. They rush to Camille's side and wrap their arms around her waist.

"*Gracias*," they say in unison.

Camille kisses the tops of their heads before releasing them back into the clutch of women, who surround them in a protective circle of love.

"*¡Adios!*" the children cry, turning around and waving one last time. Then they fly out of the bakery door and into their brand-new lives.

"They're going to be all right, aren't they?" Camille asks Alejandro.

He pulls her even closer to him. "I do believe they already are."

Camille follows Alejandro's truck in her rental car as they head west on Pico Boulevard toward his house. In a very short time the neighborhood changes from crowded inner city with old brick storefronts to quiet, palm tree–lined streets with classic Victorian and Craftsman homes. Some are sagging and in disrepair, but the majority of them appear to have been recently renovated, given their fresh paint, neatly trimmed lawns, and quaint flower gardens.

Alejandro pulls into the driveway of an obviously remodeled two-story Craftsman home. It's painted a dark gray and has a burgundy front door. The architectural design has such good bones that Camille thinks the house must be close to a hundred years old. There is a huge wraparound porch with a white wooden swing. A large bay window looks out over the front garden. Curving through the front lawn is a red brick path bordered by blue and purple delphinium.

Camille gets out of her car and stares at the property in awe. "This is your house?" she asks. "Seriously?"

"What?" he asks. "You weren't expecting a Mexican gardener to live in a house like this?"

She laughs. "Actually, to be honest, no. I was not expecting this at all. Your house is absolutely charming."

"Just like me." He unlocks the door. Although he's smiling, he can't hide the worry behind his eyes.

Graciela, Camille thinks, and her own smile fades.

"Come on inside," he says. "It's still pretty empty. I only just finished remodeling the house and I haven't bought any furniture yet, but there's a bed upstairs if you want to lie down and rest. If you get hungry, there's some tamales in the fridge that you can heat up in the microwave."

They walk into a spacious living room with gleaming hardwood floors. The light spills in through the original lead glass windows. A carved wooden mantel above the fireplace has been restored to its previous ornate glory.

He was accurate about the house being empty. There's nothing but a folding card table and two plastic chairs set in front of the bay window.

Alejandro glances at his watch and edges toward the door.

"Are you sure I can't come with you?" Camille asks. "I can wait in your truck."

"No. You need to stay here, where I know you'll be safe. I'll call you and let you know what's happening."

They quickly exchange phone numbers, and Camille walks him to the door.

"I hope you know how much it's going to drive me crazy to have to wait around here doing nothing. You make sure to call or text me with any news, okay?"

He takes her hands in his. "I will. Now, you have to swear to me you won't go anywhere. You must stay here the whole time. I'm serious, Camila. Things could get dangerous."

She holds up her right hand. "I swear."

"No matter what?"

"*No matter what.*"

"Good." He looks at her a long moment, then takes his hands and places them on either side of her head, pulls her face toward his, and kisses her so hard that her knees begin to buckle.

When he's done, he looks her right in the eyes. "Camila, I promise you I will find Graciela. And when I do, we are going to have a big celebration. Just the two of us."

Then he's gone.

CHAPTER 42

It's been over two hours and Camille still hasn't heard from Alejandro. She stares out the front window, becoming increasingly panicked with each passing minute. Her mind is reeling with all sorts of hideous images: Graciela huddled in some dark basement with a gag in her mouth, her hands tied behind her as the rope cuts off the circulation to her hands. Graciela drenched in sweat in the trunk of Little Chuy's car, breathing in hot exhaust as the temperature rises.

To keep her imagination from running rampant, Camille decides to explore Alejandro's house. Like the ticking of a metronome, her footsteps tap out a steady rhythm as she climbs the wooden staircase. She wanders down the long hall, looking into the bedrooms. All of them are beautifully remodeled and freshly painted, but completely devoid of any furniture or decor—except for the master, where, as Alejandro promised, Camille finds a bed. She lies down on it and covers herself with the comforter.

She allows herself to imagine for a moment what living with Alejandro in this house would be like. They would furnish it with overstuffed sofas and antique furniture, she decides. She'd hang filmy white curtains above the windows. The built-in shelves would be filled with books, stacks of music, and green houseplants.

During their visits to Oaxaca, they could buy colorful Mexican pottery for the kitchen and handmade woven rugs for the hardwood floors. She even pictures her mother's rosewood grand piano positioned in front of the bay window. Camille takes the fantasy as far as she can, hearing the sound of children's voices echoing throughout the house.

Oh, for God's sake, Camille, knock it off! You're being ridiculous.

Her phone buzzes; she rolls over and pries it out of her pocket. *No Caller ID.*

"Hello?" she says. Silence. *"Hello?"*

No one is there.

A moment later, the phone rings again.

"Hello? Who's there? *Hello?*"

"Miss Camille?" Graciela's voice is so quiet that Camille can barely hear it.

Camille gasps and sits up. "Graciela! Are you okay? Where are you?" She presses the phone to her ear.

"I don't know where I am," Graciela whispers. "I'm in some old house not that far from where I saw you. The guy yelled at me to stay down in the back seat so I couldn't see where we went. When he took me out of the car he made me close my eyes. I peeked a little, but I couldn't see much except the house is yellow and is kind of run-down. There are two big piles of dirt in the front yard."

"Is he there in the house with you?"

"I don't know. I'm locked in a back bedroom. The window is painted shut. I've tried, but I can't get it open."

"Whose phone are you using?"

"The lady who came to our hotel room in Tijuana gave me one. I don't know her name. She told me not to tell anyone that she gave it to me, so I hid it in my sock the whole time. It's been quiet in the house for a while now. I thought maybe the guy left so it was safe to call."

"Smart thinking," Camille says, trying to keep her voice calm. "Are you okay? Has he hurt you?"

Graciela begins to cry. "No, but he said that if I tried to escape he would kill me. Oh, Miss Camille, I'm so scared. I don't know what to do."

"Don't panic, I'll help you. Take a look around the room and see if you can find anything with an address on it. Is there a piece of paper or an envelope or something?"

"I already looked, but there's nothing in here but a bed and a dresser that's totally empty."

"Look in the closet. Or maybe under the bed."

Camille hears rustling from the other end of the line.

"There's a shoebox under the bed."

"Open it!"

"It's full of papers. There's some old letters here that all have the same address. It's 251 Agnes Street, Los Angeles."

Bingo! "Okay, that must be it. That's probably where you are—"

"I have to go. I just heard a door slam. Someone's coming!"

"Graciela, wait—"

The phone beeps three times, and then she hears only silence.

With shaking hands, Camille dials Alejandro's number. It goes immediately to voice mail. *C'mon, Alejandro—pick up already!* She hangs up and presses redial. Voice mail again. *Why the hell won't he answer?*

She tries calling three more times, with no results. She's done waiting. She types 251 Agnes Street into her phone, exits the house, and runs to her car.

She finds the weathered Victorian in less than fifteen minutes. It's exactly as Graciela described it, with peeling yellow paint and two large mounds of dirt in the front yard. There are no cars parked in the driveway, and the house looks deserted. Maybe Little Chuy hid his car somewhere in the neighborhood to keep people from knowing that he's home.

At the end of the street, she makes a U-turn and parks the car four houses down and across the street. Far enough away so she can easily see the front of the house, but not close enough for Little Chuy to notice her if he were to look out the window. She calls Alejandro once more, and again his voice mail picks up. She's just about to call again when she sees Alejandro's black truck slowly make its way down the street. He parks in front of Little Chuy's house.

Alejandro, Graciela's uncle Victor, and the *coyote* from the alley, Paco, walk up the front steps and peer through the bars of the front window. Camille must warn them that Chuy is probably waiting inside to ambush them. Just as she unclasps her seat belt to get out of the car, the front door opens and the three of them go inside the house.

Crap! She's got to do something. She gets out of the car and runs toward the house.

Just as she reaches the other side of the street, the tip of her huarache catches on the curb and she goes sprawling to the ground. She skins her knees and the palms of her hands on the sidewalk.

Camille, you are such a klutz! She sits up quickly and brushes off her knees, the burn of scraped skin stinging her palms. Out of the corner of her eye, something catches her attention—a small silver pendant and chain almost completely hidden in a patch of dead grass. Without thinking, she picks it up and tucks it into the pocket of her shorts.

She sneaks quietly onto the front porch, steering clear of the window. The sound of men's voices comes from inside the house. She recognizes Little Chuy's voice immediately. She's relieved that so far he hasn't done anything crazy, like attack Alejandro.

Little Chuy is distracted; this is the perfect opportunity for her to sneak into the back of the house and get Graciela out of there. She creeps over to the gate that leads into the backyard. It won't budge, so she decides to see if she can cut through the neighbor's yard. Luckily, the old fence between the two houses is rotted out in places. All she has to do is push a couple of pieces of wood out of the way, and she's able to climb through into Little Chuy's yard.

The backyard is disgusting. Leaning up against the fence opposite her is a line of rusty metal cans spilling over with black trash bags that have been chewed open by animals. The stench of rotting garbage is overwhelming. Camille dashes across the dead grass and past a rusted clothesline pole in the corner that squeaks noisily as it spins in the breeze.

The windows that run across the back of the house have all been painted over with the same yellow paint. Camille has no idea in which room Graciela is being held captive—or, for that matter, how she's even going to get inside the house. If she does manage to find a way in, she's terrified of what Little Chuy will do to her if he catches her there.

Feeling her resolve weaken, Camille's hands begins to tremble. Panic overtakes her. She suddenly wants to get as far away as possible from this scary, dilapidated house as she can. She turns to leave and reaches into her right pocket to grab her car keys. They're not there. Did she leave them in the ignition? With the hope that she just missed them, she digs deeper into her pockets and feels something cold between her fingers. It's the silver pendant she picked up in front of the house.

She pulls the necklace from her pocket and examines the tarnished metal. Immediately, she recognizes the familiar image on the front of the pendant: a bald man holding a small child in his arms. She turns it over and rubs the dirt away from the engraving on the back: *Saint Anthony. All is not lost.*

Her trembling ceases.

"*Let's go, Camila,*" she whispers to herself. "*You can do this. San Antonio's got your back.*"

Now all she has to do is to figure out a way to get inside that house.

CHAPTER 43

It seems as if the best way to get inside Little Chuy's house is to climb the short staircase that angles up the rear of the house and pray that the back door is unlocked.

Camille starts up the stairs. The banister wobbles and the wooden slats are rotting in places, so she steps lightly, hoping it won't collapse under her feet. When she reaches the landing, she turns the doorknob of a metal security gate oxidized with streaks of rust. Miraculously, it's unlocked. The knob turns with an almost inaudible click. She slips inside unnoticed.

The smell of decay assaults her immediately. When her eyes adjust to the dim lighting, she sees she is standing in a filthy kitchen. The worn linoleum has curled at the edges, and the geometric pattern is barely visible through the thick layer of grime. Pizza boxes, takeout cartons, and empty beer bottles line the countertops. The sink is piled high with dishes that stink of rotting food. Camille must hold her breath to keep from gagging. She hears a light rattling noise as she tiptoes across the floor and freezes. She looks down to see dozens of cockroaches skittering back to their hiding places under the baseboards.

When she reaches the dining room, she hears the voices from the front of the house becoming louder. She quickly heads in the other direction, down a narrow hallway smelling of mildew. There are two doors for the rooms that face the backyard. Not certain which one leads to where Graciela is being held, she tries turning the doorknob of the first one. She's once again surprised that it's unlocked and opens easily.

"Graciela?" she whispers. "Are you in there?" When she opens the door wider, she comes face-to-face with an old woman wearing a *huipil*. Her long white hair flows down around her shoulders like a frayed shawl. Her face is clouded with confusion.

Worried the woman is going to call out to Little Chuy, Camille covers the woman's mouth with her hand. "*¿Dónde está Graciela?*" She asks in a low voice.

The woman points a bony finger toward the room next door. Camille removes her hand from the woman's mouth, puts her finger to her lips, and slowly backs away from the doorway. But before she can close the door, the old woman reaches out and grabs her forearm with so much force that she almost cries out in pain.

The woman mumbles something in Zapotec and places her other hand into the pocket of her apron. Camille tries again to close the door, but the woman only tightens her grip. She takes her hand out of her pocket and presses something hard and flat into Camille's hand.

"*La llave,*" she croaks.

Camille feels the cold metal burn into her palm. *The key. She's giving me the key to unlock the other bedroom door.* "*Ushkenot,*" she whispers, thanking the woman in the only Zapotec word she can remember.

For a split second, the woman's watery eyes brighten. She smiles sadly and steps back into the musty darkness of the room. The door closes without a sound.

Camille quickly moves over to the next bedroom, shoves the key into the lock, and jiggles the doorknob until it opens. "Graciela?" she whispers. "Are you there?"

Camille sees a figure moving out from the shadows behind the bed. "Miss Camille?"

Graciela runs over and hugs her tightly. Her body shakes with silent tears of relief as Camille gently draws her hand across the top of her head. Camille motions for Graciela to follow her, and they sneak back into the kitchen. Camille is just about to open the back door to freedom when she hears an animated shout from the living room.

"No, Chuy—*cálmate!*" Camille can hear the fear in Alejandro's voice. Without a second thought, she opens the kitchen door and shoves Graciela out onto the landing. "Run!" she says. "Run as fast as you can and get away from here. There's a hole in the fence. Climb through it and don't stop running until you're out of this neighborhood. Then use that cell phone to call someone to pick you up. I'll meet you at your uncle Victor's house later on."

"But—"

"You heard me, Graciela! Now, *go!*"

Without another word Graciela is out the door, moving like the wind. She flies down the back steps and through the hole in the fence in less than thirty seconds. The din from the living room intensifies, and the voices blend into a frenzy of shouting. Camille is terrified that Chuy is going to do something to hurt Alejandro. She frantically opens several kitchen drawers, looking for some sort of weapon—a knife or a hammer—but there's nothing but individually wrapped plastic utensils and packets of hot sauce.

She hears Alejandro's shout again. "No, Chuy! Put it down! Don't do it!"

On the stove there is a heavy cooking pot with a layer of congealed black beans lining the bottom. She picks it up and runs toward the front of the house.

Alejandro is speaking calmly, but Camille can hear the terror in his voice. "Chuy, man, take it easy. You don't want to hurt Paco. Let him go. C'mon, Chuy, think about it."

Chuy sounds like he's lost his mind. "The hell with you, man! You get the fuck out of my house, or I'll kill this *pinche* motherfucker!"

Camille slowly peeks her head around the corner of the wall. Chuy is almost directly in front of her, facing in the opposite direction. He has his arm around Paco's neck. She can't see what he has in his hand, but she assumes it's a knife.

"This is between me and Paco! It ain't none of your business. You stay back or I'll kill you too!"

Camille's heart moves into her throat.

"All we want is the girl, Chuy," Alejandro says in a low voice.

Chuy lets out a crazy, high-pitched laugh. "You fuckin' kidding me? There's no way in hell you getting that chick back. I'm gonna do whatever I want with her. *She's my bitch now!*"

As Camille hears those words, paralyzing fear rushes through her body. She squeezes her eyes closed, trying with all her might to block out the memory that is rising to the surface of her mind. She sees Jack's enraged face screaming at her. She watches him grab her hand, hold it against the open door, and slam the sliding glass door against her fingers. One, two, three times. Camille sees her bloody hand in shreds. She hears Jack speaking the words that have been seared into her memory: *You're my bitch now, Camille!*

ENOUGH! Her eyes fly open and Jack's face disappears. She looks down at the pot in her hands. Intense rage flares from within, and adrenaline surges through her body.

Camille suddenly recalls what the *curandera* said after her cleansing in Yalálag—that she has a chance for a new life, but she needs to forgive herself first. Camille didn't understand what the *curandera* meant until right now. For fifteen years, she has blamed herself for what Jack did to her. She believed it was her fault that he mutilated her hand and destroyed her dream of becoming a concert pianist. But it was never her fault. It was all Jack's fault. And he's gone now—but she's still here.

I'm not your bitch, Jack. Not then, not now. And you're not taking anything away from me ever again.

It's time for her to take what she wants in life. And what she wants is Alejandro.

She peers around the wall into the living room again. Little Chuy still has his arm around Paco's neck. She steps into the living room so she's standing directly behind Little Chuy. Alejandro's and Victor's eyes go wide at the sight of her.

Without making a sound, Camille lifts the heavy pot above her head with both hands, sucks in her breath, and drops the pan with all of her might, striking Little Chuy on the top of his bald head. Like a marionette whose strings have been cut, his skinny, tattooed body crumples to the floor in a heap.

The pot lands with a reverberating thud. Pieces of dried black beans fly up into the air and scatter across the room.

"Hey, Little Chuy," she hisses. *"Who's the bitch now?"*

CHAPTER 44

Since the Pot o' Beans Incident, as Alejandro likes to call it, Camille has become Paco's new best friend. He won't leave her alone. He calls or texts her throughout the day to ask how she's doing, continuously thanking her for saving his life. He even returned half of the smuggling money, which Camille promptly turned over to her mother.

Camille is not going to ask Paco what happened to Little Chuy. All she needs to know is what Alejandro told her—that Little Chuy will never bother her again. She doesn't really want to know anything beyond that.

Paco has announced to anyone who will listen that he'll never be able to repay Camille for saving his life. He even told her that if she ever needs anything, he'll take care of it, no questions asked. At first, Camille laughed him off, unable to fathom what there was that Paco could do for her, as she no longer required the services of a *coyote*.

Camille has just spent the last four days holed up in her room at the Ritz Carlton with Alejandro—compliments of her mother, who graciously paid for the room for the remainder of the week so Camille and Alejandro could spend some time alone together. At first, Alejandro balked at staying there on her mother's dime, but Camille reassured him that her mother feels indebted to him for helping Camille navigate her way through Oaxaca and wants to show her appreciation.

"Wow," he said when they first arrived, looking out the window at the spectacular view of the city. "This is incredible. I've never been in a hotel room like this one before."

Camille smiled. "You mean one so luxurious?"

He turned around and faced her, his eyes shining. "No. I've stayed in fancy hotels before, some even fancier than this one. I've just never stayed in one that comes with the most beautiful redhead I've ever seen." With that, he walked over and enveloped her in his arms. "And now, *mi amor*, I think it's time for us to have that celebration I promised you."

Camille spent the next four glorious days in bed ordering room service, watching movies, and making love with the most handsome Yalalteco on the planet. The only time she ventured out all week was to rehearse with Graciela in one of the Ritz's conference rooms. Camille's mother managed to procure them a room that included a brand-new Bösendorfer piano.

Camille had never dreamed she could be so happy. She's fallen madly in love. She's getting along with her mother better than she ever has. After everything they'd been through, Graciela is going to be presented in her debut recital. The end of the race is finally in sight, and nothing is going to stop Camille from crossing over that finish line.

The morning of the orchestra rehearsal, Camille and Graciela climb the steps to the entrance of the concert hall. It's deserted but for two lone figures standing in front of the glass doors. As they get closer, Camille is surprised to see that it's Sofia Vanilovich and Amy Chen. Sofia is overdressed in a tight-fitting pink cocktail dress. Amy, with her severe bangs, tortoiseshell glasses, and pleated skirt resembles an uptight parochial student.

"Oh, it's you," Sofia says, unable to hide her dismay. "I thought that perhaps you and Graciela weren't going to make it back in time for the rehearsal."

"Hello, Sofia," Camille says, smiling a bit smugly. She links her arm through Graciela's. "Yes, we did indeed make it. As I said we would. What are you doing here?"

The smirk on Sofia's face makes her look like a snotty preteen with a secret. "Well, Camille," she says airily, "we weren't really sure what was happening with your *situation*. We wanted to be prepared in case Amy was going to have to fill in for Graciela at the last minute. Luckily, Amy is playing the same concerto as Graciela."

Always scheming. "Oh, I see. Well, we're here now and all set to rehearse. So if you'll excuse us . . ." Camille moves to open the glass door.

"Hold on a minute." Sofia places a firm hand on Camille's shoulder. "I need to have a word with you first."

Camille stiffens, her intuition setting off alarm bells. "What is it now, Sofia?"

Sofia glances briefly at Graciela. "There's something I need to discuss with you in private."

Camille turns to Graciela. "You go on in. Look for the conductor and let him know you're here. I'll catch up with you in a minute."

Graciela gives her a worried look. "Sure, Miss Camille. I'll see you inside."

Sofia has already begun to walk briskly in the other direction, her stiletto heels spiking the cement with rhythmic precision. Camille hurries to catch up with her.

"What's the problem, Sofia?" she says, unable to conceal her irritation.

As soon as they're out of Amy's earshot, Sofia abruptly turns around and faces Camille. Her features are distorted with hostility. "The *problem*," she spits, "is that I've done some detective work and discovered that you've been busy keeping a little secret. Or should I say, a *big* secret—that Graciela is not a citizen of this country. Furthermore, she doesn't even have the legal documentation to be here at all!"

Camille's insides turn cold. *How the hell did Sofia find out about this?* "Don't be ridiculous," she says, keeping her face still. "Of course she does. You've been misinformed."

Sofia narrows her eyes. "Then you won't mind presenting Graciela's documents?"

Camille's anger rises. "To whom? To you? I'm not going to *present* anything to you, Sofia. It's none of your damn business."

"Well, I'm making it my business. And if you don't come up with proof by tomorrow morning that Graciela has the legal authorization to be in this country, I'm going to inform the orchestra conductor *and* the competition committee." She turns and strides off toward the front of the hall.

Camille chases after her. "Seriously? You're going to try to ruin this experience for Graciela? Even though she won the competition fair and square?"

This stops Sophia midstride. She puts her hands on her hips and faces Camille, her lower lip sticking out like a wet slug. "*Fair and square?* What a joke. You and I both know that Amy should've won the grand prize. Graciela only won because it makes a good story that she's an underprivileged Mexican from a poor neighborhood. Obviously the judges were trying to make a point. To demonstrate to the public how open-minded they are by choosing a minority as the grand-prize winner."

Camille is incredulous. "Oh, so Graciela's winning has nothing to do with her exceptional talent and ability? Not to mention all of her hard work?"

Sofia cocks her head to one side. "Have you not heard of *reverse racism*, Camille? It's when people are so worried about offending ethnic minorities that they overcompensate. In my opinion, all of this exaggerated political correctness is ruining our great country."

Camille has the sudden urge to reach up, rip out a handful of Sofia's spiky blond hair, and shove it down her throat. "You *are* aware that Amy is of Chinese descent, right? That makes her an ethnic minority as well."

Sofia sniffs. "You know it's not the same thing, Camille. There's a difference."

"What's the difference?" Camille shouts, throwing her hands up in the air. "The color of her skin?"

Sofia's face turns stony. Camille decides to try another route. "Look, the concert is the day after tomorrow. No matter what Graciela's situation might be, she's the one being honored. I'm sure the programs have already been printed, listing her as the grand-prize winner. I don't think the competition committee is going to want to have to reprint all of the programs at the last minute."

Sofia pauses and looks Camille right in the eyes. "They might not want to, but they'll do it if Graciela can't make the concert because she's being detained by immigration."

Camille feels like she's been punched in the stomach. "I can't believe that even *you* would do something so evil."

Sofia smiles serenely. "You of all people should know that I most certainly would."

For the first time in her life, Camille realizes she is capable of murder. "*You are such a bitch!*" she screams, her voice ricocheting around the building. "You have no idea what I've been through over the past week. Do you really think you can bully me into doing what you want? Well, screw you, Sofia! There is no way in hell I'm letting you ruin this opportunity for Graciela!"

For a moment, Sofia looks afraid; she takes several steps back from Camille, her eyes wide. Then she purses her lips. "I'm sorry you can't grasp the seriousness of this situation. If it's true that Graciela is in this country illegally, then she's breaking the law. And so are you. You either bring me her papers by tomorrow, or I'm calling the authorities." She fluffs the top of her hair. "Amy and I are staying at the Four Seasons in Beverly Hills, Room 354. You have until nine tomorrow morning to show me the proof."

And with that, Sofia turns and heads back toward the concert hall, her steps as strong and steady as a John Philip Sousa march.

CHAPTER 45

Even in her distress about Sofia's plan to ruin everything, Camille enjoys watching the nearly two-hour rehearsal. If Sofia follows through with her threat to call ICE, this rehearsal might be the only chance she'll get to hear Graciela play her concerto with the orchestra.

When it's over, the conductor makes a point of coming over to compliment Camille on her teaching. He tells her he's never worked with a young pianist who was so musically gifted or who acted in such a mature and professional manner. He even hints that he'd like to ask Graciela back to perform again in the future.

All week long, Paco has been insisting that Camille come over and try his wife's famous *chiles rellenos*, saying he won't take no for an answer, so after resting up at the hotel for a few hours, she heads there for an early dinner. Everyone is coming—Alejandro, Graciela, her aunt Rosario and her uncle Victor, and even Camille's mother.

Paco's house is a modest bungalow in a quiet neighborhood near the sports coliseum. Painted a periwinkle blue, it is surrounded by a white wrought iron fence trailing with yellow climbing roses. Plastic children's toys are scattered across a neatly trimmed patch of green front lawn.

The inside of the house is small but cozy. Its white walls are covered with dozens of framed photos of weddings, baptisms, and other large family gatherings. A massive dining room table is laden with all kinds of delicious food: rice, beans, guacamole and salsa, and a huge platter of plump, homemade *chiles relleños*. Camille almost laughs aloud when she sees the centerpiece: a cake in the shape of a cooking pot, decorated with black jelly beans. "*Gracias*" is written in bright red letters across the top.

Paco's pretty, dark-haired wife, Lupe, treats Camille like an honored guest. His three young children even present her with handmade thank-you cards they've made with paint and glitter— so much glitter, in fact, that the front of Camille's white blouse now sparkles like a disco ball.

When everyone finally sits down at the table and begins passing the food, Camille stares at her empty plate. Her stomach is knotted with worry. She can't eat a single bite.

"What's the matter, Camila?" Alejandro asks. "Aren't you hungry?"

"Not really," she says. Her eyes began to tear up.

The spirited chatter around the table stops. All eyes shift to Camille.

Alejandro squeezes her hand. "What's going on, *mi amor?*"

Composing herself, Camille explains about Sofia's threat to call immigration and prevent Graciela from performing on Saturday.

Her mother's mouth flies open. "You're joking."

"Is this true, Miss Camille?" Graciela asks, her face paling.

"I'm afraid it is," Camille says. "Sofia told me that if I don't prove to her by tomorrow that you have legal residency in this country, she'll report you to the competition committee. She said she'll even contact ICE to come and arrest you."

Paco sits up in his chair, his face becoming hard. "Who the hell is this Sofia person?"

"Only one of the most despicable women on the planet," Camille's mother pipes up, her face full of fury. "She's been out to get Camille for years. This is *unbelievable!*"

Paco rubs his chin thoughtfully. "You say this woman is Russian?"

"Yes," Camille says. "She's a piano teacher in Santa Barbara, but her family is originally from Moscow. Why do you ask?"

"Does she have any family in Russia?" he asks.

"Her mother and father live in Santa Barbara, but I think she still has relatives back in Moscow. Why do you want to know?"

Paco asks Lupe to bring him a piece of paper and a pencil. When she does, he hands them to Camille. "Write down her full name and her parents' names. And any other family members whose names you know too."

"What are you going to do?" Camille asks, worried. "You're not going to kill her or anything, are you?"

Alejandro chuckles and puts his hand over hers. "Don't worry, Camila. Paco's not going to kill anyone. Just do what he tells you."

She hastily writes down Sofia's information and hands the paper over to him.

Paco stands up from the table. "Keep eating, everyone." He looks at Camille with an odd smile on his face. "I'm just gonna make a quick phone call."

The next morning, Camille finds herself in the elevator of the Four Seasons Hotel, accompanied by Paco and Alejandro.

"Paco," she says, "I'm begging you. *Please.* Just tell me what it is we're going to do."

Paco presses the button for the third floor, and the elevator door closes without a sound. "Don't worry, Camila," he says, placing his hands in his pockets and lightly bouncing back on his heels.

"We're not gonna do nothing bad. We're just gonna have a little talk with this Sofia person."

"But what am I supposed to say to her?"

"You don't have to say barely nothing," Paco says. "I'll do all the talking."

Camille glances over at Alejandro. He puts a supportive arm around her shoulder. "You need to stop worrying. Paco's got everything under control. He knows what he's doing."

"I hope so," she says. "I don't even care about the concert anymore. I just want to keep Graciela from being deported."

The elevator door slides open onto a luxurious hallway carpeted in hues of gold and green. An oversize arrangement of tiger lilies has saturated the air with a cloying scent.

Paco wrinkles his nose. "Smells like a damn funeral home in here." He looks up and down the hallway. "What room is hers?"

Camille points to the left. "354—this way."

Before they knock on Sofia's door, Paco takes hold of Camille's wrist.

"Hold up, Camila," he says. "Let me tell you what's goin' down. We gonna give this Sofia person one last shot at doing the right thing. You go into the room first and tell her that you're not gonna show her Graciela's papers. If she says she's still gonna call ICE, then you open the door and give me a thumbs-down signal. I'll take it from there. Okay?"

"Okay. But what are you going to do?"

"You'll see." He grins. "Don't worry. I got your back on this."

Alejandro puts his arm around Camille and hugs her tightly. "This is all going to be over very soon, *mi amor*, I promise you." He leans in and kisses her softly on the lips.

Paco punches Alejandro on the upper arm. "*Ay, cabrón*," he says with an obvious wink. "You gonna have plenty of time for that once we take care of business." He jerks his head toward

Sofia's door. "*Vámanos, pues.*" He and Alejandro back away from the door.

Before Camille has even finished knocking, Sofia opens the door. Her hair is wrapped in a towel, and she hasn't yet put on her makeup. "Oh, it's you," she says. "I'm still getting ready. Come in." She motions for Camille to follow her. "Amy is in the bathroom taking a shower."

Camille walks into the darkened room and is momentarily taken aback by the mess. Piles of rumpled clothing and take-out cartons are strewn about like a tornado just hit the room.

Sofia's features are set in her usual sneer. She moves a stack of music off a chair and offers Camille the seat with a languid wave of her hand. "I presume you're here because you have proof of Graciela's citizenship?"

"Actually," Camille says, sitting down, "I don't have Graciela's papers with me. But I did come here this morning to offer you one last chance to behave like a decent human being."

Sofia puts her hands on her hips and cocks her head to one side.

Camille clears her throat. "Look, Graciela won the competition because she was the best performer that day. She didn't win because she's poor, or because she's Mexican. She won because she deserved to win. For you to try to take it away from her with the threat of deportation is deplorable."

Sofia flattens her lips and stares down at her. "I knew it. You don't have Graciela's papers, do you?"

"That's not what I'm saying. What I'm trying to say is—"

"Oh, give it a rest, Camille," she says, waving her fingers dismissively in the air. "Why don't you just admit you don't have her papers because they don't exist?"

Camille fights to keep calm. "It's true I don't have her papers with me. As I told you before, I wouldn't show them to you even if I did have them. It's the principle of the matter, Sofia. There's no reason for you to threaten Graciela just because you hold a grudge against me."

Sofia tightens the sash of her robe and scowls. "Don't be such an idiot, Camille. I'm not reporting Graciela because I'm mad at you. I'm reporting her because it's the right thing to do. *It's the law.* Illegal aliens should not be allowed to stay in this country without permission, *period.* I'm not against immigration—as you know, many of my family members are immigrants from Russia. But unlike Graciela and her family, they didn't sneak into this country. They followed the rules and went through the proper channels. They did it the legal way."

Camille sighs. "So there's nothing I can say to change your mind?"

"I'm afraid not." Sofia grins so devilishly Camille could swear she sees two pointy horns sticking out from under her stiff blond hair. "In fact," she says, wagging her phone in Camille's face, "I've got the numbers of ICE and the director of the competition already programmed in my cell. As soon as you leave, I'll be making a few phone calls."

Camille moves toward the door. "Okay, Sofia. But I have a very strong feeling you're going to regret your decision." She opens the door, sticks her hand out into the hallway, and points her thumb toward the ground. A second later, Paco and Alejandro barrel into the room like a couple of bulls.

A flash of fear darkens Sofia's face and she steps back, almost tripping over a pile of bedding on the floor. Then she lets out a nervous laugh. "Seriously?" she says, her voice rising up an octave. "I knew you were pathetic, Camille, but I never thought you'd be so desperate as to go out and hire a couple of Mexican thugs to try to intimidate me."

Paco charges toward Sofia. "*Pinche puta*—what did you just call me?" His head barely reaches up to her neck.

Narrowing her eyes, Sofia holds her phone up over Paco's head with her fingers poised over the screen. "I called you a thug, which is exactly what you are. Now, go away, little bald man. I'm not afraid of you."

She turns and glares at Camille. "You better get the hell out of here, Camille. You and your little hoodlum friends need to leave right now, or I'm calling hotel security."

In two quick steps, Alejandro is next to Sofia and snatching her phone out of her hand. He nods in Paco's direction. "First of all, my friend Paco is not a hoodlum. Secondly, before you go making any phone calls, it might be in your best interest to listen to what this gentleman has to say." He takes Sofia's elbow and leads her to the edge of the bed. "Please have a seat, Sofia."

No longer laughing, Sofia sinks down onto the bed. She grabs the collar of her robe and pulls it up around her neck.

Paco sits down opposite Sofia on the other queen bed. "*Gracias, Alejandro*," he says, then pulls a folded note from his pocket and opens it. "Okay then, let's get down to it." He looks down at the paper. "Your name is Sofia Vanilla Bitch, right?"

She glares at him. "It's pronounced *Vanilovich*."

Paco smirks. "That's what I said. Vanilla Bitch. And your mother's name is Anna Kozlov?"

Sofia suddenly looks nervous. "What about her?"

"She lives with you and your father, Alexei, in Santa Barbara, right?"

"Yes, both my parents live with me. Why do you want to know?"

Paco's mustache dances under his nose when he smiles. "Well, the thing is, Sofia, sometimes it's kinda cool being a *thug*—like you just called me—because I get to meet a lot of other thugs in my line of work. And I personally know this one *thug* whose name is Popov.

He's this big bald guy with tattoos. Kinda like me, only a lot taller. And he's from Russia, just like your family."

Sofia sits perfectly still, her mouth clamped shut.

"Anyways," Paco continues, "me and Señor Popov have become friends. We even got some business deals together." He crosses two of his fingers and holds them up in front of her face. "You could say we've become pretty close."

Sofia goes white. Her hands travel back up to her neck. She begins to tug at the collar of her robe.

Paco grins with delight. "Ah, Vanilla Bitch, I see you've heard of my Russian friend." He looks at Camille and wags his finger back and forth, chuckling. "*Ay*, Camila, that name you came up with for this girl is fuckin' hilarious."

Camille laughs. "Actually, it was my mother who came up with it."

Sofia glares at Camille, her ice-blue eyes shooting daggers from across the room.

"Okay, then," Paco says, "I'll just have to tell your mother myself when I see her at Graciela's concert tomorrow night."

Sofia straightens her shoulders with false bravado. "I'm afraid Graciela won't be performing tomorrow night after all," she says airily. "Unfortunately, she's run into a difficult situation regarding her immigration status."

Paco stands up. "Hey, *Vanilla Bitch,*" he says, his voice like steel. "You stupid or something? Of course Graciela's gonna play her concert. And you're not gonna do nothing to stop her, like calling ICE, *are you?*"

Sofia isn't ready to give in. She sticks out her chin with defiance. "And what if I do?"

He laughs and sits back down on the bed. "Well, I don't think I would do that if I were you." He licks his index finger and thumb before slowly twisting one side of his mustache. "As I was sayin' before, Popov and me are real tight—plus, he owes me a big favor. In fact, he's already been nice enough to make some long-distance phone calls for me."

The fear returns to Sofia's face, and Paco laughs again.

"You know, this *vato* Popov is a pretty popular guy, even for being such a scary motherfucker. Not only does he know a lot of people here in LA, but he knows people in Russia too. And he found out some pretty crazy shit about your family."

Beads of perspiration appear above Sofia's upper lip. "Like what?" she asks, squirming.

"Well, he told me a lot of stuff about your father. How before he came to this country he did some pretty nasty shit in Russia. That he made some enemies over there. How he was involved in some crime ring but ended up leaving in a hurry. I guess he screwed over some pretty important people, huh?"

Like an albino deer caught in the headlights, Sofia's eyes go wide.

Paco runs his hand over his bald head. "Another interesting thing Popov found out is that your mother, this Anna Kozlov person, has some secrets of her own. The biggest one is that she's not a citizen of this great country of ours. In fact, she's not supposed to be here at all! Your mama don't got no green card!"

Camille gasps. "Are you serious?"

Paco snorts. "That's right, no fuckin' green card. Hell, even I got me one of those! Turns out, Sofia's mama came here almost forty years ago for a 'visit,' and then she didn't go back to Russia like she was supposed to. And because of the shit that went down in the old country, she couldn't get her papers here."

Sofia closes her eyes and lays her face in her hands.

Paco claps his hands together. "That's right, Vanilla Bitch, your mama's an *illegal alien.*" He laughs even harder, cradling his belly with his thick arms as his body shakes. He looks up at Camille and winks. "After what this bitch was about to do to Graciela, I'd call that *muy irónico*—wouldn't you, Camila?"

Unable to speak, Camille nods her head in joyous disbelief.

Paco puts his hand under Sofia's chin and tilts her face up so she's looking right into his eyes. "And one thing you should know, Vanilla Bitch. If you make one move to stop Graciela from playing her concert tomorrow night, or if you do anything to hurt my good friend Camila here, all I have to do is text my friend Popov. I do that, and not only will he let those friends of your father back in Russia know exactly where to find him, he'll also put your illegal alien mama right back on the next plane to Moscow. And as for you? Well, I'll deal with you personally."

As they turn to leave, Camille hears a door click. Amy walks out of the bathroom wearing a fluffy hotel robe, a white towel wrapped around her head. Her tortoiseshell glasses are still partially fogged up from the shower steam. She stares at them in confusion.

Camille puts up her hand and waves. "Hey, Amy, how's it going?" she says, trying to contain her obvious glee. "Make sure to arrive early for the concert tomorrow night; you'll want to get good seats for Graciela's performance!"

Amy's eyes dart over to Sofia on the bed; her sagging posture indicates complete defeat.

Camille takes Alejandro's hand and practically skips through the doorway. "And the earlier the better," she calls over her shoulder. "For some reason, I have a feeling it's going to be a full house."

EPILOGUE

Camille never imagined that she would travel to the mountains of Oaxaca once, let alone twice. Yet almost exactly one year to the day, she is driving the same winding road up to Yalálag. This time, though, she's not on a bus. And it's not raining.

"Are you okay, Camila?" Alejandro asks, concerned. Since they left Oaxaca City, he's had to stop the truck several times so she could throw up. "I never knew you had a problem with carsickness."

"I don't normally," she says, holding her head in her hands. "It must be the altitude. Or maybe I'm coming down with the flu or something."

"Do you want to stop and rest for a while?"

"No, I'm okay. We're almost there, right?"

"About an hour or so."

She manages to smile. "Let's keep going, then."

After two more stops along the side of the road so Camille can get out of the truck and dry heave, they near the place where the mudslide came down the mountain. Alejandro parks the truck on the shoulder, rolls down the windows, and turns off the engine.

The scenery is even more magnificent than Camille remembers. The sun shoots down through the branches of the pine trees like icicles of white light, illuminating the green hillsides. Cool mountain air wafts through the open windows and fills the cab with the smell of fertile earth.

"Is this where it happened?" she whispers, not wanting to shatter the silence.

"No," he says. "It's a little farther up the road. But we need to stop here because the road narrows. There's no room up there to park the truck."

"Okay." Camille opens the door and jumps down from the cab. Her feet land on a pillow of damp pine needles.

Alejandro meets her in the middle of the road. "You feel good enough to walk up there?"

She nods.

"Okay, then, *mi amor,*" he says, taking her hand. "Let's go see where it all started."

Driving almost the entire length of Mexico wasn't Alejandro's idea of the perfect honeymoon, but Camille stubbornly insisted. He suggested they go to Hawaii or New York City, but Camille made it clear she wanted to go back to Yalálag. She has a favor to repay.

A year ago, she prayed to a particular saint to help get Graciela home. She said then that if he helped her, she would return and do something big to honor him. Since June thirteenth—San Antonio's birthday—would coincide with their honeymoon, Camille decided that would be the perfect time to present San Antonio with his gift. Driving two thousand miles to Yalálag would be tough, but flying wasn't an option this time. It's pretty much impossible to board an airplane with a Steinway grand piano in your carry-on luggage.

"You want to do *what?*" her mother said, looking at her as if she'd lost her mind. Alejandro and Camille were in Santa Barbara because Camille's mother had just hired Alejandro to re-landscape her entire property. They were also going to take that time to work out the details of Camille and Alejandro's upcoming wedding.

"You heard me, Mom," Camille said, helping herself to a cup of coffee and sitting down at the kitchen table. "I want to bring a grand piano to Yalálag."

Her mother sat down next to her. "Why on earth would you go to all the trouble to take a piano there? Is there even anyone there who could play it?"

She looked up at her mother. "There will be."

"Who?" she asked.

Camille couldn't hold back her grin. "Why, Graciela, of course. Thanks to you and your connections, not to mention that hotshot immigration lawyer you hired, it looks like she should have her green card within a few months."

It was during Graciela's debut concert that the idea came to Camille. Standing in the wings of the concert hall while waiting for Graciela to take the stage, Camille peeked out from behind the curtain and was thrilled to see that the hall was packed to capacity.

Scanning the audience, she spotted Alejandro in the center of the auditorium. He was sitting with her mother on one side of him and Paco on the other, the three of them smiling and laughing like old friends. Under the golden glow of the auditorium lights, Alejandro could've passed for a handsome Mexican soap opera star with his tightly cut black suit, crisp white shirt, and paisley tie. Camille was surprised to see that Paco had spruced himself up as well. He looked quite dapper in his long-sleeved turquoise shirt, which covered the tattoos on his arms and almost managed to cover the ones on his neck.

A few seats over, two young children sat on either side of a petite, curly-haired woman. Camille was delighted to see that it was Luz, Alicia, and Little Alejandro. She also spied two figures at the very edge of the back row. Slumped in their seats and wearing equally sullen expressions were Sofia and Amy. Camille almost felt sorry for them. *Almost*.

Smiling, she glanced back at her mother, who was stunning in a silvery-blue chiffon gown. Her hair was out of its usual tight bun and curled softly around her shoulders. She looked to be having the time of her life, flirting with both men like a tipsy sorority girl at her first college frat party. She *wasn't* tipsy, though. She had recently confided to Camille that she had given up drinking when Camille went missing in Oaxaca. She'd even joined a twelve-step program.

Camille fingered the silver pendant of San Antonio around her neck. After everything they had been through, it was nothing short of a miracle that Graciela was about to come out on that stage and perform.

Paco told her he was going to get the word out about the concert, and he'd clearly done just that. More than half the audience were members of the Yalalteco community. For many, Camille surmised, this was the first classical music concert they'd ever attended. She felt badly that there were many more people back in Yalálag—including Tía Nifa—who would never get the chance to hear Graciela play the piano. Not because Graciela couldn't return there someday, but because there was no piano to be found anywhere in the entire town.

Then it came to her: if she could somehow get a piano to Yalálag, Graciela could give a concert there for all of her family and friends. It could be Camille's gift to honor San Antonio. To thank him for helping her get Graciela home.

Camille's mother stood with her hands on her hips, her mint-colored suit turning her blue eyes a pale green. She set her coffee cup on the table. "Camille, do you have any idea how much a piano costs?" she asked. "After using all your savings getting Graciela back here from Mexico, you've hardly a dime left to your name. I'd help you out myself, but I've got a wedding to pay for." She wagged her finger at Camille. "And don't you dare ask Alejandro to help you with the cost. He's already working hard enough to support you while you start up your music school in Los Angeles."

"Alejandro's not going to pay for anything," Camille said. "The Yalalteco community is having a big dance in LA in a few weeks to raise money to help me buy the piano. In fact, they've sold so many advance tickets for the fund-raiser they have over three thousand dollars already."

Her mother rolled her eyes. "Camille, three thousand dollars isn't going to get you a grand piano. Maybe a used upright. But a grand? Forget it. You're going to need fifteen to twenty thousand dollars for a decent one."

"I realize we need a lot more money than what's been raised so far," Camille said patiently. "This is just a start. It's going to take some time."

Her mother studied her. "You're serious about this, aren't you?"

"More serious than I've ever been about anything in my life, except telling Alejandro I would marry him. This is something I have to do."

Her mother stood up from the table and began to pace the kitchen floor. Camille could almost see the wheels turning in her head.

"You know, there's always someone here in Montecito who's redecorating their home. Maybe I could talk to my friends and see if they know of anyone who has a grand piano they'd be willing to sell at a reduced price. Or maybe even donate." She suddenly turned around and faced Camille. "*Wait a second!* I have the perfect solution! I'll get you a piano from Bella Vista. They're always upgrading the pianos in the studios. Maybe I can even talk them into donating one. After all I've done for that school, it's the least they could do." Her mother's eyes lit up like a Vegas slot machine. "The real problem would be getting it there. The cost of shipping it to Oaxaca would be astronomical. And all the way to Yalálag? That would cost a small fortune."

Camille looked up at her mother, another idea already forming in her mind.

"Not if we drive it ourselves."

After hiking up the road for ten minutes, Alejandro and Camille reach the spot where the bus went over the side of the road. Camille never would've recognized it. Other than a slight crevasse in the earth, there's little evidence that a mudslide came down and pushed a huge vehicle off the cliff there. The road is now leveled and spread with gravel. The thick, leafy vegetation has grown back against the steep hillsides. A parade of yellow wildflowers has sprung up along either side of the road, their petals fluttering in the breeze like the waving hands of a welcoming committee.

"Is this really where it happened?" Camille asks.

"See up there?" Alejandro asks, pointing. "You can see there's a slight gap in the mountain."

"Wow. It all looks so different now."

Alejandro smiles. "Maybe that's because you're not the same girl you were a year ago."

"That's for sure."

"Then again, it could just be that it's not pouring rain this time. If you had some mud in your eyes, you'd be able to recognize it." He gives Camille one of his mischievous smiles. "Hey, if you like, I could go hunt for a mud hole and push you down in it for old times' sake."

She playfully slaps him on the shoulder before putting her arms around his neck and drawing him close. "No, thanks. I'm good."

Alejandro is right. Camille is not the same girl she was a year ago. She's still a piano teacher, but she's not so hung up on making a name for herself anymore. She's content living in Los Angeles in Alejandro's house—*their* house, now. She's working on building a school for children who can't afford the high cost of private music lessons. When she moved to LA, she happily referred all of her mediocre students to Sofia. *They're all yours, Vanilla Bitch*, she thought as she gave the kids Sofia's contact information.

She stands with Alejandro at the edge of the road, looking down into the ravine. The undergrowth has almost completely covered it, but Camille can still see a bit of the bus's blue fender poking out from under the twisting vines. Another wave of nausea rolls through her; she takes a deep breath. She is not carsick, and she doesn't have the flu. But she's decided she'll wait to tell Alejandro the news until they get to the red gingerbread church—until they are standing together in front of San Antonio.

The *curandera* was right about yet another thing, she realizes. After the *limpia*, the old woman pointed to the tiny red dot on the egg yolk and told Camille that if she could forgive herself, she would have a chance at a new beginning. A new life.

Camille gently rests her fingers on her stomach. *A new life.* She smiles.

"Let's go, my love," she says, taking Alejandro's hand. "We've got a piano to deliver."

ACKNOWLEDGMENTS

Thank you to the incredibly supportive team of women at She Writes Press: Brooke Warner, Samantha Strom, and Lauren Wise, for your expertise in helping me navigate the complicated world of book publishing. Much thanks to Krissa Lagos, for your invaluable editorial help.

My heartfelt thanks to my Santa Barbara writing group: Ron Alexander, Brad Dobson, Minette Riordan, Ken Collier, Michael Guinn, Emily Heckman, Marilyn Lauer, Melissa Lowenstein, Adele Menichella, and Elizabeth Wolfson. Without your constructive comments, gentle criticisms, and constant encouragement during the process of writing this novel, it would never have been completed. And to think that I almost didn't show up to that first meeting all those years ago.

I'm extremely grateful to the early readers of my novel: Corrine Appelbaum, Julie Barnes, Lauri Hamer, Nancy Gnagy (I'll never forget that late night phone call!), Theresa Lueck, Nora Mireles, Leah Mireles, Isa Mireles, Cece Mireles, and René Mireles. Thank you for all of your editorial suggestions and encouragement during the writing of this novel.

Thank you to my brilliant and talented virtual friends on Facebook who later became my forever-in-the-flesh friends: Becky Aaronson, Deborah Batterman, Jayne Martin, Britton Minor, and

Rossandra White. We will be forever bound by our love of words.

My heartfelt gratitude to the Page Turners Book Club: Jane Adobbo Roberts, Ann Battles, Cindy Billings, Sheila Davies, Ellen Evans, Patricia Forrest, Amy Mathews, and Jody Vandenberg, for choosing my then-unpublished novel as our book choice and then for telling me you liked my book better than some of the other books we read.

Much love and thanks to my best friends since seventh grade: Michele Abbott, Corrine Appelbaum, Julie Barnes, Kay Bess, Kathi Carlson, Lauri Hamer, Holly Kemsley, Pam Poehler, and Sheila Starnes. I have nothing but the deepest appreciation for all of you, not only for your friendship of forty-five years but also for your continued support from the very beginning of my writing process.

Thank you, Elisabeth Ogle, for your wonderful friendship and encouragement. You always know just what to say to make it better. Special thanks to Deborah Batterman, Rossandra White, and Jessica Anya Blau for kindly and generously supporting a fellow writer.

Thank you to the Winters and Mireles families for your never-ending love and support; especially to my mother, Eleanor Winters, who has always been my biggest fan. From piano competitions to novel writing, she's been there, cheering me on with love. To my late father, Joseph R. Winters, thank you for sharing your love of language with me. I hope wherever you are, you are in possession of a crossword puzzle and a pencil.

To my daughter, Leah Mireles and my son-in-law, Jeff Borden for their invaluable help in all things digital.

I have been incredibly lucky to be the mother of four of the most amazing children: Nora, Leah, Cece, and Isa. I love you all to infinity and back. You are my world.

And lastly, my deepest love and appreciation for my husband of thirty-two years, René Mireles. Thank you for opening up my world and teaching me about your beautiful culture. You are my Alejandro. *Ushkenot*.

ABOUT THE AUTHOR

Born and raised in Santa Barbara, California, Jessica Winters Mireles holds a degree in piano performance from USC. After graduating, she began her career as a piano teacher and performer. Four children and a studio of over forty piano students later, Jessica's life changed drastically when her youngest daughter was diagnosed with leukemia at the age of two; she soon decided that life was too short to give up on her dreams of becoming a writer, and after five years of carving out some time each day from her busy schedule, she finished *Lost in Oaxaca*. Jessica's work has been published in *GreenPrints* and *Mothering* magazines. She also knows quite a bit about Oaxaca, as her husband is an indigenous Zapotec man from the highlands of Oaxaca and is a great source of inspiration. She lives with her husband and family in Santa Barbara, California.

SELECTED TITLES FROM SHE WRITES PRESS

She Writes Press is an independent publishing company
founded to serve women writers everywhere.
Visit us at www.shewritespress.com.

Magic Flute by Patricia Minger. $16.95, 978-1-63152-093-8. When a
car accident puts an end to ambitious flutist Liz Morgan's dreams, she
returns to her childhood hometown in Wales in an effort to reinvent her
path.

A Work of Art by Micayla Lally. $16.95, 978-1631521683. After their
breakup—and different ways of dealing with it—Julene and Samson
eventually find their way back to each other, but when she finds out what
he did to keep himself busy while they were apart, she wonders: Can she
trust him again?

Fire & Water by Betsy Graziani Fasbinder. $16.95, 978-1-938314-14-
8. Kate Murphy has always played by the rules—but when she meets
charismatic artist Jake Bloom, she's forced to navigate the treacherous
territory of passionate love, friendship, and family devotion.

Warming Up by Mary Hutchings Reed. $16.95, 978-1-938314-05-6.
Unemployed and depressed former musical actress Cecilia Morrison
decides to start therapy, hoping it will get her out of her slump—but
ultimately it's a teen who cons her out of sixty bucks, not her analyst,
who changes her life.

Anchor Out by Barbara Sapienza. $16.95, 978-1631521652. Quirky Fran-
ces Pia was a feminist Catholic nun, artist, and beloved sister and mother
until she fell from grace—but now, done nursing her aching mood
swings offshore in a thirty-foot sailboat, she is ready to paint her way
toward forgiveness.

Appetite by Sheila Grinell. $16.95, 978-1-63152-022-8. When twenty-
five-year-old Jenn Adler brings home a guru fiancé from Bangalore, her
parents must come to grips with the impending marriage—and its effect
on their own relationship.

Printed in the USA
CPSIA information can be obtained
at www.ICGtesting.com
JSHW021650180224
57584JS00001B/1